THE LEGEND OF
SLEEPY HOLLOW
AND OTHER STORIES

THE LEGEND OF
SLEEPY HOLLOW
AND OTHER STORIES

WASHINGTON IRVING

This edition published in 2020 by Arcturus Publishing Limited
26/27 Bickels Yard, 151–153 Bermondsey Street,
London SE1 3HA

Typesetting by Palimpsest Book Production Limited

Cover design: Peter Ridley
Cover illustration: Peter Gray
Design: Steve Flight

AD007630US

Printed in the UK

CONTENTS

INTRODUCTION

Born in New York City on 3 April 1783, Washington Irving was the youngest member of a family of merchants who prospered during the economic boom that followed the American Revolution. He was named after George Washington, who blessed him as a child.

Irving was a writer, historian, and diplomat, perhaps most famous for short stories such as "Rip Van Winkle" (1819) and "The Legend of Sleepy Hollow" (1820). When he was 19, a series of observational letters he wrote were published under the pen name Jonathan Oldstyle in the *Morning Chronicle*. He quickly became notorious for his caustic style, which was designed to ruffle feathers.

In 1804, he set forth on a grand tour of Europe. When he returned two years later, he was pressured into becoming a lawyer. His ambition, however, was to become a professional writer. In 1807, he became one of the founders of a periodical called *Salmagundi*, which lampooned those who ran New York City. It was in this magazine that Irving first affectionately called New York Gotham, meaning "Goat's Town" in Anglo-Saxon, after a village in Nottingham, England, famed for the supposed stupidity of its inhabitants. New Yorkers took the name on with good humor and it continues to be used to this day.

In 1809, Irving published *A History of New York from the Beginning of the World to the End of the Dutch Dynasty*, "written" by Diedrich Knickerbocker, a scatter-brained fictional Dutch historian. Knickerbocker became so strongly associated with the island of Manhattan and its inhabitants, that his name was taken for the local basketball team, the New York Knicks.

In 1815, Irving moved to England to help his brothers with the failing family business, an importing firm. Here, he became friendly with figures in the literary world, such as Walter Scott, his future publisher John Murray, and many others. He realized that if he were to become a successful writer, he was going to have to broaden his appeal. This rethink produced a gentler, more whimsical, and much-imitated collection of essays and short stories called *The Sketch Book of Geoffrey Crayon, Gent*, which achieved great popularity on both sides of the Atlantic. "Rip Van Winkle" and "The Legend of Sleepy Hollow" were to be found within its pages.

Though *The Sketch Book* was a great success, it was marred by the plague of piracy that ran rampant in the 19th-century publishing world. Profits from unauthorized editions went straight into the hands of literary bootleggers, leaving Irving out of pocket and hampering his ability to become a professional writer, living solely by the proceeds of his pen. Taking up the fight against bootleggers, Irving became a fierce advocate for copyright law.

In 1835, he acquired a riverfront farmhouse in Tarrytown, New York called Sunnyside to house himself, his brother and sister-in-law, and five nieces, who had become his family (he never married). This "neglected cottage," as he described it, overlooked the Hudson river near Sleepy Hollow. Irving served as Minister to Spain from 1842 to 1846, a position which left him exhausted, as he found himself caught up in the middle of much infighting at a time of huge political upheaval.

When Irving came back from Spain, he moved back into Sunnyside and continued writing until his death in 1859, an event commemorated in a poem by Longfellow. His last major project was a five-volume biography of George Washington.

Irving is often said to have been the first American author to earn a living by the pen. He certainly invented the first successful short stories to be set in America. They were folksy entertainment, atmospherically served up with lashings of wry humor. They perhaps also marked the first glimmerings of American national literature. As the critic H. R. Hawless put it in 1881: "[Irving] is the first of the American humorists, as he is almost the first of the American writers; while yet belonging to the New World, there is a quaint Old World flavor about him."

ROSCOE

——In the service of mankind to be
A guardian god below; still to employ
The mind's brave ardor in heroic aims,
Such as may raise us o'er the grovelling herd,
And make us shine for ever—that is life.
THOMSON.

One of the first places to which a stranger is taken in Liverpool is the Athenaeum. It is established on a liberal and judicious plan; it contains a good library, and spacious reading-room, and is the great literary resort of the place. Go there at what hour you may, you are sure to find it filled with grave-looking personages, deeply absorbed in the study of newspapers.

As I was once visiting this haunt of the learned, my attention was attracted to a person just entering the room. He was advanced in life, tall, and of a form that might once have been commanding, but it was a little bowed by time—perhaps by care. He had a noble Roman style of countenance; a head that would have pleased a painter; and though some slight furrows on his brow showed that wasting thought had been busy there, yet his eye beamed with the fire of a poetic soul. There was something in his whole appearance that indicated a being of a different order from the bustling race round him.

I inquired his name, and was informed that it was ROSCOE. I drew back with an involuntary feeling of veneration. This, then, was an author of celebrity; this was one of those men whose voices have gone forth to the ends of the earth; with whose minds I have communed even in the solitudes of America. Accustomed, as we are in our country, to know European writers only by their works, we cannot conceive of them, as of other men, engrossed by trivial or sordid pursuits, and jostling with the crowd of common minds in the dusty paths of life. They pass before our imaginations like superior beings, radiant with the emanations of their genius, and surrounded by a halo of literary glory.

To find, therefore, the elegant historian of the Medici mingling among the busy sons of traffic, at first shocked my poetical ideas; but it is from the very circumstances and situation in which he has been placed, that Mr. Roscoe derives his highest claims to admiration. It is interesting to notice how some minds seem almost to create themselves, springing up under every disadvantage, and working their solitary but irresistible way through a thousand obstacles. Nature seems to delight in disappointing the assiduities of art, with which it would rear legitimate endeavor to maturity; and to glory in the vigor and luxuriance of her chance productions. She scatters the seeds of genius to the winds, and though some may perish among the stony places of the world, and some be choked, by the thorns and brambles of early adversity, yet others will now and then strike root even in the clefts of the rock, struggle bravely up into sunshine, and spread over their sterile birthplace all the beauties of vegetation.

Such has been the case with Mr. Roscoe. Born in a place apparently ungenial to the growth of literary talent—in the very market-place of trade; without fortune, family connections, or patronage; self-prompted, self-sustained, and almost self-taught, he has conquered every obstacle, achieved his way to eminence, and, having become one of the ornaments of the nation, has turned the whole force of his talents and influence to advance and embellish his native town.

Indeed, it is this last trait in his character which has given him the greatest interest in my eyes, and induced me particularly to point him out to my countrymen. Eminent as are his literary merits, he is but one among the many distinguished authors of this intellectual nation. They, however, in general, live but for their own fame, or their own pleasures.

Their private history presents no lesson to the world, or, perhaps, a humiliating one of human frailty or inconsistency. At best, they are prone to steal away from the bustle and commonplace of busy existence; to indulge in the selfishness of lettered ease; and to revel in scenes of mental, but exclusive enjoyment.

Mr. Roscoe, on the contrary, has claimed none of the accorded privileges of talent. He has shut himself up in no garden of thought, nor sojourner of fancy; but has gone forth into the highways and thoroughfares of life, he has planted bowers by the wayside, for the refreshment of the pilgrim and the sojourner, and has opened pure fountains, where the laboring man may turn aside from the dust and heat of the day, and drink of the living streams of knowledge. There is a "daily beauty in his life," on which mankind may meditate, and grow better. It exhibits no lofty and almost useless, because inimitable, example of excellence; but presents a picture of active, yet simple and imitable virtues, which are within every man's reach, but which, unfortunately, are not exercised by many, or this world would be a paradise.

But his private life is peculiarly worthy the attention of the citizens of our young and busy country, where literature and the elegant arts must grow up side by side with the coarser plants of daily necessity; and must depend for their culture, not on the exclusive devotion of time and wealth; nor the quickening rays of titled patronage; but on hours and seasons snatched from the purest of worldly interests, by intelligent and public-spirited individuals.

He has shown how much may be done for a place in hours of leisure by one master-spirit, and how completely it can give its own impress to surrounding objects. Like his own Lorenzo de' Medici, on whom he seems to have fixed his eye, as on a pure model of antiquity, he has interwoven the history of his life with the history of his native town, and has made the foundations of his fame the monuments of his virtues. Wherever you go, in Liverpool, you perceive traces of his footsteps in all that is elegant and liberal. He found the tide of wealth flowing merely in the channels of traffic; he has diverted from it invigorating rills to refresh the garden of literature. By his own example and constant exertions, he has effected that union of commerce and the intellectual pursuits, so eloquently recommended in one of his latest writings;* and has practically proved how beautifully they may be brought to harmonize, and to benefit each other. The noble institutions for literary and scientific purposes, which reflect such credit on Liverpool, and are giving such an impulse to the public mind, have mostly been originated, and have all been effectively promoted, by Mr. Roscoe; and when we consider the rapidly increasing opulence and magnitude of that town, which promises to vie in commercial importance with the metropolis, it will be perceived that in awakening an ambition of mental improvement among its inhabitants, he has effected a great benefit to the cause of British literature.

In America, we know Mr. Roscoe only as the author; in Liverpool he is spoken of as the banker; and I was told of his having been unfortunate in business. I could not pity him, as I heard some rich men do. I considered him far above the reach of pity. Those who live only for the world, and in the world, may be cast down by the frowns of adversity; but a man like Roscoe is not to be overcome by the reverses of fortune. They do but drive him in upon the resources of his own mind, to the superior society of his own thoughts; which the best of men are apt sometimes to neglect, and to roam abroad in search of less worthy associates. He is independent of the world around him. He lives with antiquity, and with posterity: with antiquity, in the sweet communion of studious retirement; and with posterity, in the generous aspirings after future renown. The solitude of such a mind is its state of highest enjoyment. It is then visited by

---

* *Address on the opening of the Liverpool Institution.*

those elevated meditations which are the proper aliment of noble souls, and are, like manna, sent from heaven, in the wilderness of this world.

While my feelings were yet alive on the subject, it was my fortune to light on further traces of Mr. Roscoe. I was riding out with a gentleman, to view the environs of Liverpool, when he turned off, through a gate, into some ornamented grounds. After riding a short distance, we came to a spacious mansion of freestone, built in the Grecian style. It was not in the purest style, yet it had an air of elegance, and the situation was delightful. A fine lawn sloped away from it, studded with clumps of trees, so disposed as to break a soft fertile country into a variety of landscapes. The Mersey was seen winding a broad quiet sheet of water through an expanse of green meadow land, while the Welsh mountains, blended with clouds, and melting into distance, bordered the horizon.

This was Roscoe's favorite residence during the days of his prosperity. It had been the seat of elegant hospitality and literary retirement. The house was now silent and deserted. I saw the windows of the study, which looked out upon the soft scenery I have mentioned. The windows were closed—the library was gone. Two or three ill-favored beings were loitering about the place, whom my fancy pictured into retainers of the law. It was like visiting some classic fountain, that had once welled its pure waters in a sacred shade, but finding it dry and dusty, with the lizard and the toad brooding over the shattered marbles.

I inquired after the fate of Mr. Roscoe's library, which had consisted of scarce and foreign books, from many of which he had drawn the materials for his Italian histories. It had passed under the hammer of the auctioneer, and was dispersed about the country. The good people of the vicinity thronged liked wreckers to get some part of the noble vessel that had been driven on shore. Did such a scene admit of ludicrous associations, we might imagine something whimsical in this strange irruption in the regions of learning. Pigmies rummaging the armory of a giant, and contending for the possession of weapons which they could not wield. We might picture to ourselves some knot of speculators, debating with calculating brow over the quaint binding and illuminated margin of an obsolete author; of the air of intense, but baffled sagacity, with which some successful purchaser attempted to dive into the black-letter bargain he had secured.

It is a beautiful incident in the story of Mr. Roscoe's misfortunes, and one which cannot fail to interest the studious mind, that the parting with his books seems to have touched upon his tenderest feelings, and to have been the only circumstance that could provoke the notice of his muse. The scholar only knows how dear these silent, yet eloquent, companions of pure thoughts and innocent hours become in the season of adversity. When all that is worldly turns to dross around us, these only retain their steady value. When friends grow cold, and the converse of intimates languishes into vapid civility and commonplace, these only continue the unaltered countenance of happier days, and cheer us with that true friendship which never deceived hope, nor deserted sorrow.

I do not wish to censure; but, surely, if the people of Liverpool had been properly sensible of what was due to Mr. Roscoe and themselves, his library would never have been sold. Good worldly reasons may, doubtless, be given for the circumstance, which it would be difficult to combat with others that might seem merely fanciful; but it certainly appears to me such an opportunity as seldom occurs, of cheering a noble mind struggling under misfortunes by one of the most delicate, but most expressive tokens of public sympathy. It is difficult, however, to estimate a man of genius properly who is daily before our eyes. He becomes mingled and confounded with other men. His great qualities lose their novelty; we become too familiar with the common materials which form the basis even of the loftiest character. Some of Mr. Roscoe's townsmen may regard him merely as a man of business; others, as a politician; all find him engaged like themselves in ordinary occupations, and surpassed, perhaps, by themselves on some points of worldly wisdom. Even that amiable and unostentatious simplicity of character, which gives the nameless grace to real excellence, may cause him to be undervalued by some coarse minds, who do not know that true worth is always void of glare and pretension. But the man of letters, who speaks of Liverpool, speaks of it as the residence of Roscoe.—The intelligent traveller who visits it inquires where Roscoe is to be seen. He is the literary landmark of the place, indicating its existence to the distant scholar.— He is like Pompey's column at Alexandria, towering alone in classic dignity.

The following sonnet, addressed by Mr. Roscoe to his books, on parting with them, has already been alluded to. If anything can add effect to the pure feeling and elevated thought here displayed, it is the conviction, *that the whole is no effusion of fancy, but a faithful transcript from the writer's heart.

To My Books

As one who, destined from his friends to part,
*   Regrets his loss, but hopes again erewhile*
*   To share their converse and enjoy their smile,*
And tempers as he may affliction's dart;

Thus, loved associates, chiefs of elder art,
*   Teachers of wisdom, who could once beguile*
*   My tedious hours, and lighten every toil,*
I now resign you; nor with fainting heart;

For pass a few short years, or days, or hours,
*   And happier seasons may their dawn unfold,*

And all your sacred fellowship restore:
When, freed from earth, unlimited its powers.
Mind shall with mind direct communion hold,
And kindred spirits meet to part no more.

RIP VAN WINKLE

[The following Tale was found among the papers of the late Diedrich Knickerbocker, an old gentleman of New York, who was very curious in the Dutch History of the province and the manners of the descendants from its primitive settlers. His historical researches, however, did not lie so much among books as among men; for the former are lamentably scanty on his favorite topics; whereas he found the old burghers, and still more, their wives, rich in that legendary lore, so invaluable to true history. Whenever, therefore, he happened upon a genuine Dutch family, snugly shut up in its low-roofed farm-house, under a spreading sycamore, he looked upon it as a little clasped volume of black-letter, and studied it with the zeal of a bookworm.

The result of all these researches was a history of the province, during the reign of the Dutch governors, which he published some years since. There have been various opinions as to the literary character of his work, and, to tell the truth, it is not a whit better than it should be. Its chief merit is its scrupulous accuracy, which indeed was a little questioned on its first appearance, but has since been completely established; and it is now admitted into all historical collections, as a book of unquestionable authority.

The old gentleman died shortly after the publication of his work; and now that he is dead and gone, it cannot do much harm to his memory to say that his time might have been much better employed in weightier labors. He, however, was apt to ride his hobby his own way; and though it did now and then kick up the dust a little in the eyes of his neighbors, and grieve the spirit of some friends, for whom he felt the truest deference and affection, yet his errors and follies are remembered "more in sorrow than in anger,"* and it begins to

---

* Vide the excellent discourse of G. C. Verplanck, Esq. before the New York Historical Society.

be suspected, that he never intended to injure or offend. But however his memory may be appreciated by critics, it is still held dear among many folks, whose good opinion is well worth having; particularly by certain biscuit-makers, who have gone so far as to imprint his likeness on their New-Year cakes, and have thus given him a chance for immortality, almost equal to the being stamped on a Waterloo Medal, or a Queen Anne's farthing.]

A Posthumous Writing of Diedrich Knickerbocker

By Woden, God of Saxons,
From whence comes Wensday, that is Wodensday,
Truth is a thing that ever I will keep
Unto thylke day in which I creep into
My sepulchre———
CARTWRIGHT

Whoever has made a voyage up the Hudson must remember the Kaatskill mountains. They are a dismembered branch of the great Appalachian family, and are seen away to the west of the river, swelling up to a noble height, and lording it over the surrounding country. Every change of season, every change of weather, indeed, every hour of the day produces some change in the magical hues and shapes of these mountains; and they are regarded by all the good wives, far and near, as perfect barometers. When the weather is fair and settled, they are clothed in blue and purple, and print their bold outlines on the clear evening sky; but sometimes, when the rest of the landscape is cloudless, they will gather a hood of gray vapors about their summits, which, in the last rays of the setting sun, will glow and light up like a crown of glory.

At the foot of these fairy mountains, the voyager may have descried the light smoke curling up from a village, whose shingle roofs gleam among the trees, just where the blue tints of the upland melt away into the fresh green of the nearer landscape. It is a little village of great antiquity, having been founded by some of the Dutch colonists, in the early times of the province, just about the beginning of the government of the good Peter Stuyvesant (may he rest in peace!), and there were some of the houses of the original settlers standing within a few years, built of small yellow bricks, brought from Holland, having latticed windows and gable fronts, surmounted with weathercocks.

In that same village, and in one of these very houses (which, to tell the precise truth, was sadly time-worn and weather-beaten), there lived, many years since, while the country was yet a province of Great Britain, a simple, good-natured fellow, of the name of Rip Van Winkle. He was a descendant of the Van Winkles who figured so gallantly in the chivalrous days of Peter Stuyvesant, and accompanied him to the siege of Fort Christina. He inherited, however, but little of the martial character of his ancestors. I have observed that he was a simple, good-natured man; he was, moreover, a kind neighbor, and an obedient hen-pecked husband. Indeed, to the latter circumstance might be owing that meekness of spirit which gained him such universal popularity; for those men are apt to be obsequious and conciliating abroad, who are under the discipline of shrews at home. Their tempers, doubtless, are rendered pliant and malleable in the fiery furnace of domestic tribulation, and a curtain-lecture is worth all the sermons in the world for teaching the virtues of patience and long-suffering. A termagant wife may, therefore, in some respects, be considered a tolerable blessing, and if so, Rip Van Winkle was thrice blessed.

Certain it is, that he was a great favorite among all the good wives of the village, who, as usual with the amiable sex, took his part in all family squabbles, and never failed, whenever they talked those matters over in their evening gossipings, to lay all the blame on Dame Van Winkle. The children of the village, too, would shout with joy whenever he approached. He assisted at their sports, made their playthings, taught them to fly kites and shoot marbles, and told them long stories of ghosts, witches, and Indians. Whenever he went dodging about the village, he was surrounded by a troop of them hanging on his skirts, clambering on his back, and playing a thousand tricks on him with impunity; and not a dog would bark at him throughout the neighborhood.

The great error in Rip's composition was an insuperable aversion to all kinds of profitable labor. It could not be from the want of assiduity or perseverance; for he would sit on a wet rock, with a rod as long and heavy as a Tartar's lance, and fish all day without a murmur, even though he should not be encouraged by a single nibble. He would carry a fowling-piece on his shoulder, for hours together, trudging through woods and swamps, and up hill and down dale, to shoot a few squirrels or wild pigeons. He would never refuse to assist a neighbor even in the roughest toil, and was a foremost man in all country frolics for husking Indian corn, or building stone fences; the women of the village, too, used to employ him to run their errands, and to do such little odd jobs as their less obliging husbands would not do for them. In a word, Rip was ready to attend to anybody's business but his own; but as to doing family duty, and keeping his farm in order, he found it impossible.

In fact, he declared it was of no use to work on his farm; it was the most pestilent little piece of ground in the whole country; everything about it went wrong, in spite of him. His fences were continually falling to pieces; his cow would either go astray, or get among the cabbages; weeds were sure to grow quicker in his fields than anywhere else; the rain always made a point of setting in just as he had some out-door work to do; so that though his patrimonial estate had dwindled away under his management, acre by acre, until there was little more left than a mere patch of Indian corn and potatoes, yet it was the worst-conditioned farm in the neighborhood.

His children, too, were as ragged and wild as if they belonged to nobody. His son Rip, an urchin begotten in his own likeness, promised to inherit the habits, with the old clothes, of his father. He was generally seen trooping like a colt at his mother's heels, equipped in a pair of his father's cast-off galligaskins, which he had much ado to hold up with one hand, as a fine lady does her train in bad weather.

Rip Van Winkle, however, was one of those happy mortals, of foolish, well-oiled dispositions, who take the world easy, eat white bread or brown, whichever can be got with least thought or trouble, and would rather starve on a penny than work for a pound. If left to himself, he would have whistled life away, in perfect contentment; but his wife kept continually dinning in his ears about his idleness, his carelessness, and the ruin he was bringing on his family. Morning, noon, and night, her tongue was incessantly going, and every thing he said or did was sure to produce a torrent of household eloquence. Rip had but one way of replying to all lectures of the kind, and that, by frequent use, had grown into a habit. He shrugged his shoulders, shook his head, cast up his eyes, but said nothing. This, however, always provoked a fresh volley from his wife, so that he was fain to draw off his forces, and take to the outside of the house—the only side which, in truth, belongs to a hen-pecked husband.

Rip's sole domestic adherent was his dog Wolf, who was as much hen-pecked as his master; for Dame Van Winkle regarded them as companions in idleness, and even looked upon Wolf with an evil eye, as the cause of his master's going so often astray. True it is, in all points of spirit befitting an honorable dog, he was as courageous an animal as ever scoured the woods—but what courage can withstand the evil-doing and all-besetting terrors of a woman's tongue? The moment Wolf entered the house, his crest fell, his tail drooped to the ground, or curled between his legs, he sneaked about with a gallows air, casting many a sidelong glance at Dame Van Winkle, and at the least flourish of a broomstick or ladle, he would fly to the door with yelping precipitation.

Times grew worse and worse with Rip Van Winkle as years of matrimony rolled on; a tart temper never mellows with age, and a sharp tongue is the only edged tool that grows keener with constant use. For a long while he used to console himself, when driven from home, by frequenting a kind of perpetual club of the sages, philosophers, and other idle personages of the village, which held its sessions on a bench before a small inn, designated by a rubicund portrait of His Majesty George the Third. Here they used to sit in the shade through a long, lazy summer's day, talking listlessly over village gossip, or telling endless, sleepy stories about nothing. But it would have been worth any statesman's money to have heard the profound discussions which sometimes took place, when by chance an old newspaper fell into their hands from some passing traveller. How solemnly they would listen to the contents, as drawled out by Derrick Van Bummel, the schoolmaster, a dapper learned little man, who was not to be daunted by the most gigantic word in the dictionary; and how sagely they would deliberate upon public events some months after they had taken place.

The opinions of this junto were completely controlled by Nicholas Vedder, a patriarch of the village, and landlord of the inn, at the door of which he took his seat from morning till night, just moving sufficiently to avoid the sun, and keep in the shade of a large tree; so that the neighbors could tell the hour by his movements as accurately as by a sun-dial. It is true, he was rarely heard to speak, but smoked his pipe incessantly. His adherents, however (for every great man has his adherents), perfectly understood him, and knew how to gather his opinions. When anything that was read or related displeased him, he was observed to smoke his pipe vehemently, and to send forth, frequent, and angry puffs; but when pleased, he would inhale the smoke slowly and tranquilly, and emit it in light and placid clouds, and sometimes, taking the pipe from his mouth, and letting the fragrant vapor curl about his nose, would gravely nod his head in token of perfect approbation.

From even this stronghold the unlucky Rip was at length routed by his termagant wife, who would suddenly break in upon the tranquillity of the assemblage, and call the members all to nought; nor was that august personage, Nicholas Vedder himself, sacred from the daring tongue of this terrible virago, who charged him outright with encouraging her husband in habits of idleness.

Poor Rip was at last reduced almost to despair; and his only alternative, to escape from the labor of the farm and the clamor of his wife, was to take gun in hand, and stroll away into the woods. Here he would sometimes seat himself at the foot of a tree, and share the contents of his wallet with Wolf, with whom he sympathized as a fellow-sufferer in persecution. "Poor Wolf," he would say, "thy mistress leads thee a dog's life of it; but never mind, my lad, whilst I live thou shalt never want a friend to stand by thee!" Wolf would wag his tail, look wistfully in his master's face, and if dogs can feel pity, I verily believe he reciprocated the sentiment with all his heart.

In a long ramble of the kind, on a fine autumnal day, Rip had unconsciously scrambled to one of the highest parts of the Kaatskill mountains. He was after his favorite sport of squirrel-shooting, and the still solitudes had echoed and re-echoed with the reports of his gun. Panting and fatigued, he threw himself, late in the afternoon, on a green knoll, covered with mountain herbage, that crowned the brow of a precipice. From an opening between the trees, he could overlook all the lower country for many a mile of rich woodland. He saw at a distance the lordly Hudson, far, far below him, moving on its silent but majestic course, with the reflection of a purple cloud, or the sail of a lagging bark, here and there sleeping on its glassy bosom and at last losing itself in the blue highlands.

On the other side he looked down into a deep mountain glen, wild, lonely, and shagged, the bottom filled with fragments from the impending cliffs, and scarcely lighted by the reflected rays of the setting sun. For some time Rip lay musing on this scene; evening was gradually advancing; the mountains began to throw their long blue shadows over the valleys; he saw that it would be dark long before he could reach the village; and he heaved a heavy sigh when he thought of encountering the terrors of Dame Van Winkle.

As he was about to descend, he heard a voice from a distance hallooing: "Rip Van Winkle! Rip Van Winkle!" He looked around, but could see nothing but a crow winging its solitary flight across the mountain. He thought his fancy must have deceived him, and turned again to descend, when he heard the same cry ring through the still evening air, "Rip Van Winkle! Rip Van Winkle!"—at the same time Wolf bristled up his back, and giving a low growl, skulked to his master's side, looking fearfully down into the glen. Rip now felt a vague apprehension stealing over him; he looked anxiously in the same direction, and perceived a strange figure slowly toiling up the rocks, and bending under the weight of something he carried on his back. He was surprised to see any human being in this lonely and unfrequented place, but supposing it to be some one of the neighborhood in need of his assistance, he hastened down to yield it.

On nearer approach, he was still more surprised at the singularity of the stranger's appearance. He was a short, square-built old fellow, with thick bushy hair, and a grizzled beard. His dress was of the antique Dutch fashion—a cloth jerkin strapped round the waist— several pairs of breeches, the outer one of ample volume, decorated with rows of buttons down the sides, and bunches at the knees. He bore on his shoulders a stout keg, that seemed full of liquor, and made signs for Rip to approach and assist him with the load. Though rather shy and distrustful of this new acquaintance, Rip complied with his usual alacrity; and mutually relieving each other, they clambered up a narrow gully, apparently the dry bed of a mountain torrent. As they ascended, Rip every now and then heard long rolling peals, like distant thunder, that seemed to issue out of a deep ravine, or rather cleft between lofty rocks, toward which their rugged path conducted. He paused for an instant, but supposing it to be the muttering of one of those transient thunder-showers which often take place in the mountain heights, he proceeded. Passing through the ravine, they came to a hollow, like a small amphitheatre, surrounded by perpendicular precipices, over the brinks of which impending trees shot their branches, so that you only caught glimpses of the azure sky, and the bright evening cloud. During the whole time Rip and his companion had labored on in silence; for though the former marvelled greatly what could be the object of carrying a keg of liquor up this wild mountain, yet there was something strange and incomprehensible about the unknown, that inspired awe, and checked familiarity.

On entering the amphitheatre, new objects of wonder presented themselves. On a level spot in the centre was a company of odd-looking personages playing at ninepins. They were dressed in quaint outlandish fashion; some wore short doublets, others jerkins, with long knives in their belts, and most of them had enormous breeches, of similar style with that of the guide's. Their visages, too, were peculiar; one had a large head, broad face, and small piggish eyes; the face of another seemed to consist entirely of nose, and was surmounted by a white sugar-loaf hat, set off with a little red cock's tail. They all had beards, of various shapes and colors. There was one who seemed to be the commander. He was a stout old gentleman, with a weather-beaten countenance; he wore a laced doublet, broad belt and hanger, high-crowned hat and feather, red stockings, and high-heeled shoes, with roses in them. The whole group reminded Rip of the figures in an old Flemish painting, in the parlor of Dominie Van Schaick, the village parson, and which had been brought over from Holland at the time of the settlement.

What seemed particularly odd to Rip was, that though these folks were evidently amusing themselves, yet they maintained the gravest faces, the most mysterious silence, and were, withal, the most melancholy party of pleasure he had ever witnessed. Nothing interrupted the stillness of the scene but the noise of the balls, which, whenever they were rolled, echoed along the mountains like rumbling peals of thunder.

As Rip and his companion approached them, they suddenly desisted from their play, and stared at him with such a fixed statue-like gaze, and such strange uncouth, lack-lustre countenances, that his heart turned within him, and his knees smote together. His companion now emptied the contents of the keg into large flagons, and made signs to him to wait upon the company. He obeyed with fear and trembling; they quaffed the liquor in profound silence, and then returned to their game.

By degrees, Rip's awe and apprehension subsided. He even ventured, when no eye was fixed upon him, to taste the beverage which he found had much of the flavor of excellent Hollands. He was naturally a thirsty soul, and was soon tempted to repeat the draught. One taste provoked another; and he reiterated his visits to the flagon so often, that at length his senses were overpowered, his eyes swam in his head, his head gradually declined, and he fell into a deep sleep.

On waking, he found himself on the green knoll whence he had first seen the old man of the glen. He rubbed his eyes—it was a bright sunny morning. The birds were hopping and twittering among the bushes, and the eagle was wheeling aloft, and breasting the pure mountain breeze. "Surely," thought Rip, "I have not slept here all night." He recalled the occurrences before he fell asleep. The strange man with the keg of liquor—the mountain ravine—the wild retreat among the rocks—the woe-begone party at ninepins—the flagon—"Oh! That flagon! That wicked flagon!" thought Rip—"what excuse shall I make to Dame Van Winkle?"

He looked round for his gun, but in place of the clean well-oiled fowling-piece, he found an old firelock lying by him, the barrel encrusted with rust, the lock falling off, and the stock worm-eaten. He now suspected that the grave roisters of the mountains had put a trick upon him, and, having dosed him with liquor, had robbed him of his gun. Wolf, too, had disappeared, but he might have strayed away after a squirrel or partridge. He whistled after him and shouted his name, but all in vain; the echoes repeated his whistle and shout, but no dog was to be seen.

He determined to revisit the scene of the last evening's gambol, and if he met with any of the party, to demand his dog and gun. As he rose to walk, he found himself stiff in the joints, and wanting in his usual activity. "These mountain beds do not agree with me," thought Rip, "and if this frolic, should lay me up with a fit of the rheumatism, I shall have a blessed time with Dame Van Winkle." With some difficulty he got down into the glen: he found the gully up which he and his companion had ascended the preceding evening; but to his astonishment a mountain stream was now foaming down it, leaping from rock to rock, and filling the glen with babbling murmurs. He, however, made shift to scramble up its sides, working his toilsome way through thickets of birch, sassafras, and witch-hazel; and sometimes tripped up or entangled by the wild grape-vines that twisted their coils and tendrils from tree to tree, and spread a kind of network in his path.

At length he reached to where the ravine had opened through the cliffs to the amphitheatre; but no traces of such opening remained. The rocks presented a high impenetrable wall, over which the torrent came tumbling in a sheet of feathery foam, and fell into a broad deep basin, black from the shadows of the surrounding forest. Here, then, poor Rip was brought to a stand. He again called and whistled after his dog; he was only answered by the cawing of a flock of idle crows, sporting high in the air about a dry tree that overhung a sunny precipice; and who, secure in their elevation, seemed to look down and scoff at the poor man's perplexities. What was to be done? The morning was passing away, and Rip felt famished for want of his breakfast. He grieved to give up his dog and gun; he dreaded to meet his wife; but it would not do to starve among the mountains. He shook his head, shouldered the rusty firelock, and, with a heart full of trouble and anxiety, turned his steps homeward.

As he approached the village, he met a number of people, but none whom he new, which somewhat surprised him, for he had thought himself acquainted with every one in the country round. Their dress, too, was of a different fashion from that to which he was accustomed. They all stared at him with equal marks of surprise, and whenever they cast eyes upon him, invariably stroked their chins. The constant recurrence of this gesture, induced Rip, involuntarily, to do, the same, when, to his astonishment, he found his beard had grown a foot long!

He had now entered the skirts of the village. A troop of strange children ran at his heels, hooting after him, and pointing at his gray beard. The dogs, too, not one of which he recognized for an old acquaintance, barked at him as he passed. The very village was altered: it was larger and more populous. There were rows of houses which he had never seen before, and those which had been his familiar haunts had disappeared. Strange names were over the doors—strange faces at the windows—everything was strange. His mind now misgave him; he began to doubt whether both he and the world around him were not bewitched. Surely this was his native village, which he had left but a day before. There stood the Kaatskill mountains—there ran the silver Hudson at a distance—there was every hill and dale precisely as it had always been—Rip was sorely perplexed. "That flagon last night," thought he, "has addled my poor head sadly!"

It was with some difficulty that he found the way to his own house, which he approached with silent awe, expecting every moment to hear the shrill voice of Dame Van Winkle. He found the house gone to decay—the roof had fallen in, the windows shattered, and the doors off the hinges. A half-starved dog, that looked like Wolf, was skulking about it. Rip called him by name, but the cur snarled, showed his teeth, and passed on. This was an unkind cut indeed. "My very dog," sighed poor Rip, "has forgotten me!"

He entered the house, which, to tell the truth, Dame Van Winkle had always kept in neat order. It was empty, forlorn, and apparently abandoned. This desolateness overcame all his connubial fears—he called loudly for his wife and children—the lonely chambers rang for a moment with his voice, and then all again was silence.

He now hurried forth, and hastened to his old resort, the village inn—but it too was gone. A large rickety wooden building stood in its place, with great gaping windows, some of them broken, and mended with old hats and petticoats, and over the door was painted, "The Union Hotel, by Jonathan Doolittle." Instead of the great tree that used to shelter the quiet little Dutch inn of yore, there now was reared a tall naked pole, with something on the top that looked like a red nightcap, and from it was fluttering a flag, on which was a singular assemblage of stars and stripes—all this was strange and incomprehensible. He recognized on the sign, however, the ruby face of King George, under which he had smoked so many a peaceful pipe, but even this was singularly metamorphosed. The red coat was changed for one of blue and buff, a sword was held in the hand instead of a sceptre, the head was decorated with a cocked hat, and underneath was painted in large characters, GENERAL WASHINGTON.

There was, as usual, a crowd of folk about the door, but none that Rip recollected. The very character of the people seemed changed. There was a busy, bustling, disputatious tone about it, instead of the accustomed phlegm and drowsy tranquillity. He looked in vain for the sage Nicholas Vedder, with his broad face, double chin, and fair long pipe, uttering clouds of tobacco-smoke, instead of idle speeches; or Van Bummel, the schoolmaster, doling forth the contents of an ancient newspaper. In place of these, a lean, bilious-looking fellow, with his pockets full of handbills, was haranguing, vehemently about rights of citizens—elections—members of Congress—liberty—Bunker's hill—heroes of seventy-six—and other words, which were a perfect Babylonish jargon to the bewildered Van Winkle.

The appearance of Rip, with his long, grizzled beard, his rusty fowling-piece, his uncouth dress, and the army of women and children at his heels, soon attracted the attention of the tavern politicians. They crowded round him, eying him from head to foot, with great curiosity. The orator bustled up to him, and, drawing him partly aside, inquired "on which side he voted?" Rip stared in vacant stupidity. Another short but busy little fellow pulled him by the arm, and, rising on tiptoe, inquired in his ear, "whether he was Federal or Democrat." Rip was equally at a loss to comprehend the question; when a knowing, self-important old gentleman, in a sharp cocked hat, made his way through the crowd, putting them to the right and left with his elbows as he passed, and planting himself before Van Winkle, with one arm akimbo, the other resting on his cane, his keen eyes and sharp hat penetrating, as it were, into his very soul, demanded in an austere tone, "What brought him to the election with a gun on his shoulder, and a mob at his heels; and whether he meant to breed a riot in the village?"

"Alas! Gentlemen," cried Rip, somewhat dismayed, "I am a poor, quiet man, a native of the place, and a loyal subject of the King, God bless him!"

Here a general shout burst from the bystanders—"A tory! A tory! A spy! A refugee! Hustle him! Away with him!" It was with great difficulty that the self-important man in the cocked hat restored order; and having assumed a tenfold austerity of brow, demanded again of the unknown culprit, what he came there for, and whom he was seeking. The poor man humbly assured him that he meant no harm, but merely came there in search of some of his neighbors, who used to keep about the tavern.

"Well—who are they?—name them."

Rip bethought himself a moment, and inquired, "Where's Nicholas Vedder?"

There was a silence for a little while, when an old man replied, in a thin, piping voice, "Nicholas Vedder? Why, he is dead and gone these eighteen years! There was a wooden tombstone in the church-yard that used to tell all about him, but that's rotten and gone too."

"Where's Brom Dutcher?"

"Oh, he went off to the army in the beginning of the war; some say he was killed at the storming of Stony Point—others say he was drowned in a squall at the foot of Antony's Nose. I don't know—he never came back again."

"Where's Van Bummel, the schoolmaster?"

"He went off to the wars, too; was a great militia general, and is now in Congress."

Rip's heart died away, at hearing of these sad changes in his home and friends, and finding himself thus alone in the world. Every answer puzzled him too, by treating of such enormous lapses of time, and of matters which he could not understand: war—Congress—Stony Point—he had no courage to ask after any more friends, but cried out in despair, "Does nobody here know Rip Van Winkle?"

"Oh, Rip Van Winkle!" exclaimed two or three. "Oh, to be sure! That's Rip Van Winkle yonder, leaning against the tree."

Rip looked, and beheld a precise counterpart of himself as he went up the mountain; apparently as lazy, and certainly as ragged. The poor fellow was now completely confounded. He doubted his own identity, and whether he was himself or another man. In the midst of his bewilderment, the man in the cocked hat demanded who he was, and what was his name?

"God knows!" exclaimed he at his wit's end; "I'm not myself—I'm somebody else—that's me yonder—no—that's somebody else, got into my shoes—I was myself last night, but I fell asleep on the mountain, and they've changed my gun, and everything's changed, and I'm changed, and I can't tell what's my name, or who I am!"

The by-standers began now to look at each other, nod, wink significantly, and tap their fingers against their foreheads. There was a whisper, also, about securing the gun, and keeping the old fellow from doing mischief; at the very suggestion of which, the self-important man with the cocked hat retired with some precipitation. At this critical moment a fresh, comely woman pressed through the throng to get a peep at the gray-bearded man. She had a chubby child in her arms, which, frightened at his looks, began to cry. "Hush, Rip," cried she, "hush, you little fool; the old man won't hurt you." The name of the child, the air of the mother, the tone of her voice, all awakened a train of recollections in his mind.

"What is your name, my good woman?" asked he.

"Judith Gardenier."

"And your father's name?"

"Ah, poor man, Rip Van Winkle was his name, but it's twenty years since he went away from home with his gun, and never has been heard of since,—his dog came home without him; but whether he shot himself, or was carried away by the Indians, nobody can tell. I was then but a little girl."

Rip had but one more question to ask; but he put it with a faltering voice:

"Where's your mother?"

Oh, she too had died but a short time since; she broke a blood vessel in a fit of passion at a New England pedler.

There was a drop of comfort, at least, in this intelligence. The honest man could contain himself no longer. He caught his daughter and her child in his arms. "I am your father!" cried he—"Young Rip Van Winkle once—old Rip Van Winkle now!—Does nobody know poor Rip Van Winkle!"

All stood amazed, until an old woman, tottering out from among the crowd, put her hand to her brow, and peering under it in his face for a moment exclaimed, "Sure enough! It is Rip Van Winkle—it is himself. Welcome home again, old neighbor. Why, where have you been these twenty long years?"

Rip's story was soon told, for the whole twenty years had been to him but as one night. The neighbors stared when they heard it; some were seen to wink at each other, and put their tongues in their cheeks; and the self-important man in the cocked hat, who, when the alarm was over, had returned to the field, screwed down the corners of his mouth, and shook his head—upon which there was a general shaking of the head throughout the assemblage.

It was determined, however, to take the opinion of old Peter Vanderdonk, who was seen slowly advancing up the road. He was a descendant of the historian of that name, who wrote one of the earliest accounts of the province. Peter was the most ancient inhabitant of the village, and well versed in all the wonderful events and traditions of the neighborhood. He recollected Rip at once, and corroborated his story in the most satisfactory manner. He assured the company that it was a fact, handed down from his ancestor, the historian, that the Kaatskill mountains had always been haunted by strange beings. That it was affirmed that the great Hendrick Hudson, the first discoverer of the river and country, kept a kind of vigil there every twenty years, with his crew of the *Half-moon*; being permitted in this way to revisit the scenes of his enterprise, and keep a guardian eye upon the river and the great city called by his name. That his father had once seen them in their old Dutch dresses playing at ninepins in the hollow of the mountain; and that he himself had heard, one summer afternoon, the sound of their balls, like distant peals of thunder.

To make a long story short, the company broke up, and returned to the more important concerns of the election. Rip's daughter took him home to live with her; she had a snug, well-furnished house, and a stout cheery farmer for a husband, whom Rip recollected for one of the urchins that used to climb upon his back. As to Rip's son and heir, who was the ditto of himself, seen leaning against the tree, he was employed to work on the farm; but evinced an hereditary disposition to attend to anything else but his business.

Rip now resumed his old walks and habits; he soon found many of his former cronies, though all rather the worse for the wear and tear of time; and preferred making friends among the rising generation, with whom he soon grew into great favor.

Having nothing to do at home, and being arrived at that happy age when a man can be idle with impunity, he took his place once more on the bench, at the inn door, and was reverenced as one of the patriarchs of the village, and a chronicle of the old times "before the war." It was some time before he could get into the regular track of gossip, or could be made to comprehend the strange events that had taken place during his torpor. How that there had been a revolutionary war—that the country had thrown off the yoke of old England—and that, instead of being a subject to His Majesty George the Third, he was now a free citizen of the United States. Rip, in fact, was no politician; the changes of states and empires made but little impression on him; but there was one species of despotism under which he had long groaned, and that was—petticoat government. Happily, that was at an end; he had got his neck out of the yoke of matrimony, and could go in and out whenever he pleased, without dreading the tyranny of Dame Van Winkle. Whenever her name was mentioned, however, he shook his head, shrugged his shoulders, and cast up his eyes; which might pass either for an expression of resignation to his fate, or joy at his deliverance.

He used to tell his story to every stranger that arrived at Mr. Doolittle's hotel. He was observed, at first, to vary on some points every time he told it, which was, doubtless, owing to his having so recently awaked. It at last settled down precisely to the tale I have related, and not a man, woman, or child in the neighborhood, but knew it by heart. Some always pretended to doubt the reality of it, and insisted that Rip had been out of his head, and that this was one point on which he always remained flighty. The old Dutch inhabitants, however, almost universally gave it full credit. Even to this day, they never hear a thunderstorm of a summer afternoon about the Kaatskill, but they say Hendrick Hudson and his crew are at their game of ninepins; and it is a common wish of all hen-pecked husbands in the neighborhood, when life hangs heavy on their hands, that they might have a quieting draught out of Rip Van Winkle's flagon.

NOTE—The foregoing Tale, one would suspect, had been suggested to Mr. Knickerbocker by a little German superstition about the Emperor Frederick *der Rothbart* and the Kypphäuser mountain; the subjoined note, however, which had appended to the tale, shows that it is an absolute fact, narrated with his usual fidelity.

"The story of Rip Van Winkle may seem incredible to many, but nevertheless I give it my full belief, for I know the vicinity of our old Dutch settlements to have been very subject to marvellous events and appearances. Indeed, I have heard many stranger stories than this, in the villages along the Hudson; all of which were too well authenticated to admit of a doubt. I have even talked with Rip Van Winkle myself, who, when last I saw him, was a very venerable old man, and so perfectly rational and consistent on every other point, that I think no conscientious person could refuse to take this into the bargain; nay, I have seen a certificate on the subject taken before a country justice, and signed with cross, in the justice's own handwriting. The story, therefore, is beyond the possibility of doubt.

D. K."

POSTSCRIPT

The following are travelling notes from a memorandum-book of Mr. Knickerbocker:

The Kaatsber, or Catskill Mountains, have always been a region full of fable. The Indians considered them the abode of spirits, who influenced the weather, spreading sunshine or clouds over the landscape, and sending good or bad hunting seasons. They were ruled by an old squaw spirit, said to be their mother. She dwelt on the highest peak of the Catskills, and had charge of the doors of day and night to open and shut them at the proper hour. She hung up the new moons in the skies, and cut up the old ones into stars. In times of drought, if properly propitiated, she would spin light summer clouds out of cobwebs and morning dew, and send them off from the crest of the mountain, flake after flake, like flakes of carded cotton, to float in the air; until, dissolved by the heat of the sun, they would fall in gentle showers, causing the grass to spring, the fruits to ripen, and the corn to grow an inch an hour. If displeased, however, she would brew up clouds black as ink, sitting in the midst of them like a bottle-bellied spider in the midst of its web; and when these clouds broke, woe betide the valleys!

In old times, say the Indian traditions, there was a kind of Manitou or Spirit, who kept about the wildest recesses of the Catskill mountains, and took a mischievous pleasure in wreaking all kind of evils and vexations upon the red men. Sometimes he would assume the form of a bear, a panther, or a deer, lead the bewildered hunter a weary chase through tangled forests and among ragged rocks, and then spring off with a loud ho! ho! leaving him aghast on the brink of a beetling precipice or raging torrent.

The favorite abode of this Manitou is still shown. It is a rock or cliff on the loneliest port of the mountains, and, from the flowering vines which clamber about it, and the wild flowers which abound in its neighborhood, is known by the name of the Garden Rock. Near the foot of it is a small lake, the haunt of the solitary bittern, with water-snakes basking in the sun on the leaves of the pond-lilies which lie on the surface. This place was held in great awe by the Indians, insomuch that the boldest hunter would not pursue his game within its precincts. Once upon a time, however, a hunter who had lost his way penetrated to the Garden Rock, where he beheld a number of gourds placed in the crotches of trees. One of these he seized and made off with it, but in the hurry of his retreat he let it fall among the rocks, when a great stream gushed forth, which washed him away and swept him down precipices, where he was dished to pieces, and the stream made its way to the Hudson, and continues to flow to the present day, being the identical stream known by the name of the Kaaterskill.

THE MUTABILITY OF LITERATURE

A Colloquy in Westminster Abbey

I know that all beneath the moon decays,
And what by mortals in this world is brought,
In time's great periods shall return to nought.
I know that all the muses' heavenly lays,
With toil of sprite which are so dearly bought,
As idle sounds, of few or none are sought—
That there is nothing lighter than mere praise.
DRUMMOND OF HAWTHORNDEN.

There are certain half-dreaming moods of mind in which we naturally steal away from noise and glare, and seek some quiet haunt where we may indulge our reveries and build our air castles undisturbed. In such a mood I was loitering about the old gray cloisters of Westminster Abbey, enjoying that luxury of wandering thought which one is apt to dignify with the name of reflection, when suddenly an irruption of madcap boys from Westminster school, playing at football, broke in upon the monastic stillness of the place, making the vaulted passages and mouldering tombs echo with their merriment. I sought to take refuge from their noise by penetrating still deeper into the solitudes of the pile, and applied to one of the vergers for admission to the library. He conducted me through a portal rich with the crumbling sculpture of former ages, which opened upon a gloomy passage leading to the chapter-house and the chamber in which Doomsday Book is deposited. Just within the passage is a small door on the left. To this the verger applied a key; it was double locked, and opened with some difficulty, as if seldom used. We now ascended a dark narrow staircase, and, passing through a second door, entered the library.

I found myself in a lofty antique hall, the roof supported by massive joists of old English oak. It was soberly lighted by a row of Gothic windows at a considerable height from the floor, and which apparently opened upon the roofs of the cloisters. An ancient picture of some reverend dignitary of the church in his robes hung over the fireplace. Around the hall and in a small gallery were the books, arranged in carved oaken cases. They consisted principally of old polemical writers, and were much more worn by time than use. In the centre of the library was a solitary table with two or three books on it, an inkstand without ink, and a few pens parched by long disuse. The place seemed fitted for quiet study and profound meditation. It was buried deep among the massive walls of the abbey and shut up from the tumult of the world. I could only hear now and then the shouts of the school-boys faintly swelling from the cloisters, and the sound of a bell tolling for prayers echoing soberly along the roofs of the abbey. By degrees the shouts of merriment grew fainter and fainter, and at length died away; the bell ceased to toll, and a profound silence reigned through the dusky hall.

I had taken down a little thick quarto, curiously bound in parchment, with brass clasps, and seated myself at the table in a venerable elbow-chair. Instead of reading, however, I was beguiled by the solemn monastic air and lifeless quiet of the place, into a train of musing. As I looked around upon the old volumes in their mouldering covers, thus ranged on the shelves and apparently never disturbed in their repose, I could not but consider the library a kind of literary catacomb, where authors, like mummies, are piously entombed and left to blacken and moulder in dusty oblivion.

How much, thought I, has each of these volumes, now thrust aside with such indifference, cost some aching head! how many weary days! how many sleepless nights! How have their authors buried themselves in the solitude of cells and cloisters, shut themselves up from the face of man, and the still more blessed face of Nature; and devoted themselves to painful research and intense reflection! And all for what? To occupy an inch of dusty shelf—to have the titles of their works read now and then in a future age by some drowsy churchman or casual straggler like myself, and in another age to be lost even to remembrance. Such is the amount of this boasted immortality. A mere temporary rumor, a local sound; like the tone of that bell which has tolled among these towers, filling the ear for a moment, lingering transiently in echo, and then passing away, like a thing that was not!

While I sat half-murmuring, half-meditating, these unprofitable speculations with my head resting on my hand, I was thrumming with the other hand upon the quarto, until I accidentally loosened the clasps; when, to my utter astonishment, the little book gave two or three yawns, like one awaking from a deep sleep, then a husky hem, and at length began to talk. At first its voice was very hoarse and broken, being much troubled by a cobweb which some studious spider had woven across it, and having probably contracted a cold from long exposure to the chills and damps of the abbey. In a short time, however, it became more distinct, and I soon found it an exceedingly fluent, conversable little tome. Its language, to be sure, was rather quaint and obsolete, and its pronunciation what, in the present day, would be deemed barbarous; but I shall endeavor, as far as I am able, to render it in modern parlance.

It began with railings about the neglect of the world, about merit being suffered to languish in obscurity, and other such commonplace topics of literary repining, and complained bitterly that it had not been opened for more than two centuries—that the dean only looked now and then into the library, sometimes took down a volume or two, trifled with them for a few moments, and then returned them to their shelves. "What a plague do they mean?" said the little quarto, which I began to perceive was somewhat choleric—"what a plague do they mean by keeping several thousand volumes of us shut up here, and watched by a set of old vergers, like so many beauties in a harem, merely to be looked at now and then by the dean? Books were written to give pleasure and to be enjoyed; and I would have a rule passed that the dean should pay each of us a visit at least once a year; or, if he is not equal to the task, let them once in a while turn loose the whole school of Westminster among us, that at any rate we may now and then have an airing."

"Softly, my worthy friend," replied I; "you are not aware how much better you are off than most books of your generation. By being stored away in this ancient library you are like the treasured remains of those saints and monarchs which lie enshrined in the adjoining chapels, while the remains of their contemporary mortals, left to the ordinary course of nature, have long since returned to dust."

"Sir," said the little tome, ruffling his leaves and looking big, "I was written for all the world, not for the bookworms of an abbey. I was intended to circulate from hand to hand, like other great contemporary works; but here have I been clasped up for more than two centuries, and might have silently fallen a prey to these worms that are playing the very vengeance with my intestines if you had not by chance given me an opportunity of uttering a few last words before I go to pieces."

"My good friend," rejoined I, "had you been left to the circulation of which you speak, you would long ere this have been no more. To judge from your physiognomy, you are now well stricken in years: very few of your contemporaries can be at present in existence, and those few owe their longevity to being immured like yourself in old libraries; which, suffer me to add, instead of likening to harems, you might more properly and gratefully have compared to those infirmaries attached to religious establishments for the benefit of the old and decrepit, and where, by quiet fostering and no employment, they often endure to an amazingly good-for-nothing old age. You talk of your contemporaries as if in circulation. Where do we meet with their works? What do we hear of Robert Groteste of Lincoln? No one could have toiled harder than he for immortality. He is said to have written nearly two hundred volumes. He built, as it were, a pyramid of books to perpetuate his name: but, alas! the pyramid has long since fallen, and only a few fragments are scattered in various libraries, where they are scarcely disturbed even by the antiquarian. What do we hear of Giraldus Cambrensis, the historian, antiquary, philosopher, theologian, and poet? He declined two bishoprics that he might shut himself up and write for posterity; but posterity never inquires after his labors. What of Henry of Huntingdon, who, besides a learned history of England, wrote a treatise on the contempt of the world, which the world has revenged by forgetting him? What is quoted of Joseph of Exeter, styled the miracle of his age in classical composition? Of his three great heroic poems, one is lost forever, excepting a mere fragment; the others are known only to a few of the curious in literature; and as to his love verses and epigrams, they have entirely disappeared. What is in current use of John Wallis the Franciscan, who acquired the name of the tree of life? Of William of Malmsbury—of Simeon of Durham—of Benedict of Peterborough—of John Hanvill of St. Albans—of——"

"Prithee, friend," cried the quarto in a testy tone, "how old do you think me? You are talking of authors that lived long before my time, and wrote either in Latin or French, so that they in a manner expatriated themselves, and deserved to be forgotten;* but I, sir, was ushered into the world from the press of the renowned Wynkyn de Worde. I was written in my own native tongue, at a time when the language had become fixed; and indeed I was considered a model of pure and elegant English."

(I should observe that these remarks were couched in such intolerably antiquated terms, that I have had infinite difficulty in rendering them into modern phraseology.)

---

* "In Latin and French hath many soueraine wittes had great delyte to endite, and have many noble thinges fulfilde, but certes there ben some that speaken their poisye in French, of which speche the Frenchmen have as good a fantasye as we have in hearying of Frenchmen's Englishe."—Chaucer's *Testament of Love*.

"I cry you mercy," said I, "for mistaking your age; but it matters little. Almost all the writers of your time have likewise passed into forgetfulness, and De Worde's publications are mere literary rarities among book-collectors. The purity and stability of language, too, on which you found your claims to perpetuity, have been the fallacious dependence of authors of every age, even back to the times of the worthy Robert of Gloucester, who wrote his history in rhymes of mongrel Saxon.* Even now many talk of Spenser's 'well of pure English undefiled,' as if the language ever sprang from a well or fountain-head, and was not rather a mere confluence of various tongues perpetually subject to changes and intermixtures. It is this which has made English literature so extremely mutable, and the reputation built upon it so fleeting. Unless thought can be committed to something more permanent and unchangeable than such a medium, even thought must share the fate of everything else, and fall into decay. This should serve as a check upon the vanity and exultation of the most popular writer. He finds the language in which he has embarked his fame gradually altering and subject to the dilapidations of time and the caprice of fashion. He looks back and beholds the early authors of his country, once the favorites of their day, supplanted by modern writers. A few short ages have covered them with obscurity, and their merits can only be relished by the quaint taste of the bookworm. And such, he anticipates, will be the fate of his own work, which, however it may be admired in its day and held up as a model of purity, will in the course of years grow antiquated

---

* Holinshed in his Chronicle, observes, "afterwards, also, by deligent travell of Geffry Chaucer and John Gowre, in the time of Richard the Second, and after them of John Scogan and John Lydgate, monke of Berrie, our said toong was brought to an excellent passe, notwithstanding that it never came unto the type of perfection until the time of Queen Elizabeth, wherein John Jewell, Bishop of Sarum, John Fox, and sundrie learned and excellent writers, have fully accomplished the ornature of the same, to their great praise and immortal commendation."

and obsolete, until it shall become almost as unintelligible in its native land as an Egyptian obelisk or one of those Runic inscriptions said to exist in the deserts of Tartary." "I declare," added I, with some emotion, "when I contemplate a modern library, filled with new works in all the bravery of rich gilding and binding, I feel disposed to sit down and weep, like the good Xerxes, when he surveyed his army, pranked out in all the splendor of military array, and reflected that in one hundred years not one of them would be in existence!"

"Ah," said the little quarto, with a heavy sigh, "I see how it is: these modern scribblers have superseded all the good old authors. I suppose nothing is read nowadays but Sir Philip Sidney's *Arcadia*, Sackville's stately plays and Mirror for Magistrates, or the fine-spun euphuisms of the 'unparalleled John Lyly.'"

"There you are again mistaken," said I; "the writers whom you suppose in vogue, because they happened to be so when you were last in circulation, have long since had their day. Sir Philip Sidney's *Arcadia*, the immortality of which was so fondly predicted by his admirers,* and which, in truth, was full of noble thoughts, delicate images, and graceful turns of language, is now scarcely ever mentioned. Sackville has strutted into obscurity; and even Lyly, though his writings were once the delight of a court, and apparently perpetuated by a proverb, is now scarcely known even by name. A whole crowd of authors who wrote and wrangled at the time, have likewise gone down with all their writings and their controversies. Wave after wave of succeeding literature has rolled over them, until

---

* "*Live ever sweete booke; the simple image of his gentle witt, and the golden-pillar of his noble courage; and ever notify unto the world that thy writer was the secretary of eloquence, the breath of the muses, the honey-bee of the daintyest flowers of witt and arte, the pith of morale and intellectual virtues, the arme of Bellona in the field, the tonge of Suada in the chamber, the spirits of Practise in esse, and the paragon of excellency in print.*"—Harvey, Pierce's Supererogation.

they are buried so deep, that it is only now and then that some industrious diver after fragments of antiquity brings up a specimen for the gratification of the curious.

"For my part," I continued, "I consider this mutability of language a wise precaution of Providence for the benefit of the world at large, and of authors in particular. To reason from analogy, we daily behold the varied and beautiful tribes of vegetables springing up, flourishing, adorning the fields for a short time, and then fading into dust, to make way for their successors. Were not this the case, the fecundity of nature would be a grievance instead of a blessing. The earth would groan with rank and excessive vegetation, and its surface become a tangled wilderness. In like manner, the works of genius and learning decline and make way for subsequent productions. Language gradually varies, and with it fade away the writings of authors who have flourished their allotted time; otherwise the creative powers of genius would overstock the world, and the mind would be completely bewildered in the endless mazes of literature. Formerly there were some restraints on this excessive multiplication. Works had to be transcribed by hand, which was a slow and laborious operation; they were written either on parchment, which was expensive, so that one work was often erased to make way for another; or on papyrus, which was fragile and extremely perishable. Authorship was a limited and unprofitable craft, pursued chiefly by monks in the leisure and solitude of their cloisters. The accumulation of manuscripts was slow and costly, and confined almost entirely to monasteries. To these circumstances it may, in some measure, be owing that we have not been inundated by the intellect of antiquity—that the fountains of thought have not been broken up, and modern genius drowned in the deluge. But the inventions of paper and the press have put an end to all these restraints. They have made every one a writer, and enabled every mind to pour itself into print, and diffuse itself over the whole intellectual world. The consequences are alarming. The stream of literature has swollen into a torrent—

augmented into a river—expanded into a sea. A few centuries since five or six hundred manuscripts constituted a great library; but what would you say to libraries, such as actually exist, containing three or four hundred thousand volumes; legions of authors at the same time busy; and the press going on with fearfully increasing activity, to double and quadruple the number? Unless some unforeseen mortality should break out among the progeny of the muse, now that she has become so prolific, I tremble for posterity. I fear the mere fluctuation of language will not be sufficient. Criticism may do much; it increases with the increase of literature, and resembles one of those salutary checks on population spoken of by economists. All possible encouragement, therefore, should be given to the growth of critics, good or bad. But I fear all will be in vain; let criticism do what it may, writers will write, printers will print, and the world will inevitably be overstocked with good books. It will soon be the employment of a lifetime merely to learn their names. Many a man of passable information at the present day reads scarcely anything but reviews, and before long a man of erudition will be little better than a mere walking catalogue."

"My very good sir," said the little quarto, yawning most drearily in my face, "excuse my interrupting you, but I perceive you are rather given to prose. I would ask the fate of an author who was making some noise just as I left the world. His reputation, however, was considered quite temporary. The learned shook their heads at him, for he was a poor, half-educated varlet, that knew little of Latin, and nothing of Greek, and had been obliged to run the country for deer-stealing. I think his name was Shakespeare. I presume he soon sunk into oblivion."

"On the contrary," said I, "it is owing to that very man that the literature of his period has experienced a duration beyond the ordinary term of English literature. There rise authors now and then who seem proof against the mutability of language because they have rooted themselves in the unchanging principles of human nature. They are like gigantic trees that we sometimes see on the banks of a stream, which by their vast and deep roots, penetrating through the mere surface and laying hold on the very foundations of the earth, preserve the soil around them from being swept away by the ever-flowing current, and hold up many a neighboring plant, and perhaps worthless weed, to perpetuity. Such is the case with Shakespeare, whom we behold defying the encroachments of time, retaining in modern use the language and literature of his day, and giving duration to many an indifferent author, merely from having flourished in his vicinity. But even he, I grieve to say, is gradually assuming the tint of age, and his whole form is overrun by a profusion of commentators, who, like clambering vines and creepers, almost bury the noble plant that upholds them."

Here the little quarto began to heave his sides and chuckle, until at length he broke out into a plethoric fit of laughter that had well nigh choked him by reason of his excessive corpulency. "Mighty well!" cried he, as soon as he could recover breath, "mighty well! and so you would persuade me that the literature of an age is to be perpetuated by a vagabond deer-stealer! by a man without learning! by a poet! forsooth—a poet!" And here he wheezed forth another fit of laughter.

I confess that I felt somewhat nettled at this rudeness, which, however, I pardoned on account of his having flourished in a less polished age. I determined, nevertheless, not to give up my point.

"Yes," resumed I positively, "a poet; for of all writers he has the best chance for immortality. Others may write from the head, but he writes from the heart, and the heart will always understand him. He is the faithful portrayer of nature, whose features are always the same and always interesting. Prose writers are voluminous and unwieldy; their pages crowded with commonplaces, and their thoughts expanded into tediousness. But with the true poet every thing is terse, touching, or brilliant. He gives the choicest thoughts in the choicest language. He illustrates them by everything that he sees most striking in nature and art. He enriches them by pictures of human life, such as it is passing before him. His writings, therefore, contain the spirit, the aroma, if I may use the phrase, of the age in which he lives. They are caskets which inclose within a small compass the wealth of the language—its family jewels, which are thus transmitted in a portable form to posterity. The setting may occasionally be antiquated, and require now and then to be renewed, as in the case of Chaucer; but the brilliancy and intrinsic value of the gems continue unaltered. Cast a look back over the long reach of literary history. What vast valleys of dullness, filled with monkish legends and academical controversies! What bogs of theological speculations! What dreary wastes of metaphysics! Here and there only do we behold the heaven-illumined bards, elevated like beacons on their widely-separated heights, to transmit the pure light of poetical intelligence from age to age."*

I was just about to launch forth into eulogiums upon the poets of the day when the sudden opening of the door caused me to turn my head. It was the verger, who came to inform me that it was time to close the library. I sought to have a parting word with the quarto, but the worthy little tome was silent; the clasps were closed: and it looked perfectly unconscious of all that had passed. I have been to the library two or three times since, and have endeavored to draw it into further conversation, but in vain; and whether all this rambling

---

* *Thorow earth and waters deepe,*
The pen by skill doth passe:
And featly nyps the worldes abuse,
And shoes us in a glasse,
The vertu and the vice
Of every wight alyve;
The honey comb that bee doth make
Is not so sweet in hyve,
As are the golden leves
That drops from poet's head!
Which doth surmount our common talke
As farre as dross doth lead.   —*Churchyard.*

colloquy actually took place, or whether it was another of those old day-dreams to which I am subject, I have never, to this moment, been able to discover.

THE SPECTRE BRIDEGROOM

A Traveller's Tale*

He that supper for is dight,
He lyes full cold, I trow, this night!
Yestreen to chamber I him led,
This night Gray-Steel has made his bed!
Sir Eger, Sir Grahame, and Sir Gray-Steel.

On the summit of one of the heights of the Odenwald, a wild and romantic tract of Upper Germany that lies not far from the confluence of the Main and the Rhine, there stood many, many years since the castle of the Baron Von Landshort. It is now quite fallen to decay, and almost buried among beech trees and dark firs; above which, however, its old watch-tower may still be seen struggling, like the former possessor I have mentioned, to carry a high head and look down upon the neighboring country.

The baron was a dry branch of the great family of Katzenellenbogen,† and inherited the relics of the property and all the pride, of his ancestors. Though the warlike disposition of his predecessors had much impaired the family possessions, yet the baron still endeavored to keep up some show of former state. The times were peaceable, and the German nobles in general had abandoned their inconvenient old castles, perched like eagles' nests among the

---

* The erudite reader, well versed in good-for-nothing lore, will perceive that the above Tale must have been suggested to the old Swiss by a little French anecdote, a circumstance said to have taken place in Paris.

† i.e., Cat's Elbow—the name of a family of those parts, and very powerful in former times. The appellation, we are told, was given in compliment to a peerless dame of the family, celebrated for a fine arm.

mountains, and had built more convenient residences in the valleys; still, the baron remained proudly drawn up in his little fortress, cherishing with hereditary inveteracy all the old family feuds, so that he was on ill terms with some of his nearest neighbors, on account of disputes that had happened between their great-great-grandfathers.

The baron had but one child, a daughter, but Nature, when she grants but one child, always compensates by making it a prodigy; and so it was with the daughter of the baron. All the nurses, gossips, and country cousins assured her father that she had not her equal for beauty in all Germany; and who should know better than they? She had, moreover, been brought up with great care under the superintendence of two maiden aunts, who had spent some years of their early life at one of the little German courts, and were skilled in all branches of knowledge necessary to the education of a fine lady. Under their instructions she became a miracle of accomplishments. By the time she was eighteen she could embroider to admiration, and had worked whole histories of the saints in tapestry with such strength of expression in their countenances that they looked like so many souls in purgatory. She could read without great difficulty, and had spelled her way through several Church legends and almost all the chivalric wonders of the Heldenbuch. She had even made considerable proficiency in writing; could sign her own name without missing a letter, and so legibly that her aunts could read it without spectacles. She excelled in making little elegant good-for-nothing, lady-like knicknacks of all kinds, was versed in the most abstruse dancing of the day, played a number of airs on the harp and guitar, and knew all the tender ballads of the Minnelieders by heart.

Her aunts, too, having been great flirts and coquettes in their younger days, were admirably calculated to be vigilant guardians and strict censors of the conduct of their niece; for there is no duenna so rigidly prudent and inexorably decorous as a superannuated coquette. She was rarely suffered out of their sight; never went beyond the domains of the castle unless well attended, or rather well watched; had continual lectures read to her about strict decorum and implicit obedience; and, as to the men—pah!—she was taught to hold them at such a distance and in such absolute distrust that, unless properly authorized, she would not have cast a glance upon the handsomest cavalier in the world—no, not if he were even dying at her feet.

The good effects of this system were wonderfully apparent. The young lady was a pattern of docility and correctness. While others were wasting their sweetness in the glare of the world, and liable to be plucked and thrown aside by every hand, she was coyly blooming into fresh and lovely womanhood under the protection of those immaculate spinsters, like a rosebud blushing forth among guardian thorns. Her aunts looked upon her with pride and exultation, and vaunted that, though all the other young ladies in the world might go astray, yet thank Heaven, nothing of the kind could happen to the heiress of Katzenellenbogen.

But, however scantily the Baron Von Landshort might be provided with children, his household was by no means a small one; for Providence had enriched him with abundance of poor relations. They, one and all, possessed the affectionate disposition common to humble relatives—were wonderfully attached to the baron, and took every possible occasion to come in swarms and enliven the castle. All family festivals were commemorated by these good people at the baron's expense; and when they were filled with good cheer they would declare that there was nothing on earth so delightful as these family meetings, these jubilees of the heart.

The baron, though a small man, had a large soul, and it swelled with satisfaction at the consciousness of being the greatest man in the little world about him. He loved to tell long stories about the stark old warriors whose portraits looked grimly down from the walls around, and he found no listeners equal to those who fed at his expense. He was much given to the marvellous and a firm believer in all those supernatural tales with which every mountain and valley in Germany abounds. The faith of his guests exceeded even his own: they listened to every tale of wonder with open eyes and mouth, and never failed to be astonished, even though repeated for the hundredth time. Thus lived the Baron Von Landshort, the oracle of his table, the absolute monarch of his little territory, and happy, above all things, in the persuasion that he was the wisest man of the age.

At the time of which my story treats there was a great family gathering at the castle on an affair of the utmost importance: it was to receive the destined bridegroom of the baron's daughter. A negotiation had been carried on between the father and an old nobleman of Bavaria to unite the dignity of their houses by the marriage of their children. The preliminaries had been conducted with proper punctilio. The young people were betrothed without seeing each other, and the time was appointed for the marriage ceremony. The young Count Von Altenburg had been recalled from the army for the purpose, and was actually on his way to the baron's to receive his bride. Missives had even been received from him from Würtzburg , where he was accidentally detained, mentioning the day and hour when he might be expected to arrive.

The castle was in a tumult of preparation to give him a suitable welcome. The fair bride had been decked out with uncommon care. The two aunts had superintended her toilet, and quarrelled the whole morning about every article of her dress. The young lady had taken advantage of their contest to follow the bent of her own taste; and fortunately it was a good one. She looked as lovely as youthful bridegroom could desire; and the flutter of expectation heightened the lustre of her charms.

The suffusions that mantled her face and neck, the gentle heaving of the bosom, the eye now and then lost in reverie, all betrayed the soft tumult that was going on in her little heart. The aunts were continually hovering around her, for maiden aunts are apt to take great interest in affairs of this nature. They were giving her a world of staid counsel how to deport herself, what to say, and in what manner to receive the expected lover.

The baron was no less busied in preparations. He had, in truth, nothing exactly to do; but he was naturally a fuming, bustling little man, and could not remain passive when all the world was in a hurry. He worried from top to bottom of the castle with an air of infinite anxiety; he continually called the servants from their work to exhort them to be diligent; and buzzed about every hall and chamber, as idly restless and importunate as a blue-bottle fly on a warm summer's day.

In the mean time the fatted calf had been killed; the forests had rung with the clamor of the huntsmen; the kitchen was crowded with good cheer; the cellars had yielded up whole oceans of *Rhein-wein* and *Ferne-wein*; and even the great Heidelberg tun had been laid under contribution. Everything was ready to receive the distinguished guest with *Saus und Braus* in the true spirit of German hospitality; but the guest delayed to make his appearance. Hour rolled after hour. The sun, that had poured his downward rays upon the rich forest of the Odenwald, now just gleamed along the summits of the mountains. The baron mounted the highest tower and strained his eyes in hopes of catching a distant sight of the count and his attendants. Once he thought he beheld them; the sound of horns came floating from the valley, prolonged by the mountain echoes. A number of horsemen were seen far below slowly advancing along the road; but when they had nearly reached the foot of the mountain they suddenly struck off in a different direction. The last ray of sunshine departed, the bats began to flit by in the twilight, the road grew dimmer and dimmer to the view, and nothing appeared stirring in it but now and then a peasant lagging homeward from his labor.

While the old castle of Landshort was in this state of perplexity a very interesting scene was transacting in a different part of the Odenwald.

The young Count Von Altenburg was tranquilly pursuing his route in that sober jog-trot way in which a man travels toward matrimony when his friends have taken all the trouble and uncertainty of courtship off his hands and a bride is waiting for him as certainly as a dinner at the end of his journey. He had encountered at Würtzburg a youthful companion-in-arms with whom he had seen some service on the frontiers—Herman Von Starkenfaust, one of the stoutest hands and worthiest hearts of German chivalry—who was now returning from the army. His father's castle was not far distant from the old fortress of Landshort, although an hereditary feud rendered the families hostile and strangers to each other.

In the warm-hearted moment of recognition the young friends related all their past adventures and fortunes, and the count gave the whole history of his intended nuptials with a young lady whom he had never seen, but of whose charms he had received the most enrapturing descriptions.

As the route of the friends lay in the same direction, they agreed to perform the rest of their journey together, and that they might do it the more leisurely, set off from Würtzburg at an early hour, the count having given directions for his retinue to follow and overtake him.

They beguiled their wayfaring with recollections of their military scenes and adventures; but the count was apt to be a little tedious now and then about the reputed charms of his bride and the felicity that awaited him.

In this way they had entered among the mountains of the Odenwald, and were traversing one of its most lonely and thickly wooded passes. It is well known that the forests of Germany have always been as much infested by robbers as its castles by spectres; and at this time the former were particularly numerous, from the hordes of disbanded soldiers wandering about the country. It will not appear extraordinary, therefore, that the cavaliers were attacked by a gang of these stragglers, in the midst of the forest. They defended themselves with bravery, but were nearly overpowered when the count's retinue arrived to their assistance. At sight of them the robbers fled, but not until the count had received a mortal wound. He was slowly and carefully conveyed back to the city of Würtzburg, and a friar summoned from a neighboring convent who was famous for his skill in administering to both soul and body; but half of his skill was superfluous; the moments of the unfortunate count were numbered.

With his dying breath he entreated his friend to repair instantly to the castle of Landshort and explain the fatal cause of his not keeping his appointment with his bride. Though not the most ardent of lovers, he was one of the most punctilious of men, and appeared earnestly solicitous that his mission should be speedily and courteously executed. "Unless this is done," said he, "I shall not sleep quietly in my grave." He repeated these last words with peculiar solemnity. A request at a moment so impressive admitted no hesitation. Starkenfaust endeavored to soothe him to calmness, promised faithfully to execute his wish, and gave him his hand in solemn pledge. The dying man pressed it in acknowledgment, but soon lapsed into delirium—raved about his bride, his engagements, his plighted word—ordered his horse, that he might ride to the castle of Landshort, and expired in the fancied act of vaulting into the saddle.

Starkenfaust bestowed a sigh and a soldier's tear on the untimely fate of his comrade and then pondered on the awkward mission he had undertaken. His heart was heavy and his head perplexed; for he was to present himself an unbidden guest among hostile people, and to damp their festivity with tidings fatal to their hopes. Still, there were certain whisperings of curiosity in his bosom to see this far-famed beauty of Katzenellenbogen, so cautiously shut up from the world; for he was a passionate admirer of the sex, and there was a dash of eccentricity and enterprise in his character that made him fond of all singular adventure.

Previous to his departure he made all due arrangements with the holy fraternity of the convent for the funeral solemnities of his friend, who was to be buried in the cathedral of Würtzburg near some of his illustrious relatives, and the mourning retinue of the count took charge of his remains.

It is now high time that we should return to the ancient family of Katzenellenbogen, who were impatient for their guest, and still more for their dinner, and to the worthy little baron, whom we left airing himself on the watch-tower.

Night closed in, but still no guest arrived. The baron descended from the tower in despair. The banquet, which had been delayed from hour to hour, could no longer be postponed. The meats were already overdone, the cook in an agony, and the whole household had the look of a garrison, that had been reduced by famine. The baron was obliged reluctantly to give orders for the feast without the presence of the guest. All were seated at table, and just on the point of commencing, when the sound of a horn from without the gate gave notice of the approach of a stranger. Another long blast filled the old courts of the castle with its echoes, and was answered by the warder from the walls. The baron hastened to receive his future son-in-law.

The drawbridge had been let down, and the stranger was before the gate. He was a tall gallant cavalier, mounted on a black steed. His countenance was pale, but he had a beaming, romantic eye and an air of stately melancholy. The baron was a little mortified that he should have come in this simple, solitary style. His dignity for a moment was ruffled, and he felt disposed to consider it a want of proper respect for the important occasion and the important family with which he was to be connected. He pacified himself, however, with the conclusion that it must have been youthful impatience which had induced him thus to spur on sooner than his attendants.

"I am sorry," said the stranger, "to break in upon you thus unseasonably—"

Here the baron interrupted him with a world of compliments and greetings, for, to tell the truth, he prided himself upon his courtesy and eloquence. The stranger attempted once or twice to stem the torrent of words, but in vain, so he bowed his head and suffered it to flow on. By the time the baron had come to a pause they had reached the inner court of the castle, and the stranger was again about to speak, when he was once more interrupted by the appearance of the female part of the family, leading forth the shrinking and blushing bride. He gazed on her for a moment as one entranced; it seemed as if his whole soul beamed forth in the gaze and rested upon that lovely form. One of the maiden aunts whispered something in her ear; she made an effort to speak; her moist blue eye was timidly raised, gave a shy glance of inquiry on the stranger, and was cast again to the ground. The words died away, but there was a sweet smile playing about her lips, and a soft dimpling of the cheek that showed her glance had not been unsatisfactory. It was impossible for a girl of the fond age of eighteen, highly predisposed for love and matrimony, not to be pleased with so gallant a cavalier.

The late hour at which the guest had arrived left no time for parley. The baron was peremptory, and deferred all particular conversation until the morning, and led the way to the untasted banquet.

It was served up in the great hall of the castle. Around the walls hung the hard-favored portraits of the heroes of the house of Katzenellenbogen, and the trophies which they had gained in the field, and in the chase. Hacked corselets, splintered jousting spears, and tattered banners were mingled with the spoils of sylvan warfare: the jaws of the wolf and the tusks of the boar grinned horribly among crossbows and battle-axes, and a huge pair of antlers branched immediately over the head of the youthful bridegroom.

The cavalier took but little notice of the company or the entertainment. He scarcely tasted the banquet, but seemed absorbed in admiration of his bride. He conversed in a low tone that could not be overheard, for the language of love is never loud; but where is the female ear so dull that it cannot catch the softest whisper of the lover? There was a mingled tenderness and gravity in his manner that appeared to have a powerful effect upon the young lady. Her color came and went as she listened with deep attention. Now and then she made some blushing reply, and when his eye was turned away she would steal a sidelong glance at his romantic countenance, and heave a gentle sigh of tender happiness. It was evident that the young couple were completely enamored. The aunts, who were deeply versed in the mysteries of the heart, declared that they had fallen in love with each other at first sight.

The feast went on merrily, or at least noisily, for the guests were all blessed with those keen appetites that attend upon light purses and mountain air. The baron told his best and longest stories, and never had he told them so well or with such great effect. If there was anything marvellous, his auditors were lost in astonishment; and if anything facetious, they were sure to laugh exactly in the right place. The baron, it is true, like most great men, was too dignified to utter any joke but a dull one; it was always enforced, however, by a bumper of excellent Hockheimer, and even a dull joke at one's own table, served up with jolly old wine, is irresistible. Many good things were said by poorer and keener wits that would not bear repeating, except on similar occasions; many sly speeches whispered in ladies' ears that almost convulsed them with suppressed laughter; and a song or two roared out by a poor but merry and broad-faced cousin of the baron that absolutely made the maiden aunts hold up their fans.

Amidst all this revelry the stranger guest maintained a most singular and unseasonable gravity. His countenance assumed a deeper cast of dejection as the evening advanced, and, strange as it may appear, even the baron's jokes seemed only to render him the more melancholy. At times he was lost in thought, and at times there was a perturbed and restless wandering of the eye that bespoke a mind but ill at ease. His conversations with the bride became more and more earnest and mysterious. Lowering clouds began to steal over the fair serenity of her brow, and tremors to run through her tender frame.

All this could not escape the notice of the company. Their gayety was chilled by the unaccountable gloom of the bridegroom; their spirits were infected; whispers and glances were interchanged, accompanied by shrugs and dubious shakes of the head. The song and the laugh grew less and less frequent: there were dreary pauses in the conversation, which were at length succeeded by wild tales and supernatural legends. One dismal story produced another still more dismal, and the baron nearly frightened some of the ladies into hysterics with the history of the goblin horseman that carried away the fair Leonora—a dreadful story which has since been put into excellent verse, and is read and believed by all the world.

The bridegroom listened to this tale with profound attention. He kept his eyes steadily fixed on the baron, and, as the story drew to a close, began gradually to rise from his seat, growing taller and taller, until in the baron's entranced eye he seemed almost to tower into a giant. The moment the tale was finished he heaved a deep sigh and took a solemn farewell of the company. They were all amazement. The baron was perfectly thunderstruck.

"What! Going to leave the castle at midnight? Why, everything was prepared for his reception; a chamber was ready for him if he wished to retire."

The stranger shook his head mournfully and mysteriously: "I must lay my head in a different chamber to-night."

There was something in this reply and the tone in which it was uttered that made the baron's heart misgive him; but he rallied his forces and repeated his hospitable entreaties.

The stranger shook his head silently, but positively, at every offer, and, waving his farewell to the company, stalked slowly out of the hall. The maiden aunts were absolutely petrified; the bride hung her head and a tear stole to her eye.

The baron followed the stranger to the great court of the castle, where the black charger stood pawing the earth and snorting with impatience. When they had reached the portal, whose deep archway was dimly lighted by a cresset, the stranger paused, and addressed the baron in a hollow tone of voice, which the vaulted roof rendered still more sepulchral.

"Now that we are alone," said he, "I will impart to you the reason of my going. I have a solemn, an indispensable engagement—"

"Why," said the baron, "cannot you send some one in your place?"

"It admits of no substitute—I must attend it in person; I must away to Würtzburg cathedral—"

"Ay," said the baron, plucking up spirit, "but not until to-morrow— to-morrow you shall take your bride there."

"No! no!" replied the stranger, with tenfold solemnity, "my engagement is with no bride—the worms! The worms expect me! I am a dead man—I have been slain by robbers—my body lies at Würtzburg—at midnight I am to be buried—the grave is waiting for me—I must keep my appointment!"

He sprang on his black charger, dashed over the drawbridge, and the clattering of his horse's hoofs was lost in the whistling of the night blast.

The baron returned to the hall in the utmost consternation, and related what had passed. Two ladies fainted outright, others sickened at the idea of having banqueted with a spectre. It was the opinion of some that this might be the wild huntsman, famous in German legend. Some talked of mountain sprites, of wood-demons, and of other supernatural beings with which the good people of Germany have been so grievously harassed since time immemorial. One of the poor relations ventured to suggest that it might be some sportive evasion of the young cavalier, and that the very gloominess of the caprice seemed to accord with so melancholy a personage. This, however, drew on him, the indignation of the whole company, and especially of the baron, who looked upon him as little better than an infidel; so that he was fain to abjure his heresy as speedily as possible and come into the faith of the true believers.

But, whatever may have been the doubts entertained, they were completely put to an end by the arrival next day of regular missives confirming the intelligence of the young count's murder and his interment in Würtzburg cathedral.

The dismay at the castle may well be imagined. The baron shut himself up in his chamber. The guests, who had come to rejoice with him, could not think of abandoning him in his distress. They wandered about the courts or collected in groups in the hall, shaking their heads and shrugging their shoulders at the troubles of so good a man, and sat longer than ever at table, and ate and drank more stoutly than ever, by way of keeping up their spirits. But the situation of the widowed bride was the most pitiable. To have lost a husband before she had even embraced him—and such a husband! If the very spectre could be so gracious and noble, what must have been the living man? She filled the house with lamentations.

On the night of the second day of her widowhood she had retired to her chamber, accompanied by one of her aunts, who insisted on sleeping with her. The aunt, who was one of the best tellers of ghost-stories in all Germany, had just been recounting one of her longest, and had fallen asleep in the very midst of it. The chamber was remote and overlooked a small garden. The niece lay pensively gazing at the beams of the rising moon as they trembled on the leaves of an aspen tree before the lattice. The castle clock had just tolled midnight when a soft strain of music stole up from the garden. She rose hastily from her bed and stepped lightly to the window. A tall figure stood among the shadows of the trees. As it raised its head a beam of moonlight fell upon the countenance. Heaven and earth! She beheld the Spectre Bridegroom! A loud shriek at that moment burst upon her ear, and her aunt, who had been awakened by the music and had followed her silently to the window, fell into her arms. When she looked again the spectre had disappeared.

Of the two females, the aunt now required the most soothing, for she was perfectly beside herself with terror. As to the young lady, there was something even in the spectre of her lover that seemed endearing. There was still the semblance of manly beauty, and, though the shadow of a man is but little calculated to satisfy the affections of a lovesick girl, yet where the substance is not to be had even that is consoling. The aunt declared she would never sleep in that chamber again; the niece, for once, was refractory, and declared as strongly that she would sleep in no other in the castle: the consequence was, that she had to sleep in it alone; but she drew a promise from her aunt not to relate the story of the spectre, lest she should be denied the only melancholy pleasure left her on earth—that of inhabiting the chamber over which the guardian shade of her lover kept its nightly vigils.

How long the good old lady would have observed this promise is uncertain, for she dearly loved to talk of the marvellous, and there is a triumph in being the first to tell a frightful story; it is, however, still quoted in the neighborhood as a memorable instance of female secrecy that she kept it to herself for a whole week, when she was suddenly absolved from all further restraint by intelligence brought to the breakfast-table one morning that the young lady was not to be found. Her room was empty—the bed had not been slept in—the window was open and the bird had flown!

The astonishment and concern with which the intelligence was received can only be imagined by those who have witnessed the agitation which the mishaps of a great man cause among his friends. Even the poor relations paused for a moment from the indefatigable labors of the trencher, when the aunt, who had at first been struck speechless, wrung her hands and shrieked out, "The goblin! The goblin! She's carried away by the goblin!"

In a few words she related the fearful scene of the garden, and concluded that the spectre must have carried off his bride. Two of the domestics corroborated the opinion, for they had heard the clattering of a horse's hoofs down the mountain about midnight, and had no doubt that it was the spectre on his black charger bearing her away to the tomb. All present were struck with the direful probability for events of the kind are extremely common in Germany, as many well-authenticated histories bear witness.

What a lamentable situation was that of the poor baron! What a heartrending dilemma for a fond father and a member of the great family of Katzenellenbogen! His only daughter had either been rapt away to the grave, or he was to have some wood-demon for a son-in-law, and perchance a troop of goblin grandchildren. As usual, he was completely bewildered, and all the castle in an uproar. The men were ordered to take horse and scour every road and path and glen of the Odenwald. The baron himself had just drawn on his jack-boots, girded on his sword, and was about to mount his steed to sally forth on the doubtful quest, when he was brought to a pause by a new apparition. A lady was seen approaching the castle mounted on a palfrey, attended by a cavalier on horseback. She galloped up to the gate, sprang from her horse, and, falling at the baron's feet, embraced his knees. It was his lost daughter, and her companion— the Spectre Bridegroom! The baron was astounded. He looked at his daughter, then at the spectre, and almost doubted the evidence of his senses. The latter, too, was wonderfully improved in his appearance since his visit to the world of spirits. His dress was splendid, and set off a noble figure of manly symmetry. He was no longer pale and melancholy. His fine countenance was flushed with the glow of youth, and joy rioted in his large dark eye.

The mystery was soon cleared up. The cavalier (for, in truth, as you must have known all the while, he was no goblin) announced himself as Sir Herman Von Starkenfaust. He related his adventure with the young count. He told how he had hastened to the castle to deliver the unwelcome tidings, but that the eloquence of the baron had interrupted him in every attempt to tell his tale. How the sight of the bride had completely captivated him and that to pass a few hours near her he had tacitly suffered the mistake to continue. How he had been sorely perplexed in what way to make a decent retreat, until the baron's goblin stories had suggested his eccentric exit. How, fearing the feudal hostility of the family, he had repeated his visits by stealth—had haunted the garden beneath the young lady's window—had wooed—had won—had borne away in triumph—and, in a word, had wedded the fair.

Under any other circumstances the baron would have been inflexible, for he was tenacious of paternal authority and devoutly obstinate in all family feuds; but he loved his daughter; he had lamented her as lost; he rejoiced to find her still alive; and, though her husband was of a hostile house, yet, thank heaven, he was not a goblin. There was something, it must be acknowledged, that did not exactly accord with his notions of strict veracity in the joke the knight had passed upon him of his being a dead man; but several old friends present, who had served in the wars, assured him that every stratagem was excusable in love, and that the cavalier was entitled to especial privilege, having lately served as a trooper.

Matters, therefore, were happily arranged. The baron pardoned the young couple on the spot. The revels at the castle were resumed. The poor relations overwhelmed this new member of the family with loving-kindness; he was so gallant, so generous—and so rich. The aunts, it is true, were somewhat scandalized that their system of strict seclusion and passive obedience should be so badly exemplified, but attributed it all to their negligence in not having the windows grated. One of them was particularly mortified at having her marvellous story marred, and that the only spectre she had ever seen should turn out a counterfeit; but the niece seemed perfectly happy at having found him substantial flesh and blood. And so the story ends.

THE LEGEND OF SLEEPY HOLLOW

Found Among the Papers of
the Late Diedrich Knickerbocker

A pleasing land of drowsy head it was,
Of dreams that wave before the half-shut eye;
And of gay castles in the clouds that pass,
Forever flushing round a summer sky.
CASTLE OF INDOLENCE.

In the bosom of one of those spacious coves which indent the eastern shore of the Hudson, at that broad expansion of the river denominated by the ancient Dutch navigators the Tappan Zee, and where they always prudently shortened sail and implored the protection of St. Nicholas when they crossed, there lies a small market town or rural port, which by some is called Greensburgh, but which is more generally and properly known by the name of Tarry Town. This name was given, we are told, in former days, by the good housewives of the adjacent country, from the inveterate propensity of their husbands to linger about the village tavern on market days. Be that as it may, I do not vouch for the fact, but merely advert to it, for the sake of being precise and authentic. Not far from this village, perhaps about two miles, there is a little valley or rather lap of land among high hills, which is one of the quietest places in the whole world. A small brook glides through it, with just murmur enough to lull one to repose; and the occasional whistle of a quail or tapping of a woodpecker is almost the only sound that ever breaks in upon the uniform tranquillity.

I recollect that, when a stripling, my first exploit in squirrel-shooting was in a grove of tall walnut-trees that shades one side of the valley. I had wandered into it at noontime, when all nature is peculiarly quiet, and was startled by the roar of my own gun, as it broke the Sabbath stillness around and was prolonged and reverberated by the angry echoes. If ever I should wish for a retreat whither I might steal from the world and its distractions, and dream quietly away the remnant of a troubled life, I know of none more promising than this little valley.

From the listless repose of the place, and the peculiar character of its inhabitants, who are descendants from the original Dutch settlers, this sequestered glen has long been known by the name of SLEEPY HOLLOW, and its rustic lads are called the Sleepy Hollow Boys throughout all the neighboring country. A drowsy, dreamy influence seems to hang over the land, and to pervade the very atmosphere. Some say that the place was bewitched by a high German doctor, during the early days of the settlement; others, that an old Indian chief, the prophet or wizard of his tribe, held his powwows there before the country was discovered by Master Hendrick Hudson. Certain it is, the place still continues under the sway of some witching power, that holds a spell over the minds of the good people, causing them to walk in a continual reverie. They are given to all kinds of marvellous beliefs, are subject to trances and visions, and frequently see strange sights, and hear music and voices in the air. The whole neighborhood abounds with local tales, haunted spots, and twilight superstitions; stars shoot and meteors glare oftener across the valley than in any other part of the country, and the nightmare, with her whole ninefold, seems to make it the favorite scene of her gambols.

The dominant spirit, however, that haunts this enchanted region, and seems to be commander-in-chief of all the powers of the air, is the apparition of a figure on horseback, without a head. It is said by some to be the ghost of a Hessian trooper, whose head had been carried away by a cannonball, in some nameless battle during the Revolutionary War, and who is ever and anon seen by the country folk hurrying along in the gloom of night, as if on the wings of the wind. His haunts are not confined to the valley, but extend at times to the adjacent roads, and especially to the vicinity of a church at no great distance. Indeed, certain of the most authentic historians of those parts, who have been careful in collecting and collating the floating facts concerning this spectre, allege that the body of the trooper having been buried in the churchyard, the ghost rides forth to the scene of battle in nightly quest of his head, and that the rushing speed with which he sometimes passes along the Hollow, like a midnight blast, is owing to his being belated, and in a hurry to get back to the churchyard before daybreak.

Such is the general purport of this legendary superstition, which has furnished materials for many a wild story in that region of shadows; and the spectre is known at all the country firesides, by the name of the Headless Horseman of Sleepy Hollow.

It is remarkable that the visionary propensity I have mentioned is not confined to the native inhabitants of the valley, but is unconsciously imbibed by every one who resides there for a time. However wide awake they may have been before they entered that sleepy region, they are sure, in a little time, to inhale the witching influence of the air, and begin to grow imaginative, to dream dreams, and see apparitions.

I mention this peaceful spot with all possible laud, for it is in such little retired Dutch valleys, found here and there embosomed in the great State of New York, that population, manners, and customs remain fixed, while the great torrent of migration and improvement, which is making such incessant changes in other parts of this restless country, sweeps by them unobserved. They are like those little nooks of still water, which border a rapid stream, where we may see the straw and bubble riding quietly at anchor, or slowly revolving in their mimic harbor, undisturbed by the rush of the passing current. Though many years have elapsed since I trod the drowsy shades of Sleepy Hollow, yet I question whether I should not still find the same trees and the same families vegetating in its sheltered bosom.

In this by-place of nature there abode, in a remote period of American history, that is to say, some thirty years since, a worthy wight of the name of Ichabod Crane, who sojourned, or, as he expressed it, "tarried," in Sleepy Hollow, for the purpose of instructing the children of the vicinity. He was a native of Connecticut, a State which supplies the Union with pioneers for the mind as well as for the forest, and sends forth yearly its legions of frontier woodmen and country schoolmasters. The cognomen of Crane was not inapplicable to his person. He was tall, but exceedingly lank, with narrow shoulders, long arms and legs, hands that dangled a mile out of his sleeves, feet that might have served for shovels, and his whole frame most loosely hung together. His head was small, and flat at top, with huge ears, large green glassy eyes, and a long snipe nose, so that it looked like a weathercock perched upon his spindle neck to tell which way the wind blew. To see him striding along the profile of a hill on a windy day, with his clothes bagging and fluttering about him, one might have mistaken him for the genius of famine descending upon the earth, or some scarecrow eloped from a cornfield.

His schoolhouse was a low building of one large room, rudely constructed of logs; the windows partly glazed, and partly patched with leaves of old copybooks. It was most ingeniously secured at vacant hours, by a withe twisted in the handle of the door, and stakes set against the window shutters; so that though a thief might get in with perfect ease, he would find some embarrassment in getting out;—an idea most probably borrowed by the architect, Yost Van Houten, from the mystery of an eelpot. The schoolhouse stood in a rather lonely but pleasant situation, just at the foot of a woody hill, with a brook running close by, and a formidable birch-tree growing at one end of it. From hence the low murmur of his pupils' voices, conning over their lessons, might be heard on a drowsy summer's day, like the hum of a beehive; interrupted now and then by the authoritative voice of the master, in the tone of menace or command, or, peradventure, by the appalling sound of the birch, as he urged some tardy loiterer along the flowery path of knowledge. Truth to say, he was a conscientious man, and ever bore in mind the golden maxim, "Spare the rod and spoil the child." Ichabod Crane's scholars certainly were not spoiled.

I would not have it imagined, however, that he was one of those cruel potentates of the school who joy in the smart of their subjects; on the contrary, he administered justice with discrimination rather than severity; taking the burden off the backs of the weak, and laying it on those of the strong. Your mere puny stripling, that winced at the least flourish of the rod, was passed by with indulgence; but the claims of justice were satisfied by inflicting a double portion on some little tough wrong-headed, broad-skirted Dutch urchin, who sulked and swelled and grew dogged and sullen beneath the birch. All this he called "doing his duty" by their parents; and he never inflicted a chastisement without following it by the assurance, so consolatory to the smarting urchin, that "he would remember it and thank him for it the longest day he had to live."

When school hours were over, he was even the companion and playmate of the larger boys; and on holiday afternoons would convoy some of the smaller ones home, who happened to have pretty sisters, or good housewives for mothers, noted for the comforts of the cupboard. Indeed, it behooved him to keep on good terms with his pupils. The revenue arising from his school was small, and would have been scarcely sufficient to furnish him with daily bread, for he was a huge feeder, and, though lank, had the dilating powers of an anaconda; but to help out his maintenance, he was, according to country custom in those parts, boarded and lodged at the houses of the farmers whose children he instructed. With these he lived successively a week at a time, thus going the rounds of the neighborhood, with all his worldly effects tied up in a cotton handkerchief.

That all this might not be too onerous on the purses of his rustic patrons, who are apt to consider the costs of schooling a grievous burden, and schoolmasters as mere drones, he had various ways of rendering himself both useful and agreeable. He assisted the farmers occasionally in the lighter labors of their farms, helped to make hay, mended the fences, took the horses to water, drove the cows from pasture, and cut wood for the winter fire. He laid aside, too, all the dominant dignity and absolute sway with which he lorded it in his little empire, the school, and became wonderfully gentle and ingratiating. He found favor in the eyes of the mothers by petting the children, particularly the youngest; and like the lion bold, which whilom so magnanimously the lamb did hold, he would sit with a child on one knee, and rock a cradle with his foot for whole hours together.

In addition to his other vocations, he was the singing-master of the neighborhood, and picked up many bright shillings by instructing the young folks in psalmody. It was a matter of no little vanity to him on Sundays, to take his station in front of the church gallery, with a band of chosen singers; where, in his own mind, he completely carried away the palm from the parson. Certain it is, his voice resounded far above all the rest of the congregation; and there are peculiar quavers still to be heard in that church, and which may even be heard half a mile off, quite to the opposite side of the millpond, on a still Sunday morning, which are said to be legitimately descended from the nose of Ichabod Crane. Thus, by divers little makeshifts, in that ingenious way which is commonly denominated "by hook and by crook," the worthy pedagogue got on tolerably enough, and was thought, by all who understood nothing of the labor of headwork, to have a wonderfully easy life of it.

The schoolmaster is generally a man of some importance in the female circle of a rural neighborhood; being considered a kind of idle, gentlemanlike personage, of vastly superior taste and accomplishments to the rough country swains, and, indeed, inferior in learning only to the parson. His appearance, therefore, is apt to occasion some little stir at the tea-table of a farmhouse, and the addition of a supernumerary dish of cakes or sweetmeats, or, peradventure, the parade of a silver teapot. Our man of letters, therefore, was peculiarly happy in the smiles of all the country damsels. How he would figure among them in the churchyard, between services on Sundays; gathering grapes for them from the wild vines that overran the surrounding trees; reciting for their amusement all the epitaphs on the tombstones; or sauntering, with a whole bevy of them, along the banks of the adjacent millpond; while the more bashful country bumpkins hung sheepishly back, envying his superior elegance and address.

From his half-itinerant life, also, he was a kind of travelling gazette, carrying the whole budget of local gossip from house to house, so that his appearance was always greeted with satisfaction. He was, moreover, esteemed by the women as a man of great erudition, for he had read several books quite through, and was a perfect master of Cotton Mather's *History of New England Witchcraft*, in which, by the way, he most firmly and potently believed.

He was, in fact, an odd mixture of small shrewdness and simple credulity. His appetite for the marvellous, and his powers of digesting it, were equally extraordinary; and both had been increased by his residence in this spellbound region. No tale was too gross or monstrous for his capacious swallow. It was often his delight, after his school was dismissed in the afternoon, to stretch himself on the rich bed of clover bordering the little brook that whimpered by his schoolhouse, and there con over old Mather's direful tales, until the gathering dusk of evening made the printed page a mere mist before his eyes. Then, as he wended his way by swamp and stream and awful woodland, to the farmhouse where he happened to be quartered, every sound of nature, at that witching hour, fluttered his excited imagination; the moan of the whip-poor-will from the hillside, the boding cry of the tree toad, that harbinger of storm, the dreary hooting of the screech owl, or the sudden rustling in the thicket of birds frightened from their roost. The fireflies, too, which sparkled most vividly in the darkest places, now and then startled him, as one of uncommon brightness would stream across his path; and if, by chance, a huge blockhead of a beetle came winging his blundering flight against him, the poor varlet was ready to give up the ghost, with the idea that he was struck with a witch's token. His only resource on such occasions, either to drown thought or drive away evil spirits, was to sing psalm tunes and the good people of Sleepy Hollow, as they sat by their doors of an evening, were often filled with awe at hearing his nasal melody, "in linked sweetness long drawn out," floating from the distant hill, or along the dusky road.

Another of his sources of fearful pleasure was to pass long winter evenings with the old Dutch wives, as they sat spinning by the fire, with a row of apples roasting and spluttering along the hearth, and listen to their marvellous tales of ghosts and goblins, and haunted fields, and haunted brooks, and haunted bridges, and haunted houses, and particularly of the headless horseman, or Galloping Hessian of the Hollow, as they sometimes called him. He would delight them equally by his anecdotes of witchcraft, and of the direful omens and portentous sights and sounds in the air, which prevailed in the earlier times of Connecticut; and would frighten them woefully with speculations upon comets and shooting stars; and with the alarming fact that the world did absolutely turn round, and that they were half the time topsy-turvy!

But if there was a pleasure in all this, while snugly cuddling in the chimney corner of a chamber that was all of a ruddy glow from the crackling wood fire, and where, of course, no spectre dared to show its face, it was dearly purchased by the terrors of his subsequent walk homewards. What fearful shapes and shadows beset his path, amidst the dim and ghastly glare of a snowy night! With what wistful look did he eye every trembling ray of light streaming across the waste fields from some distant window! How often was he appalled by some shrub covered with snow, which, like a sheeted spectre, beset his very path! How often did he shrink with curdling awe at the sound of his own steps on the frosty crust beneath his feet; and dread to look over his shoulder, lest he should behold some uncouth being tramping close behind him! And how often was he thrown into complete dismay by some rushing blast, howling among the trees, in the idea that it was the Galloping Hessian on one of his nightly scourings!

All these, however, were mere terrors of the night, phantoms of the mind that walk in darkness; and though he had seen many spectres in his time, and been more than once beset by Satan in divers shapes, in his lonely perambulations, yet daylight put an end to all these evils; and he would have passed a pleasant life of it, in despite of the Devil and all his works, if his path had not been crossed by a being that causes more perplexity to mortal man than ghosts, goblins, and the whole race of witches put together, and that was—a woman.

Among the musical disciples who assembled, one evening in each week, to receive his instructions in psalmody, was Katrina Van Tassel, the daughter and only child of a substantial Dutch farmer. She was a blooming lass of fresh eighteen; plump as a partridge; ripe and melting and rosy-cheeked as one of her father's peaches, and universally famed, not merely for her beauty, but her vast expectations. She was withal a little of a coquette, as might be perceived even in her dress, which was a mixture of ancient and modern fashions, as most suited to set off her charms. She wore the ornaments of pure yellow gold, which her great-great-grandmother had brought over from Saardam; the tempting stomacher of the olden time, and withal a provokingly short petticoat, to display the prettiest foot and ankle in the country round.

Ichabod Crane had a soft and foolish heart towards the sex; and it is not to be wondered at that so tempting a morsel soon found favor in his eyes, more especially after he had visited her in her paternal mansion. Old Baltus Van Tassel was a perfect picture of a thriving, contented, liberal-hearted farmer. He seldom, it is true, sent either his eyes or his thoughts beyond the boundaries of his own farm; but within those everything was snug, happy and well-conditioned. He was satisfied with his wealth, but not proud of it; and piqued himself upon the hearty abundance, rather than the style in which he lived. His stronghold was situated on the banks of the Hudson, in one of those green, sheltered, fertile nooks in which the Dutch farmers are so fond of nestling. A great elm tree spread its broad branches over it, at the foot of which bubbled up a spring of the softest and sweetest water, in a little well formed of a barrel; and then stole sparkling away through the grass, to a neighboring brook, that babbled along among alders and dwarf willows. Hard by the farmhouse was a vast barn, that might have served for a church; every window and crevice of which seemed bursting forth with the treasures of the farm; the flail was busily resounding within it from morning to night; swallows and martins skimmed twittering about the eaves; and rows of pigeons, some with one eye turned up, as if watching the weather, some with their heads under their wings or buried in their bosoms, and others swelling, and cooing, and bowing about their dames, were enjoying the sunshine on the roof. Sleek unwieldy porkers were grunting in the repose and abundance of their pens, from whence sallied forth, now and then, troops of sucking pigs, as if to snuff the air. A stately squadron of snowy geese were riding in an adjoining pond, convoying whole fleets of ducks; regiments of turkeys were gobbling through the farmyard, and Guinea fowls fretting about it, like ill-tempered housewives, with their peevish, discontented cry. Before the barn door strutted the gallant cock, that pattern of a husband, a warrior and a fine gentleman, clapping his burnished wings and crowing in the pride and gladness of his heart—sometimes tearing up the earth with his feet, and then generously calling his ever-hungry family of wives and children to enjoy the rich morsel which he had discovered.

The pedagogue's mouth watered as he looked upon this sumptuous promise of luxurious winter fare. In his devouring mind's eye, he pictured to himself every roasting-pig running about with a pudding in his belly, and an apple in his mouth; the pigeons were snugly put to bed in a comfortable pie, and tucked in with a coverlet of crust; the geese were swimming in their own gravy; and the ducks pairing cosily in dishes, like snug married couples, with a decent competency of onion sauce. In the porkers he saw carved out the future sleek side of bacon, and juicy relishing ham; not a turkey but he beheld daintily trussed up, with its gizzard under its wing, and, peradventure, a necklace of savory sausages; and even bright chanticleer himself lay sprawling on his back, in a side dish, with uplifted claws, as if craving that quarter which his chivalrous spirit disdained to ask while living.

As the enraptured Ichabod fancied all this, and as he rolled his great green eyes over the fat meadow lands, the rich fields of wheat, of rye, of buckwheat, and Indian corn, and the orchards burdened with ruddy fruit, which surrounded the warm tenement of Van Tassel, his heart yearned after the damsel who was to inherit these domains, and his imagination expanded with the idea, how they might be readily turned into cash, and the money invested in immense tracts of wild land, and shingle palaces in the wilderness. Nay, his busy fancy already realized his hopes, and presented to him the blooming Katrina, with a whole family of children, mounted on the top of a wagon loaded with household trumpery, with pots and kettles dangling beneath; and he beheld himself bestriding a pacing mare, with a colt at her heels, setting out for Kentucky, Tennessee—or the Lord knows where!

When he entered the house, the conquest of his heart was complete. It was one of those spacious farmhouses, with high-ridged but lowly sloping roofs, built in the style handed down from the first Dutch settlers; the low projecting eaves forming a piazza along the front, capable of being closed up in bad weather. Under this were hung flails, harness, various utensils of husbandry, and nets for fishing in the neighboring river. Benches were built along the sides for summer use; and a great spinning-wheel at one end, and a churn at the other, showed the various uses to which this important porch might be devoted. From this piazza the wondering Ichabod entered the hall, which formed the centre of the mansion, and the place of usual residence. Here rows of resplendent pewter, ranged on a long dresser, dazzled his eyes. In one corner stood a huge bag of wool, ready to be spun; in another, a quantity of linsey-woolsey just from the loom; ears of Indian corn, and strings of dried apples and peaches, hung in gay festoons along the walls, mingled with the gaud of red peppers; and a door left ajar gave him a peep into the best parlor, where the claw-footed chairs and dark mahogany tables shone like mirrors; and irons, with their accompanying shovel and tongs, glistened from their covert of asparagus tops; mock-oranges and conch-shells decorated the mantelpiece; strings of various colored birds' eggs were suspended above it; a great ostrich egg was hung from the centre of the room, and a corner cupboard, knowingly left open, displayed immense treasures of old silver and well-mended china.

From the moment Ichabod laid his eyes upon these regions of delight, the peace of his mind was at an end, and his only study was how to gain the affections of the peerless daughter of Van Tassel. In this enterprise, however, he had more real difficulties than generally fell to the lot of a knight-errant of yore, who seldom had anything but giants, enchanters, fiery dragons, and such like easily conquered adversaries, to contend with and had to make his way merely through gates of iron and brass, and walls of adamant to the castle keep, where the lady of his heart was confined; all which he achieved as easily as a man would carve his way to the centre of a Christmas pie; and then the lady gave him her hand as a matter of course. Ichabod, on the contrary, had to win his way to the heart of a country coquette, beset with a labyrinth of whims and caprices, which were forever presenting new difficulties and impediments; and he had to encounter a host of fearful adversaries of real flesh and blood, the numerous rustic admirers, who beset every portal to her heart, keeping a watchful and angry eye upon each other, but ready to fly out in the common cause against any new competitor.

Among these, the most formidable was a burly, roaring, roystering blade, of the name of Abraham, or, according to the Dutch abbreviation, Brom Van Brunt, the hero of the country round, which rang with his feats of strength and hardihood. He was broad-shouldered and double-jointed, with short curly black hair, and a bluff but not unpleasant countenance, having a mingled air of fun and arrogance. From his Herculean frame and great powers of limb he had received the nickname of BROM BONES, by which he was universally known. He was famed for great knowledge and skill in horsemanship, being as dexterous on horseback as a Tartar. He was foremost at all races and cockfights; and, with the ascendancy which bodily strength always acquires in rustic life, was the umpire in all disputes, setting his hat on one side, and giving his decisions with an air and tone that admitted of no gainsay or appeal. He was always ready for either a fight or a frolic; but had more mischief than ill-will in his composition; and with all his overbearing roughness, there was a strong dash of waggish good humor at bottom. He had three or four boon companions, who regarded him as their model, and at the head of whom he scoured the country, attending every scene of feud or merriment for miles round. In cold weather he was distinguished by a fur cap, surmounted with a flaunting fox's tail; and when the folks at a country gathering descried this well-known crest at a distance, whisking about among a squad of hard riders, they always stood by for a squall. Sometimes his crew would be heard dashing along past the farmhouses at midnight, with whoop and halloo, like a troop of Don Cossacks; and the old dames, startled out of their sleep, would listen for a moment till the hurry-scurry had clattered by, and then exclaim, "Ay, there goes Brom Bones and his gang!" The neighbors looked upon him with a mixture of awe, admiration, and good-will; and, when any madcap prank or rustic brawl occurred in the vicinity, always shook their heads, and warranted Brom Bones was at the bottom of it.

This rantipole hero had for some time singled out the blooming Katrina for the object of his uncouth gallantries, and though his amorous toyings were something like the gentle caresses and endearments of a bear, yet it was whispered that she did not altogether discourage his hopes. Certain it is, his advances were signals for rival candidates to retire, who felt no inclination to cross a lion in his amours; insomuch, that when his horse was seen tied to Van Tassel's paling, on a Sunday night, a sure sign that his master was courting, or, as it is termed, "sparking," within, all other suitors passed by in despair, and carried the war into other quarters.

Such was the formidable rival with whom Ichabod Crane had to contend, and, considering all things, a stouter man than he would have shrunk from the competition, and a wiser man would have despaired. He had, however, a happy mixture of pliability and perseverance in his nature; he was in form and spirit like a supple-jack—yielding, but tough; though he bent, he never broke; and though he bowed beneath the slightest pressure, yet, the moment it was away—jerk!—he was as erect, and carried his head as high as ever.

To have taken the field openly against his rival would have been madness; for he was not a man to be thwarted in his amours, any more than that stormy lover, Achilles. Ichabod, therefore, made his advances in a quiet and gently insinuating manner. Under cover of his character of singing-master, he made frequent visits at the farmhouse; not that he had anything to apprehend from the meddlesome interference of parents, which is so often a stumbling-block in the path of lovers. Balt Van Tassel was an easy indulgent soul; he loved his daughter better even than his pipe, and, like a reasonable man and an excellent father, let her have her way in everything. His notable little wife, too, had enough to do to attend to her housekeeping and manage her poultry; for, as she sagely observed, ducks and geese are foolish things, and must be looked after, but girls can take care of themselves. Thus, while the busy dame bustled about the house, or plied her spinning-wheel at one end of the piazza, honest Balt would sit smoking his evening pipe at the other, watching the achievements of a little wooden warrior, who, armed with a sword in each hand, was most valiantly fighting the wind on the pinnacle of the barn. In the meantime, Ichabod would carry on his suit with the daughter by the side of the spring under the great elm, or sauntering along in the twilight, that hour so favorable to the lover's eloquence.

I profess not to know how women's hearts are wooed and won. To me they have always been matters of riddle and admiration. Some seem to have but one vulnerable point, or door of access; while others have a thousand avenues, and may be captured in a thousand different ways. It is a great triumph of skill to gain the former, but a still greater proof of generalship to maintain possession of the latter, for man must battle for his fortress at every door and window. He who wins a thousand common hearts is therefore entitled to some renown; but he who keeps undisputed sway over the heart of a coquette is indeed a hero. Certain it is, this was not the case with the redoubtable Brom Bones; and from the moment Ichabod Crane made his advances, the interests of the former evidently declined: his horse was no longer seen tied to the palings on Sunday nights, and a deadly feud gradually arose between him and the preceptor of Sleepy Hollow.

Brom, who had a degree of rough chivalry in his nature, would fain have carried matters to open warfare and have settled their pretensions to the lady, according to the mode of those most concise and simple reasoners, the knights-errant of yore—by single combat; but Ichabod was too conscious of the superior might of his adversary to enter the lists against him; he had overheard a boast of Bones, that he would "double the schoolmaster up, and lay him on a shelf of his own schoolhouse;" and he was too wary to give him an opportunity. There was something extremely provoking in this obstinately pacific system; it left Brom no alternative but to draw upon the funds of rustic waggery in his disposition, and to play off boorish practical jokes upon his rival. Ichabod became the object of whimsical persecution to Bones and his gang of rough riders. They harried his hitherto peaceful domains; smoked out his singing school by stopping up the chimney; broke into the schoolhouse at night, in spite of its formidable fastenings of withe and window stakes, and turned everything topsy-turvy, so that the poor schoolmaster began to think all the witches in the country held their meetings there. But what was still more annoying, Brom took all opportunities of turning him into ridicule in presence of his mistress, and had a scoundrel dog whom he taught to whine in the most ludicrous manner, and introduced as a rival of Ichabod's, to instruct her in psalmody.

In this way matters went on for some time, without producing any material effect on the relative situations of the contending powers. On a fine autumnal afternoon, Ichabod, in pensive mood, sat enthroned on the lofty stool from whence he usually watched all the concerns of his little literary realm. In his hand he swayed a ferule, that sceptre of despotic power; the birch of justice reposed on three nails behind the throne, a constant terror to evil doers, while on the desk before him might be seen sundry contraband articles and prohibited weapons, detected upon the persons of idle urchins, such as half-munched apples, popguns, whirligigs, fly-cages, and whole legions of rampant little paper gamecocks. Apparently there had been some appalling act of justice recently inflicted, for his scholars were all busily intent upon their books, or slyly whispering behind them with one eye kept upon the master; and a kind of buzzing stillness reigned throughout the schoolroom. It was suddenly interrupted by the appearance of a negro in tow-cloth jacket and trousers, a round-crowned fragment of a hat, like the cap of Mercury, and mounted on the back of a ragged, wild, half-broken colt, which he managed with a rope by way of halter. He came clattering up to the school door with an invitation to Ichabod to attend a merry-making or "quilting frolic," to be held that evening at Mynheer Van Tassel's; and having delivered his message with that air of importance, and effort at fine language, which a negro is apt to display on petty embassies of the kind, he dashed over the brook, and was seen scampering away up the hollow, full of the importance and hurry of his mission.

All was now bustle and hubbub in the late quiet schoolroom. The scholars were hurried through their lessons without stopping at trifles; those who were nimble skipped over half with impunity, and those who were tardy had a smart application now and then in the rear, to quicken their speed or help them over a tall word. Books were flung aside without being put away on the shelves, inkstands were overturned, benches thrown down, and the whole school was turned loose an hour before the usual time, bursting forth like a legion of young imps, yelping and racketing about the green in joy at their early emancipation.

The gallant Ichabod now spent at least an extra half hour at his toilet, brushing and furbishing up his best, and indeed only suit of rusty black, and arranging his locks by a bit of broken looking-glass that hung up in the schoolhouse. That he might make his appearance before his mistress in the true style of a cavalier, he borrowed a horse from the farmer with whom he was domiciliated, a choleric old Dutchman of the name of Hans Van Ripper, and, thus gallantly mounted, issued forth like a knight-errant in quest of adventures. But it is meet I should, in the true spirit of romantic story, give some account of the looks and equipments of my hero and his steed. The animal he bestrode was a broken-down plough-horse, that had outlived almost everything but its viciousness. He was gaunt and shagged, with a ewe neck, and a head like a hammer; his rusty mane and tail were tangled and knotted with burrs; one eye had lost its pupil, and was glaring and spectral, but the other had the gleam of a genuine devil in it. Still he must have had fire and mettle in his day, if we may judge from the name he bore of Gunpowder. He had, in fact, been a favorite steed of his master's, the choleric Van Ripper, who was a furious rider, and had infused, very probably, some of his own spirit into the animal; for, old and broken-down as he looked, there was more of the lurking devil in him than in any young filly in the country.

Ichabod was a suitable figure for such a steed. He rode with short stirrups, which brought his knees nearly up to the pommel of the saddle; his sharp elbows stuck out like grasshoppers'; he carried his whip perpendicularly in his hand, like a sceptre, and as his horse jogged on, the motion of his arms was not unlike the flapping of a pair of wings. A small wool hat rested on the top of his nose, for so his scanty strip of forehead might be called, and the skirts of his black coat fluttered out almost to the horse's tail. Such was the appearance of Ichabod and his steed as they shambled out of the gate of Hans Van Ripper, and it was altogether such an apparition as is seldom to be met with in broad daylight.

It was, as I have said, a fine autumnal day; the sky was clear and serene, and nature wore that rich and golden livery which we always associate with the idea of abundance. The forests had put on their sober brown and yellow, while some trees of the tenderer kind had been nipped by the frosts into brilliant dyes of orange, purple, and scarlet. Streaming files of wild ducks began to make their appearance high in the air; the bark of the squirrel might be heard from the groves of beech and hickory-nuts, and the pensive whistle of the quail at intervals from the neighboring stubble field.

The small birds were taking their farewell banquets. In the fulness of their revelry, they fluttered, chirping and frolicking from bush to bush, and tree to tree, capricious from the very profusion and variety around them. There was the honest cock robin, the favorite game of stripling sportsmen, with its loud querulous note; and the twittering blackbirds flying in sable clouds; and the golden-winged woodpecker with his crimson crest, his broad black gorget, and splendid plumage; and the cedar bird, with its red-tipt wings and yellow-tipt tail and its little monteiro cap of feathers; and the blue jay, that noisy coxcomb, in his gay light blue coat and white underclothes, screaming and chattering, nodding and bobbing and bowing, and pretending to be on good terms with every songster of the grove.

As Ichabod jogged slowly on his way, his eye, ever open to every symptom of culinary abundance, ranged with delight over the treasures of jolly autumn. On all sides he beheld vast store of apples; some hanging in oppressive opulence on the trees; some gathered into baskets and barrels for the market; others heaped up in rich piles for the cider-press. Farther on he beheld great fields of Indian corn, with its golden ears peeping from their leafy coverts, and holding out the promise of cakes and hasty-pudding; and the yellow pumpkins lying beneath them, turning up their fair round bellies to the sun, and giving ample prospects of the most luxurious of pies; and anon he passed the fragrant buckwheat fields breathing the odor of the beehive, and as he beheld them, soft anticipations stole over his mind of dainty slapjacks, well buttered, and garnished with honey or treacle, by the delicate little dimpled hand of Katrina Van Tassel.

Thus feeding his mind with many sweet thoughts and "sugared suppositions," he journeyed along the sides of a range of hills which look out upon some of the goodliest scenes of the mighty Hudson. The sun gradually wheeled his broad disk down in the west. The wide bosom of the Tappan Zee lay motionless and glassy, excepting that here and there a gentle undulation waved and prolonged the blue shadow of the distant mountain. A few amber clouds floated in the sky, without a breath of air to move them. The horizon was of a fine golden tint, changing gradually into a pure apple green, and from that into the deep blue of the mid-heaven. A slanting ray lingered on the woody crests of the precipices that overhung some parts of the river, giving greater depth to the dark gray and purple of their rocky sides. A sloop was loitering in the distance, dropping slowly down with the tide, her sail hanging uselessly against the mast; and as the reflection of the sky gleamed along the still water, it seemed as if the vessel was suspended in the air.

It was toward evening that Ichabod arrived at the castle of the Heer Van Tassel, which he found thronged with the pride and flower of the adjacent country. Old farmers, a spare leathern-faced race, in homespun coats and breeches, blue stockings, huge shoes, and magnificent pewter buckles. Their brisk, withered little dames, in close-crimped caps, long-waisted short gowns, homespun petticoats, with scissors and pincushions, and gay calico pockets hanging on the outside. Buxom lasses, almost as antiquated as their mothers, excepting where a straw hat, a fine ribbon, or perhaps a white frock, gave symptoms of city innovation. The sons, in short square-skirted coats, with rows of stupendous brass buttons, and their hair generally queued in the fashion of the times, especially if they could procure an eel-skin for the purpose, it being esteemed throughout the country as a potent nourisher and strengthener of the hair.

Brom Bones, however, was the hero of the scene, having come to the gathering on his favorite steed Daredevil, a creature, like himself, full of mettle and mischief, and which no one but himself could manage. He was, in fact, noted for preferring vicious animals, given to all kinds of tricks which kept the rider in constant risk of his neck, for he held a tractable, well-broken horse as unworthy of a lad of spirit.

Fain would I pause to dwell upon the world of charms that burst upon the enraptured gaze of my hero, as he entered the state parlor of Van Tassel's mansion. Not those of the bevy of buxom lasses, with their luxurious display of red and white; but the ample charms of a genuine Dutch country tea-table, in the sumptuous time of autumn. Such heaped up platters of cakes of various and almost indescribable kinds, known only to experienced Dutch housewives! There was the doughty doughnut, the tender oly koek, and the crisp and crumbling cruller; sweet cakes and short cakes, ginger cakes and honey cakes, and the whole family of cakes. And then there were apple pies, and peach pies, and pumpkin pies; besides slices of ham and smoked beef; and moreover delectable dishes of preserved plums, and peaches, and pears, and quinces; not to mention broiled shad and roasted chickens; together with bowls of milk and cream, all mingled higgledy-piggledy, pretty much as I have enumerated them, with the motherly teapot sending up its clouds of vapor from the midst—Heaven bless the mark! I want breath and time to discuss this banquet as it deserves, and am too eager to get on with my story. Happily, Ichabod Crane was not in so great a hurry as his historian, but did ample justice to every dainty.

He was a kind and thankful creature, whose heart dilated in proportion as his skin was filled with good cheer, and whose spirits rose with eating, as some men's do with drink. He could not help, too, rolling his large eyes round him as he ate, and chuckling with the possibility that he might one day be lord of all this scene of almost unimaginable luxury and splendor. Then, he thought, how soon he'd turn his back upon the old schoolhouse; snap his fingers in the face of Hans Van Ripper, and every other niggardly patron, and kick any itinerant pedagogue out of doors that should dare to call him comrade!

Old Baltus Van Tassel moved about among his guests with a face dilated with content and good humor, round and jolly as the harvest moon. His hospitable attentions were brief, but expressive, being confined to a shake of the hand, a slap on the shoulder, a loud laugh, and a pressing invitation to "fall to, and help themselves."

And now the sound of the music from the common room, or hall, summoned to the dance. The musician was an old gray-headed negro, who had been the itinerant orchestra of the neighborhood for more than half a century. His instrument was as old and battered as himself. The greater part of the time he scraped on two or three strings, accompanying every movement of the bow with a motion of the head; bowing almost to the ground, and stamping with his foot whenever a fresh couple were to start.

Ichabod prided himself upon his dancing as much as upon his vocal powers. Not a limb, not a fibre about him was idle; and to have seen his loosely hung frame in full motion, and clattering about the room, you would have thought St. Vitus himself, that blessed patron of the dance, was figuring before you in person. He was the admiration of all the negroes; who, having gathered, of all ages and sizes, from the farm and the neighborhood, stood forming a pyramid of shining black faces at every door and window, gazing with delight at the scene, rolling their white eyeballs, and showing grinning rows of ivory from ear to ear. How could the flogger of urchins be otherwise than animated and joyous? The lady of his heart was his partner in the dance, and smiling graciously in reply to all his amorous oglings; while Brom Bones, sorely smitten with love and jealousy, sat brooding by himself in one corner.

When the dance was at an end, Ichabod was attracted to a knot of the sager folks, who, with Old Van Tassel, sat smoking at one end of the piazza, gossiping over former times, and drawing out long stories about the war.

This neighborhood, at the time of which I am speaking, was one of those highly favored places which abound with chronicle and great men. The British and American line had run near it during the war; it had, therefore, been the scene of marauding and infested with refugees, cowboys, and all kinds of border chivalry. Just sufficient time had elapsed to enable each story-teller to dress up his tale with a little becoming fiction, and, in the indistinctness of his recollection, to make himself the hero of every exploit.

There was the story of Doffue Martling, a large blue-bearded Dutchman, who had nearly taken a British frigate with an old iron nine-pounder from a mud breastwork, only that his gun burst at the sixth discharge. And there was an old gentleman who shall be nameless, being too rich a mynheer to be lightly mentioned, who, in the battle of White Plains, being an excellent master of defence, parried a musket-ball with a small sword, insomuch that he absolutely felt it whiz round the blade, and glance off at the hilt; in proof of which he was ready at any time to show the sword, with the hilt a little bent. There were several more that had been equally great in the field, not one of whom but was persuaded that he had a considerable hand in bringing the war to a happy termination.

But all these were nothing to the tales of ghosts and apparitions that succeeded. The neighborhood is rich in legendary treasures of the kind. Local tales and superstitions thrive best in these sheltered, long-settled retreats; but are trampled underfoot by the shifting throng that forms the population of most of our country places. Besides, there is no encouragement for ghosts in most of our villages, for they have scarcely had time to finish their first nap and turn themselves in their graves, before their surviving friends have travelled away from the neighborhood; so that when they turn out at night to walk their rounds, they have no acquaintance left to call upon. This is perhaps the reason why we so seldom hear of ghosts except in our long-established Dutch communities.

The immediate cause, however, of the prevalence of supernatural stories in these parts, was doubtless owing to the vicinity of Sleepy Hollow. There was a contagion in the very air that blew from that haunted region; it breathed forth an atmosphere of dreams and fancies infecting all the land. Several of the Sleepy Hollow people were present at Van Tassel's, and, as usual, were doling out their wild and wonderful legends. Many dismal tales were told about funeral trains, and mourning cries and wailings heard and seen about the great tree where the unfortunate Major André was taken, and which stood in the neighborhood. Some mention was made also of the woman in white, that haunted the dark glen at Raven Rock, and was often heard to shriek on winter nights before a storm, having perished there in the snow. The chief part of the stories, however, turned upon the favorite spectre of Sleepy Hollow, the Headless Horseman, who had been heard several times of late, patrolling the country; and, it was said, tethered his horse nightly among the graves in the churchyard.

The sequestered situation of this church seems always to have made it a favorite haunt of troubled spirits. It stands on a knoll, surrounded by locust-trees and lofty elms, from among which its decent, whitewashed walls shine modestly forth, like Christian purity beaming through the shades of retirement. A gentle slope descends from it to a silver sheet of water, bordered by high trees, between which, peeps may be caught at the blue hills of the Hudson. To look upon its grass-grown yard, where the sunbeams seem to sleep so quietly, one would think that there at least the dead might rest in peace. On one side of the church extends a wide woody dell, along which raves a large brook among broken rocks and trunks of fallen trees. Over a deep black part of the stream, not far from the church, was formerly thrown a wooden bridge; the road that led to it, and the bridge itself, were thickly shaded by overhanging trees, which cast a gloom about it, even in the daytime; but occasioned a fearful darkness at night. Such was one of the favorite haunts of the Headless Horseman, and the place where he was most frequently encountered. The tale was told of old Brouwer, a most heretical disbeliever in ghosts, how he met the Horseman returning from his foray into Sleepy Hollow, and was obliged to get up behind him; how they galloped over bush and brake, over hill and swamp, until they reached the bridge; when the Horseman suddenly turned into a skeleton, threw old Brouwer into the brook, and sprang away over the tree-tops with a clap of thunder.

This story was immediately matched by a thrice marvellous adventure of Brom Bones, who made light of the Galloping Hessian as an arrant jockey. He affirmed that on returning one night from the neighboring village of Sing Sing, he had been overtaken by this midnight trooper; that he had offered to race with him for a bowl of punch, and should have won it too, for Daredevil beat the goblin horse all hollow, but just as they came to the church bridge, the Hessian bolted, and vanished in a flash of fire.

All these tales, told in that drowsy undertone with which men talk in the dark, the countenances of the listeners only now and then receiving a casual gleam from the glare of a pipe, sank deep in the mind of Ichabod. He repaid them in kind with large extracts from his invaluable author, Cotton Mather, and added many marvellous events that had taken place in his native State of Connecticut, and fearful sights which he had seen in his nightly walks about Sleepy Hollow.

The revel now gradually broke up. The old farmers gathered together their families in their wagons, and were heard for some time rattling along the hollow roads, and over the distant hills. Some of the damsels mounted on pillions behind their favorite swains, and their light-hearted laughter, mingling with the clatter of hoofs, echoed along the silent woodlands, sounding fainter and fainter, until they gradually died away—and the late scene of noise and frolic was all silent and deserted. Ichabod only lingered behind, according to the custom of country lovers, to have a *tête-à-tête* with the heiress; fully convinced that he was now on the high road to success. What passed at this interview I will not pretend to say, for in fact I do not know. Something, however, I fear me, must have gone wrong, for he certainly sallied forth, after no very great interval, with an air quite desolate and chapfallen. Oh, these women! These women! Could that girl have been playing off any of her coquettish tricks? Was her encouragement of the poor pedagogue all a mere sham to secure her conquest of his rival? Heaven only knows, not I! Let it suffice to say, Ichabod stole forth with the air of one who had been sacking a hen-roost, rather than a fair lady's heart. Without looking to the right or left to notice the scene of rural wealth, on which he had so often gloated, he went straight to the stable, and with several hearty cuffs and kicks roused his steed most uncourteously from the comfortable quarters in which he was soundly sleeping, dreaming of mountains of corn and oats, and whole valleys of timothy and clover.

It was the very witching time of night that Ichabod, heavy-hearted and crestfallen, pursued his travels homewards, along the sides of the lofty hills which rise above Tarry Town, and which he had traversed so cheerily in the afternoon. The hour was as dismal as himself. Far below him the Tappan Zee spread its dusky and indistinct waste of waters, with here and there the tall mast of a sloop, riding quietly at anchor under the land. In the dead hush of midnight, he could even hear the barking of the watchdog from the opposite shore of the Hudson; but it was so vague and faint as only to give an idea of his distance from this faithful companion of man. Now and then, too, the long-drawn crowing of a cock, accidentally awakened, would sound far, far off, from some farmhouse away among the hills—but it was like a dreaming sound in his ear. No signs of life occurred near him, but occasionally the melancholy chirp of a cricket, or perhaps the guttural twang of a bull-frog from a neighboring marsh, as if sleeping uncomfortably and turning suddenly in his bed.

All the stories of ghosts and goblins that he had heard in the afternoon now came crowding upon his recollection. The night grew darker and darker; the stars seemed to sink deeper in the sky, and driving clouds occasionally hid them from his sight. He had never felt so lonely and dismal. He was, moreover, approaching the very place where many of the scenes of the ghost stories had been laid. In the centre of the road stood an enormous tulip-tree, which towered like a giant above all the other trees of the neighborhood, and formed a kind of landmark. Its limbs were gnarled and fantastic, large enough to form trunks for ordinary trees, twisting down almost to the earth, and rising again into the air. It was connected with the tragical story of the unfortunate André, who had been taken prisoner hard by; and was universally known by the name of Major André's tree. The common people regarded it with a mixture of respect and superstition, partly out of sympathy for the fate of its ill-starred namesake, and partly from the tales of strange sights, and doleful lamentations, told concerning it.

As Ichabod approached this fearful tree, he began to whistle; he thought his whistle was answered; it was but a blast sweeping sharply through the dry branches. As he approached a little nearer, he thought he saw something white, hanging in the midst of the tree: he paused and ceased whistling but, on looking more narrowly, perceived that it was a place where the tree had been scathed by lightning, and the white wood laid bare. Suddenly he heard a groan—his teeth chattered, and his knees smote against the saddle: it was but the rubbing of one huge bough upon another, as they were swayed about by the breeze. He passed the tree in safety, but new perils lay before him.

About two hundred yards from the tree, a small brook crossed the road, and ran into a marshy and thickly-wooded glen, known by the name of Wiley's Swamp. A few rough logs, laid side by side, served for a bridge over this stream. On that side of the road where the brook entered the wood, a group of oaks and chestnuts, matted thick with wild grape-vines, threw a cavernous gloom over it. To pass this bridge was the severest trial. It was at this identical spot that the unfortunate André was captured, and under the covert of those chestnuts and vines were the sturdy yeomen concealed who surprised him. This has ever since been considered a haunted stream, and fearful are the feelings of the schoolboy who has to pass it alone after dark.

As he approached the stream, his heart began to thump; he summoned up, however, all his resolution, gave his horse half a score of kicks in the ribs, and attempted to dash briskly across the bridge; but instead of starting forward, the perverse old animal made a lateral movement, and ran broadside against the fence. Ichabod, whose fears increased with the delay, jerked the reins on the other side, and kicked lustily with the contrary foot: it was all in vain; his steed started, it is true, but it was only to plunge to the opposite side of the road into a thicket of brambles and alder bushes. The schoolmaster now bestowed both whip and heel upon the starveling ribs of old Gunpowder, who dashed forward, snuffling and snorting, but came to a stand just by the bridge, with a suddenness that had nearly sent his rider sprawling over his head. Just at this moment a plashy tramp by the side of the bridge caught the sensitive ear of Ichabod. In the dark shadow of the grove, on the margin of the brook, he beheld something huge, misshapen and towering. It stirred not, but seemed gathered up in the gloom, like some gigantic monster ready to spring upon the traveller.

The hair of the affrighted pedagogue rose upon his head with terror. What was to be done? To turn and fly was now too late; and besides, what chance was there of escaping ghost or goblin, if such it was, which could ride upon the wings of the wind? Summoning up, therefore, a show of courage, he demanded in stammering accents, "Who are you?" He received no reply. He repeated his demand in a still more agitated voice. Still there was no answer. Once more he cudgelled the sides of the inflexible Gunpowder, and, shutting his eyes, broke forth with involuntary fervor into a psalm tune. Just then the shadowy object of alarm put itself in motion, and with a scramble and a bound stood at once in the middle of the road. Though the night was dark and dismal, yet the form of the unknown might now in some degree be ascertained. He appeared to be a horseman of large dimensions, and mounted on a black horse of powerful frame. He made no offer of molestation or sociability, but kept aloof on one side of the road, jogging along on the blind side of old Gunpowder, who had now got over his fright and waywardness.

Ichabod, who had no relish for this strange midnight companion, and bethought himself of the adventure of Brom Bones with the Galloping Hessian, now quickened his steed in hopes of leaving him behind. The stranger, however, quickened his horse to an equal pace. Ichabod pulled up, and fell into a walk, thinking to lag behind—the other did the same.

His heart began to sink within him; he endeavored to resume his psalm tune, but his parched tongue clove to the roof of his mouth, and he could not utter a stave. There was something in the moody and dogged silence of this pertinacious companion that was mysterious and appalling. It was soon fearfully accounted for. On mounting a rising ground, which brought the figure of his fellow-traveller in relief against the sky, gigantic in height, and muffled in a cloak, Ichabod was horror-struck on perceiving that he was headless!—but his horror was still more increased on observing that the head, which should have rested on his shoulders, was carried before him on the pommel of his saddle! His terror rose to desperation; he rained a shower of kicks and blows upon Gunpowder, hoping by a sudden movement to give his companion the slip; but the spectre started full jump with him. Away, then, they dashed through thick and thin; stones flying and sparks flashing at every bound. Ichabod's flimsy garments fluttered in the air, as he stretched his long lank body away over his horse's head, in the eagerness of his flight.

They had now reached the road which turns off to Sleepy Hollow; but Gunpowder, who seemed possessed with a demon, instead of keeping up it, made an opposite turn, and plunged headlong dowhill to the left. This road leads through a sandy hollow shaded by trees for about a quarter of a mile, where it crosses the bridge famous in goblin story; and just beyond swells the green knoll on which stands the whitewashed church.

As yet the panic of the steed had given his unskillful rider an apparent advantage in the chase, but just as he had got halfway through the hollow, the girths of the saddle gave way, and he felt it slipping from under him. He seized it by the pommel, and endeavored to hold it firm, but in vain; and had just time to save himself by clasping old Gunpowder round the neck, when the saddle fell to the earth, and he heard it trampled under foot by his pursuer. For a moment the terror of Hans Van Ripper's wrath passed across his mind—for it was his Sunday saddle; but this was no time for petty fears; the goblin was hard on his haunches; and (unskilful rider that he was!) he had much ado to maintain his seat; sometimes slipping on one side, sometimes on another, and sometimes jolted on the high ridge of his horse's backbone, with a violence that he verily feared would cleave him asunder.

An opening in the trees now cheered him with the hopes that the church bridge was at hand. The wavering reflection of a silver star in the bosom of the brook told him that he was not mistaken. He saw the walls of the church dimly glaring under the trees beyond. He recollected the place where Brom Bones's ghostly competitor had disappeared. "If I can but reach that bridge," thought Ichabod, "I am safe." Just then he heard the black steed panting and blowing close behind him; he even fancied that he felt his hot breath. Another convulsive kick in the ribs, and old Gunpowder sprang upon the bridge; he thundered over the resounding planks; he gained the opposite side; and now Ichabod cast a look behind to see if his pursuer should vanish, according to rule, in a flash of fire and brimstone. Just then he saw the goblin rising in his stirrups, and in the very act of hurling his head at him. Ichabod endeavored to dodge the horrible missile, but too late. It encountered his cranium with a tremendous crash—he was tumbled headlong into the dust, and Gunpowder, the black steed, and the goblin rider, passed by like a whirlwind.

The next morning the old horse was found without his saddle, and with the bridle under his feet, soberly cropping the grass at his master's gate. Ichabod did not make his appearance at breakfast; dinner-hour came, but no Ichabod. The boys assembled at the schoolhouse, and strolled idly about the banks of the brook; but no schoolmaster. Hans Van Ripper now began to feel some uneasiness about the fate of poor Ichabod, and his saddle. An inquiry was set on foot, and after diligent investigation they came upon his traces. In one part of the road leading to the church was found the saddle trampled in the dirt; the tracks of horses' hoofs deeply dented in the road, and evidently at furious speed, were traced to the bridge, beyond which, on the bank of a broad part of the brook, where the water ran deep and black, was found the hat of the unfortunate Ichabod, and close beside it a shattered pumpkin.

The brook was searched, but the body of the schoolmaster was not to be discovered. Hans Van Ripper as executor of his estate, examined the bundle which contained all his worldly effects. They consisted of two shirts and a half; two stocks for the neck; a pair or two of worsted stockings; an old pair of corduroy small-clothes; a rusty razor; a book of psalm tunes full of dogs' ears; and a broken pitch-pipe. As to the books and furniture of the schoolhouse, they belonged to the community, excepting Cotton Mather's *History of Witchcraft*, a *New England Almanac*, and a book of dreams and fortune-telling; in which last was a sheet of foolscap much scribbled and blotted in several fruitless attempts to make a copy of verses in honor of the heiress of Van Tassel. These magic books and the poetic scrawl were forthwith consigned to the flames by Hans Van Ripper; who, from that time forward, determined to send his children no more to school, observing that he never knew any good come of this same reading and writing. Whatever money the schoolmaster possessed, and he had received his quarter's pay but a day or two before, he must have had about his person at the time of his disappearance.

The mysterious event caused much speculation at the church on the following Sunday. Knots of gazers and gossips were collected in the churchyard, at the bridge, and at the spot where the hat and pumpkin had been found. The stories of Brouwer, of Bones, and a whole budget of others were called to mind; and when they had diligently considered them all, and compared them with the symptoms of the present case, they shook their heads, and came to the conclusion that Ichabod had been carried off by the Galloping Hessian. As he was a bachelor, and in nobody's debt, nobody troubled his head any more about him; the school was removed to a different quarter of the hollow, and another pedagogue reigned in his stead.

It is true, an old farmer, who had been down to New York on a visit several years after, and from whom this account of the ghostly adventure was received, brought home the intelligence that Ichabod Crane was still alive; that he had left the neighborhood partly through fear of the goblin and Hans Van Ripper, and partly in mortification at having been suddenly dismissed by the heiress; that he had changed his quarters to a distant part of the country; had kept school and studied law at the same time; had been admitted to the bar; turned politician; electioneered; written for the newspapers; and finally had been made a justice of the Ten Pound Court. Brom Bones, too, who, shortly after his rival's disappearance conducted the blooming Katrina in triumph to the altar, was observed to look exceedingly knowing whenever the story of Ichabod was related, and always burst into a hearty laugh at the mention of the pumpkin; which led some to suspect that he knew more about the matter than he chose to tell.

The old country wives, however, who are the best judges of these matters, maintain to this day that Ichabod was spirited away by supernatural means; and it is a favorite story often told about the neighborhood round the winter evening fire. The bridge became more than ever an object of superstitious awe; and that may be the reason why the road has been altered of late years, so as to approach the church by the border of the millpond. The schoolhouse being deserted soon fell to decay, and was reported to be haunted by the ghost of the unfortunate pedagogue and the plough-boy, loitering homeward of a still summer evening, has often fancied his voice at a distance, chanting a melancholy psalm tune among the tranquil solitudes of Sleepy Hollow.

POSTSCRIPT

Found in the Handwriting of Mr. Knickerbocker.

The preceding tale is given almost in the precise words in which I heard it related at a Corporation meeting at the ancient city of Manhattoes, at which were present many of its sagest and most illustrious burghers. The narrator was a pleasant, shabby, gentlemanly old fellow, in pepper-and-salt clothes, with a sadly humorous face, and one whom I strongly suspected of being poor—he made such efforts to be entertaining. When his story was concluded, there was much laughter and approbation, particularly from two or three deputy aldermen, who had been asleep the greater part of the time. There was, however, one tall, dry-looking old gentleman, with beetling eyebrows, who maintained a grave and rather severe face throughout, now and then folding his arms, inclining his head, and looking down upon the floor, as if turning a doubt over in his mind. He was one of your wary men, who never laugh but upon good grounds—when they have reason and law on their side. When the mirth of the rest of the company had subsided, and silence was restored, he leaned one arm on the elbow of his chair, and sticking the other akimbo, demanded, with a slight, but exceedingly sage motion of the head, and contraction of the brow, what was the moral of the story, and what it went to prove?

The story-teller, who was just putting a glass of wine to his lips, as a refreshment after his toils, paused for a moment, looked at his inquirer with an air of infinite deference, and, lowering the glass slowly to the table, observed that the story was intended most logically to prove—

"That there is no situation in life but has its advantages and pleasures—provided we will but take a joke as we find it:

"That, therefore, he that runs races with goblin troopers is likely to have rough riding of it.

"*Ergo*, for a country schoolmaster to be refused the hand of a Dutch heiress is a certain step to high preferment in the state."

The cautious old gentleman knit his brows tenfold closer after this explanation, being sorely puzzled by the ratiocination of the syllogism, while, methought, the one in pepper-and-salt eyed him with something of a triumphant leer. At length he observed that all this was very well, but still he thought the story a little on the extravagant—there were one or two points on which he had his doubts.

"Faith, sir," replied the story-teller, "as to that matter, I don't believe one-half of it myself."

D. K.

THE STUDENT OF SALAMANCA

What a life doe I lead with my master; nothing but blowing
of bellowes, beating of spirits, and scraping of croslets! It is
a very secret science, for none almost can understand the
language of it. Sublimation, almigation, calcination,
rubification, albification, and fermentation; with as many
termes unpossible to be uttered as the arte to be compassed.
—LILLY'S *GALLATHEA*.

Once upon a time, in the ancient city of Granada, there sojourned
a young man of the name of Antonio de Castros. He wore the garb
of a student of Salamanca, and was pursuing a course of reading in
the library of the university; and, at intervals of leisure, indulging
his curiosity by examining those remains of Moorish magnificence
for which Granada is renowned.

Whilst occupied in his studies, he frequently noticed an old man
of singular appearance, who was likewise a visitor to the library. He
was lean and withered, though apparently more from study than from
age. His eyes, though bright and visionary, were sunk in his head,
and thrown into shade by overhanging eyebrows. His dress was
always the same: a black doublet; a short black cloak, very rusty
and threadbare; a small ruff and a large overshadowing hat.

His appetite for knowledge seemed insatiable. He would pass
whole days in the library, absorbed in study, consulting a multiplicity
of authors, as though he were pursuing some interesting subject
through all its ramifications; so that, in general, when evening came,
he was almost buried among books and manuscripts.

The curiosity of Antonio was excited, and he inquired of the attendants concerning the stranger. No one could give him any information,
excepting that he had been for some time past a casual frequenter of

the library; that his reading lay chiefly among works treating of the occult sciences, and that he was particularly curious in his inquiries after Arabian manuscripts. They added, that he never held communication with any one, excepting to ask for particular works; that, after a fit of studious application, he would disappear for several days, and even weeks, and when he revisited the library, he would look more withered and haggard than ever. The student felt interested by this account; he was leading rather a desultory life, and had all that capricious curiosity which springs up in idleness. He determined to make himself acquainted with this bookworm, and find out who and what he was.

The next time that he saw the old man at the library, he commenced his approaches by requesting permission to look into one of the volumes with which the unknown appeared to have done. The latter merely bowed his head, in token of assent. After pretending to look through the volume with great attention, he returned it with many acknowledgements.

The stranger made no reply.

"May I ask, señor," said Antonio, with some hesitation, "may I ask what you are searching after in all these books?"

The old man raised his head, with an expression of surprise, at having his studies interrupted for the first time, and by so intrusive a question. He surveyed the student with a side glance from head to foot: "Wisdom, my son," said he, calmly; "and the search requires every moment of my attention." He then cast his eyes upon his book, and resumed his studies.

"But, father," said Antonio, "cannot you spare a moment to point out the road to others? It is to experienced travellers like you, that we strangers in the paths of knowledge must look for directions on our journey."

The stranger looked disturbed: "I have not time enough, my son, to learn," said he, "much less to teach. I am ignorant myself of the path of true knowledge; how then can I show it to others?"

"Well, but, father—"

"Señor," said the old man, mildly, but earnestly, "you must see that I have but few steps more to the grave. In that short space have I to accomplish the whole business of my existence. I have no time for words; every word is as one grain of sand of my glass wasted. Suffer me to be alone."

There was no replying to so complete a closing of the door of intimacy. The student found himself calmly but totally repulsed. Though curious and inquisitive, yet he was naturally modest, and on after-thoughts he blushed at his own intrusion. His mind soon became occupied by other objects. He passed several days wandering among the mouldering piles of Moorish architecture, those melancholy monuments of an elegant and voluptuous people. He paced the deserted halls of the Alhambra, the paradise of the Moorish kings. He visited the great court of the lions, famous for the perfidious massacre of the gallant Abencerrages. He gazed with admiration at its mosaic cupolas, gorgeously painted in gold and azure; its basins of marble, its alabaster vase, supported by lions, and storied with inscriptions.

His imagination kindled as he wandered among these scenes. They were calculated to awaken all the enthusiasm of a youthful mind. Most of the halls have anciently been beautified by fountains. The fine taste of the Arabs delighted in the sparkling purity and reviving freshness of water; and they erected, as it were, altars on every side, to that delicate element. Poetry mingles with architecture in the Alhambra. It breathes along the very walls. Wherever Antonio turned his eye, he beheld inscriptions in Arabic, wherein the perpetuity of Moorish power and splendor within these walls was confidently predicted. Alas! How has the prophecy been falsified! Many of the basins, where the fountains had once thrown up their sparkling showers, were dry and dusty. Some of the palaces were turned into gloomy convents, and the barefoot monk paced through these courts, which had once glittered with the array, and echoed to the music, of Moorish chivalry.

In the course of his rambles, the student more than once encountered the old man of the library. He was always alone, and so full of thought as not to notice any one about him. He appeared to be intent upon studying those half-buried inscriptions, which, are found, here and there, among the Moorish ruins, and seem to murmur from the earth the tale of former greatness. The greater part of these have since been translated; but they were supposed by many at the time, to contain symbolical revelations, and golden maxims of the Arabian sages and astrologers. As Antonio saw the stranger apparently deciphering these inscriptions, he felt an eager longing to make his acquaintance, and to participate in his curious researches; but the repulse he had met with at the library deterred him from making any further advances.

He had directed his steps one evening to the sacred mount, which overlooks the beautiful valley watered by the Darro, the fertile plain of the Vega, and all that rich diversity of vale and mountain that surrounds Granada with an earthly paradise. It was twilight when he found himself at the place, where, at the present day, are situated the chapels, known by the name of the Sacred Furnaces. They are so called from grottoes, in which some of the primitive saints are said to have been burnt. At the time of Antonio's visit, the place was an object of much curiosity. In an excavation of these grottoes, several manuscripts had recently been discovered, engraved on plates of lead. They were written in the Arabian language, excepting one, which was in unknown characters. The Pope had issued a bull, forbidding any one, under pain of excommunication, to speak of these manuscripts. The prohibition had only excited the greater curiosity; and many reports were whispered about, that these manuscripts contained treasures of dark and forbidden knowledge.

As Antonio was examining the place from whence these mysterious manuscripts had been drawn, he again observed the old man of the library wandering among the ruins. His curiosity was now fully awakened; the time and place served to stimulate it. He resolved to watch this groper after secret and forgotten lore, and to trace him to his habitation. There was something like adventure in the thing, that charmed his romantic disposition. He followed the stranger, therefore, at a little distance; at first cautiously, but he soon observed him to be so wrapped in his own thoughts, as to take little heed of external objects.

They passed along the skirts of the mountain, and then by the shady banks of the Darro. They pursued their way, for some distance from Granada, along a lonely road that led among the hills. The gloom of evening was gathering, and it was quite dark when the stranger stopped at the portal of a solitary mansion.

It appeared to be a mere wing, or ruined fragment, of what had once been a pile of some consequence. The walls were of great thickness; the windows narrow, and generally secured by iron bars. The door was of planks, studded with iron spikes, and had been of great strength, though at present it was much decayed. At one end of the mansion was a ruinous tower, in the Moorish style of architecture. The edifice had probably been a country retreat, or castle of pleasure, during the occupation of Granada by the Moors, and rendered sufficiently strong to withstand any casual assault in those warlike times.

The old man knocked at the portal. A light appeared at a small window just above it, and a female head looked out: it might have served as a model for one of Raphael's saints. The hair was beautifully braided, and gathered in a silken net; and the complexion, as well as could be judged from the light, was that soft, rich brunette, so becoming in southern beauty.

"It is I, my child," said the old man. The face instantly disappeared, and soon after a wicket-door in the large portal opened. Antonio, who had ventured near to the building, caught a transient sight of a delicate female form. A pair of fine black eyes darted a look of surprise at seeing a stranger hovering near, and the door was precipitately closed.

There was something in this sudden gleam of beauty that wonderfully struck the imagination of the student. It was like a brilliant, flashing from its dark casket. He sauntered about, regarding the gloomy pile with increasing interest. A few simple, wild notes, from among some rocks and trees at a little distance, attracted his attention. He found there a group of Gitanas, a vagabond gipsy race, which at that time abounded in Spain, and lived in hovels and caves of the hills about the neighborhood of Granada. Some were busy about a fire, and others were listening to the uncouth music which one of their companions, seated on a ledge of the rock, was making with a split reed.

Antonio endeavored to obtain some information of them, concerning the old building and its inhabitants. The one who appeared to be their spokesman was a gaunt fellow, with a subtle gait, a whispering voice, and a sinister roll of the eye. He shrugged his shoulders on the student's inquiries, and said that all was not right in that building. An old man inhabited it, whom nobody knew, and whose family appeared to be only a daughter and a female servant. He and his companions, he added, lived up among the neighboring hills; and as they had been about at night, they had often seen strange lights, and heard strange sounds from the tower. Some of the country people, who worked in the vineyards among the hills, believed the old man to be one that dealt in the black art, and were not over-fond of passing near the tower at night; "but for our parts," said the Gitano, "we are not a people that trouble ourselves much with fears of that kind."

The student endeavored to gain more precise information, but they had none to furnish him. They began to be solicitous for a compensation for what they had already imparted; and, recollecting the loneliness of the place, and the vagabond character of his companions, he was glad to give them a gratuity, and to hasten homewards.

He sat down to his studies, but his brain was too full of what he had seen and heard; his eye was upon the page, but his fancy still returned to the tower; and he was continually picturing the little window, with the beautiful head peeping out; or the door half open, and the nymph-like form within. He retired to bed, but the same object haunted his dreams. He was young and susceptible; and the excited state of his feelings, from wandering among the abodes of departed grace and gallantry, had predisposed him for a sudden impression from female beauty.

The next morning, he strolled again in the direction of the tower. It was still more forlorn, by the broad glare of day, than in the gloom of evening. The walls were crumbling, and weeds and moss were growing in every crevice. It had the look of a prison, rather than a dwelling-house. In one angle, however, he remarked a window which seemed an exception to the surrounding squalidness. There was a curtain drawn within it, and flowers standing on the window-stone. Whilst he was looking at it, the curtain was partially withdrawn, and a delicate white arm, of the most beautiful roundness, was put forth to water the flowers.

The student made a noise, to attract the attention of the fair florist. He succeeded. The curtain was further drawn, and he had a glance of the same lovely face he had seen the evening before; it was but a mere glance—the curtain again fell, and the casement closed. All this was calculated to excite the feelings of a romantic youth. Had he seen the unknown under other circumstances, it is probable that he would not have been struck with her beauty; but this appearance of being shut up and kept apart, gave her the value of a treasured gem. He passed and repassed before the house several times in the course of the day, but saw nothing more. He was there again in the evening. The whole aspect of the house was dreary. The narrow windows emitted no rays of cheerful light, to indicate that there was social life within. Antonio listened at the portal, but no sound of voices reached his ear. Just then he heard the clapping to of a distant door, and fearing to be detected in the unworthy act of eavesdropping, he precipitately drew off to the opposite side of the road, and stood in the shadow of a ruined archway.

He now remarked a light from a window in the tower. It was fitful and changeable; commonly feeble and yellowish, as if from a lamp; with an occasional glare of some vivid metallic color, followed by a dusky glow. A column of dense smoke would now and then rise in the air, and hang like a canopy over the tower. There was altogether such a loneliness and seeming mystery about the building and its inhabitants, that Antonio was half inclined to indulge the country people's notions, and to fancy it the den of some powerful sorcerer, and the fair damsel he had seen to be some spellbound beauty.

After some time had elapsed, a light appeared in the window where he had seen the beautiful arm. The curtain was down, but it was so thin that he could perceive the shadow of some one passing and re-passing between it and the light. He fancied that he could distinguish that the form was delicate; and, from the alacrity of its movements, it was evidently youthful. He had not a doubt but this was the bedchamber of his beautiful unknown.

Presently he heard the sound of a guitar, and a female voice singing. He drew near cautiously, and listened. It was a plaintive Moorish ballad, and he recognized in it the lamentations of one of the Abencerrages on leaving the walls of lovely Granada. It was full of passion and tenderness. It spoke of the delights of early life; the hours of love it had enjoyed on the banks of the Darro, and among the blissful abodes of the Alhambra. It bewailed the fallen honors of the Abencerrages, and imprecated vengeance on their oppressors. Antonio was affected by the music. It singularly coincided with the place. It was like the voice of past times echoed in the present, and breathing among the monuments of its departed glory.

The voice ceased; after a time the light disappeared, and all was still. "She sleeps!" said Antonio, fondly. He lingered about the building, with the devotion with which a lover lingers about the bower of sleeping beauty. The rising moon threw its silver beams on the gray walls, and glittered on the casement. The late gloomy landscape gradually became flooded with its radiance. Finding, therefore, that he could no longer move about in obscurity, and fearful that his loiterings might be observed, he reluctantly retired.

The curiosity which had at first drawn the young man to the tower, was now seconded by feelings of a more romantic kind. His studies were almost entirely abandoned. He maintained a kind of blockade of the old mansion; he would take a book with him, and pass a great part of the day under the trees in its vicinity; keeping a vigilant eye upon it, and endeavoring to ascertain what were the walks of his mysterious charmer. He found, however, that she never went out except to mass, when she was accompanied by her father. He waited at the door of the church, and offered her the holy water, in the hope of touching her hand; a little office of gallantry common in Catholic countries. She, however, modestly declined without raising her eyes to see who made the offer, and always took it herself from the font. She was attentive in her devotion; her eyes were never taken from the altar or the priest; and, on returning home, her countenance was almost entirely concealed by her mantilla.

Antonio had now carried on the pursuit for several days, and was hourly getting more and more interested in the chase, but never a step nearer to the game. His lurkings about the house had probably been noticed, for he no longer saw the fair face at the window, nor the white arm put forth to water the flowers. His only consolation was to repair nightly to his post of observation, and listen to her warbling; and if by chance he could catch a sight of her shadow, passing and repassing before the window, he thought himself most fortunate.

As he was indulging in one of these evening vigils, which were complete revels of the imagination, the sound of approaching footsteps made him withdraw into the deep shadow of the ruined archway opposite to the tower. A cavalier approached, wrapped in a large Spanish cloak. He paused under the window of the tower, and after a little while began a serenade, accompanied by his guitar, in the usual style of Spanish gallantry. His voice was rich and manly; he touched the instrument with skill, and sang with amorous and impassioned eloquence. The plume of his hat was buckled by jewels that sparkled in the moon-beams; and as he played on the guitar, his cloak falling off from one shoulder, showed him to be richly dressed. It was evident that he was a person of rank.

The idea now flashed across Antonio's mind, that the affections of his unknown beauty might be engaged. She was young, and doubtless susceptible; and it was not in the nature of Spanish females to be deaf and insensible to music and admiration. The surmise brought with it a feeling of dreariness. There was a pleasant dream of several days suddenly dispelled. He had never before experienced anything of the tender passion; and, as its morning dreams are always delightful, he would fain have continued in the delusion.

"But what have I to do with her attachments?" thought he; "I have no claim on her heart, nor even on her acquaintance. How do I know that she is worthy of affection? Or if she is, must not so gallant a lover as this, with his jewels, his rank, and his detestable music, have completely captivated her? What idle humor is this that I have fallen into? I must again to my books. Study, study, will soon chase away all these idle fancies!"

The more he thought, however, the more he became entangled in the spell which his lively imagination had woven round him; and now that a rival had appeared, in addition to the other obstacles that environed this enchanted beauty, she appeared ten times more lovely and desirable. It was some slight consolation to him to perceive that the gallantry of the unknown met with no apparent return from the tower. The light at the window was extinguished. The curtain remained undrawn, and none of the customary signals were given to intimate that the serenade was accepted.

The cavalier lingered for some time about the place, and sang several other tender airs with a taste and feeling that made Antonio's heart ache; at length he slowly retired. The student remained with folded arms, leaning against the ruined arch, endeavoring to summon up resolution enough to depart; but there was a romantic fascination that still enchained him to the place. "It is the last time," said he, willing to compromise between his feelings and his judgment, "it is the last time; then let me enjoy the dream a few moments longer."

As his eye ranged about the old building to take a farewell look, he observed the strange light in the tower, which he had noticed on a former occasion. It kept beaming up, and declining, as before. A pillar of smoke rose in the air, and hung in sable volumes. It was evident the old man was busied in some of those operations that had gained him the reputation of a sorcerer throughout the neighborhood.

Suddenly an intense and brilliant glare shone through the casement, followed by a loud report, and then a fierce and ruddy glow. A figure appeared at the window, uttering cries of agony or alarm, but immediately disappeared, and a body of smoke and flame whirled out of the narrow aperture. Antonio rushed to the portal, and knocked at it with vehemence. He was only answered by loud shrieks, and found that the females were already in helpless consternation. With an exertion of desperate strength he forced the wicket from its hinges, and rushed into the house.

He found himself in a small vaulted hall, and, by the light of the moon which entered at the door, he saw a staircase to the left. He hurried up it to a narrow corridor, through which was rolling a volume of smoke. He found here the two females in a frantic state of alarm; one of them clasped her hands, and implored him to save her father.

The corridor terminated in a spiral flight of steps, leading up to the tower. He sprang up it to a small door, through the chinks of which came a glow of light, and smoke was spuming out. He burst it open, and found himself in an antique vaulted chamber, furnished with a furnace and various chemical apparatus. A shattered retort lay on the stone floor; a quantity of combustibles, nearly consumed, with various half-burnt books and papers, were sending up an expiring flame, and filling the chamber with stifling smoke. Just within the threshold lay the reputed conjurer. He was bleeding, his clothes were scorched, and he appeared lifeless. Antonio caught him up, and bore him down the stairs to a chamber, in which there was a light, and laid him on a bed. The female domestic was dispatched for such appliances as the house afforded; but the daughter threw herself frantically beside her parent, and could not be reasoned out of her alarm. Her dress was all in disorder; her dishevelled hair hung in rich confusion about her neck and bosom, and never was there beheld a lovelier picture of terror and affliction.

The skilful assiduities of the scholar soon produced signs of returning animation in his patient. The old man's wounds, though severe, were not dangerous. They had evidently been produced by the bursting of the retort; in his bewilderment he had been enveloped in the stifling metallic vapors, which had overpowered his feeble frame, and had not Antonio arrived to his assistance, it is possible he might never have recovered.

By slow degrees he came to his senses. He looked about with a bewildered air at the chamber, the agitated group around, and the student who was leaning over him.

"Where am I?" said he wildly.

At the sound of his voice, his daughter uttered a faint exclamation of delight. "My poor Inez!" said he, embracing her; then, putting his hand to his head, and taking it away stained with blood, he seemed suddenly to recollect himself, and to be overcome with emotion.

"Ah!" cried he, "all is over with me! all gone! all vanished! gone in a moment! the labor of a lifetime lost!"

His daughter attempted to soothe him, but he became slightly delirious, and raved incoherently about malignant demons, and about the habitation of the green lion being destroyed. His wounds being dressed, and such other remedies administered as his situation required, he sunk into a state of quiet. Antonio now turned his attention to the daughter, whose sufferings had been little inferior to those of her father. Having with great difficulty succeeded in tranquillizing her fears, he endeavored to prevail upon her to retire, and seek the repose so necessary to her frame, proffering to remain by her father until morning. "I am a stranger," said he, "it is true, and my offer may appear intrusive; but I see you are lonely and helpless, and I cannot help venturing over the limits of mere ceremony. Should you feel any scruple or doubt, however, say but a word, and I will instantly retire."

There was a frankness, a kindness, and a modesty, mingled in Antonio's deportment, that inspired instant confidence; and his simple scholar's garb was a recommendation in the house of poverty. The females consented to resign the sufferer to his care, as they would be the better able to attend to him on the morrow. On retiring, the old domestic was profuse in her benedictions; the daughter only looked her thanks; but as they shone through the tears that filled her fine black eyes, the student thought them a thousand times the most eloquent.

Here, then, he was, by a singular turn of chance, completely housed within this mysterious mansion. When left to himself, and the bustle of the scene was over, his heart throbbed as he looked round the chamber in which he was sitting. It was the daughter's room, the promised land toward which he had cast so many a longing gaze. The furniture was old, and had probably belonged to the building in its prosperous days; but everything was arranged with propriety. The flowers that he had seen her attend stood in the window; a guitar leaned against a table, on which stood a crucifix, and before it lay a missal and a rosary. There reigned an air of purity and serenity about this little nestling-place of innocence; it was the emblem of a chaste and quiet mind. Some few articles of female dress lay on the chairs; and there was the very bed on which she had slept—the pillow on which her soft cheek had reclined! The poor scholar was treading enchanted ground; for what fairy land has more of magic in it, than the bedchamber of innocence and beauty?

From various expressions of the old man in his ravings, and from what he had noticed on a subsequent visit to the tower, to see that the fire was extinguished, Antonio had gathered that his patient was an alchemist. The philosopher's stone was an object eagerly sought after by visionaries in those days; but in consequence of the superstitious prejudices of the times, and the frequent persecutions of its votaries, they were apt to pursue their experiments in secret; in lonely houses, in caverns and ruins, or in the privacy of cloistered cells.

In the course of the night, the old man had several fits of restlessness and delirium; he would call out upon Theophrastus, and Geber, and Albertus Magnus, and other sages of his art; and anon would murmur about fermentation and projection, until, toward daylight, he once more sunk into a salutary sleep. When the morning sun darted his rays into the casement, the fair Inez, attended by the female domestic, came blushing into the chamber. The student now took his leave, having himself need of repose, but obtaining ready permission to return and inquire after the sufferer.

When he called again, he found the alchemist languid and in pain, but apparently suffering more in mind than in body. His delirium had left him, and he had been informed of the particulars of his deliverance, and of the subsequent attentions of the scholar. He could do little more than look his thanks, but Antonio did not require them;

his own heart repaid him for all that he had done, and he almost rejoiced in the disaster that had gained him an entrance into this mysterious habitation. The alchemist was so helpless as to need much assistance; Antonio remained with him, therefore, the greater part of the day. He repeated his visit the next day, and the next. Every day his company seemed more pleasing to the invalid; and every day he felt his interest in the latter increasing. Perhaps the presence of the daughter might have been at the bottom of this solicitude.

He had frequent and long conversations with the alchemist. He found him, as men of his pursuits were apt to be, a mixture of enthusiasm and simplicity; of curious and extensive reading on points of little utility, with great inattention to the everyday occurrences of life, and profound ignorance of the world. He was deeply versed in singular and obscure branches of knowledge, and much given to visionary speculations. Antonio, whose mind was of a romantic cast, had himself given some attention to the occult sciences, and he entered upon these themes with an ardor that delighted the philosopher. Their conversations frequently turned upon astrology, divination, and the great secret. The old man would forget his aches and wounds, rise up like a spectre in his bed, and kindle into eloquence on his favorite topics. When gently admonished of his situation, it would but prompt him to another sally of thought.

"Alas, my son!" he would say, "is not this very decrepitude and suffering another proof of the importance of those secrets with which we are surrounded? Why are we trammelled by disease, withered by old age, and our spirits quenched, as it were, within us, but because we have lost those secrets of life and youth which were known to our parents before their fall? To regain these, have philosophers been ever since aspiring; but just as they are on the point of securing the precious secrets for ever, the brief period of life is at an end; they die, and with them all their wisdom and experience. 'Nothing,' as De Nuysment observes, 'nothing is wanting for man's perfection but a longer life, less crossed with sorrows and maladies, to the attaining of the full and perfect knowledge of things.'"

At length Antonio so far gained on the heart of his patient, as to draw from him the outlines of his story.

Felix de Vasques, the alchemist, was a native of Castile, and of an ancient and honorable line. Early in life he had married a beautiful female, a descendant from one of the Moorish families. The marriage displeased his father, who considered the pure Spanish blood contaminated by this foreign mixture. It is true, the lady traced her descent from one of the Abencerrages, the most gallant of Moorish cavaliers, who had embraced the Christian faith on being exiled from the walls of Granada.

The injured pride of the father, however, was not to be appeased. He never saw his son afterwards, and on dying left him but a scanty portion of his estate; bequeathing the residue, in the piety and bitterness of his heart, to the erection of convents, and the performance of masses for souls in purgatory. Don Felix resided for a long time in the neighborhood of Valladolid, in a state of embarrassment and obscurity. He devoted himself to intense study, having, while at the university of Salamanca, imbibed a taste for the secret sciences. He was enthusiastic and speculative; he went on from one branch of knowledge to another, until he became zealous in the search after the grand Arcanum.

He had at first engaged in the pursuit with the hopes of raising himself from his present obscurity, and resuming the rank and dignity to which his birth entitled him; but, as usual, it ended in absorbing every thought, and becoming the business of his existence. He was at length aroused from this mental abstraction, by the calamities of his household. A malignant fever swept off his wife and all his children, excepting an infant daughter. These losses for a time overwhelmed and stupefied him. His home had in a manner died away from around him, and he felt lonely and forlorn. When his spirit revived within him, he determined to abandon the scene of his humiliation and disaster; to bear away the child that was still left him beyond the scene of contagion, and never to return to Castile until he should be enabled to reclaim the honors of his line.

He had ever since been wandering and unsettled in his abode. Sometimes the resident of populous cities, at other times of absolute solitudes. He had searched libraries, meditated on inscriptions, visited adepts of different countries, and sought to gather and concentrate the rays which had been thrown by various minds upon the secrets of alchemy. He had at one time travelled quite to Padua to search for the manuscripts of Pietro d'Abano, and to inspect an urn which had been dug up near Este, supposed to have been buried by Maximus Olybius, and to have contained the grand elixir.*

While at Padua, he had met with an adept versed in Arabian lore, who talked of the invaluable manuscripts that must remain in the Spanish libraries, preserved from the spoils of the Moorish academies and universities; of the probability of meeting with precious unpublished writings of Geber, and Alfarabius, and Avicenna, the great physicians of the Arabian schools, who, it was well known, had treated much of alchemy; but, above all, he spoke of the Arabian tablets of lead, which had recently been dug up in the neighborhood of Granada, and which, it was confidently believed among adepts, contained the lost secrets of the art.

---

* This urn was found in 1533. It contained a lesser one, in which was a burning lamp betwixt two small vials, the one of gold, the other of silver, both of them full of a very clear liquor. On the largest was an inscription, stating that Maximus Olybius shut up in this small vessel elements which he had prepared with great toil. There were many disquisitions among the learned on the subject. It was the most received opinion, that this Maximus Olybius was an inhabitant of Padua, that he had discovered the great secret, and that these vessels contained liquor, one to transmute metals to gold, and other to silver. The peasants who found the urns, imagining this precious liquor to be common water, spilt every drop, so that the art of transmuting metals remains as much a secret as ever.

The indefatigable alchemist once more bent his steps for Spain, full of renovated hope. He had made his way to Granada: he had wearied himself in the study of Arabic, in deciphering inscriptions, in rummaging libraries, and exploring every possible trace left by the Arabian sages.

In all his wanderings he had been accompanied by Inez; through the rough and the smooth, the pleasant and the adverse; never complaining, but rather seeking to soothe his cares by her innocent and playful caresses. Her instruction had been the employment and the delight of his hours of relaxation. She had grown up while they were wandering, and had scarcely ever known any home but by his side. He was family, friends, home, everything to her. He had carried her in his arms, when they first began their wayfaring; had nestled her, as an eagle does its young, among the rocky heights of the Sierra Morena; she had sported about him in childhood, in the solitudes of the Bateucas; had followed him, as a lamb does the shepherd, over the rugged Pyrenees, and into the fair plains of Languedoc; and now she was grown up to support his feeble steps among the ruined abodes of her maternal ancestors.

His property had gradually wasted away, in the course of his travels and his experiments. Still hope, the constant attendant of the alchemist, had led him on; ever on the point of reaping the reward of his labors, and ever disappointed. With the credulity that often attended his art, he attributed many of his disappointments to the machination of the malignant spirits that beset the paths of the alchemist and torment him in his solitary labors. "It is their constant endeavor," he observed, "to close up every avenue to those sublime truths, which would enable man to rise above the abject state into which he has fallen, and to return to his original perfection." To the evil offices of these demons, he attributed his late disaster. He had been on the very verge of the glorious discovery; never were the indications more completely auspicious; all was going on prosperously, when, at the critical moment which should have crowned his labors with success, and have placed him at the very summit of human power and felicity, the bursting of a retort had reduced his laboratory and himself to ruins.

"I must now," said he, "give up at the very threshold of success. My books and papers are burnt; my apparatus is broken. I am too old to bear up against these evils. The ardor that once inspired me is gone; my poor frame is exhausted by study and watchfulness, and this last misfortune has hurried me towards the grave." He concluded in a tone of deep dejection. Antonio endeavored to comfort and reassure him; but the poor alchemist had for once awakened to a consciousness of the worldly ills that were gathering around him, and had sunk into despondency. After a pause, and some thoughtfulness and perplexity of brow, Antonio ventured to make a proposal.

"I have long," said he, "been filled with a love for the secret sciences, but have felt too ignorant and diffident to give myself up to them. You have acquired experience; you have amassed the knowledge of a lifetime; it were a pity it should be thrown away. You say you are too old to renew the toils of the laboratory; suffer me to undertake them. Add your knowledge to my youth and activity, and what shall we not accomplish? As a probationary fee, and a fund on which to proceed, I will bring into the common stock a sum of gold, the residue of a legacy, which has enabled me to complete my education. A poor scholar cannot boast much; but I trust we shall soon put ourselves beyond the reach of want; and if we should fail, why, I must depend, like other scholars, upon my brains to carry me through the world."

The philosopher's spirits, however, were more depressed than the student had imagined. This last shock, following in the rear of so many disappointments, had almost destroyed the reaction of his mind. The fire of an enthusiast, however, is never so low but that it may be blown again into a flame. By degrees, the old man was cheered and reanimated by the buoyancy and ardor of his sanguine companion. He at length agreed to accept of the services of the student, and once more to renew his experiments. He objected, however, to using the student's gold, notwithstanding that his own was nearly exhausted; but this objection was soon overcome; the student insisted on making it a common stock and common cause;— and then how absurd was any delicacy about such a trifle, with men who looked forward to discovering the philosopher's stone!

While, therefore, the alchemist was slowly recovering, the student busied himself in getting the laboratory once more in order. It was strewed with the wrecks of retorts and alembics, with old crucibles, boxes and phials of powders and tinctures, and half-burnt books and manuscripts.

As soon as the old man was sufficiently recovered, the studies and experiments were renewed. The student became a privileged and frequent visitor, and was indefatigable in his toils in the laboratory. The philosopher daily derived new zeal and spirits from the animation of his disciple. He was now enabled to prosecute the enterprise with continued exertion, having so active a coadjutor to divide the toil. While he was poring over the writings of Sandivogius, and Philalethes, and Dominus de Nuysment, and endeavoring to comprehend the symbolical language in which they have locked up their mysteries, Antonio would occupy himself among the retorts and crucibles, and keep the furnace in a perpetual glow.

With all his zeal, however, for the discovery of the golden art, the feelings of the student had not cooled as to the object that first drew him to this ruinous mansion. During the old man's illness, he had frequent opportunities of being near the daughter; and every day made him more sensible to her charms. There was a pure simplicity, and an almost passive gentleness, in her manners; yet with all this was mingled something, whether mere maiden shyness, or a consciousness of high descent, or a dash of Castilian pride, or perhaps all united, that prevented undue familiarity, and made her difficult of approach. The danger of her father, and the measures to be taken for his relief, had at first overcome this coyness and reserve, but as he recovered and her alarm subsided, she seemed to shrink from the familiarity she had indulged with the youthful stranger, and to become every day more shy and silent.

Antonio had read many books, but this was the first volume of womankind that he had ever studied. He had been captivated with the very title-page; but the further he read, the more he was delighted. She seemed formed to love; her soft black eye rolled languidly under its long silken lashes, and wherever it turned, it would linger and repose; there was tenderness in every beam. To him alone she was reserved and distant. Now that the common cares of the sick-room were at an end, he saw little more of her than before his admission to the house. Sometimes he met her on his way to and from the laboratory, and at such times there was ever a smile and a blush; but, after a simple salutation, she glided on and disappeared.

"'Tis plain," thought Antonio, "my presence is indifferent, if not irksome to her. She has noticed my admiration, and is determined to discourage it; nothing but a feeling of gratitude prevents her treating me with marked distaste—and then has she not another lover, rich, gallant, splendid, musical? How can I suppose she would turn her eyes from so brilliant a cavalier, to a poor obscure student, raking among the cinders of her father's laboratory?"

Indeed, the idea of the amorous serenader continually haunted his mind. He felt convinced that he was a favored lover; yet, if so, why did he not frequent the tower?—why did he not make his approaches by noon-day? There was mystery in this eavesdropping and musical courtship. Surely Inez could not be encouraging a secret intrigue! Oh! No! she was too artless, too pure, too ingenuous! But then the Spanish females were so prone to love and intrigue; and music and moonlight were so seductive, and Inez had such a tender soul languishing in every look. "Oh!" would the poor scholar exclaim, clasping his hands, "oh, that I could but once behold those loving eyes beaming on me with affection!"

It is incredible to those who have not experienced it, on what scanty aliment human life and human love may be supported. A dry crust, thrown now and then to a starving man, will give him a new lease of existence; and a faint smile, or a kind look, bestowed at casual intervals, will keep a lover loving on, when a man in his sober senses would despair.

When Antonio found himself alone in the laboratory, his mind would be haunted by one of these looks, or smiles, which he had received in passing. He would set it in every possible light, and argue on it with all the self-pleasing, self-teasing logic of a lover.

The country around him was enough to awaken that voluptuousness of feeling so favorable to the growth of passion. The window of the tower rose above the trees of the romantic valley of the Darro, and looked down upon some of the loveliest scenery of the Vega, where groves of citron and orange were refreshed by cool springs and brooks of the purest water.

The Xenel and the Darro wound their shining streams along the plain, and gleamed from among its bowers. The surrounding hills were covered with vineyards, and the mountains, crowned with snow, seemed to melt into the blue sky. The delicate airs that played about the tower were perfumed by the fragrance of myrtle and orange blossoms, and the ear was charmed with the fond warbling of the nightingale, which, in these happy regions, sings the whole day long. Sometimes, too, there was the idle song of the muleteer, sauntering along the solitary road; or the notes of the guitar, from some group of peasants dancing in the shade. All these were enough to fill the head of the young lover with poetic fancies; and Antonio would picture to himself how he could loiter among those happy groves, and wander by those gentle rivers, and love away his life with Inez.

He felt at times impatient at his own weakness, and would endeavor to brush away these cobwebs of the mind. He would turn his thoughts, with sudden effort, to his occult studies, or occupy himself in some perplexing process; but often, when he had partially succeeded in fixing his attention, the sound of Inez's lute, or the soft notes of her voice, would come stealing upon the stillness of the chamber, and, as it were, floating round the tower. There was no great art in her performance; but Antonio thought he had never heard music comparable to this. It was perfect witchcraft to hear her warble forth some of her national melodies; those little Spanish romances and Moorish ballads, that transport the hearer, in idea, to the banks of the Guadalquivir, or the walls of the Alhambra, and make him dream of beauties, and balconies, and moonlight serenades.

Never was poor student more sadly beset than Antonio. Love is a troublesome companion in a study, at the best of tunes; but in the laboratory of an alchemist, his intrusion is terribly disastrous. Instead of attending to the retorts and crucibles, and watching the process of some experiment intrusted to his charge, the student would get entranced in one of these love-dreams, from which he would often be aroused by some fatal catastrophe. The philosopher, on returning from his researches in the libraries, would find everything gone wrong, and Antonio in despair over the ruins of the whole day's work. The old man, however, took all quietly, for his had been a life of experiment and failure.

"We must have patience, my son," would he say, "as all the great masters that have gone before us have had. Errors, and accidents, and delays are what we have to contend with. Did not Pontanus err two hundred times, before he could obtain even the matter on which to found his experiments? The great Flamel, too, did he not labor four-and-twenty years, before he ascertained the first agent? What difficulties and hardships did not Cartilaceus encounter, at the very threshold of his discoveries? And Bernard de Treves, even after he had attained a knowledge of all the requisites, was he not delayed full three years? What you consider accidents, my son, are the machinations of our invisible enemies. The treasures and golden secrets of nature are surrounded by spirits hostile to man. The air about us teems with them. They lurk in the fire of the furnace, in the bottom of the crucible, and the alembic, and are ever on the alert to take advantage of those moments when our minds are wandering from intense meditation on the great truth that we are seeking. We must only strive the more to purify ourselves from, those gross and earthly feelings which becloud the soul, and prevent her from piercing into nature's arcana."

"Alas!" thought Antonio, "if to be purified from all earthly feeling requires that I should cease to love Inez, I fear I shall never discover the philosopher's stone!"

In this way, matters went on for some time, at the alchemist's. Day after day was sending the student's gold in vapor up the chimney; every blast of the furnace made him a ducat the poorer, without apparently helping him a jot nearer to the golden secret. Still the young man stood by, and saw piece after piece disappearing without a murmur: he had daily an opportunity of seeing Inez, and felt as if her favor would be better than silver or gold, and that every smile was worth a ducat.

Sometimes, in the cool of the evening, when the toils of the laboratory happened to be suspended, he would walk with the alchemist in what had once been a garden belonging to the mansion. There were still the remains of terraces and balustrades, and here and there a marble urn, or mutilated statue overturned, and buried among weeds and flowers run wild. It was the favorite resort of the alchemist in his hours of relaxation, where he would give full scope to his visionary flights. His mind was tinctured with the Rosicrucian doctrines. He believed in elementary beings; some favorable, others adverse to his pursuits; and, in the exaltation of his fancy, had often imagined that he held communion with them in his solitary walks, about the whispering groves and echoing walls of this old garden.

When accompanied by Antonio, he would prolong these evening recreations. Indeed, he sometimes did it out of consideration for his disciple, for he feared lest his too close application, and his incessant seclusion in the tower, should be injurious to his health. He was delighted and surprised by this extraordinary zeal and perseverance in so young a tyro, and looked upon him as destined to be one of the great luminaries of the art. Lest the student should repine at the time lost in these relaxations, the good alchemist would fill them up with wholesome knowledge, in matters connected with their pursuits; and would walk up and down the alleys with his disciple, imparting oral instruction, like an ancient philosopher. In all his visionary schemes, these breathed a spirit of lofty, though chimerical philanthropy, that won the admiration of the scholar. Nothing sordid nor sensual, nothing petty nor selfish, seemed to enter into his views, in respect to the grand discoveries he was anticipating. On the contrary, his imagination kindled with conceptions of widely dispensated happiness. He looked forward to the time when he should be able to go about the earth, relieving the indigent, comforting the distressed; and, by his unlimited means, devising and executing plans for the complete extirpation of poverty, and all its attendant sufferings and crimes. Never were grander schemes for general good, for the distribution of boundless wealth and universal competence, devised than by this poor, indigent alchemist in his ruined tower.

Antonio would attend these peripatetic lectures with all the ardor of a devotee; but there was another circumstance which may have given a secret charm to them. The garden was the resort also of Inez, where she took her walks of recreation; the only exercise that her secluded life permitted. As Antonio was duteously pacing by the side of his instructor, he would often catch a glimpse of the daughter, walking pensively about the alleys in the soft twilight. Sometimes they would meet her unexpectedly, and the heart of the student would throb with agitation. A blush, too, would crimson the cheek of Inez, but still she passed on and never joined them.

He had remained one evening until rather a late hour with the alchemist in this favorite resort. It was a delightful night after a sultry day, and the balmy air of the garden was peculiarly reviving. The old man was seated on a fragment of a pedestal, looking like a part of the ruin on which he sat. He was edifying his pupil by long lessons of wisdom from the stars, as they shone out with brilliant lustre in the dark-blue vault of a southern sky; for he was deeply versed in Behmen, and other of the Rosicrucians, and talked much of the signature of earthly things and passing events, which may be discerned in the heavens; of the power of the stars over corporeal beings, and their influence on the fortunes of the sons of men.

By degrees the moon rose and shed her gleaming light among the groves. Antonio apparently listened with fixed attention to the sage, but his ear was drinking in the melody of Inez's voice, who was singing to her lute in one of the moonlight glades of the garden. The old man, having exhausted his theme, sat gazing in silent reverie at the heavens. Antonio could not resist an inclination to steal a look at this coy beauty, who was thus playing the part of the nightingale, so sequestered and musical. Leaving the alchemist in his celestial reverie, he stole gently along one of the alleys. The music had ceased, and he thought he heard the sound of voices. He came to an angle of a copse that had screened a kind of green recess, ornamented by a marble fountain. The moon shone full upon the place, and by its light he beheld his unknown, serenading rival at the feet of Inez. He was detaining her by the hand, which he covered with kisses; but at sight of Antonio he started up and half drew his sword, while Inez, disengaged, fled back to the house.

All the jealous doubts and fears of Antonio were now confirmed. He did not remain to encounter the resentment of his happy rival at being thus interrupted, but turned from the place in sudden wretchedness of heart. That Inez should love another, would have been misery enough; but that she should be capable of a dishonorable amour, shocked him to the soul. The idea of deception in so young and apparently artless a being, brought with it that sudden distrust in human nature, so sickening to a youthful and ingenuous mind; but when he thought of the kind, simple parent she was deceiving, whose affections all centred in her, he felt for a moment a sentiment of indignation, and almost of aversion.

He found the alchemist still seated in his visionary contemplation of the moon. "Come hither, my son," said he, with his usual enthusiasm, "come, read with me in this vast volume of wisdom, thus nightly unfolded for our perusal. Wisely did the Chaldean sages affirm, that the heaven is as a mystic page, uttering speech to those who can rightly understand; warning them of good and evil, and instructing them in the secret decrees of fate."

The student's heart ached for his venerable master; and, for a moment, he felt the futility of his occult wisdom. "Alas! Poor old man!" thought he, "of what avails all thy study? Little dost thou dream, while busied in airy speculations among the stars, what a treason against thy happiness is going on under thine eyes; as it were, in thy very bosom!—Oh Inez! Inez! Where shall we look for truth and innocence, where shall we repose confidence in woman, if even you can deceive?"

It was a trite apostrophe, such as every lover makes when he finds his mistress not quite such a goddess as he had painted her. With the student, however, it sprung from honest anguish of heart. He returned to his lodgings, in pitiable confusion of mind. He now deplored the infatuation that had led him on until his feelings were so thoroughly engaged. He resolved to abandon his pursuits at the tower, and trust to absence to dispel the fascination by which he had been spellbound. He no longer thirsted after the discovery of the grand elixir: the dream of alchemy was over; for, without Inez, what was the value of the philosopher's stone?

He rose, after a sleepless night, with the determination of taking his leave of the alchemist, and tearing himself from Granada. For several days did he rise with the same resolution, and every night saw him come back to his pillow, to repine at his want of resolution, and to make fresh determinations for the morrow. In the meanwhile, he saw less of Inez than ever. She no longer walked in the garden, but remained almost entirely in her apartment. When she met him, she blushed more than usual; and once hesitated, as if she would have spoken; but, after a temporary embarrassment, and still deeper blushes, she made some casual observation, and retired. Antonio read, in this confusion, a consciousness of fault, and of that fault's being discovered. "What could she have wished to communicate? Perhaps to account for the scene in the garden;—but how can she account for it, or why should she account for it to me? What am I to her?—or rather, what is she to me?" exclaimed he, impatiently, with a new resolution to break through these entanglements of the heart, and fly from this enchanted spot forever.

He was returning that very night to his lodgings, full of this excellent determination, when, in a shadowy part of the road, he passed a person whom he recognized, by his height and form, for his rival: he was going in the direction of the tower. If any lingering doubts remained, here was an opportunity of settling them completely. He determined to follow this unknown cavalier, and, under favor of the darkness, observe his movements. If he obtained access to the tower, or in any way a favorable reception, Antonio felt as if it would be a relief to his mind, and would enable him to fix his wavering resolution.

The unknown, as he came near the tower, was more cautious and stealthy in his approaches. He was joined under a clump of trees by another person, and they had much whispering together. A light was burning in the chamber of Inez; the curtain was down, but the casement was left open, as the night was warm. After some time, the light was extinguished. A considerable interval elapsed. The cavalier and his companion remained under covert of the trees, as if keeping watch. At length they approached the tower, with silent and cautious steps. The cavalier received a dark-lantern from his companion, and threw off his cloak. The other then softly brought something from the clump of trees, which Antonio perceived to be a light ladder: he placed it against the wall, and the serenader gently ascended. A sickening sensation came over Antonio. Here was indeed a confirmation of every fear. He was about to leave the place, never to return, when he heard a stifled shriek from Inez's chamber.

In an instant, the fellow that stood at the foot of the ladder lay prostrate on the ground. Antonio wrested a stiletto from his nerveless hand, and hurried up the ladder. He sprang in at the window, and found Inez struggling in the grasp of his fancied rival; the latter, disturbed from his prey, caught up his lantern, turned its light full upon Antonio, and, drawing his sword, made a furious assault; luckily the student saw the light gleam along the blade, and parried the thrust with the stiletto. A fierce, but unequal combat ensued. Antonio fought exposed to the full glare of the light, while his antagonist was in shadow: his stiletto, too, was but a poor defence against a rapier. He saw that nothing would save him but closing with his adversary, and getting within his weapon: he rushed furiously upon him, and gave him a severe blow with the stiletto; but received a wound in return from the shortened sword. At the same moment, a blow was inflicted from behind, by the confederate, who had ascended the ladder; it felled him to the floor, and his antagonists made their escape.

By this time, the cries of Inez had brought her father and the domestic into the room. Antonio was found weltering in his blood, and senseless. He was conveyed to the chamber of the alchemist, who now repaid in kind the attentions which the student had once bestowed upon him. Among his varied knowledge he possessed some skill in surgery, which at this moment was of more value than even his chemical lore. He stanched and dressed the wounds of his disciple, which on examination proved less desperate than he had at first apprehended. For a few days, however, his case was anxious, and attended with danger. The old man watched over him with the affection of a parent. He felt a double debt of gratitude towards him, on account of his daughter and himself; he loved him too as a faithful and zealous disciple; and he dreaded lest the world, should be deprived of the promising talents of so aspiring an alchemist.

An excellent constitution soon medicined his wounds; and there was a balsam in the looks and words of Inez, that had a healing effect on the still severer wounds which he carried in his heart. She displayed the strongest interest in his safety; she called him her deliverer, her preserver. It seemed as if her grateful disposition sought, in the warmth of its acknowledgments, to repay him for past coldness. But what most contributed to Antonio's recovery, was her explanation concerning his supposed rival. It was some time since he had first beheld her at church, and he had ever since persecuted her with his attentions. He had beset her in her walks, until she had been obliged to confine herself to the house, except when accompanied by her father. He had besieged her with letters, serenades, and every art by which he could urge a vehement, but clandestine and dishonorable suit. The scene in the garden was as much of a surprise to her as to Antonio. Her persecutor had been attracted by her voice, and had found his way over a ruined part of the wall. He had come upon her unawares; was detaining her by force, and pleading his insulting passion, when the appearance of the student interrupted him, and enabled her to make her escape. She had forborne to mention to her father the persecution which she suffered; she wished to spare him unavailing anxiety and distress, and had determined to confine herself more rigorously to the house; though it appeared that even here she had not been safe from his daring enterprise.

Antonio inquired whether she knew the name of this impetuous admirer? She replied that he had made his advances under a fictitious name; but that she had heard him once called by the name of Don Ambrosio de Loxa.

Antonio knew him, by report, for one of the most determined and dangerous libertines in all Granada. Artful, accomplished, and, if he chose to be so, insinuating; but daring and headlong in the pursuit of his pleasures; violent and implacable in his resentments. He rejoiced to find that Inez had been proof against his seductions, and had been inspired with aversion by his splendid profligacy; but he trembled to think of the dangers she had run, and he felt solicitude about the dangers that must yet environ her.

At present, however, it was probable the enemy had a temporary quietus. The traces of blood had been found for some distance from the ladder, until they were lost among thickets; and as nothing had been heard or seen of him since, it was concluded that he had been seriously wounded.

As the student recovered from his wounds, he was enabled to join Inez and her father in their domestic intercourse. The chamber in which they usually met had probably been a saloon of state in former times. The floor was of marble; the walls partially covered with remains of tapestry; the chairs, richly carved and gilt, were crazed with age, and covered with tarnished and tattered brocade. Against the wall hung a long rusty rapier, the only relic that the old man retained of the chivalry of his ancestors. There might have been something to provoke a smile, in the contrast between the mansion and its inhabitants; between present poverty and the graces of departed grandeur; but the fancy of the student had thrown so much romance about the edifice and its inmates, that everything was clothed with charms. The philosopher, with his broken-down pride, and his strange pursuits, seemed to comport with the melancholy ruin he inhabited; and there was a native elegance of spirit about the daughter, that showed she would have graced the mansion in its happier days.

What delicious moments were these to the student! Inez was no longer coy and reserved. She was naturally artless and confiding; though the kind of persecution she had experienced from one admirer had rendered her, for a time, suspicious and circumspect toward the other. She now felt an entire confidence in the sincerity and worth of Antonio, mingled with an overflowing gratitude. When her eyes met his, they beamed with sympathy and kindness; and Antonio, no longer haunted by the idea of a favored rival, once more aspired to success.

At these domestic meetings, however, he had little opportunity of paying his court, except by looks. The alchemist, supposing him, like himself, absorbed in the study of alchemy, endeavored to cheer the tediousness of his recovery by long conversations on the art. He even brought several of his half-burnt volumes, which the student had once rescued from the flames, and rewarded him for their preservation, by reading copious passages. He would entertain him with the great and good acts of Flamel, which he effected through means of the philosopher's stone, relieving widows and orphans, founding hospitals, building churches, and what not; or with the interrogatories of King Kalid, and the answers of Morienus, the Roman hermit of Jerusalem; or the profound questions which Elardus, a necromancer of the province of Catalonia, put to the devil, touching the secrets of alchemy, and the devil's replies.

All these were couched, in occult language, almost unintelligible to the unpractised ear of the disciple. Indeed, the old man delighted in the mystic phrases and symbolical jargon in which the writers that have treated of alchemy have wrapped their communications; rendering them incomprehensible except to the initiated. With what rapture would he elevate his voice at a triumphant passage, announcing the grand discovery! "Thou shalt see," would he exclaim, in the words of Henry Kuhnrade,* "the stone of the philosophers (our king) go forth of the

---

* Amphitheatre of the Eternal Wisdom.

bed-chamber of his glassy sepulchre into the theatre of this world; that is to say, regenerated and made perfect, a shining carbuncle, a most temperate splendor, whose most subtle and depurated parts are inseparable, united into one with a concordial mixture, exceeding equal, transparent as crystal, shining red like a ruby, permanently coloring or ringing, fixt in all temptations or trials; yea, in the examination of the burning sulphur itself, and the devouring waters, and in the most vehement persecution of the fire, always incombustible and permanent as a salamander!"

The student had a high veneration for the fathers of alchemy, and a profound respect for his instructor; but what was Henry Kuhnrade, Geber, Lully, or even Albertus Magnus himself, compared to the countenance of Inez, which presented such a page of beauty to his perusal? While, therefore, the good alchemist was doling out knowledge by the hour, his disciple would forget books, alchemy, everything but the lovely object before him. Inez, too, unpractised in the science of the heart, was gradually becoming fascinated by the silent attentions of her lover. Day by day, she seemed more and more perplexed by the kindling and strangely pleasing emotions of her bosom. Her eye was often cast down in thought. Blushes stole to her cheek without any apparent cause, and light, half-suppressed sighs would follow these short fits of musing. Her little ballads, though the same that she had always sung, yet breathed a more tender spirit. Either the tones of her voice were more soft and touching, or some passages were delivered with a feeling she had never before given them. Antonio, beside his love for the abstruse sciences, had a pretty turn for music; and never did philosopher touch the guitar more tastefully. As, by degrees, he conquered the mutual embarrassment that kept them asunder, he ventured to accompany Inez in some of her songs. He had a voice full of fire and tenderness: as he sang, one would have thought, from the kindling blushes of his companion, that he had been pleading his own passion in her ear. Let those who would keep two youthful hearts asunder, beware of music. Oh! This leaning over chairs, and conning the same music-book, and entwining of voices, and melting away in harmonies!—the German waltz is nothing to it.

The worthy alchemist saw nothing of all this. His mind could admit of no idea that was not connected with the discovery of the grand arcanum, and he supposed his youthful coadjutor equally devoted. He was a mere child as to human nature; and, as to the passion of love, whatever he might once have felt of it, he had long since forgotten that there was such an idle passion in existence. But, while he dreamed, the silent amour went on. The very quiet and seclusion of the place were favorable to the growth of romantic passion. The opening bud of love was able to put forth leaf by leaf, without an adverse wind to check its growth. There was neither officious friendship to chill by its advice, nor insidious envy to wither by its sneers, nor an observing world to look on and stare it out of countenance. There was neither declaration, nor vow, nor any other form of Cupid's canting school. Their hearts mingled together, and understood each other without the aid of language. They lapsed into the full current of affection, unconscious of its depth, and thoughtless of the rocks that might lurk beneath its surface. Happy lovers! Who wanted nothing to make their felicity complete, but the discovery of the philosopher's stone!

At length, Antonio's health was sufficiently restored to enable him to return to his lodgings in Granada. He felt uneasy, however, at leaving the tower, while lurking danger might surround its almost defenceless inmates. He dreaded lest Don Ambrosio, recovered from his wounds, might plot some new attempt, by secret art, or open violence. From all that he had heard, he knew him to be too implacable to suffer his defeat to pass unavenged, and too rash and fearless, when his arts were unavailing, to stop at any daring deed in the accomplishment of his purposes. He urged his apprehensions to the alchemist and his daughter, and proposed that they should abandon the dangerous vicinity of Granada.

"I have relations," said he, "in Valencia, poor indeed, but worthy and affectionate. Among them you will find friendship and quiet, and we may there pursue our labors unmolested." He went on to paint the beauties and delights of Valencia, with all the fondness of a native, and all the eloquence with which a lover paints the fields and groves which he is picturing as the future scenes of his happiness. His eloquence, backed by the apprehensions of Inez, was successful with the alchemist, who, indeed, had led too unsettled a life to be particular about the place of his residence; and it was determined, that, as soon as Antonio's health was perfectly restored, they should abandon the tower, and seek the delicious neighborhood of Valencia.*

To recruit his strength, the student suspended his toils in the laboratory, and spent the few remaining days, before departure, in taking a farewell look at the enchanting environs of Granada. He felt returning health and vigor, as he inhaled the pure temperate breezes that play about its hills; and the happy state of his mind contributed to his rapid recovery. Inez was often the companion of his walks. Her descent, by the mother's side, from one of the ancient Moorish families, gave her an interest in this once favorite seat of Arabian power. She gazed with enthusiasm upon its magnificent monuments, and her memory was filled with the traditional tales and ballads of Moorish chivalry. Indeed, the solitary life she had led, and the visionary turn of her father's mind, had produced an effect upon

---

* Here are the strongest silks, the sweetest wines, the excellent'st almonds, the best oyls, and beautifull'st females of all Spain. The very bruit animals make themselves beds of rosemary, and other fragrant flowers hereabouts; and when one is at sea, if the winde blow from the shore, he may smell this soyl before he come in sight of it, many leagues off, by the strong odoriferous scent it casts. As it is the most pleasant, so it is also the temperat'st clime of all Spain, and they commonly call it the second Italy; which made the Moors, whereof many thousands were disterr'd, and banish'd hence to Barbary, to think that Paradise was in that part of the heavens which hung over this citie.   —HOWELL'S LETTERS.

her character, and given it a tinge of what, in modern days, would be termed romance. All this was called into full force by this new passage; for, when a woman first begins to love, life is all romance to her.

In one of their evening strolls, they had ascended to the mountain of the Sun, where is situated the Generaliffe, the palace of pleasure, in the days of Moorish dominion, but now a gloomy convent of Capuchins. They had wandered about its garden, among groves of orange, citron, and cypress, where the waters, leaping in torrents, or gushing in fountains, or tossed aloft in sparkling jets, fill the air with music and freshness.

There is a melancholy mingled with all the beauties of this garden, that gradually stole over the feelings of the lovers. The place is full of the sad story of past times. It was the favorite abode of the lovely queen of Granada, where she was surrounded by the delights of a gay and voluptuous court. It was here, too, amidst her own bowers of roses, that her slanderers laid the base story of her dishonor, and struck a fatal blow to the line of the gallant Abencerrages.

The whole garden has a look of ruin and neglect. Many of the fountains are dry and broken; the streams have wandered from their marble channels, and are choked by weeds and yellow leaves. The reed whistles to the wind, where it had once sported among roses, and shaken perfume from the orange-blossom. The convent-bell flings its sullen sound, or the drowsy vesper-hymn floats along these solitudes, which once resounded with the song, and the dance, and the lover's serenade. Well may the Moors lament over the loss of this earthly paradise; well may they remember it in their prayers, and beseech Heaven to restore it to the faithful; well may their ambassadors smite their breasts when they behold these monuments of their race, and sit down and weep among the fading glories of Granada!

It is impossible to wander about these scenes of departed love and gayety, and not feel the tenderness of the heart awakened. It was then that Antonio first ventured to breathe his passion, and to express by words what his eyes had long since so eloquently revealed. He made his avowal with fervor, but with frankness. He had no gay prospects to hold out: he was a poor scholar, dependent on his "good spirits to feed and clothe him." But a woman in love is no interested calculator. Inez listened to him with downcast eyes, but in them was a humid gleam that showed her heart was with him. She had no prudery in her nature; and she had not been sufficiently in society to acquire it. She loved him with all the absence of worldliness of a genuine woman; and, amidst timid smiles and blushes, he drew from her a modest acknowledgment of her affection.

They wandered about the garden, with that sweet intoxication of the soul which none but happy lovers know. The world about them was all fairy land; and, indeed, it spread forth one of its fairest scenes before their eyes, as if to fulfil their dream of earthly happiness. They looked out from between groves of orange, upon the towers of Granada below them; the magnificent plain of the Vega beyond, streaked with evening sunshine, and the distant hills tinted with rosy and purple hues: it seemed an emblem of the happy future, that love and hope were decking out for them.

As if to make the scene complete, a group of Andalusians struck up a dance, in one of the vistas of the garden, to the guitars of two wandering musicians. The Spanish music is wild and plaintive, yet the people dance to it with spirit and enthusiasm. The picturesque figures of the dancers; the girls with their hair in silken nets that hung in knots and tassels down their backs, their mantillas floating round their graceful forms, their slender feet peeping from under their basquinas, their arms tossed up in the air to play the castanets, had a beautiful effect on this airy height, with the rich evening landscape spreading out below them.

When the dance was ended, two of the parties approached Antonio and Inez; one of them began a soft and tender Moorish ballad, accompanied by the other on the lute. It alluded to the story of the garden, the wrongs of the fair queen of Granada, and the misfortunes of the Abencerrages. It was one of those old ballads that abound in this part of Spain, and live, like echoes, about the ruins of Moorish greatness. The heart of Inez was at that moment open to every tender impression; the tears rose into her eyes, as she listened to the tale. The singer approached nearer to her; she was striking in her appearance; young, beautiful, with a mixture of wildness and melancholy in her fine black eyes. She fixed them mournfully and expressively on Inez, and, suddenly varying her manner, sang another ballad, which treated of impending danger and treachery. All this might have passed for a mere accidental caprice of the singer, had there not been something in her look, manner, and gesticulation that made it pointed and startling.

Inez was about to ask the meaning of this evidently personal application of the song, when she was interrupted by Antonio, who gently drew her from the place. Whilst she had been lost in attention to the music, he had remarked a group of men, in the shadows of the trees, whispering together. They were enveloped in the broad hats and great cloaks so much worn by the Spanish, and, while they were regarding himself and Inez attentively, seemed anxious to avoid observation. Not knowing what might be their character or intention, he hastened to quit a place where the gathering shadows of evening might expose them to intrusion and insult. On their way down the hill, as they passed through the wood of elms, mingled with poplars and oleanders, that skirts the road leading from the Alhambra, he again saw these men apparently following at a distance; and he afterwards caught sight of them among the trees on the banks of the Darro. He said nothing on the subject to Inez, nor her father, for he would not awaken unnecessary alarm; but he felt at a loss how to ascertain or to avert any machinations that might be devising against the helpless inhabitants of the tower.

He took his leave of them late at night, full of this perplexity. As he left the dreary old pile, he saw someone lurking in the shadow of the wall, apparently watching his movements. He hastened after the figure, but it glided away, and disappeared among some ruins. Shortly after he heard a low whistle, which was answered from a little distance. He had no longer a doubt but that some mischief was on foot, and turned to hasten back to the tower, and put its inmates on their guard. He had scarcely turned, however, before he found himself suddenly seized from behind by someone of Herculean strength. His struggles were in vain; he was surrounded by armed men. One threw a mantle over him that stifled his cries, and enveloped him in its folds; and he was hurried off with irresistible rapidity.

The next day passed without the appearance of Antonio at the alchemist's. Another, and another day succeeded, and yet he did not come; nor had anything been heard of him at his lodgings. His absence caused, at first, surprise and conjecture, and at length alarm. Inez recollected the singular intimations of the ballad-singer upon the mountain, which seemed to warn her of impending danger, and her mind was full of vague forebodings. She sat listening to every sound at the gate, or footstep on the stairs. She would take up her guitar and strike a few notes, but it would not do; her heart was sickening with suspense and anxiety. She had never before felt what it was to be really lonely. She now was conscious of the force of that attachment which had taken possession of her breast; for never do we know how much we love, never do we know how necessary the object of our love is to our happiness, until we experience the weary void of separation.

The philosopher, too, felt the absence of his disciple almost as sensibly as did his daughter. The animating buoyancy of the youth had inspired him with new ardor, and had given to his labors the charm of full companionship. However, he had resources and consolations of which his daughter was destitute. His pursuits were of a nature to occupy every thought, and keep the spirits in a state of continual excitement. Certain indications, too, had lately manifested themselves, of the most favorable nature. Forty days and forty nights had the process gone on successfully; the old man's hopes were constantly rising, and he now considered the glorious moment once more at hand, when he should obtain not merely the major lunaria, but likewise the tinctura solaris, the means of multiplying gold, and of prolonging existence. He remained, therefore, continually shut up in his laboratory, watching his furnace; for a moment's inadvertency might once more defeat all his expectations.

He was sitting one evening at one of his solitary vigils, wrapped up in meditation; the hour was late, and his neighbor, the owl, was hooting from the battlement of the tower, when he heard the door open behind him. Supposing it to be his daughter coming to take her leave of him for the night, as was her frequent practice, he called her by name, but a harsh voice met his ear in reply. He was grasped by the arms, and, looking up, perceived three strange men in the chamber. He attempted to shake them off, but in vain. He called for help, but they scoffed at his cries. "Peace, dotard!" cried one: "think'st thou the servants of the most holy inquisition are to be daunted by thy clamors? Comrades, away with him!"

Without heeding his remonstrances and entreaties, they seized upon his books and papers, took some note of the apartment, and the utensils, and then bore him off a prisoner.

Inez, left to herself, had passed a sad and lonely evening; seated by a casement which looked into the garden, she had pensively watched star after star sparkle out of the blue depths of the sky, and was indulging a crowd of anxious thoughts about her lover, until the rising tears began to flow. She was suddenly alarmed by the sound of voices, that seemed to come from a distant part of the mansion. There was, not long after, a noise of several persons descending the stairs. Surprised at these unusual sounds in their lonely habitation, she remained for a few moments in a state of trembling, yet indistinct apprehension, when the servant rushed into the room, with terror in her countenance, and informed her that her father was carried off by armed men.

Inez did not stop to hear further, but flew downstairs to overtake them. She had scarcely passed the threshold, when she found herself in the grasp of strangers. "Away! away!" cried she, wildly, "do not stop me—let me follow my father."

"We come to conduct you to him, señora," said one of the men, respectfully.

"Where is he, then?"

"He is gone to Granada," replied the man: "an unexpected circumstance requires his presence there immediately; but he is among friends."

"We have no friends in Granada," said Inez, drawing back; but then the idea of Antonio rushed into her mind; something relating to him might have call her father thither. "Is Señor Antonio de Castros with him?" demanded she, with agitation.

"I know not, señora," replied the man. "It is very possible. I only know that your father is among friends, and is anxious for you to follow him."

"Let us go, then," cried she, eagerly. The men led her a little distance to where a mule was waiting, and, assisting her to mount, they conducted her slowly towards the city.

Granada was on that evening a scene of fanciful revel. It was one of the festivals of the Maestranza, an association of the nobility to keep up some of the gallant customs of ancient chivalry. There had been a representation of a tournament in one of the squares; the streets would still occasionally resound with the beat of a solitary drum, or the bray of a trumpet from some straggling party of revellers. Sometimes they were met by cavaliers, richly dressed in ancient costumes, attended by their squires; and at one time they passed in sight of a palace brilliantly illuminated, from whence came the mingled sounds of music and the dance. Shortly after, they came to the square where the mock tournament had been held. It was thronged by the populace, recreating themselves among booths and stalls where refreshments were sold, and the glare of torches showed the temporary galleries, and gay-coloured awnings, and armorial trophies, and other paraphernalia of the show. The conductors of Inez endeavored to keep out of observation, and to traverse a gloomy part of the square; but they were detained at one place by the pressure of a crowd surrounding a party of wandering musicians, singing one of those ballads of which the Spanish populace are so passionately fond. The torches which were held by some of the crowd, threw a strong mass of light upon Inez, and the sight of so beautiful a being, without mantilla or veil, looking so bewildered, and conducted by men who seemed to take no gratification in the surrounding gayety, occasioned expressions of curiosity. One of the ballad-singers approached, and striking her guitar with peculiar earnestness, began to sing a doleful air, full of sinister forebodings. Inez started with surprise. It was the same ballad-singer that had addressed her in the garden of the Generaliffe.

It was the same air that she had then sung. It spoke of impending dangers; they seemed, indeed, to be thickening around her. She was anxious to speak with the girl, and to ascertain whether she really had a knowledge of any definite evil that was threatening her; but, as she attempted to address her, the mule, on which she rode, was suddenly seized, and led forcibly through the throng by one of her conductors, while she saw another addressing menacing words to the ballad-singer. The latter raised her hand with a warning gesture, as Inez lost sight of her.

While she was yet lost in perplexity, caused by this singular occurrence, they stopped at the gate of a large mansion. One of her attendants knocked, the door was opened, and they entered a paved court. "Where are we?" demanded Inez, with anxiety. "At the house of a friend, señora," replied the man. "Ascend this staircase with me, and in a moment you will meet your father."

They ascended a staircase, that led to a suite of splendid apartments. They passed through several, until they came to an inner chamber. The door opened—someone approached; but what was her terror at perceiving, not her father, but Don Ambrosio!

The men who had seized upon the alchemist had, at least, been more honest in their professions. They were, indeed, familiars of the inquisition. He was conducted in silence to the gloomy prison of that horrible tribunal. It was a mansion whose very aspect withered joy, and almost shut out hope. It was one of those hideous abodes which the bad passions of men conjure up in this fair world, to rival the fancied dens of demons and the accursed.

Day after day went heavily by, without anything to mark the lapse of time, but the decline and reappearance of the light that feebly glimmered through the narrow window of the dungeon in which the unfortunate alchemist was buried rather than confined. His mind was harassed with uncertainties and fears about his daughter, so helpless and inexperienced. He endeavored to gather tidings of her from the man who brought his daily portion of food. The fellow stared, as if astonished at being asked a question in that mansion of silence and mystery, but departed without saying a word. Every succeeding attempt was equally fruitless.

The poor alchemist was oppressed by many griefs; and it was not the least, that he had been again interrupted in his labors on the very point of success. Never was alchemist so near attaining the golden secret—a little longer, and all his hopes would have been realized. The thoughts of these disappointments afflicted him more even than the fear of all that he might suffer from the merciless inquisition. His waking thoughts would follow him into his dreams. He would be transported in fancy to his laboratory, busied again among retorts and alembics, and surrounded by Lully, by D'Abano, by Olybius, and the other masters of the sublime art. The moment of projection would arrive; a seraphic form would rise out of the furnace, holding forth a vessel containing the precious elixir; but, before he could grasp the prize, he would awake, and find himself in a dungeon.

All the devices of inquisitorial ingenuity were employed to ensnare the old man, and to draw from him evidence that might be brought against himself, and might corroborate certain secret information that had been given against him. He had been accused of practising necromancy and judicial astrology, and a cloud of evidence had been secretly brought forward to substantiate the charge. It would be tedious to enumerate all the circumstances, apparently corroborative, which had been industriously cited by the secret accuser. The silence which prevailed about the tower, its desolateness, the very quiet of its inhabitants, had been adduced as proofs that something sinister was perpetrated within. The alchemist's conversations and soliloquies in the garden had been overheard and misrepresented. The lights and strange appearances at night, in the tower, were given with violent exaggerations. Shrieks and yells were said to have been heard from thence at midnight, when, it was confidently asserted, the old man raised familiar spirits by his incantations, and even compelled the dead to rise from their graves, and answer to his questions.

The alchemist, according to the custom of the inquisition, was kept in complete ignorance of his accuser; of the witnesses produced against him; even of the crimes of which he was accused. He was examined generally, whether he knew why he was arrested, and was conscious of any guilt that might deserve the notice of the holy office? He was examined as to his country, his life, his habits, his pursuits, his actions, and opinions. The old man was frank and simple in his replies; he was conscious of no guilt, capable of no art, practised in no dissimulation. After receiving a general admonition to bethink himself whether he had not committed any act deserving of punishment and to prepare, by confession, to secure the well-known mercy of the tribunal, he was remanded to his cell.

He was now visited in his dungeon by crafty familiars of the inquisition, who, under pretence of sympathy and kindness, came to beguile the tediousness of his imprisonment with friendly conversation. They casually introduced the subject of alchemy, on which they touched with great caution and pretended indifference. There was no need of such craftiness. The honest enthusiast had no suspicion in his nature: the moment they touched upon his favorite theme, he forgot his misfortunes and imprisonment, and broke forth into rhapsodies about the divine science.

The conversation was artfully turned to the discussion of elementary beings. The alchemist readily avowed his belief in them; and that there had been instances of their attending upon philosophers, and administering to their wishes. He related many miracles said to have been performed by Apollonius Thyaneus, through the aid of spirits or demons; insomuch that he was set up by the heathens in opposition to the Messiah; and was even regarded with reverence by many Christians. The familiars eagerly demanded whether he believed Apollonius to be a true and worthy philosopher. The unaffected piety of the alchemist protected him even in the midst of his simplicity; for he condemned Apollonius as a sorcerer and an imposter. No art could draw from him an admission that he had ever employed or invoked spiritual agencies in the prosecution of his pursuits, though he believed himself to have been frequently impeded by their invisible interference.

The inquisitors were sorely vexed at not being able to inveigle him into a confession of a criminal nature; they attributed their failure to craft, to obstinacy, to every cause but the right one, namely, that the harmless visionary had nothing guilty to confess. They had abundant proof of a secret nature against him; but it was the practice of the inquisition to endeavor to procure confession from the prisoners. An *auto da fé* was at hand; the worthy fathers were eager for his conviction, for they were always anxious to have a good number of culprits condemned to the stake, to grace these solemn triumphs. He was at length brought to a final examination.

The chamber of trial was spacious and gloomy. At one end was a huge crucifix, the standard of the inquisition. A long table extended through the centre of the room, at which sat the inquisitors and their secretary; at the other end, a stool was placed for the prisoner.

He was brought in, according to custom, bare-headed and bare-legged. He was enfeebled by confinement and affliction; by constantly brooding over the unknown fate of his child, and the disastrous interruption of his experiments. He sat bowed down and listless; his head sunk upon his breast; his whole appearance that of one "past hope, abandoned, and by himself given over."

The accusation alleged against him was now brought forward in a specific form; he was called upon by name, Felix de Vasquez, formerly of Castile, to answer to the charges of necromancy and demonology. He was told that the charges were amply substantiated; and was asked whether he was ready, by full confession, to throw himself upon the well-known mercy of the holy inquisition.

The philosopher testified some slight surprise at the nature of the accusation, but simply replied, "I am innocent."

"What proof have you to give of your innocence?"

"It rather remains for you to prove your charges," said the old man. "I am a stranger and a sojourner in the land, and know no one out of the doors of my dwelling. I can give nothing in my vindication but the word of a nobleman and a Castilian."

The inquisitor shook his head, and went on to repeat the various inquiries that had before been made as to his mode of life and pursuits. The poor alchemist was too feeble and too weary at heart to make any but brief replies. He requested that some man of science might examine his laboratory, and all his books and papers, by which it would be made abundantly evident that he was merely engaged in the study of alchemy.

To this the inquisitor observed, that alchemy had become a mere covert for secret and deadly sins. That the practisers of it were apt to scruple at no means to satisfy their inordinate greediness of gold. Some had been known to use spells and impious ceremonies; to conjure the aid of evil spirits; nay, even to sell their souls to the enemy of mankind, so that they might riot in boundless wealth while living.

The poor alchemist had heard all patiently, or, at least, passively. He had disdained to vindicate his name otherwise than by his word; he had smiled at the accusations of sorcery, when applied merely to himself; but when the sublime art, which had been the study and passion of his life, was assailed, he could no longer listen in silence. His head gradually rose from his bosom; a hectic color came in faint streaks to his cheek; played about there, disappeared, returned, and at length kindled into a burning glow. The clammy dampness dried from his forehead; his eyes, which had nearly been extinguished, lighted up again, and burned with their wonted and visionary fires. He entered into a vindication of his favorite art. His voice at first was feeble and broken; but it gathered strength as he proceeded, until it rolled in a deep and sonorous volume. He gradually rose from his seat, as he rose with his subject; he threw back the scanty black mantle which had hitherto wrapped his limbs; the very uncouthness of his form and looks gave an impressive effect to what he uttered; it was as though a corpse had become suddenly animated.

He repelled with scorn the aspersions cast upon alchemy by the ignorant and vulgar. He affirmed it to be the mother of all art and science, citing the opinions of Paracelsus, Sandivogius, Raymond Lully, and others, in support of his assertions. He maintained that it was pure and innocent and honorable both in its purposes and means. What were its objects? The perpetuation of life and youth, and the production of gold. "The elixir vitæ," said he, "is no charmed potion, but merely a concentration of those elements of vitality which nature has scattered through her works.

The philosopher's stone, or tincture, or powder, as it is variously called, is no necromantic talisman, but consists simply of those particles which gold contains within itself for its reproduction; for gold, like other things, has its seed within itself, though bound up with inconceivable firmness, from the vigor of innate fixed salts and sulphurs. In seeking to discover the elixir of life, then," continued he, "we seek only to apply some of nature's own specifics against the disease and decay to which our bodies are subjected; and what else does the physician, when he tasks his art, and uses subtle compounds and cunning distillations, to revive our languishing powers, and avert the stroke of death for a season?

"In seeking to multiply the precious metals, also, we seek but to germinate and multiply, by natural means, a particular species of nature's productions; and what else does the husbandman, who consults times and seasons, and, by what might be deemed a natural magic, from the mere scattering of his hand, covers a whole plain with golden vegetation? The mysteries of our art, it is true, are deeply and darkly hidden; but it requires so much the more innocence and purity of thought, to penetrate unto them. No, father! The true alchemist must be pure in mind and body; he must be temperate, patient, chaste, watchful, meek, humble, devout. 'My son,' says Hermes Trismegestes, the great master of our art, 'my son, I recommend you above all things to fear God.' And indeed it is only by devout castigation of the senses, and purification of the soul that the alchemist is enabled to enter into the sacred chambers of truth. 'Labor, pray, and read,' is the motto of our science. As De Nuysment well observes, 'These high and singular favors are granted unto none, save only unto the sons of God, (that is to say, the virtuous and devout), who, under his paternal benediction, have obtained the opening of the same, by the helping hand of the queen of arts, divine Philosophy.' Indeed, so sacred has the nature of this knowledge been considered, that we are told it has four times been expressly communicated by God to man, having made a part of that cabalistical wisdom which was revealed to Adam to console him for the loss of Paradise; and to Moses in the bush, and to Solomon in a dream, and to Esdras by the angel.

"So far from demons and malign spirits being the friends and abettors of the alchemist, they are the continual foes with which he has to contend. It is their constant endeavor to shut up the avenues to those truths which would enable him to rise above the abject state into which he has fallen, and return to that excellence which was his original birthright. For what would be the effect of this length of days, and this abundant wealth, but to enable the possessor to go on from art to art, from science to science, with energies unimpaired by sickness, uninterrupted by death? For this have sages and philosophers shut themselves up in cells and solitudes; buried themselves in caves and dens of the earth; turning from the joys of life, and the pleasance of the world; enduring scorn, poverty, persecution. For this was Raymond Lully stoned to death in Mauritania. For this did the immortal Pietro D'Abano suffer persecution at Padua, and, when he escaped from his oppressors by death, was despitefully burnt in effigy. For this have illustrious men of all nations intrepidly suffered martyrdom. For this, if unmolested, have they assiduously employed the latest hour of life, the expiring throb of existence; hoping to the last that they might yet seize upon the prize for which they had struggled, and pluck themselves back even from the very jaws of the grave!

"For, when once the alchemist shall have attained the object of his toils; when the sublime secret shall be revealed to his gaze, how glorious will be the change in his condition! How will he emerge from his solitary retreat, like the sun breaking forth from the darksome chamber of the night, and darting his beams throughout the earth! Gifted with perpetual youth and boundless riches, to what heights of wisdom may he attain! How may he carry on, uninterrupted, the thread of knowledge, which has hitherto been snapped at the death of each philosopher! And, as the increase of wisdom is the increase of virtue, how may he become the benefactor of his fellow-men; dispensing, with liberal but cautious and discriminating hand, that inexhaustible wealth which is at his disposal; banishing poverty, which is the cause of so much sorrow and wickedness; encouraging the arts; promoting discoveries, and enlarging all the means of virtuous enjoyment! His life will be the connecting band of generations. History will live in his recollection; distant ages will speak with his tongue. The nations of the earth will look to him as their preceptor, and kings will sit at his feet and learn wisdom. Oh glorious! Oh celestial alchemy!"

Here he was interrupted by the inquisitor, who had suffered him to go on thus far, in hopes of gathering something from his unguarded enthusiasm. "Señor" said he, "this is all rambling, visionary talk. You are charged with sorcery, and in defence you give us a rhapsody about alchemy. Have you nothing better than this to offer in your defence?"

The old man slowly resumed his seat, but did not deign a reply. The fire that had beamed in his eye gradually expired. His cheek resumed its wonted paleness; but he did not relapse into inanity. He sat with a steady, serene, patient look. Like one prepared not to contend, but to suffer.

His trial continued for a long time, with cruel mockery of justice, for no witnesses were ever in this court confronted with the accused, and the latter had continually to defend himself in the dark. Some unknown and powerful enemy had alleged charges against the unfortunate alchemist, but who he could not imagine. Stranger and sojourner as he was in the land, solitary and harmless in his pursuits, how could he have provoked such hostility? The tide of secret testimony, however, was too strong against him; he was convicted of the crime of magic, and condemned to expiate his sins at the stake, at the approaching *auto da fé*.

While the unhappy alchemist was undergoing his trial at the inquisition, his daughter was exposed to trials no less severe. Don Ambrosio, into whose hands she had fallen, was, as has before been intimated, one of the most daring and lawless profligates in all Granada. He was a man of hot blood and fiery passions, who stopped at nothing in the gratification of his desires; yet with all this he possessed manners, address, and accomplishments, that had made him eminently successful among the sex. From the palace to the cottage he had extended his amorous enterprises; his serenades harassed the slumbers of half the husbands in Granada; no balcony was too high for his adventurous attempts, nor any cottage too lowly for his perfidious seductions. Yet he was as fickle as he was ardent; success had made him vain and capricious; he had no sentiment to attach him to the victim of his arts; and many a pale cheek and fading eye, languishing amidst the sparkling of jewels, and many a breaking heart, throbbing under the rustic bodice, bore testimony to his triumphs and his faithlessness.

He was sated, however, by easy conquests, and wearied of a life of continual and prompt gratification. There had been a degree of difficulty and enterprise in the pursuit of Inez that he had never before experienced. It had aroused him from the monotony of mere sensual life, and stimulated him with the charm of adventure. He had become an epicure in pleasure; and now that he had this coy beauty in his power, he was determined to protract his enjoyment, by the gradual conquest of her scruples and downfall of her virtue. He was vain of his person and address, which he thought no woman could long withstand; and it was a kind of trial of skill to endeavor to gain, by art and fascination, what he was secure of obtaining at any time by violence.

When Inez, therefore, was brought into his presence by his emissaries, he affected not to notice her terror and surprise, but received her with formal and stately courtesy. He was too wary a fowler to flutter the bird when just entangled in the net. To her eager and wild inquiries about her father, he begged her not to be alarmed; that he was safe, and had been there, but was engaged elsewhere in an affair of moment, from which he would soon return; in the meantime, he had left word that she should await his return in patience. After some stately expressions of general civility, Don Ambrosio made a ceremonious bow and retired.

The mind of Inez was full of trouble and perplexity. The stately formality of Don Ambrosio was so unexpected as to check the accusations and reproaches that were springing to her lips. Had he had evil designs, would he have treated her with such frigid ceremony when he had her in his power? But why, then, was she brought to his house? Was not the mysterious disappearance of Antonio connected with this? A thought suddenly darted into her mind. Antonio had again met with Don Ambrosio—they had fought—Antonio was wounded—perhaps dying! It was him to whom her father had gone—it was at his request that Don Ambrosio had sent for them, to soothe his dying moments! These, and a thousand such horrible suggestions, harassed her mind; but she tried in vain to get information from the domestics; they knew nothing but that her father had been there, had gone, and would soon return.

Thus passed a night of tumultuous thought, and vague yet cruel apprehensions. She knew not what to do or what to believe—whether she ought to fly, or to remain; but if to fly, how was she to extricate herself? and where was she to seek her father? As the day dawned without any intelligence of him, her alarm increased; at length a message was brought from him, saying that circumstances prevented his return to her, but begging her to hasten to him without delay.

With an eager and throbbing heart did she set forth with the men that were to conduct her. She little thought, however, that she was merely changing her prison-house. Don Ambrosio had feared lest she should be traced to his residence in Granada; or that he might be interrupted there before he could accomplish his plan of seduction. He had her now conveyed, therefore, to a mansion which he possessed in one of the mountain solitudes in the neighborhood of Granada; a lonely, but beautiful retreat. In vain, on her arrival, did she look around for her father or Antonio; none but strange faces met her eye: menials, profoundly respectful, but who knew nor saw anything but what their master pleased.

She had scarcely arrived before Don Ambrosio made his appearance, less stately in his manner, but still treating her with the utmost delicacy and deference. Inez was too much agitated and alarmed to be baffled by his courtesy, and became vehement in her demand to be conducted to her father.

Don Ambrosio now put on an appearance of the greatest embarrassment and emotion. After some delay, and much pretended confusion, he at length confessed that the seizure of her father was all a stratagem; a mere false alarm, to procure him the present opportunity of having access to her, and endeavoring to mitigate that obduracy, and conquer that repugnance, which he declared had almost driven him to distraction.

He assured her that her father was again at home in safety, and occupied in his usual pursuits; having been fully satisfied that his daughter was in honorable hands, and would soon be restored to him. It was in vain that she threw herself at his feet, and implored to be set at liberty; he only replied by gentle entreaties, that she would pardon the seeming violence he had to use; and that she would trust a little while to his honor. "You are here," said he, "absolute mistress of everything: nothing shall be said or done to offend you; I will not even intrude upon your ear the unhappy passion that is devouring my heart. Should you require it, I will even absent myself from your presence; but, to part with you entirely at present, with your mind full of doubts and resentments, would be worse than death to me. No, beautiful Inez, you must first know me a little better, and know by my conduct that my passion for you is as delicate and respectful as it is vehement."

The assurance of her father's safety had relieved Inez from one cause of torturing anxiety, only to render her fears the more violent on her own account. Don Ambrosio, however, continued to treat her with artful deference, that insensibly lulled her apprehensions. It is true she found herself a captive, but no advantage appeared to be taken of her helplessness. She soothed herself with the idea that a little while would suffice to convince Don Ambrosio of the fallacy of his hopes, and that he would be induced to restore her to her home. Her transports of terror and affliction, therefore, subsided, in a few days, into a passive, yet anxious melancholy, with which she awaited the hoped-for event.

In the meanwhile, all those artifices were employed that are calculated to charm the senses, ensnare the feelings, and dissolve the heart into tenderness. Don Ambrosio was a master of the subtle arts of seduction. His very mansion breathed an enervating atmosphere of languor and delight. It was here, amidst twilight saloons and dreamy chambers, buried among groves of orange and myrtle, that he shut himself up at times from the prying world, and gave free scope to the gratification of his pleasures.

The apartments were furnished in the most sumptuous and voluptuous manner; the silken couches swelled to the touch, and sunk in downy softness beneath the slightest pressure. The paintings and statues, all told some classic tale of love, managed, however, with an insidious delicacy; which, while it banished the grossness that might disgust, was the more calculated to excite the imagination. There the blooming Adonis was seen, not breaking away to pursue the boisterous chase, but crowned with flowers, and languishing in the embraces of celestial beauty. There Acis wooed his Galatea in the shade, with the Sicilian sea spreading in halcyon serenity before them. There were depicted groups of fauns and dryads, fondly reclining in summer bowers, and listening to the liquid piping of the reed; or the wanton satyrs, surprising some wood-nymph during her noontide slumber. There, too, on the storied tapestry, might be seen the chaste Diana, stealing, in the mystery of moonlight, to kiss the sleeping Endymion; while Cupid and Psyche, entwined in immortal marble, breathed on each other's lips the early kiss of love.

The ardent rays of the sun were excluded from these balmy halls; soft and tender music from unseen musicians floated around, seeming to mingle with the perfumes that were exhaled from a thousand flowers. At night, when the moon shed a fairy light over the scene, the tender serenade would rise from among the bowers of the garden, in which the fine voice of Don Ambrosio might often be distinguished; or the amorous flute would be heard along the mountain, breathing in its pensive cadences the very soul of a lover's melancholy.

Various entertainments were also devised to dispel her loneliness, and to charm away the idea of confinement. Groups of Andalusian dancers performed, in the splendid saloons, the various picturesque dances of their country; or represented little amorous ballets, which turned upon some pleasing scene of pastoral coquetry and courtship. Sometimes there were bands of singers, who, to the romantic guitar, warbled forth ditties full of passion and tenderness.

Thus all about her enticed to pleasure and voluptuousnesss; but the heart of Inez turned with distaste from this idle mockery. The tears would rush into her eyes, as her thoughts reverted from this scene of profligate splendor, to the humble but virtuous home from whence she had been betrayed; or if the witching power of music ever soothed her into a tender reverie, it was to dwell with fondness on the image of Antonio. But if Don Ambrosio, deceived by this transient calm, should attempt at such time to whisper his passion, she would start as from a dream, and recoil from him with involuntary shuddering.

She had passed one long day of more than ordinary sadness, and in the evening a band of these hired performers were exerting all the animating powers of song and dance to amuse her. But while the lofty saloon resounded with their warblings, and the light sound of feet upon its marble pavement kept time to the cadence of the song, poor Inez, with her face buried in the silken couch on which she reclined, was only rendered more wretched by the sound of gayety.

At length her attention was caught by the voice of one of the singers, that brought with it some indefinite recollections. She raised her head, and cast an anxious look at the performers, who, as usual, were at the lower end of the saloon.

One of them advanced a little before the others. It was a female, dressed in a fanciful, pastoral garb, suited to the character she was sustaining; but her countenance was not to be mistaken. It was the same ballad-singer that had twice crossed her path, and given her mysterious intimations of the lurking mischief that surrounded her. When the rest of the performances were concluded, she seized a tambourine, and, tossing it aloft, danced alone to the melody of her own voice. In the course of her dancing, she approached to where Inez reclined: and as she struck the tambourine, contrived dexterously to throw a folded paper on the couch. Inez seized it with avidity, and concealed it in her bosom. The singing and dancing were at an end; the motley crew retired; and Inez, left alone, hastened with anxiety to unfold the paper thus mysteriously conveyed. It was written in an agitated, and almost illegible handwriting: "Be on your guard! You are surrounded by treachery. Trust not to the forbearance of Don Ambrosio; you are marked out for his prey. An humble victim to his perfidy gives you this warning; she is encompassed by too many dangers to be more explicit. Your father is in the dungeons of the inquisition!"

The brain of Inez reeled, as she read this dreadful scroll. She was less filled with alarm at her own danger, than horror at her father's situation. The moment Don Ambrosio appeared, she rushed and threw herself at his feet, imploring him to save her father. Don Ambrosio stared with astonishment; but immediately regaining his self-possession, endeavored to soothe her by his blandishments, and by assurances that her father was in safety. She was not to be pacified;

her fears were too much aroused to be trifled with. She declared her knowledge of her father's being a prisoner of the inquisition, and reiterated her frantic supplications that he would save him.

Don Ambrosio paused for a moment in perplexity, but was too adroit to be easily confounded. "That your father is a prisoner," replied he, "I have long known. I have concealed it from you, to save you from fruitless anxiety. You now know the real reason of the restraint I have put upon your liberty: I have been protecting instead of detaining you. Every exertion has been made in your father's favor; but I regret to say, the proofs of the offences of which he stands charged have been too strong to be controverted. Still," added he, "I have it in my power to save him; I have influence, I have means at my beck; it may involve me, it is true, in difficulties, perhaps in disgrace; but what would I not do, in the hope of being rewarded by your favor? Speak, beautiful Inez," said he, his eyes kindling with sudden eagerness; "it is with you to say the word that seals your father's fate. One kind word—say but you will be mine, and you will behold me at your feet, your father at liberty and in affluence, and we shall all be happy!"

Inez drew back from him with scorn and disbelief. "My father," exclaimed she, "is too innocent and blameless to be convicted of crime; this is some base, some cruel artifice!" Don Ambrosio repeated his asseverations, and with them also his dishonorable proposals; but his eagerness overshot its mark: her indignation and her incredulity were alike awakened by his base suggestions; and he retired from her presence, checked and awed by the sudden pride and dignity of her demeanor.

The unfortunate Inez now became a prey to the most harrowing anxieties. Don Ambrosio saw that the mask had fallen from his face, and that the nature of his machinations was revealed. He had gone too far to retrace his steps, and assume the affectation of tenderness and respect; indeed, he was mortified and incensed at her insensibility to his attractions, and now only sought to subdue her through her fears. He daily represented to her the dangers that threatened her father, and that it was in his power alone to avert them. Inez was still incredulous. She was too ignorant of the nature of the inquisition, to know that even innocence was not always a protection from its cruelties; and she confided too surely in the virtue of her father, to believe that any accusation could prevail against him.

At length Don Ambrosio, to give an effectual blow to her confidence, brought her the proclamation of the approaching *auto da fé*, in which the prisoners were enumerated. She glanced her eye over it, and beheld her father's name, condemned to the stake for sorcery!

For a moment she stood transfixed with horror. Don Ambrosio seized upon the transient calm. "Think, now, beautiful Inez," said he, with a tone of affected tenderness, "his life is still in your hands; one word from you, one kind word, and I can yet save him."

"Monster! Wretch!" cried she, coming to herself, and recoiling from him with insuperable abhorrence: "'Tis you that are the cause of this—'tis you that are his murderer!" Then, wringing her hands, she broke forth into exclamations of the most frantic agony.

The perfidious Ambrosio saw the torture of her soul, and anticipated from it a triumph. He saw that she was in no mood, during her present paroxysm, to listen to his words; but he trusted that the horrors of lonely rumination would break down her spirit, and subdue her to his will. In this, however, he was disappointed. Many were the vicissitudes of mind of the wretched Inez; at one time, she would embrace his knees, with piercing supplications; at another, she would shrink with nervous horror at his very approach; but any intimation of his passion only excited the same emotion of loathing and detestation.

At length the fatal day drew nigh. "To-morrow," said Don Ambrosio, as he left her one evening, "to-morrow is the *auto da fé*. To-morrow you will hear the sound of the bell that tolls your father to his death. You will almost see the smoke that rises from the funeral pile. I leave you to yourself. It is yet in my power to save him. Think whether you can stand to-morrow's horrors without shrinking! Think whether you can endure the after-reflection, that you were the cause of his death, and that merely through a perversity in refusing proffered happiness."

What a night it was to Inez! Her heart already harassed and almost broken, by repeated and protracted anxieties; her strength wasted and enfeebled. On every side, horrors awaited her; her father's death, her own dishonor. There seemed no escape from misery or perdition. "Is there no relief from man—no pity in heaven?" exclaimed she. "What—what have we done, that we should be thus wretched?"

As the dawn approached, the fever of her mind arose to agony; a thousand times did she try the doors and windows of her apartment, in the desperate hope of escaping. Alas! With all the splendor of her prison, it was too faithfully secured for her weak hands to work deliverance. Like a poor bird, that beats its wings against its gilded cage, until it sinks panting in despair, so she threw herself on the floor in hopeless anguish. Her blood grew hot in her veins, her tongue was parched, her temples throbbed with violence, she gasped rather than breathed; it seemed as if her brain was on fire. "Blessed Virgin!" exclaimed she, clasping her hands and turning up her strained eyes, "look down with pity, and support me in this dreadful hour!"

Just as the day began to dawn, she heard a key turn softly in the door of her apartment. She dreaded lest it should be Don Ambrosio; and the very thought of him gave her a sickening pang. It was a female clad in a rustic dress, with her face concealed by her mantilla. She stepped silently into the room, looked cautiously round, and then, uncovering her face, revealed the well-known features of the ballad-singer. Inez uttered an exclamation of surprise, almost of joy. The unknown started back, pressed her finger on her lips enjoining silence, and beckoned her to follow. She hastily wrapped herself in her veil, and obeyed. They passed with quick, but noiseless steps through an antechamber, across a spacious hall, and along a corridor;

all was silent; the household was yet locked in sleep. They came to a door, to which the unknown applied a key. Inez's heart misgave her; she knew not but some new treachery was menacing her; she laid her cold hand on the stranger's arm: "Whither are you leading me?" said she. "To liberty," replied the other, in a whisper.

"Do you know the passages about this mansion?"

"But too well!" replied the girl, with a melancholy shake of the head. There was an expression of sad veracity in her countenance, that was not to be distrusted. The door opened on a small terrace, which was overlooked by several windows of the mansion.

"We must move across this quickly," said the girl, "or we may be observed."

They glided over it, as if scarce touching the ground. A flight of steps led down into the garden; a wicket at the bottom was readily unbolted: they passed with breathless velocity along one of the alleys, still in sight of the mansion, in which, however, no person appeared to be stirring. At length they came to a low private door in the wall, partly hidden by a fig-tree. It was secured by rusty bolts, that refused to yield to their feeble efforts.

"Holy Virgin!" exclaimed the stranger, "what is to be done? One moment more, and we may be discovered."

She seized a stone that lay near by: a few blows, and the bolt flew back; the door grated harshly as they opened it, and the next moment they found themselves in a narrow road.

"Now," said the stranger, "for Granada as quickly as possible! The nearer we approach it, the safer we shall be; for the road will be more frequented."

The imminent risk they ran of being pursued and taken, gave supernatural strength to their limbs; they flew, rather than ran. The day had dawned; the crimson streaks on the edge of the horizon gave tokens of the approaching sunrise; already the light clouds that floated in the western sky were tinged with gold and purple; though the broad plain of the Vega, which now began to open upon their view, was covered with the dark haze of morning. As yet they only passed a few straggling peasants on the road, who could have yielded them no assistance in case of their being overtaken. They continued to hurry forward, and had gained a considerable distance, when the strength of Inez, which had only been sustained by the fever of her mind, began to yield to fatigue: she slackened her pace, and faltered.

"Alas!" said she, "my limbs fail me! I can go no farther!"

"Bear up, bear up," replied her companion, cheeringly; "a little farther, and we shall be safe. Look! Yonder is Granada, just showing itself in the valley below us. A little farther, and we shall come to the main road, and then we shall find plenty of passengers to protect us."

Inez, encouraged, made fresh efforts to get forward, but her weary limbs were unequal to the eagerness of her mind; her mouth and throat were parched by agony and terror: she gasped for breath, and leaned for support against a rock. "It is all in vain!" exclaimed she; "I feel as though I should faint."

"Lean on me," said the other; "let us get into the shelter of yon thicket, that will conceal us from the view; I hear the sound of water, which will refresh you."

With much difficulty they reached the thicket, which overhung a small mountain-stream, just where its sparkling waters leaped over the rock and fell into a natural basin. Here Inez sank upon the ground, exhausted. Her companion brought water in the palms of her hands, and bathed her pallid temples. The cooling drops revived her; she was enabled to get to the margin of the stream, and drink of its crystal current; then, reclining her head on the bosom of her deliverer, she was first enabled to murmur forth her heartfelt gratitude.

"Alas!" said the other, "I deserve no thanks; I deserve not the good opinion you express. In me you behold a victim of Don Ambrosio's arts. In early years he seduced me from the cottage of my parents. Look! at the foot of yonder blue mountain, in the distance, lies my native village: but it is no longer a home for me. From thence he lured me, when I was too young for reflection; he educated me, taught me various accomplishments, made me sensible to love, to splendor, to refinement; then, having grown weary of me, he neglected me, and cast me upon the world. Happily the accomplishments he taught me have kept me from utter want; and the love with which he inspired me has kept me from further degradation. Yes! I confess my weakness; all his perfidy and wrongs cannot efface him from my heart. I have been brought up to love him; I have no other idol: I know him to be base, yet I cannot help adoring him. I am content to mingle among the hireling throng that administer to his amusements, that I may still hover about him, and linger in those halls where I once reigned mistress. What merit, then, have I in assisting your escape? I scarce know whether I am acting from sympathy and a desire to rescue another victim from his power; or jealousy, and an eagerness to remove too powerful a rival!"

While she was yet speaking, the sun rose in all its splendor; first lighting up the mountain summits, then stealing down height by height, until its rays gilded the domes and towers of Granada, which they could partially see from between the trees, below them. Just then the heavy tones of a bell came sounding from a distance, echoing, in sullen clang, along the mountain. Inez turned pale at the sound. She knew it to be the great bell of the cathedral, rung at sunrise on the day of the *auto da fé*, to give note of funeral preparation. Every stroke beat upon her heart, and inflicted an absolute, corporeal pang. She started up wildly. "Let us begone!" cried she; "there is not a moment for delay!"

"Stop!" exclaimed the other; "yonder are horsemen coming over the brow of that distant height; if I mistake not, Don Ambrosio is at their head. Alas! 'tis he! we are lost. Hold!" continued she; "give me your scarf and veil; wrap yourself in this mantilla. I will fly up yon footpath that leads to the heights. I will let the veil flutter as I ascend; perhaps they may mistake me for you, and they must dismount to follow me. Do you hasten forward: you will soon reach the main road. You have jewels on your fingers: bribe the first muleteer you meet, to assist you on your way."

All this was said with hurried and breathless rapidity. The exchange of garments was made in an instant. The girl darted up the mountain-path, her white veil fluttering among the dark shrubbery, while Inez, inspired with new strength, or rather new terror, flew to the road, and trusted to Providence to guide her tottering steps to Granada.

All Granada was in agitation on the morning of this dismal day. The heavy bell of the cathedral continued to utter its clanging tones, that pervaded every part of the city, summoning all persons to the tremendous spectacle that was about to be exhibited. The streets through which the procession was to pass were crowded with the populace. The windows, the roofs, every place that could admit a face or a foothold, were alive with spectators. In the great square, a spacious scaffolding, like an amphitheatre, was erected, where the sentences of the prisoners were to be read, and the sermon of faith to be preached; and close by were the stakes prepared, where the condemned were to be burnt to death. Seats were arranged for the great, the gay, the beautiful; for such is the horrible curiosity of human nature, that this cruel sacrifice was attended with more eagerness than a theatre, or even a bull-feast.

As the day advanced, the scaffolds and balconies were filled with expecting multitudes; the sun shone brightly upon fair faces and gallant dresses; one would have thought it some scene of elegant festivity, instead of an exhibition of human agony and death. But what a different spectacle and ceremony was this, from those which Granada exhibited in the days of her Moorish splendor! "Her galas, her tournaments, her sports of the ring, her fêtes of St. John, her music, her Zambras, and admirable tilts of canes! Her serenades,

her concerts, her songs in Generaliffe! The costly liveries of the
Abencerrages, their exquisite inventions, the skill and valor of the
Alabaces, the superb dresses of the Zegries, Mazas, and Gomeles!"*all
these were at an end. The days of chivalry were over. Instead of the
prancing cavalcade, with neighing steed and lively trumpet; with
burnished lance, and helm, and buckler; with rich confusion of plume,
and scarf, and banner, where purple, and scarlet, and green, and
orange, and every gay color, were mingled with cloth of gold and
fair embroidery; instead of this, crept on the gloomy pageant of
superstition, in cowl and sackcloth; with cross and coffin, and frightful
symbols of human suffering. In place of the frank, hardy knight,
open and brave, with his lady's favor in his casque, and amorous
motto on his shield, looking, by gallant deeds, to win the smile of
beauty, came the shaven, unmanly monk, with downcast eyes, and
head and heart bleached in the cold cloister, secretly exulting in this
bigot triumph.

The sound of the bells gave notice that the dismal procession
was advancing. It passed slowly through the principal streets of the
city, bearing in advance the awful banner of the Holy Office. The
prisoners walked singly, attended by confessors, and guarded by
familiars of the inquisition. They were clad in different garments,
according to the nature of their punishments; those who were to
suffer death wore the hideous Samarra, painted with flames and
demons. The procession was swelled by choirs of boys, different
religious orders and public dignitaries, and above all, by the fathers
of the faith, moving "with slow pace, and profound gravity, truly
triumphing as becomes the principal generals of that great victory."†

As the sacred banner of the inquisition advanced, the countless
throng sunk on their knees before it; they bowed their faces to the

---

* RODD'S *CIVIL WARS OF GRANADA*.
† GONSALVIUS, p. 135.

very earth as it passed, and then slowly rose again, like a great undulating billow. A murmur of tongues prevailed as the prisoners approached, and eager eyes were strained, and fingers pointed, to distinguish the different orders of penitents, whose habits denoted the degree of punishment they were to undergo. But as those drew near whose frightful garb marked them as destined to the flames, the noise of the rabble subsided; they seemed almost to hold in their breath; filled with that strange and dismal interest with which we contemplate a human being on the verge of suffering and death.

It is an awful thing—a voiceless, noiseless multitude! The hushed and gazing stillness of the surrounding thousands, heaped on walls, and gates, and roofs, and hanging, as it were, in clusters, heightened the effect of the pageant that moved drearily on. The low murmuring of the priests could now be heard in prayer and exhortation, with the faint responses of the prisoners, and now and then the voices of the choir at a distance, chanting the litanies of the saints.

The faces of the prisoners were ghastly and disconsolate. Even those who had been pardoned, and wore the Sanbenito, or penitential garment, bore traces of the horrors they had undergone. Some were feeble and tottering, from long confinement; some crippled and distorted by various tortures; every countenance was a dismal page, on which might be read the secrets of their prison-house. But in the looks of those condemned to death, there was something fierce and eager. They seemed men harrowed up by the past, and desperate as to the future. They were anticipating, with spirits fevered by despair, and fixed and clenched determination, the vehement struggle with agony and death which they were shortly to undergo. Some cast now and then a wild and anguished look about them, upon the shining day; the "sun-bright palaces," the gay, the beautiful world, which they were soon to quit forever; or a glance of sudden indignation at the thronging thousands, happy in liberty and life, who seemed, in contemplating their frightful situation, to exult in their own comparative security.

One among the condemned, however, was an exception to these remarks. It was an aged man, somewhat bowed down, with a serene, though dejected countenance, and a beaming, melancholy eye. It was the alchemist. The populace looked upon him with a degree of compassion, which they were not prone to feel towards criminals condemned by the inquisition; but when they were told that he was convicted of the crime of magic, they drew back with awe and abhorrence.

The procession had reached the grand square. The first part had already mounted the scaffolding, and the condemned were approaching. The press of the populace became excessive, and was repelled, as it were, in billows by the guards. Just as the condemned were entering the square, a shrieking was heard among the crowd. A female, pale, frantic, dishevelled, was seen struggling through the multitude. "My father! My father!" was all the cry she uttered, but it thrilled through every heart. The crowd instinctively drew back, and made way for her as she advanced.

The poor alchemist had made his peace with Heaven, and, by a hard struggle, had closed his heart upon the world, when the voice of his child called him once more back to worldly thought and agony. He turned towards the well-known voice; his knees smote together; he endeavored to stretch forth his pinioned arms, and felt himself clasped in the embraces of his child. The emotions of both were too agonizing for utterance. Convulsive sobs and broken exclamations, and embraces more of anguish than tenderness, were all that passed between them. The procession was interrupted for a moment. The astonished monks and familiars were filled with involuntary respect, at the agony of natural affection. Ejaculations of pity broke from the crowd, touched by the filial piety, the extraordinary and hopeless anguish, of so young and beautiful a being.

Every attempt to soothe her, and prevail on her to retire, was unheeded; at length they endeavored to separate her from her father by force. The movement roused her from her temporary abandonment. With a sudden paroxysm of fury, she snatched a sword from one of the familiars. Her late pale countenance was flushed with rage, and fire flashed from her once soft and languishing eyes. The guards shrunk back with awe. There was something in this filial frenzy, this feminine tenderness wrought up to desperation, that touched even their hardened hearts. They endeavored to pacify her, but in vain. Her eye was eager and quick, as the she-wolf's guarding her young. With one arm she pressed her father to her bosom, with the other she menaced every one that approached.

The patience of the guards was soon exhausted. They had held back in awe, but not in fear. With all her desperation the weapon was soon wrested from her feeble hand, and she was borne shrieking and struggling among the crowd. The rabble murmured compassion; but such was the dread inspired by the inquisition, that no one attempted to interfere.

The procession again resumed its march. Inez was ineffectually struggling to release herself from the hands of the familiars that detained her, when suddenly she saw Don Ambrosio before her. "Wretched girl!" exclaimed he with fury, "why have you fled from your friends? Deliver her," said he to the familiars, "to my domestics; she is under my protection."

His creatures advanced to seize her. "Oh, no! oh, no!" cried she, with new terrors, and clinging to the familiars, "I have fled from no friends. He is not my protector! He is the murderer of my father!"

The familiars were perplexed; the crowd pressed on, with eager curiosity. "Stand off!" cried the fiery Ambrosio, dashing the throng from around him. Then turning to the familiars, with sudden moderation, "My friends," said he, "deliver this poor girl to me. Her distress has turned her brain; she has escaped from her friends and protectors this morning; but a little quiet and kind treatment will restore her to tranquillity."

"I am not mad! I am not mad!" cried she, vehemently. "Oh, save me!—save me from these men! I have no protector on earth but my father, and him they are murdering!"

The familiars shook their heads; her wildness corroborated the assertions of Don Ambrosio, and his apparent rank commanded respect and belief. They relinquished their charge to him, and he was consigning the struggling Inez to his creatures.

"Let go your hold, villain!" cried a voice from among the crowd, and Antonio was seen eagerly tearing his way through the press of people.

"Seize him! Seize him!" cried Don Ambrosio to the familiars, "'tis an accomplice of the sorcerer's."

"Liar!" retorted Antonio, as he thrust the mob to the right and left, and forced himself to the spot.

The sword of Don Ambrosio flashed in an instant from the scabbard; the student was armed, and equally alert. There was a fierce clash of weapons: the crowd made way for them as they fought, and closed again, so as to hide them from the view of Inez. All was tumult and confusion for a moment; when there was a kind of shout from the spectators, and the mob again opening, she beheld, as she thought, Antonio weltering in his blood.

This new shock was too great for her already overstrained intellect. A giddiness seized upon her; every thing seemed to whirl before her eyes; she gasped some incoherent words, and sunk senseless upon the ground.

Days, weeks, elapsed, before Inez returned to consciousness. At length she opened her eyes, as if out of a troubled sleep. She was lying upon a magnificent bed, in a chamber richly furnished with pier-glasses, and massive tables inlaid with silver, of exquisite workmanship. The walls were covered with tapestry; the cornices richly gilded; through the door, which stood open, she perceived a superb saloon, with statues and crystal lustres, and a magnificent suite of apartments beyond. The casements of the room were open to admit the soft breath of summer, which stole in, laden with perfumes from a neighboring garden; from whence, also, the refreshing sound of fountains and the sweet notes of birds came in mingled music to her ear.

Female attendants were moving, with noiseless step, about the chamber; but she feared to address them. She doubted whether this was not all delusion, or whether she was not still in the palace of Don Ambrosio, and that her escape, and all its circumstances, had not been but a feverish dream. She closed her eyes again, endeavoring to recall the past, and to separate the real from the imaginary. The last scenes of consciousness, however, rushed too forcibly, with all their horrors, to her mind to be doubted, and she turned shuddering from the recollection, to gaze once more on the quiet and serene magnificence around her. As she again opened her eyes, they rested on an object that at once dispelled every alarm. At the head of her bed sat a venerable form, watching over her with a look of fond anxiety—it was her father!

I will not attempt to describe the scene that ensued; nor the moments of rapture which more than repaid all the sufferings that her affectionate heart had undergone. As soon as their feelings had become more calm, the alchemist stepped out of the room to introduce a stranger, to whom he was indebted for his life and liberty. He returned, leading in Antonio, no longer in his poor scholar's garb, but in the rich dress of a nobleman.

The feelings of Inez were almost overpowered by these sudden reverses, and it was some time before she was sufficiently composed to comprehend the explanation of this seeming romance.

It appeared that the lover, who had sought her affections in the lowly guise of a student, was only son and heir of a powerful grandee of Valencia. He had been placed at the university of Salamanca; but a lively curiosity, and an eagerness for adventure, had induced him to abandon the university, without his father's consent, and to visit various parts of Spain. His rambling inclination satisfied, he had remained incognito for a time at Granada, until, by further study and self-regulation, he could prepare himself to return home with credit, and atone for his transgressions against paternal authority.

How hard he had studied, does not remain on record. All that we know is his romantic adventure of the tower. It was at first a mere youthful caprice, excited by a glimpse of a beautiful face. In becoming a disciple of the alchemist, he probably thought of nothing more than pursuing a light love affair. Further acquaintance, however, had completely fixed his affections; and he had determined to conduct Inez and her father to Valencia, and to trust to her merits to secure his father's consent to their union.

In the meantime, he had been traced to his concealment. His father had received intelligence of his being entangled in the snares of a mysterious adventurer and his daughter, and likely to become the dupe of the fascinations of the latter. Trusty emissaries had been despatched to seize upon him by main force, and convey him without delay to the paternal home.

What eloquence he had used with his father, to convince him of the innocence, the honor, and the high descent of the alchemist, and of the exalted worth of his daughter, does not appear. All that we know is, that the father, though a very passionate, was a very reasonable man, as appears by his consenting that his son should return to Granada, and conduct Inez as his affianced bride to Valencia.

Away, then, Don Antonio hurried back, full of joyous anticipations. He still forbore to throw off his disguise, fondly picturing to himself what would be the surprise of Inez, when, having won her heart and hand as a poor wandering scholar, he should raise her and her father at once to opulence and splendor.

On his arrival he had been shocked at finding the tower deserted by its inhabitants. In vain he sought for intelligence concerning them; a mystery hung over their disappearance which he could not penetrate, until he was thunderstruck, on accidentally reading a list of the prisoners at the impending *auto da fé*, to find the name of his venerable master among the condemned.

It was the very morning of the execution. The procession was already on its way to the grand square. Not a moment was to be lost. The grand inquisitor was a relation of Don Antonio, though they had never met. His first impulse was to make himself known; to exert all his family influence, the weight of his name, and the power of his eloquence, in vindication of the alchemist. But the grand inquisitor was already proceeding, in all his pomp, to the place where the fatal ceremony was to be performed. How was he to be approached? Antonio threw himself into the crowd, in a fever of anxiety, and was forcing his way to the scene of horror, where he arrived just in time to rescue Inez, as has been mentioned.

It was Don Ambrosio that fell in their contest. Being desperately wounded, and thinking his end approaching, he had confessed to an attending father of the inquisition, that he was the sole cause of the alchemist's condemnation, and that the evidence on which it was grounded was altogether false. The testimony of Don Antonio came in corroboration of this avowal; and his relationship to the grand inquisitor had, in all probability, its proper weight. Thus was the poor alchemist snatched, in a manner, from the very flames; and so great had been the sympathy awakened in his case, that for once a populace rejoiced at being disappointed of an execution.

The residue of the story may readily be imagined, by every one versed in this valuable kind of history. Don Antonio espoused the lovely Inez, and took her and her father with him to Valencia. As she had been a loving and dutiful daughter, so she proved a true and tender wife. It was not long before Don Antonio succeeded to his father's titles and estates, and he and his fair spouse were renowned for being the handsomest and happiest couple in all Valencia.

As to Don Ambrosio, he partially recovered to the enjoyment of a broken constitution and a blasted name, and hid his remorse and disgrace in a convent; while the poor victim of his arts, who had assisted Inez in her escape, unable to conquer the early passion that he had awakened in her bosom, though convinced of the baseness of the object, retired from the world, and became an humble sister in a nunnery.

The worthy alchemist took up his abode with his children. A pavilion, in the garden of their palace, was assigned to him as a laboratory, where he resumed his researches with renovated ardor, after the grand secret. He was now and then assisted by his son-in-law; but the latter slackened grievously in his zeal and diligence, after marriage. Still he would listen with profound gravity and attention to the old man's rhapsodies, and his quotations from Paracelsus, Sandivogius, and Pietro D'Abano, which daily grew longer and longer. In this way the good alchemist lived on quietly and comfortably, to what is called a good old age, that is to say, an age that is good for nothing; and unfortunately for mankind, was hurried out of life in his ninetieth year, just as he was on the point of discovering the Philosopher's Stone.

THE ADVENTURE OF MY UNCLE

Many years since, a long time before the French Revolution, my uncle had passed several months at Paris. The English and French were on better terms, in those days, than at present, and mingled cordially together in society. The English went abroad to spend money then, and the French were always ready to help them: they go abroad to save money at present, and that they can do without French assistance. Perhaps the travelling English were fewer and choicer then, than at present, when the whole nation has broke loose, and inundated the continent. At any rate, they circulated more readily and currently in foreign society, and my uncle, during his residence in Paris, made many very intimate acquaintances among the French noblesse.

Some time afterwards, he was making a journey in the winter-time, in that part of Normandy called the Pays de Caux, when, as evening was closing in, he perceived the turrets of an ancient chateau rising out of the trees of its walled park, each turret with its high conical roof of gray slate, like a candle with an extinguisher on it.

"To whom does that chateau belong, friend?" cried my uncle to a meagre, but fiery postilion, who, with tremendous jack boots and cocked hat, was floundering on before him.

"To Monseigneur the Marquis de ——," said the postilion, touching his hat, partly out of respect to my uncle, and partly out of reverence to the noble name pronounced. My uncle recollected the Marquis for a particular friend in Paris, who had often expressed a wish to see him at his paternal chateau. My uncle was an old traveller, one that knew how to turn things to account. He revolved for a few moments in his mind how agreeable it would be to his friend the Marquis to be surprised in this sociable way by a pop visit; and how much more agreeable to himself to get into snug quarters in a chateau, and have a relish of the Marquis's well-known kitchen, and a smack of his superior champagne and burgundy; rather than take up with the miserable lodgment, and miserable fare of a country inn. In a few minutes, therefore, the meagre postilion was cracking his whip like a very devil, or like a true Frenchman, up the long straight avenue that led to the chateau.

You have no doubt all seen French chateaus, as everybody travels in France nowadays. This was one of the oldest; standing naked and alone, in the midst of a desert of gravel walks and cold stone terraces; with a cold-looking formal garden, cut into angles and rhomboids; and a cold leafless park, divided geometrically by straight alleys; and two or three noseless, cold-looking statues without any clothing; and fountains spouting cold water enough to make one's teeth chatter. At least, such was the feeling they imparted on the wintry day of my uncle's visit; though, in hot summer weather, I'll warrant there was glare enough to scorch one's eyes out.

The smacking of the postilion's whip, which grew more and more intense the nearer they approached, frightened a flight of pigeons out of a dove-cot, and rooks out of the roofs; and finally a crew of servants out of the chateau, with the Marquis at their head. He was enchanted to see my uncle; for his chateau, like the house of our worthy host, had not many more guests at the time than it could accommodate. So he kissed my uncle on each cheek, after the French fashion, and ushered him into the castle.

The Marquis did the honors of his house with the urbanity of his country. In fact, he was proud of his old family chateau; for part of it was extremely old. There was a tower and chapel that had been built almost before the memory of man; but the rest was more modern; the castle having been nearly demolished during the wars of the league. The Marquis dwelt upon this event with great satisfaction, and seemed really to entertain a grateful feeling towards Henry the Fourth, for having thought his paternal mansion worth battering down. He had many stories to tell of the prowess of his ancestors, and several skull-caps, helmets, and cross-bows to show; and divers huge boots and buff jerkins, that had been worn by the leaguers. Above all, there was a two-handled sword, which he could hardly wield; but which he displayed as a proof that there had been giants in his family.

In truth, he was but a small descendant from such great warriors. When you looked at their bluff visages and brawny limbs, as depicted in their portraits, and then at the little Marquis, with his spindle shanks; his sallow lantern visage, flanked with a pair of powdered ear-locks, or *ailes de pigeon*, that seemed ready to fly away with it, you would hardly believe him to be of the same race. But when you looked at the eyes that sparkled out like a beetle's from each side of his hooked nose, you saw at once that he inherited all the fiery spirit of his fore-fathers. In fact, a Frenchman's spirit never exhales, however his body may dwindle. It rather rarefies, and grows more inflammable, as the earthly particles diminish; and I have seen valor enough in a little fiery-hearted French dwarf, to have furnished out a tolerable giant.

When once the Marquis, as he was wont, put on one of the old helmets that were stuck up in his hall; though his head no more filled it than a dry pea its peascod; yet his eyes sparkled from the bottom of the iron cavern with the brilliancy of carbuncles, and when he poised the ponderous two-handled sword of his ancestors, you would have thought you saw the doughty little David wielding the sword of Goliath, which was unto him like a weaver's beam.

However, gentlemen, I am dwelling too long on this description of the Marquis and his chateau; but you must excuse me; he was an old friend of my uncle's, and whenever my uncle told the story, he was always fond of talking a great deal about his host.—Poor little Marquis! He was one of that handful of gallant courtiers, who made such a devoted, but hopeless stand in the cause of their sovereign, in the chateau of the Tuileries, against the irruption of the mob, on the sad tenth of August. He displayed the valor of a *preux* French chevalier to the last; flourished feebly his little court sword with a *ça-ça*! in face of a whole legion of *sans-culottes*; but was pinned to the wall like a butterfly, by the pike of a *poissarde*, and his heroic soul was borne up to heaven on his *ailes de pigeon*.

But all this has nothing to do with my story. To the point, then. When the hour arrived for retiring for the night, my uncle was shown to his room, in a venerable old tower. It was the oldest part of the chateau, and had in ancient times been the Donjon or stronghold; of course the chamber was none of the best. The Marquis had put him there, however, because he knew him to be a traveller of taste, and fond of antiquities; and also because the better apartments were already occupied. Indeed, he perfectly reconciled my uncle to his quarters by mentioning the great personages who had once inhabited them, all of whom were in some way or other connected with the family. If you would take his word for it, John Baliol, or, as he called him, Jean de Bailleul, had died of chagrin in this very chamber on hearing of the success of his rival, Robert the Bruce, at the battle of Bannockburn; and when he added that the Duke de Guise had slept in it during the wars of the league, my uncle was fain to felicitate himself upon being honored with such distinguished quarters.

The night was shrewd and windy, and the chamber none of the warmest. An old, long-faced, long-bodied servant in quaint livery, who attended upon my uncle, threw down an armful of wood beside the fireplace, gave a queer look about the room, and then wished him *bon repos*, with a grimace and a shrug that would have been suspicious from any other than an old French servant. The chamber had indeed a wild, crazy look, enough to strike any one who had read romances with apprehension and foreboding. The windows were high and narrow, and had once been loop-holes, but had been rudely enlarged, as well as the extreme thickness of the walls would permit; and the ill-fitted casements rattled to every breeze. You would have thought, on a windy night, some of the old leaguers were tramping and clanking about the apartment in their huge boots and rattling spurs. A door which stood ajar, and like a true French door would stand ajar, in spite of every reason and effort to the contrary, opened upon a long, dark corridor, that led the Lord knows whither, and seemed just made for ghosts to air themselves in, when they turned out of their graves at midnight. The wind would spring up into a hoarse murmur through this passage, and creak the door to and fro, as if some dubious ghost were balancing in its mind whether to come in or not. In a word, it was precisely the kind of comfortless apartment that a ghost, if ghost there were in the chateau, would single out for its favorite lounge.

My uncle, however, though a man accustomed to meet with strange adventures, apprehended none at the time. He made several attempts to shut the door, but in vain. Not that he apprehended any thing, for he was too old a traveller to be daunted by a wild-looking apartment; but the night, as I have said, was cold and gusty, something like the present, and the wind howled about the old turret, pretty much as it does round this old mansion at this moment; and the breeze from the long dark corridor came in as damp and chilly as if from a dungeon. My uncle, therefore, since he could not close the door, threw a quantity of wood on the fire, which soon sent up a flame in the great wide-mouthed chimney that illumined the whole chamber, and made the shadow of the tongs on the opposite wall, look like a long-legged giant. My uncle now clambered on top of the half score of mattresses which form a French bed, and which stood in a deep recess; then tucking himself snugly in, and burying himself up to the chin in the bedclothes, he lay looking at the fire, and listening to the wind, and chuckling to think how knowingly he had come over his friend the Marquis for a night's lodgings: and so he fell asleep.

He had not taken above half of his first nap, when he was awakened by the clock of the chateau, in the turret over his chamber, which struck midnight. It was just such an old clock as ghosts are fond of. It had a deep, dismal tone, and struck so slowly and tediously that my uncle thought it would never have done. He counted and counted till he was confident he counted thirteen, and then it stopped.

The fire had burnt low, and the blaze of the last faggot was almost expiring, burning in small blue flames, which now and then lengthened up into little white gleams. My uncle lay with his eyes half closed, and his nightcap drawn almost down to his nose. His fancy was already wandering, and began to mingle up the present scene with the crater of Vesuvius, the French opera, the Coliseum at Rome, Dolly's chop-house in London, and all the farrago of noted places with which the brain of a traveller is crammed—in a word, he was just falling asleep.

Suddenly he was aroused by the sound of footsteps that appeared to be slowly pacing along the corridor. My uncle, as I have often heard him say himself, was a man not easily frightened; so he lay quiet, supposing that this might be some other guest; or some servant on his way to bed. The footsteps, however, approached the door; the door gently opened; whether of its own accord, or whether pushed open, my uncle could not distinguish: a figure all in white glided in. It was a female, tall and stately in person, and of a most commanding air. Her dress was of an ancient fashion, ample in volume and sweeping the floor. She walked up to the fireplace without regarding my uncle; who raised his nightcap with one hand, and stared earnestly at her. She remained for some time standing by the fire, which flashing up at intervals cast blue and white gleams of light that enabled my uncle to remark her appearance minutely.

Her face was ghastly pale, and perhaps rendered still more so by the bluish light of the fire. It possessed beauty, but its beauty was saddened by care and anxiety. There was the look of one accustomed to trouble, but of one whom trouble could not cast down nor subdue; for there was still the predominating air of proud, unconquerable resolution. Such, at least, was the opinion formed by my uncle, and he considered himself a great physiognomist.

The figure remained, as I said, for some time by the fire, putting out first one hand, then the other, then each foot, alternately, as if warming itself; for your ghosts, if ghost it really was, are apt to be cold. My uncle furthermore remarked that it wore high-heeled shoes, after an ancient fashion, with paste or diamond buckles, that sparkled as though they were alive. At length the figure turned gently round, casting a glassy look about the apartment, which, as it passed over my uncle, made his blood run cold, and chilled the very marrow in his bones. It then stretched its arms towards heaven, clasped its hands, and wringing them in a supplicating manner, glided slowly out of the room.

My uncle lay for some time meditating on this visitation, for (as he remarked when he told me the story) though a man of firmness, he was also a man of reflection, and did not reject a thing because it was out of the regular course of events. However, being, as I have before said, a great traveller, and accustomed to strange adventures, he drew his nightcap resolutely over his eyes, turned his back to the door, hoisted the bedclothes high over his shoulders, and gradually fell asleep.

How long he slept he could not say, when he was awakened by the voice of some one at his bedside. He turned round and beheld the old French servant, with his ear-locks in tight buckles on each side of a long, lantern face, on which habit had deeply wrinkled an everlasting smile. He made a thousand grimaces and asked a thousand pardons for disturbing Monsieur, but the morning was considerably advanced. While my uncle was dressing, he called vaguely to mind the visitor of the preceding night. He asked the ancient domestic what lady was in the habit of rambling about this part of the chateau at night. The old valet shrugged his shoulders as high as his head, laid one hand on his bosom, threw open the other with every finger extended; made a most whimsical grimace, which he meant to be complimentary:

"It was not for him to know anything of *les braves fortunes* of Monsieur."

My uncle saw there was nothing satisfactory to be learnt in this quarter. After breakfast he was walking with the Marquis through the modern apartments of the chateau; sliding over the well-waxed floors of silken saloons, amidst furniture rich in gilding and brocade; until they came to a long picture gallery, containing many portraits, some in oil and some in chalks.

Here was an ample field for the eloquence of his host, who had all the family pride of a nobleman of the *ancien régime*. There was not a grand name in Normandy, and hardly one in France, that was not, in some way or other, connected with his house. My uncle stood listening with inward impatience, resting sometimes on one leg, sometimes on the other, as the little Marquis descanted, with his usual fire and vivacity, on the achievements of his ancestors, whose portraits hung along the wall; from the martial deeds of the stern warriors in steel, to the gallantries and intrigues of the blue-eyed gentlemen, with fair smiling faces, powdered ear-locks, laced ruffles, and pink and blue silk coats and breeches; not forgetting the conquests of the lovely shepherdesses, with hoop petticoats and waists no thicker than an hour glass, who appeared ruling over their sheep and their swains with dainty crooks decorated with fluttering ribbons.

In the midst of his friend's discourse my uncle's eyes rested on a full-length portrait, which struck him as being the very counterpart of his visitor of the preceding night.

"Methinks," said he, pointing to it, "I have seen the original of this portrait."

"*Pardonnez moi*," replied the Marquis politely, "that can hardly be, as the lady has been dead more than a hundred years. That was the beautiful Duchess de Longueville, who figured during the minority of Louis the Fourteenth."

"And was there anything remarkable in her history."

Never was question more unlucky. The little Marquis immediately threw himself into the attitude of a man about to tell a long story. In fact, my uncle had pulled upon himself the whole history of the civil war of the Fronde, in which the beautiful Duchess had played so distinguished a part. Turenne, Coligni, Mazarin, were called up from their graves to grace his narration; nor were the affairs of the Barricadoes, nor the chivalry of the Port Cochères forgotten. My uncle began to wish himself a thousand leagues off from the Marquis and his merciless memory, when suddenly the little man's recollections took a more interesting turn. He was relating the imprisonment of the Duke de Longueville, with the Princes Condé and Conti, in the chateau of Vincennes, and the ineffectual efforts of the Duchess to rouse the sturdy Normans to their rescue. He had come to that part where she was invested by the royal forces in the chateau of Dieppe, and in imminent danger of falling into their hands.

"The spirit of the Duchess," proceeded the Marquis, "rose with her trials. It was astonishing to see so delicate and beautiful a being buffet so resolutely with hardships. She determined on a desperate means of escape. One dark unruly night, she issued secretly out of a small postern gate of the castle, which the enemy had neglected to guard. She was followed by her female attendants, a few domestics, and some gallant cavaliers who still remained faithful to her fortunes. Her object was to gain a small port about two leagues distant, where she had privately provided a vessel for her escape in case of emergency.

"The little band of fugitives were obliged to perform the distance on foot. When they arrived at the port the wind was high and stormy, the tide contrary, the vessel anchored far off in the road, and no means of getting on board, but by a fishing-shallop which lay tossing like a cockle-shell on the edge of the surf. The Duchess determined to risk the attempt. The seamen endeavored to dissuade her, but the imminence of her danger on shore, and the magnanimity of her spirit urged her on. She had to be borne to the shallop in the arms of a mariner. Such was the violence of the wind and waves, that he faltered, lost his foothold, and let his precious burden fall into the sea.

"The Duchess was nearly drowned; but partly through her own struggles, partly by the exertions of the seamen, she got to land. As soon as she had a little recovered strength, she insisted on renewing the attempt. The storm, however, had by this time become so violent as to set all efforts at defiance. To delay, was to be discovered and taken prisoner. As the only resource left, she procured horses; mounted with her female attendants, *en croupe*, behind the gallant gentlemen who accompanied her; and scoured the country to seek some temporary asylum.

"While the Duchess," continued the Marquis, laying his forefinger on my uncle's breast to arouse his flagging attention, "while the Duchess, poor lady, was wandering amid the tempest in this disconsolate manner, she arrived at this chateau. Her approach caused some uneasiness; for the clattering of a troop of horse, at dead of night, up the avenue of a lonely chateau, in those unsettled times, and in a troubled part of the country, was enough to occasion alarm.

"A tall, broad-shouldered chasseur, armed to the teeth, galloped ahead, and announced the name of the visitor. All uneasiness was dispelled. The household turned out with flambeaux to receive her, and never did torches gleam on a more weather-beaten, travel-stained band than came tramping into the court. Such pale, careworn faces, such bedraggled dresses, as the poor Duchess and her females presented, each seated behind her cavalier; while half-drenched, half-drowsy pages and attendants seemed ready to fall from their horses with sleep and fatigue.

"The Duchess was received with a hearty welcome by my ancestors. She was ushered into the Hall of the chateau, and the fires soon crackled and blazed to cheer herself and her train; and every spit and stew-pan was put in requisition to prepare ample refreshments for the wayfarers.

"She had a right to our hospitalities," continued the little Marquis, drawing himself up with a slight degree of stateliness, "for she was related to our family. I'll tell you how it was: Her father, Henry de Bourbon, Prince of Condé—"

"But did the Duchess pass the night in the chateau?" said my uncle rather abruptly, terrified at the idea of getting involved in one of the Marquis's genealogical discussions.

"Oh, as to the Duchess, she was put into the apartment you occupied last night; which, at that time, was a kind of state apartment. Her followers were quartered in the chambers opening upon the neighboring corridor, and her favorite page slept in an adjoining closet. Up and down the corridor walked the great chasseur, who had announced her arrival, and who acted as a kind of sentinel or guard. He was a dark, stern, powerful-looking fellow, and as the light of a lamp in the corridor fell upon his deeply-marked face and sinewy form, he seemed capable of defending the castle with his single arm.

"It was a rough, rude night; about this time of the year.— *apropos!*—now I think of it, last night was the anniversary of her visit. I may well remember the precise date, for it was a night not to be forgotten by our house. There is a singular tradition concerning it in our family." Here the Marquis hesitated, and a cloud seemed to gather about his bushy eyebrows. "There is a tradition—that a strange occurrence took place that night—a strange, mysterious, inexplicable occurrence."

Here he checked himself and paused.

"Did it relate to that lady?" inquired my uncle, eagerly.

"It was past the hour of midnight," resumed the Marquis—"when the whole chateau—"

Here he paused again—my uncle made a movement of anxious curiosity.

"Excuse me," said the Marquis—a slight blush streaking his sullen visage. "There are some circumstances connected with our family history which I do not like to relate. That was a rude period. A time of great crimes among great men: for you know high blood, when it runs wrong, will not run tamely like blood of the *canaille*— poor lady!—But I have a little family pride, that—excuse me—we will change the subject if you please."

My uncle's curiosity was piqued. The pompous and magnificent introduction had led him to expect something wonderful in the story to which it served as a kind of avenue. He had no idea of being cheated out of it by a sudden fit of unreasonable squeamishness. Besides, being a traveller, in quest of information, considered it his duty to inquire into everything.

The Marquis, however, evaded every question.

"Well," said my uncle, a little petulantly, "whatever you may think of it, I saw that lady last night."

The Marquis stepped back and gazed at him with surprise.

"She paid me a visit in my bedchamber."

The Marquis pulled out his snuff-box with a shrug and a smile; taking it no doubt for an awkward piece of English pleasantry, which politeness required him to be charmed with. My uncle went on gravely, however, and related the whole circumstance. The Marquis heard him through with profound attention, holding his snuff-box unopened in his hand. When the story was finished he tapped on the lid of his box deliberately; took a long sonorous pinch of snuff—

"Bah!" said the Marquis, and walked towards the other end of the gallery.—

Here the narrator paused. The company waited for some time for him to resume his narrative; but he continued silent.

"Well," said the inquisitive gentleman, "and what did your uncle say then?"

"Nothing," replied the other.

"And what did the Marquis say farther?"

"Nothing."

"And is that all?"

"That is all," said the narrator, filling a glass of wine.

"I surmise," said the shrewd old gentleman with the waggish nose—"I surmise it was the old housekeeper walking her rounds to see that all was right."

"Bah!" said the narrator, "my uncle was too much accustomed to strange sights not to know a ghost from a housekeeper!"

There was a murmur round the table half of merriment, half of disappointment. I was inclined to think the old gentleman had really an afterpart of his story in reserve; but he sipped his wine and said nothing more; and there was an odd expression about his dilapidated countenance that left me in doubt whether he were in drollery or earnest.

"Egad," said the knowing gentleman with the flexible nose, "this story of your uncle puts me in mind of one that used to be told of an aunt of mine, by the mother's side; though I don't know that it will bear a comparison; as the good lady was not quite so prone to meet with strange adventures. But at any rate, you shall have it."

THE ADVENTURE OF MY AUNT

My aunt was a lady of large frame, strong mind, and great resolution: she was what might be termed a very manly woman. My uncle was a thin, puny little man, very meek and acquiescent, and no match for my aunt. It was observed that he dwindled and dwindled gradually away, from the day of his marriage. His wife's powerful mind was too much for him; it wore him out. My aunt, however, took all possible care of him, had half the doctors in town to prescribe for him, made him take all their prescriptions, *willy nilly*, and dosed him with physic enough to cure a whole hospital. All was in vain. My uncle grew worse and worse the more dosing and nursing he underwent, until in the end he added another to the long list of matrimonial victims, who have been killed with kindness.

"And was it his ghost that appeared to her?" asked the inquisitive gentleman, who had questioned the former story-teller.

"You shall hear," replied the narrator:—My aunt took on mightily for the death of her poor dear husband! Perhaps she felt some compunction at having given him so much physic, and nursed him into his grave. At any rate, she did all that a widow could do to honor his memory. She spared no expense in either the quantity or quality of her mourning weeds; she wore a miniature of him about her neck, as large as a little sun-dial; and she had a full-length portrait of him always hanging in her bed-chamber. All the world extolled her conduct to the skies; and it was determined, that a woman who behaved so well to the memory of one husband, deserved soon to get another.

It was not long after this that she went to take up her residence in an old country seat in Derbyshire, which had long been in the care of merely a steward and housekeeper. She took most of her servants with her, intending to make it her principal abode. The house stood in a lonely, wild part of the country among the gray Derbyshire hills; with a murderer hanging in chains on a bleak height in full view.

The servants from town were half frightened out of their wits, at the idea of living in such a dismal, pagan-looking place; especially when they got together in the servants' hall in the evening, and compared notes on all the hobgoblin stories they had picked up in the course of the day. They were afraid to venture alone about the forlorn black-looking chambers. My ladies' maid, who was troubled with nerves, declared she could never sleep alone in such a "gashly, rummaging old building;" and the footman, who was a kind-hearted young fellow, did all in his power to cheer her up.

My aunt, herself, seemed to be struck with the lonely appearance of the house. Before she went to bed, therefore, she examined well the fastenings of the doors and windows, locked up the plate with her own hands, and carried the keys, together with a little box of money and jewels, to her own room; for she was a notable woman, and always saw to all things herself. Having put the keys under her pillow, and dismissed her maid, she sat by her toilet arranging her hair; for, being, in spite of her grief for my uncle, rather a buxom widow, she was a little particular about her person. She sat for a little while looking at her face in the glass, first on one side, then on the other, as ladies are apt to do, when they would ascertain if they have been in good looks; for a roistering country squire of the neighborhood, with whom she had flirted when a girl, had called that day to welcome her to the country.

All of a sudden she thought she heard something move behind her. She Looked hastily round, but there was nothing to be seen. Nothing but the grimly painted portrait of her poor dear man, which had been hung against the wall. She gave a heavy sigh to his memory, as she was accustomed to do, whenever she spoke of him in company; and went on adjusting her night-dress. Her sigh was re-echoed; or answered by a long-drawn breath. She looked round again, but no one was to be seen. She ascribed these sounds to the wind, oozing through the rat-holes of the old mansion; and proceeded leisurely to put her hair in papers, when, all at once, she thought she perceived one of the eyes of the portrait move.

"The back of her head being towards it!" said the story-teller with the ruined head, giving a knowing wink on the sound side of his visage—"good!"

"Yes, sir!" replied drily the narrator, "her back being towards the portrait, but her eye fixed on its reflection in the glass."

Well, as I was saying, she perceived one of the eyes of the portrait move. So strange a circumstance, as you may well suppose, gave her a sudden shock. To assure herself cautiously of the fact, she put one hand to her forehead, as if rubbing it; peeped through her fingers, and moved the candle with the other hand. The light of the taper gleamed on the eye, and was reflected from it. She was sure it moved. Nay, more, it seemed to give her a wink, as she had sometimes known her husband to do when living! It struck a momentary chill to her heart; for she was a lone woman, and felt herself fearfully situated.

The chill was but transient. My aunt, who was almost as resolute a personage as your uncle, sir, (turning to the old story-teller,) became instantly calm and collected. She went on adjusting her dress. She even hummed a favorite air, and did not make a single false note. She casually overturned a dressing-box; took a candle and picked up the articles leisurely, one by one, from the floor, pursued a rolling pin-cushion that was making the best of its way under the bed; then opened the door; looked for an instant into the corridor, as if in doubt whether to go; and then walked quietly out.

She hastened down-stairs, ordered the servants to arm themselves with the first weapons that came to hand, placed herself at their head, and returned almost immediately.

Her hastily levied army presented a formidable force. The steward had a rusty blunderbuss; the coachman a loaded whip; the footman a pair of horse-pistols; the cook a huge chopping-knife, and the butler a bottle in each hand. My aunt led the van with a red-hot poker; and, in my opinion, she was the most formidable of the party. The waiting-maid brought up the rear, dreading to stay alone in the servants' hall, smelling to a broken bottle of volatile salts, and expressing her terror of the ghostesses.

"Ghosts!" said my aunt resolutely, "I'll singe their whiskers for them!"

They entered the chamber. All was still and undisturbed as when she left it. They approached the portrait of my uncle.

"Pull me down that picture!" cried my aunt.

A heavy groan, and a sound like the chattering of teeth, was heard from the portrait. The servants shrunk back. The maid uttered a faint shriek, and clung to the footman.

"Instantly!" added my aunt, with a stamp of the foot.

The picture was pulled down, and from a recess behind it, in which had formerly stood a clock, they hauled forth a round-shouldered, black-bearded varlet, with a knife as long as my arm, but trembling all over like an aspen leaf.

"Well, and who was he? No ghost, I suppose!" said the inquisitive gentleman.

"A Knight of the Post," replied the narrator, "who had been smitten with the worth of the wealthy widow; or rather a marauding Tarquin, who had stolen into her chamber to violate her purse and rifle her strong box when all the house should be asleep. In plain terms," continued he, "the vagabond was a loose idle fellow of the neighborhood, who had once been a servant in the house, and had been employed to assist in arranging it for the reception of its mistress. He confessed that he had contrived his hiding-place for his nefarious purposes, and had borrowed an eye from the portrait by way of a reconnoitring-hole."

"And what did they do with him—did they hang him?" resumed the questioner.

"Hang him!—how could they?" exclaimed a beetle-browed barrister, with a hawk's nose—"the offence was not capital—no robbery nor assault had been committed—no forcible entry or breaking into the premises—"

"My aunt," said the narrator, "was a woman of spirit, and apt to take the law into her own hands. She had her own notions of cleanliness also. She ordered the fellow to be drawn through the horse-pond to cleanse away all offences, and then to be well rubbed down with an oaken towel."

"And what became of him afterwards?" said the inquisitive gentleman.

"I do not exactly know—I believe he was sent on a voyage of improvement to Botany Bay."

"And your aunt," said the inquisitive gentleman; "I'll warrant she took care to make her maid sleep in the room with her after that."

"No, sir, she did better—she gave her hand shortly after to the roistering squire; for she used to observe it was a dismal thing for a woman to sleep alone in the country."

"She was right," observed the inquisitive gentleman, nodding his head sagaciously—"but I am sorry they did not hang that fellow."

It was agreed on all hands that the last narrator had brought his tale to the most satisfactory conclusion; though a country clergyman present regretted that the uncle and aunt, who figured in the different stories, had not been married together. They certainly would have been well matched.

"But I don't see, after all," said the inquisitive gentleman, "that there was any ghost in this last story."

"Oh, if it's ghosts you want, honey," cried the Irish Captain of Dragoons, "if it's ghosts you want, you shall have a whole regiment of them. And since these gentlemen have been giving the adventures of their uncles and aunts, faith and I'll even give you a chapter too, out of my own family-history."*

---

* 'The Bold Dragoon, or the Adventure of my Grandfather' is omitted

THE ADVENTURE
OF THE GERMAN STUDENT

On a stormy night, in the tempestuous times of the French revolution, a young German was returning to his lodgings, at a late hour, across the old part of Paris. The lightning gleamed, and the loud claps of thunder rattled through the lofty narrow streets—but I should first tell you something about this young German.

Gottfried Wolfgang was a young man of good family. He had studied for some time at Göttingen, but being of a visionary and enthusiastic character, he had wandered into those wild and speculative doctrines which have so often bewildered German students. His secluded life, his intense application, and the singular nature of his studies, had an effect on both mind and body. His health was impaired; his imagination diseased. He had been indulging in fanciful speculations on spiritual essences, until, like Swedenborg, he had an ideal world of his own around him. He took up a notion, I do not know from what cause, that there was an evil influence hanging over him; an evil genius or spirit seeking to ensnare him and ensure his perdition. Such an idea working on his melancholy temperament, produced the most gloomy effects. He became haggard and desponding. His friends discovered the mental malady preying upon him, and determined that the best cure was a change of scene; he was sent, therefore, to finish his studies amidst the splendors and gayeties of Paris.

Wolfgang arrived at Paris at the breaking out of the revolution. The popular delirium at first caught his enthusiastic mind, and he was captivated by the political and philosophical theories of the day: but the scenes of blood which followed shocked his sensitive nature, and made him more than ever a recluse. He shut himself up in a solitary apartment in the *Pays Latin,* the quarter of students. There, in a gloomy street not far from the monastic walls of the Sorbonne, he pursued his favorite speculations. Sometimes he spent hours together in the great libraries of Paris, those catacombs of departed authors, rummaging among their hordes of dusty and obsolete works in quest of food for his unhealthy appetite. He was, in a manner, a literary ghoul, feeding in the charnel-house of decayed literature.

Wolfgang, though solitary and recluse, was of an ardent temperament, but for a time it operated merely upon his imagination. He was too shy and ignorant of the world to make any advances to the fair, but he was a passionate admirer of female beauty, and in his lonely chamber would often lose himself in reveries on forms and faces which he had seen, and his fancy would deck out images of loveliness far surpassing the reality.

While his mind was in this excited and sublimated state, a dream produced an extraordinary effect upon him. It was of a female face of transcendent beauty. So strong was the impression made, that he dreamt of it again and again. It haunted his thoughts by day, his slumbers by night; in fine, he became passionately enamoured of this shadow of a dream. This lasted so long that it became one of those fixed ideas which haunt the minds of melancholy men, and are at times mistaken for madness.

Such was Gottfried Wolfgang, and such his situation at the time I mentioned. He was returning home late one stormy night, through some of the old and gloomy streets of the *Marais,* the ancient part of Paris. The loud claps of thunder rattled among the high houses of the narrow streets. He came to the Place de Grève, the square where public executions are performed. The lightning quivered about the pinnacles of the ancient Hôtel de Ville, and shed flickering gleams over the open space in front. As Wolfgang was crossing the square, he shrank back with horror at finding himself close by the guillotine. It was the height of the reign of terror, when this dreadful instrument of death stood ever ready, and its scaffold was continually running with the blood of the virtuous and the brave. It had that very day been actively employed in the work of carnage, and there it stood in grim array, amidst a silent and sleeping city, waiting for fresh victims.

Wolfgang's heart sickened within him, and he was turning shuddering from the horrible engine, when he beheld a shadowy form, cowering as it were at the foot of the steps which led up to the scaffold. A succession of vivid flashes of lightning revealed it more distinctly. It was a female figure, dressed in black. She was seated on one of the lower steps of the scaffold, leaning forward, her face hid in her lap; and her long dishevelled tresses hanging to the ground, streaming with the rain which fell in torrents. Wolfgang paused. There was something awful in this solitary monument of woe. The female had the appearance of being above the common order. He knew the times to be full of vicissitude, and that many a fair head, which had once been pillowed on down, now wandered houseless. Perhaps this was some poor mourner whom the dreadful axe had rendered desolate, and who sat here heart-broken on the strand of existence, from which all that was dear to her had been launched into eternity.

He approached, and addressed her in the accents of sympathy. She raised her head and gazed wildly at him. What was his astonishment at beholding, by the bright glare of the lightning, the very face which had haunted him in his dreams. It was pale and disconsolate, but ravishingly beautiful.

Trembling with violent and conflicting emotions, Wolfgang again accosted her. He spoke something of her being exposed at such an hour of the night, and to the fury of such a storm, and offered to conduct her to her friends. She pointed to the guillotine with a gesture of dreadful signification.

"I have no friend on earth!" said she.

"But you have a home," said Wolfgang.

"Yes—in the grave!"

The heart of the student melted at the words.

"If a stranger dare make an offer," said he, "without danger of being misunderstood, I would offer my humble dwelling as a shelter; myself as a devoted friend. I am friendless myself in Paris, and a stranger in the land; but if my life could be of service, it is at your disposal, and should be sacrificed before harm or indignity should come to you."

There was an honest earnestness in the young man's manner that had its effect. His foreign accent, too, was in his favor; it showed him not to be a hackneyed inhabitant of Paris. Indeed, there is an eloquence in true enthusiasm that is not to be doubted. The homeless stranger confided herself implicitly to the protection of the student.

He supported her faltering steps across the Pont Neuf, and by the place where the statue of Henry the Fourth had been overthrown by the populace. The storm had abated and the thunder rumbled at a distance. All Paris was quiet; that great volcano of human passion slumbered for a while, to gather fresh strength for the next day's eruption. The student conducted his charge through the ancient streets of the *Pays Latin,* and by the dusky walls of the Sorbonne, to the great dingy hotel which he inhabited. The old portress who admitted them stared with surprise at the unusual sight of the melancholy Wolfgang with a female companion.

On entering his apartment, the student, for the first time, blushed at the scantiness and indifference of his dwelling. He had but one chamber— an old-fashioned saloon—heavily carved, and fantastically furnished with the remains of former magnificence, for it was one of those hotels in the quarter of the Luxembourg palace, which had once belonged to nobility. It was lumbered with books and papers, and all the usual apparatus of a student, and his bed stood in a recess at one end.

When lights were brought, and Wolfgang had a better opportunity of contemplating the stranger, he was more than ever intoxicated by her beauty. Her face was pale, but of a dazzling fairness, set off by a profusion of raven hair that hung clustering about it. Her eyes were large and brilliant, with a singular expression approaching almost to wildness. As far as her black dress permitted her shape to be seen, it was of perfect symmetry. Her whole appearance was highly striking, though she was dressed in the simplest style. The only thing approaching to an ornament which she wore, was a broad black band round her neck, clasped by diamonds.

The perplexity now commenced with the student how to dispose of the helpless being thus thrown upon his protection. He thought of abandoning his chamber to her, and seeking shelter for himself elsewhere. Still he was so fascinated by her charms, there seemed to be such a spell upon his thoughts and senses, that he could not tear himself from her presence. Her manner, too, was singular and unaccountable. She spoke no more of the guillotine. Her grief had abated. The attentions of the student had first won her confidence, and then, apparently, her heart. She was evidently an enthusiast like himself, and enthusiasts soon understand each other.

In the infatuation of the moment, Wolfgang avowed his passion for her. He told her the story of his mysterious dream, and how she had possessed his heart before he had even seen her. She was strangely affected by his recital, and acknowledged to have felt an impulse towards him equally unaccountable. It was the time for wild theory and wild actions. Old prejudices and superstitions were done away; everything was under the sway of the "Goddess of Reason." Among other rubbish of the old times, the forms and ceremonies of marriage began to be considered superfluous bonds for honorable minds. Social compacts were the vogue. Wolfgang was too much of a theorist not to be tainted by the liberal doctrines of the day.

"Why should we separate?" said he; "our hearts are united; in the eye of reason and honor we are as one. What need is there of sordid forms to bind high souls together?"

The stranger listened with emotion: she had evidently received illumination at the same school.

"You have no home or family," continued he, "let me be everything to you, or rather let us be everything to one another. If form is necessary, form shall be observed—there is my hand. I pledge myself to you forever."

"Forever?" said the stranger, solemnly.

"Forever!" repeated Wolfgang.

The stranger clasped the hand extended to her: "Then I am yours," murmured she, and sank upon his bosom.

The next morning the student left his bride sleeping, and sallied forth at an early hour to seek more spacious apartments suitable to the change in his situation. When he returned, he found the stranger lying with her head hanging over the bed, and one arm thrown over it. He spoke to her, but received no reply. He advanced to awaken her from her uneasy posture. On taking her hand, it was cold—there was no pulsation—her face was pallid and ghastly. In a word, she was a corpse.

Horrified and frantic, he alarmed the house. A scene of confusion ensued. The police was summoned. As the officer of police entered the room, he started back on beholding the corpse.

"Great heaven!" cried he, "how did this woman come here?"

"Do you know anything about her?" said Wolfgang eagerly.

"Do I?" exclaimed the officer: "she was guillotined yesterday."

He stepped forward; undid the black collar round the neck of the corpse, and the head rolled on the floor!

The student burst into a frenzy. "The fiend! The fiend has gained possession of me!" shrieked he; "I am lost forever."

They tried to soothe him, but in vain. He was possessed with the frightful belief that an evil spirit had reanimated the dead body to ensnare him. He went distracted, and died in a mad-house.

Here the old gentleman with the haunted head finished his narrative.

"And is this really a fact?" said the inquisitive gentleman.

"A fact not to be doubted," replied the other. "I had it from the best authority. The student told it to me himself. I saw him in a mad-house in Paris."

THE ADVENTURE OF
THE MYSTERIOUS STRANGER

Many years since, when I was a young man, and had just left Oxford, I was sent on the grand tour to finish my education. I believe my parents had tried in vain to inoculate me with wisdom; so they sent me to mingle with society, in hopes I might take it the natural way. Such, at least, appears to be the reason for which nine tenths of our youngsters are sent abroad. In the course of my tour I remained some time at Venice. The romantic character of the place delighted me; I was very much amused by the air of adventure and intrigue that prevailed in this region of masks and gondolas; and I was exceedingly smitten by a pair of languishing black eyes, that played upon my heart from under an Italian mantle. So I persuaded myself that I was lingering at Venice to study men and manners. At least I persuaded my friends so, and that answered all my purposes.

Indeed, I was a little prone to be struck by peculiarities in character and conduct, and my imagination was so full of romantic associations with Italy, that I was always on the lookout for adventure. Everything chimed in with such a humor in this old mermaid of a city. My suite of apartments were in a proud, melancholy palace on the grand canal, formerly the residence of a magnifico, and sumptuous with the traces of decayed grandeur. My gondolier was one of the shrewdest of his class, active, merry, intelligent, and, like his brethren, secret as the grave; that is to say, secret to all the world except his master. I had not had him a week before he put me behind all the curtains in Venice. I liked the silence and mystery of the place, and when I sometimes saw from my window a black gondola gliding mysteriously along in the dusk of the evening, with nothing visible but its little glimmering lantern, I would jump into my own zendeletta, and give a signal for pursuit—"But I am running away from my subject with the recollection of youthful follies," said the Baronet, checking himself. "Let me come to the point."

Among my familiar resorts was a Cassino under the Arcades on one side of the grand square of St. Mark. Here I used frequently to lounge and take my ice on those warm summer nights when in Italy everybody lives abroad until morning. I was seated here one evening, when a group of Italians took their seat at a table on the opposite side of the saloon. Their conversation was gay and animated, and carried on with Italian vivacity and gesticulation. I remarked among them one young man, however, who appeared to take no share, and find no enjoyment in the conversation; though he seemed to force himself to attend to it. He was tall and slender, and of extremely prepossessing appearance. His features were fine, though emaciated. He had a profusion of black glossy hair that curled lightly about his head, and contrasted with the extreme paleness of his countenance. His brow was haggard; deep furrows seemed to have been ploughed into his visage by care, not by age, for he was evidently in the prime of youth. His eye was full of expression and fire, but wild and unsteady. He seemed to be tormented by some strange fancy or apprehension. In spite of every effort to fix his attention on the conversation of his companions, I noticed that every now and then he would turn his head slowly round, give a glance over his shoulder, and then withdraw it with a sudden jerk, as if something painful had met his eye. This was repeated at intervals of about a minute, and he appeared hardly to have got over one shock, before I saw him slowly preparing to encounter another.

After sitting some time in the casino, the party paid for the refreshments they had taken, and departed. The young man was the last to leave the saloon, and I remarked him glancing behind him in the same way, just as he passed out at the door. I could not resist the impulse to rise and follow him; for I was at an age when a romantic feeling of curiosity is easily awakened. The party walked slowly down the arcades, talking and laughing as they went. They crossed the Piazzetta, but paused in the middle of it to enjoy the scene. It was one of those moonlight nights so brilliant and clear in the pure atmosphere of Italy. The moonbeams streamed on the tall tower of St. Mark, and lighted up the magnificent front and swelling domes of the cathedral. The party expressed their delight in animated terms. I kept my eye upon the young man. He alone seemed abstracted and self-occupied. I noticed the same singular, and, as it were, furtive glance over the shoulder that had attracted my attention in the casino. The party moved on, and I followed; they passed along the walks called the Broglio; turned the corner of the Ducal Palace, and getting into a gondola, glided swiftly away.

The countenance and conduct of this young man dwelt upon my mind. There was something in his appearance that interested me exceedingly. I met him a day or two after in a gallery of paintings. He was evidently a connoisseur, for he always singled out the most masterly productions, and the few remarks drawn from him by his companions showed an intimate acquaintance with the art. His own taste, however, ran on singular extremes. On Salvator Rosa in his most savage and solitary scenes; on Raphael, Titian, and Correggio in their softest delineations of female beauty. On these he would occasionally gaze with transient enthusiasm. But this seemed only a momentary forgetfulness. Still would recur that cautious glance behind, and always quickly withdrawn, as though something terrible had met his view.

I encountered him frequently afterwards. At the theatre, at balls, at concerts; at the promenades in the gardens of San Georgio; at the grotesque exhibitions in the square of St. Mark; among the throng of merchants on the exchange by the Rialto. He seemed, in fact, to seek crowds; to hunt after bustle and amusement; yet never to take any interest in either the business or gayety of the scene. Ever an air of painful thought, of wretched abstraction; and ever that strange and recurring movement, of glancing fearfully over the shoulder.

I did not know at first but this might be caused by apprehension of arrest; or perhaps from dread of assassination. But, if so, why should he go thus continually abroad; why expose himself at all times and in all places?

I became anxious to know this stranger. I was drawn to him by that romantic sympathy that sometimes draws young men towards each other. His melancholy threw a charm about him in my eyes, which was no doubt heightened by the touching expression of his countenance, and the manly graces of his person; for manly beauty has its effect even upon man. I had an Englishman's habitual diffidence and awkwardness of address to contend with; but I subdued it, and from frequently meeting him in the casino, gradually edged myself into his acquaintance. I had no reserve on his part to contend with. He seemed on the contrary to court society; and in fact to seek anything rather than be alone.

When he found I really took an interest in him he threw himself entirely upon my friendship. He clung to me like a drowning man. He would walk with me for hours up and down the place of St. Mark—or he would sit until night was far advanced in my apartments; he took rooms under the same roof with me; and his constant request was, that I would permit him, when it did not incommode me, to sit by me in my saloon. It was not that he seemed to take a particular delight in my conversation; but rather that he craved the vicinity of a human being; and above all, of a being that sympathized with him. "I have often heard," said he, "of the sincerity of Englishmen—thank God I have one at length for a friend!"

Yet he never seemed disposed to avail himself of my sympathy other than by mere companionship. He never sought to unbosom himself to me; there appeared to be a settled corroding anguish in his bosom that neither could be soothed "by silence nor by speaking."

A devouring melancholy preyed upon his heart, and seemed to be drying up the very blood in his veins. It was not a soft melancholy—

the disease of the affections; but a parching, withering agony. I could see at times that his mouth was dry and feverish; he almost panted rather than breathed; his eyes were bloodshot; his cheeks pale and livid; with now and then faint streaks athwart them—baleful gleams of the fire that was consuming his heart. As my arm was within his, I felt him press it at times with a convulsive motion to his side; his hands would clinch themselves involuntarily, and a kind of shudder would run through his frame.

I reasoned with him about his melancholy, and sought to draw from him the cause—he shrunk from all confiding. "Do not seek to know it," said he, "you could not relieve it if you knew it; you would not even seek to relieve it. On the contrary, I should lose your sympathy; and that," said he, pressing my hand convulsively, "that I feel has become too dear to me to risk."

I endeavored to awaken hope within him. He was young; life had a thousand pleasures in store for him; there is a healthy reaction in the youthful heart; it medicines all its own wounds; "Come, come," said I, "there is no grief so great that youth cannot outgrow it."—"No! no!" said he, clinching his teeth, and striking repeatedly, with the energy of despair, upon his bosom—"It is here—here—deep-rooted; draining my heart's blood. It grows and grows, while my heart withers and withers! I have a dreadful monitor that gives me no repose—that follows me step by step; and will follow me step by step, until it pushes me into my grave!"

As he said this he gave involuntarily one of those fearful glances over his shoulder, and shrunk back with more than usual horror. I could not resist the temptation to allude to this movement, which I supposed to be some mere malady of the nerves. The moment I mentioned it his face became crimsoned and convulsed—he grasped me by both hands—

"For God's sake," exclaimed he, with a piercing agony of voice—"never allude to that again; let us avoid this subject, my friend; you cannot relieve me, indeed you cannot relieve me; but you may add to the torments I suffer;—At some future day you shall know all."

I never resumed the subject; for however much my curiosity might be aroused, I felt too true compassion for his sufferings to increase them by my intrusion. I sought various ways to divert his mind, and to arouse him from the constant meditations in which he was plunged. He saw my efforts, and seconded them as far as in his power, for there was nothing moody or wayward in his nature; on the contrary, there was something frank, generous, unassuming, in his whole deportment. All the sentiments that he uttered were noble and lofty. He claimed no indulgence; he asked no toleration. He seemed content to carry his load of misery in silence, and only sought to carry it by my side. There was a mute beseeching manner about him, as if he craved companionship as a charitable boon; and a tacit thankfulness in his looks, as if he felt grateful to me for not repulsing him.

I felt this melancholy to be infectious. It stole over my spirits; interfered with all my gay pursuits, and gradually saddened my life; yet I could not prevail upon myself to shake off a being who seemed to hang upon me for support. In truth, the generous traits of character that beamed through all this gloom had penetrated to my heart. His bounty was lavish and open-handed; his charity melting and spontaneous. Not confined to mere donations, which often humiliate as much as they relieve. The tone of his voice, the beam of his eye, enhanced every gift, and surprised the poor suppliant with that rarest and sweetest of charities, the charity not merely of the hand, but of the heart. Indeed, his liberality seemed to have something in it of self-abasement and expiation. He humbled himself, in a manner, before the mendicant. "What right have I to ease and affluence," would he murmur to himself, "when innocence wanders in misery and rags?"

The carnival-time arrived. I had hoped that the gay scenes which then presented themselves might have some cheering effect. I mingled with him in the motley throng that crowded the place of St. Mark. We frequented operas, masquerades, balls. All in vain. The evil kept growing on him; he became more and more haggard and agitated. Often, after we had returned from one of these scenes of revelry, I have entered his room, and found him lying on his face on the sofa; his hands clinched in his fine hair, and his whole countenance bearing traces of the convulsions of his mind.

The carnival passed away; the time of Lent succeeded; passion-week arrived. We attended one evening a solemn service in one of the churches; in the course of which a grand piece of vocal and instrumental music was performed relating to the death of our Saviour.

I had remarked that he was always powerfully affected by music; on this occasion he was so in an extraordinary degree. As the peeling notes swelled through the lofty aisles, he seemed to kindle up with fervor. His eyes rolled upwards, until nothing but the whites were visible; his hands were clasped together, until the fingers were deeply imprinted in the flesh. When the music expressed the dying agony, his face gradually sunk upon his knees; and at the touching words resounding through the church, "*Jesu mori*," sobs burst from him uncontrolled. I had never seen him weep before; his had always been agony rather than sorrow. I augered well from the circumstance, and let him weep on uninterrupted. When the service was ended we left the church. He hung on my arm as we walked homewards, with something of a softer and more subdued manner; instead of that nervous agitation I had been accustomed to witness. He alluded to the service we had heard. "Music," said he, "is indeed the voice of heaven; never before have I felt more impressed by the story of the atonement of our Saviour. Yes, my friend," said he, clasping his hands with a kind of transport, "I know that my Redeemer liveth!"

We parted for the night. His room was not far from mine, and I heard him for some time busied in it. I fell asleep, but was awakened before daylight. The young man stood by my bedside, dressed for travelling. He held a sealed packet and a large parcel in his hand, which he laid on the table.

"Farewell, my friend," said he, "I am about to set forth on a long journey; but, before I go, I leave with you these remembrances. In this packet you will find the particulars of my story. When you read them, I shall be far away; do not remember me with aversion. You have been, indeed, a friend to me. You have poured oil into a broken heart,—but you could not heal it.—Farewell!—let me kiss your hand—I am unworthy to embrace you." He sunk on his knees, seized my hand in despite of my efforts to the contrary, and covered it with kisses. I was so surprised by all this scene that I had not been able to say a word.—"But we shall meet again," said I, hastily, as I saw him hurrying towards the door. "Never—never in this world!" said he, solemnly.—He sprang once more to my bedside—seized my hand, pressed it to his heart and to his lips, and rushed out of the room.

Here the Baronet paused. He seemed lost in thought, and sat looking upon the floor and drumming with his fingers on the arm of his chair.

"And did this mysterious personage return?" said the inquisitive gentleman. "Never!" replied the Baronet, with a pensive shake of the head: "I never saw him again."

"And pray what has all this to do with the picture?" inquired the old gentleman with the nose

"True!" said the questioner; "Is it the portrait of this crack-brained Italian?"

"No!" said the Baronet drily, not half liking the appellation given to his hero; "but this picture was inclosed in the parcel he left with me. The sealed packet contained its explanation. There was a request on the outside that I would not open it until six months had elapsed. I kept my promise, in spite of my curiosity. I have a translation of it by me, and had meant to read it, by way of accounting for the mystery of the chamber, but I fear I have already detained the company too long."

Here there was a general wish expressed to have the manuscript read; particularly on the part of the inquisitive gentleman. So the worthy Baronet drew out a fairly written manuscript, and wiping his spectacles, read aloud the following story.

THE STORY OF THE YOUNG ITALIAN

I was born at Naples. My parents, though of noble rank, were limited in fortune, or rather my father was ostentatious beyond his means, and expended so much in his palace, his equipage, and his retinue, that he was continually straitened in his pecuniary circumstances. I was a younger son, and looked upon with indifference by my father, who, from a principle of family pride, wished to leave all his property to my elder brother.

I showed, when quite a child, an extreme sensibility. Everything affected me violently. While yet an infant in my mother's arms, and before I had learnt to talk, I could be wrought upon to a wonderful degree of anguish or delight by the power of music. As I grew older my feelings remained equally acute, and I was easily transported into paroxysms of pleasure or rage. It was the amusement of my relatives and of the domestics to play upon this irritable temperament. I was moved to tears, tickled to laughter, provoked to fury, for the entertainment of company, who were amused by such a tempest of mighty passion in a pigmy frame. They little thought, or perhaps little heeded the dangerous sensibilities they were fostering. I thus became a little creature of passion, before reason was developed. In a short time I grew too old to be a plaything, and then I became a torment. The tricks and passions I had been teased into became irksome, and I was disliked by my teachers for the very lessons they had taught me.

My mother died; and my power as a spoiled child was at an end. There was no longer any necessity to humor or tolerate me, for there was nothing to be gained by it, as I was no favorite of my father. I therefore experienced the fate of a spoiled child in such situation, and was neglected or noticed only to be crossed and contradicted. Such was the early treatment of a heart, which, if I am judge of it at all, was naturally disposed to the extremes of tenderness and affection.

My father, as I have already said, never liked me—in fact, he never understood me; he looked upon me as wilful and wayward, as deficient in natural affection. It was the stateliness of his own manner, the loftiness and grandeur of his own look that had repelled me from his arms. I always pictured him to myself as I had seen him clad in his senatorial robes, rustling with pomp and pride. The magnificence of his person had daunted my strong imagination. I could never approach him with the confiding affection of a child.

My father's feelings were wrapped up in my elder brother. He was to be the inheritor of the family title and the family dignity, and everything was sacrificed to him—I, as well as everything else. It was determined to devote me to the church, that so my humors and myself might be removed out of the way, either of tasking my father's time and trouble, or interfering with the interests of my brother. At an early age, therefore, before my mind had dawned upon the world and its delights, or known anything of it beyond the precincts of my father's palace, I was sent to a convent, the superior of which was my uncle, and was confided entirely to his care.

My uncle was a man totally estranged from the world: he had never relished, for he had never tasted its pleasures; and he deemed rigid self-denial as the great basis of Christian virtue. He considered every one's temperament like his own; or at least he made them conform to it. His character and habits had an influence over the fraternity of which he was superior. A more gloomy, saturnine set of beings were never assembled together. The convent, too, was calculated to awaken sad and solitary thoughts. It was situated in a gloomy gorge of those mountains away south of Vesuvius. All distant views were shut out by sterile volcanic heights. A mountain stream raved beneath its walls, and eagles screamed about its turrets.

I had been sent to this place at so tender an age as soon to lose all distinct recollection of the scenes I had left behind. As my mind expanded, therefore, it formed its idea of the world from the convent and its vicinity, and a dreary world it appeared to me. An early tinge of melancholy was thus infused into my character; and the dismal stories of the monks, about devils and evil spirits, with which they affrighted my young imagination, gave me a tendency to superstition, which I could never effectually shake off. They took the same delight to work upon my ardent feelings that had been so mischievously exercised by my father's household.

I can recollect the horrors with which they fed my heated fancy during an eruption of Vesuvius. We were distant from that volcano, with mountains between us; but its convulsive throes shook the solid foundations of nature. Earthquakes threatened to topple down our convent towers. A lurid, baleful light hung in the heavens at night, and showers of ashes, borne by the wind, fell in our narrow valley. The monks talked of the earth being honey-combed beneath us; of streams of molten lava raging through its veins; of caverns of sulphurous flames roaring in the centre, the abodes of demons and the damned; of fiery gulfs ready to yawn beneath our feet. All these tales were told to the doleful accompaniment of the mountain's thunders, whose low bellowing made the walls of our convent vibrate.

One of the monks had been a painter, but had retired from the world, and embraced this dismal life in expiation of some crime. He was a melancholy man, who pursued his art in the solitude of his cell, but made it a source of penance to him. His employment was to portray, either on canvas or in waxen models, the human face and human form, in the agonies of death and in all the stages of dissolution and decay. The fearful mysteries of the charnel house were unfolded in his labors—the loathsome banquet of the beetle and the worm.—I turn with shuddering even from the recollection of his works. Yet, at that time, my strong, but ill-directed imagination seized with ardor upon his instructions in his art. Anything was a variety from the dry studies and monotonous duties of the cloister. In a little while I became expert with my pencil, and my gloomy productions were thought worthy of decorating some of the altars of the chapel.

In this dismal way was a creature of feeling and fancy brought up. Everything genial and amiable in my nature was repressed and nothing brought out but what was unprofitable and ungracious. I was ardent in my temperament; quick, mercurial, impetuous, formed to be a creature all love and adoration; but a leaden hand was laid on all my finer qualities. I was taught nothing but fear and hatred. I hated my uncle, I hated the monks, I hated the convent in which I was immured. I hated the world, and I almost hated myself, for being, as I supposed, so hating and hateful an animal.

When I had nearly attained the age of sixteen, I was suffered, on one occasion, to accompany one of the brethren on a mission to a distant part of the country. We soon left behind us the gloomy valley in which I had been pent up for so many years, and after a short journey among the mountains, emerged upon the voluptuous landscape that spreads itself about the Bay of Naples. Heavens! How transported was I, when I stretched my gaze over a vast reach of delicious sunny country, gay with groves and vineyards; with Vesuvius rearing its forked summit to my right; the blue Mediterranean to my left, with its enchanting coast, studded with shining towns and sumptuous villas; and Naples, my native Naples, gleaming far, far in the distance.

Good God! Was this the lovely world from which I had been excluded! I Had reached that age when the sensibilities are in all their bloom and freshness. Mine had been checked and chilled. They now burst forth with the suddenness of a retarded spring. My heart, hitherto unnaturally shrunk up, expanded into a riot of vague, but delicious emotions. The beauty of nature intoxicated, bewildered me.

The song of the peasants; their cheerful looks; their happy avocations; the picturesque gayety of their dresses; their rustic music; their dances; all broke upon me like witchcraft. My soul responded to the music; my heart danced in my bosom. All the men appeared amiable, all the women lovely.

I returned to the convent, that is to say, my body returned but my heart and soul never entered there again. I could not forget this glimpse of a beautiful and a happy world—a world so suited to my natural character. I had felt so happy while in it; so different a being from what I felt myself while in the convent—that tomb of the living. I contrasted the countenances of the beings I had seen, full of fire and freshness and enjoyment, with the pallid, leaden, lack-lustre visages of the monks; the music of the dance, with the droning chant of the chapel. I had before found the exercises of the cloister wearisome; they now became intolerable. The dull round of duties wore away my spirit; my nerves became irritated by the fretful tinkling of the convent bell; evermore dinging among the mountain echoes; evermore calling me from my repose at night, my pencil by day, to attend to some tedious and mechanical ceremony of devotion.

I was not of a nature to meditate long, without putting my thoughts into action. My spirit had been suddenly aroused, and was now all awake within me. I watched my opportunity, fled from the convent, and made my way on foot to Naples. As I entered its gay and crowded streets, and beheld the variety and stir of life around me, the luxury of palaces, the splendor of equipages, and the pantomimic animation of the motley populace, I seemed as if awakened to a world of enchantment, and solemnly vowed that nothing should force me back to the monotony of the cloister.

I had to inquire my way to my father's palace, for I had been so young on leaving it, that I knew not its situation. I found some difficulty in getting admitted to my father's presence, for the domestics scarcely knew that there was such a being as myself in existence, and my monastic dress did not operate in my favor. Even my father entertained no recollection of my person. I told him my name, threw myself at his feet, implored his forgiveness, and entreated that I might not be sent back to the convent.

He received me with the condescension of a patron rather than the kindness of a parent. He listened patiently, but coldly, to my tale of monastic grievances and disgusts, and promised to think what else could be done for me. This coldness blighted and drove back all the frank affection of my nature that was ready to spring forth at the least warmth of parental kindness. All my early feelings towards my father revived; I again looked up to him as the stately magnificent being that had daunted my childish imagination, and felt as if I had no pretensions to his sympathies. My brother engrossed all his care and love; he inherited his nature, and carried himself towards me with a protecting rather than a fraternal air. It wounded my pride, which was great. I could brook condescension from my father, for I looked up to him with awe as a superior being, but I could not brook patronage from a brother, who, I felt, was intellectually my inferior. The servants perceived that I was an unwelcome intruder in the paternal mansion, and, menial-like, they treated me with neglect. Thus baffled at every point; my affections outraged wherever they would attach themselves, I became sullen, silent, and despondent. My feelings driven back upon myself, entered and preyed upon my own heart. I remained for some days an unwelcome guest rather than a restored son in my father's house. I was doomed never to be properly known there. I was made, by wrong treatment, strange even to myself; and they judged of me from my strangeness.

I was startled one day at the sight of one of the monks of my convent, gliding out of my father's room. He saw me, but pretended not to notice me; and this very hypocrisy made me suspect something. I had become sore and susceptible in my feelings; everything inflicted a wound on them. In this state of mind I was treated with marked disrespect by a pampered minion, the favorite servant of my father. All the pride and passion of my nature rose in an instant, and I struck him to the earth.

My father was passing by; he stopped not to inquire the reason, nor indeed could he read the long course of mental sufferings which were the real cause. He rebuked me with anger and scorn; he summoned all the haughtiness of his nature, and grandeur of his look, to give weight to the contumely with which he treated me. I felt I had not deserved it—I felt that I was not appreciated—I felt that I had that within me which merited better treatment; my heart swelled against a father's injustice. I broke through my habitual awe of him. I replied to him with impatience; my hot spirit flushed in my cheek and kindled in my eye, but my sensitive heart swelled as quickly, and before I had half vented my passion I felt it suffocated and quenched in my tears. My father was astonished and incensed at this turning of the worm, and ordered me to my chamber. I retired in silence, choking with contending emotions.

I had not been long there when I overheard voices in an adjoining apartment. It was a consultation between my father and the monk, about the means of getting me back quietly to the convent. My resolution was taken. I had no longer a home nor a father. That very night I left the paternal roof. I got on board a vessel about making sail from the harbor, and abandoned myself to the wide world. No matter to what port she steered; any part of so beautiful a world was better than my convent. No matter where I was cast by fortune; any place would be more a home to me than the home I had left behind. The vessel was bound to Genoa. We arrived there after a voyage of a few days.

As I entered the harbor, between the moles which embrace it, and beheld the amphitheatre of palaces and churches and splendid gardens, rising one above another, I felt at once its title to the appellation of

Genoa the Superb. I landed on the mole an utter stranger, without knowing what to do, or whither to direct my steps. No matter; I was released from the thraldom of the convent and the humiliations of home. When I traversed the Strada Balbi and the Strada Nuova, those streets of palaces, and gazed at the wonders of architecture around me; when I wandered at close of day, amid a gay throng of the brilliant and the beautiful, through the green alleys of the Aqua Verde, or among the colonnades and terraces of the magnificent Doria gardens, I thought it impossible to be ever otherwise than happy in Genoa.

A few days sufficed to show me my mistake. My scanty purse was exhausted, and for the first time in my life I experienced the sordid distress of penury. I had never known the want of money, and had never adverted to the possibility of such an evil. I was ignorant of the world and all its ways; and when first the idea of destitution came over my mind its effect was withering. I was wandering pensively through the streets which no longer delighted my eyes, when chance led my stops into the magnificent church of the Annunciata.

A celebrated painter of the day was at that moment superintending the placing of one of his pictures over an altar. The proficiency which I had acquired in his art during my residence in the convent had made me an enthusiastic amateur. I was struck, at the first glance, with the painting. It was the face of a Madonna. So innocent, so lovely, such a divine expression of maternal tenderness! I lost for the moment all recollection of myself in the enthusiasm of my art. I clasped my hands together, and uttered an ejaculation of delight. The painter perceived my emotion. He was flattered and gratified by it. My air and manner pleased him, and he accosted me. I felt too much the want of friendship to repel the advances of a stranger, and there was something in this one so benevolent and winning that in a moment he gained my confidence.

I told him my story and my situation, concealing only my name and rank. He appeared strongly interested by my recital; invited me to his house, and from that time I became his favorite pupil. He thought he perceived in me extraordinary talents for the art, and his encomiums awakened all my ardor. What a blissful period of my existence was it that I passed beneath his roof. Another being seemed created within me, or rather, all that was amiable and excellent was drawn out. I was as recluse as ever I had been at the convent, but how different was my seclusion. My time was spent in storing my mind with lofty and poetical ideas; in meditating on all that was striking and noble in history or fiction; in studying and tracing all that was sublime and beautiful in nature. I was always a visionary, imaginative being, but now my reveries and imaginings all elevated me to rapture.

I looked up to my master as to a benevolent genius that had opened to me a region of enchantment. I became devotedly attached to him. He was not a native of Genoa, but had been drawn thither by the solicitation of several of the nobility, and had resided there but a few years, for the completion of certain works he had undertaken. His health was delicate, and he had to confide much of the filling up of his designs to the pencils of his scholars. He considered me as particularly happy in delineating the human countenance; in seizing upon characteristic, though fleeting expressions and fixing them powerfully upon my canvas. I was employed continually, therefore, in sketching faces, and often when some particular grace or beauty or expression was wanted in a countenance, it was entrusted to my pencil. My benefactor was fond of bringing me forward; and partly, perhaps, through my actual skill, and partly by his partial praises, I began to be noted for the expression of my countenances.

Among the various works which he had undertaken, was an historical piece for one of the palaces of Genoa, in which were to be introduced the likenesses of several of the family. Among these was one entrusted to my pencil. It was that of a young girl, who as yet was in a convent for her education. She came out for the purpose of sitting for the picture. I first saw her in an apartment of one of the sumptuous palaces of Genoa. She stood before a casement that looked out upon the bay, a stream of vernal sunshine fell upon her, and shed a kind of glory round her as it lit up the rich crimson chamber. She was but sixteen years of age—and oh, how lovely! The scene broke upon me like a mere vision of spring and youth and beauty. I could have fallen down and worshipped her. She was like one of those fictions of poets and painters, when they would express the *beau ideal* that haunts their minds with shapes of indescribable perfection.

I was permitted to sketch her countenance in various positions, and I fondly protracted the study that was undoing me. The more I gazed on her the more I became enamoured; there was something almost painful in my intense admiration. I was but nineteen years of age; shy, diffident, and inexperienced. I was treated with attention and encouragement, for my youth and my enthusiasm in my art had won favor for me; and I am inclined to think that there was something in my air and manner that inspired interest and respect. Still the kindness with which I was treated could not dispel the embarrassment into which my own imagination threw me when in presence of this lovely being. It elevated her into something almost more than mortal. She seemed too exquisite for earthly use; too delicate and exalted for human attainment. As I sat tracing her charms on my canvas, with my eyes occasionally riveted on her features, I drank in delicious poison that made me giddy. My heart alternately gushed with tenderness, and ached with despair. Now I became more than ever sensible of the violent fires that had lain dormant at the bottom of my soul. You who are born in a more temperate climate and under a cooler sky, have little idea of the violence of passion in our southern bosoms.

A few days finished my task; Bianca returned to her convent, but her image remained indelibly impressed upon my heart. It dwelt on my imagination; it became my pervading idea of beauty. It had an effect even upon my pencil; I became noted for my felicity in depicting female loveliness; it was but because I multiplied the image of Bianca. I soothed, and yet fed my fancy, by introducing her in all the productions of my master. I have stood with delight in one of the chapels of the Annunciata, and heard the crowd extol the seraphic beauty of a saint which I had painted; I have seen them bow down in adoration before the painting: they were bowing before the loveliness of Bianca.

I existed in this kind of dream, I might almost say delirium, for upwards of a year. Such is the tenacity of my imagination that the image which was formed in it continued in all its power and freshness. Indeed, I was a solitary, meditative being, much given to reverie, and apt to foster ideas which had once taken strong possession of me. I was roused from this fond, melancholy, delicious dream by the death of my worthy benefactor. I cannot describe the pangs his death occasioned me. It left me alone and almost broken-hearted. He bequeathed to me his little property; which, from the liberality of his disposition and his expensive style of living, was indeed but small; and he most particularly recommended me, in dying, to the protection of a nobleman who had been his patron.

The latter was a man who passed for munificent. He was a lover and an encourager of the arts, and evidently wished to be thought so. He fancied he saw in me indications of future excellence; my pencil had already attracted attention; he took me at once under his protection; seeing that I was overwhelmed with grief, and incapable of exerting myself in the mansion of my late benefactor, he invited me to sojourn for a time in a villa which he possessed on the border of the sea, in the picturesque neighborhood of Sestri di Ponente.

I found at the villa the Count's only son, Filippo: he was nearly of my age, prepossessing in his appearance, and fascinating in his manners; he attached himself to me, and seemed to court my good opinion. I thought there was something of profession in his kindness, and of caprice in his disposition; but I had nothing else near me to attach myself to, and my heart felt the need of something to repose itself upon. His education had been neglected; he looked upon me as his superior in mental powers and acquirements, and tacitly acknowledged my superiority. I felt that I was his equal in birth, and that gave an independence to my manner which had its effect. The caprice and tyranny I saw sometimes exercised on others, over whom he had power, were never manifested towards me. We became intimate friends, and frequent companions. Still I loved to be alone, and to indulge in the reveries of my own imagination, among the beautiful scenery by which I was surrounded.

The villa stood in the midst of ornamented grounds, finely decorated with statues and fountains, and laid out into groves and alleys and shady bowers. It commanded a wide view of the Mediterranean, and the picturesque Ligurian coast. Everything was assembled here that could gratify the taste or agreeably occupy the mind. Soothed by the tranquillity of this elegant retreat, the turbulence of my feelings gradually subsided, and, blending with the romantic spell that still reigned over my imagination, produced a soft voluptuous melancholy.

I had not been long under the roof of the count, when our solitude was enlivened by another inhabitant. It was a daughter of a relation of the count, who had lately died in reduced circumstances, bequeathing this only child to his protection. I had heard much of her beauty from Filippo, but my fancy had become so engrossed by one idea of beauty as not to admit of any other. We were in the central saloon of the villa when she arrived. She was still in mourning, and approached, leaning on the count's arm. As they ascended the marble portico, I was struck by the elegance of her figure and movement, by the grace with which the *mezzaro*, the bewitching veil of Genoa, was folded about her slender form.

They entered. Heavens! What was my surprise when I beheld Bianca before me. It was herself; pale with grief; but still more matured

in loveliness than when I had last beheld her. The time that had elapsed
had developed the graces of her person; and the sorrow she had undergone had diffused over her countenance an irresistible tenderness.

She blushed and trembled at seeing me, and tears rushed into her
eyes, for she remembered in whose company she had been accustomed
to behold me. For my part, I cannot express what were my emotions.
By degrees I overcame the extreme shyness that had formerly paralyzed
me in her presence. We were drawn together by sympathy of situation.
We had each lost our best friend in the world; we were each, in some
measure thrown upon the kindness of others. When I came to know
her intellectually, all my ideal picturings of her were confirmed. Her
newness to the world, her delightful susceptibility to everything beautiful and agreeable in nature, reminded me of my own emotions when
first I escaped from the convent. Her rectitude of thinking delighted
my judgment; the sweetness of her nature wrapped itself around my
heart; and then her young and tender and budding loveliness, sent a
delicious madness to my brain.

I gazed upon her with a kind of idolatry, as something more than
mortal; and I felt humiliated at the idea of my comparative unworthiness.
Yet she was mortal; and one of mortality's most susceptible and loving
compounds; for she loved me!

How first I discovered the transporting truth I cannot recollect.
I believe it stole upon me by degrees, as a wonder past hope or
belief. We were both at such a tender and loving age; in constant
intercourse with each other; mingling in the same elegant pursuits;
for music, poetry, and painting were our mutual delights, and we
were almost separated from society, among lovely and romantic
scenery! Is it strange that two young hearts thus brought together
should readily twine round each other?

Oh, gods! What a dream—a transient dream—of unalloyed
delight then passed over my soul! Then it was that the world around
me was indeed a paradise, for I had a woman—lovely, delicious

woman, to share it with me. How often have I rambled over the picturesque shores of Sestri, or climbed its wild mountains, with the coast gemmed with villas, and the blue sea far below me, and the slender Faro of Genoa on its romantic promontory in the distance; and as I sustained the faltering steps of Bianca, have thought there could no unhappiness enter into so beautiful a world. Why, oh, why is this budding season of life and love so transient—why is this rosy cloud of love that sheds such a glow over the morning of our days so prone to brew up into the whirlwind and the storm!

I was the first to awaken from this blissful delirium of the affections. I had gained Bianca's heart: what was I to do with it? I had no wealth nor prospects to entitle me to her hand. Was I to take advantage of her ignorance of the world, of her confiding affection, and draw her down to my own poverty? Was this requiting the hospitality of the count?—was this requiting the love of Bianca?

Now first I began to feel that even successful love may have its bitterness. A corroding care gathered about my heart. I moved about the palace like a guilty being. I felt as if I had abused its hospitality— as if I were a thief within its walls. I could no longer look with unembarrassed mien in the countenance of the Count. I accused myself of perfidy to him, and I thought he read it in my looks, and began to distrust and despise me. His manner had always been ostentatious and condescending, it now appeared cold and haughty. Filippo, too, became reserved and distant; or at least I suspected him to be so. Heavens! was this mere coinage of my brain: was I to become suspicious of all the world?—a poor surmising wretch; watching looks and gestures; and torturing myself with misconstructions. Or if true—was I to remain beneath a roof where I was merely tolerated, and linger there on sufferance? "This is not to be endured!" exclaimed I; "I will tear myself from this state of self-abasement; I will break through this fascination and fly—Fly?—whither?—from the world?—for where is the world when I leave Bianca behind me?"

My spirit was naturally proud, and swelled within me at the idea of being looked upon with contumely. Many times I was on the point of declaring my family and rank, and asserting my equality, in the presence of Bianca, when I thought her relatives assumed an air of superiority. But the feeling was transient. I considered myself discarded and condemned by my family; and had solemnly vowed never to own relationship to them, until they themselves should claim it.

The struggle of my mind preyed upon my happiness and my health. It seemed as if the uncertainty of being loved would be less intolerable than thus to be assured of it, and yet not dare to enjoy the conviction. I was no longer the enraptured admirer of Bianca; I no longer hung in ecstasy on the tones of her voice, nor drank in with insatiate gaze the beauty of her countenance. Her very smiles ceased to delight me, for I felt culpable in having won them.

She could not but be sensible of the change in me, and inquired the cause with her usual frankness and simplicity. I could not evade the inquiry, for my heart was full to aching. I told her all the conflict of my soul; my devouring passion, my bitter self-upbraiding. "Yes!" said I, "I am unworthy of you. I am an offcast from my family—a wanderer—a nameless, homeless wanderer, with nothing but poverty for my portion, and yet I have dared to love you—have dared to aspire to your love!"

My agitation moved her to tears; but she saw nothing in my situation so hopeless as I had depicted it. Brought up in a convent, she knew nothing of the world—its wants—its cares: and, indeed, what woman is a worldly casuist in matters of the heart! Nay, more, she kindled into a sweet enthusiasm when she spoke of my fortunes and myself. We had dwelt together on the works of the famous masters. I had related to her their histories; the high reputation, the influence, the magnificence to which they had attained. The companions of princes, the favorites of kings, the pride and boast of nations. All this she applied to me. Her love saw nothing in their greatest productions that I was not able to achieve; and when I saw the lovely creature glow with fervor, and her whole countenance radiant with the visions of my glory, which seemed breaking upon her, I was snatched up for the moment into the heaven of her own imagination.

I am dwelling too long upon this part of my story; yet I cannot help lingering over a period of my life, on which, with all its cares and conflicts, I look back with fondness; for as yet my soul was unstained by a crime. I do not know what might have been the result of this struggle between pride, delicacy, and passion, had I not read in a Neapolitan gazette an account of the sudden death of my brother. It was accompanied by an earnest inquiry for intelligence concerning me, and a prayer, should this notice meet my eye, that I would hasten to Naples, to comfort an infirm and afflicted father.

I was naturally of an affectionate disposition; but my brother had never been as a brother to me; I had long considered myself as disconnected from him, and his death caused me but little emotion. The thoughts of my father, infirm and suffering, touched me, however, to the quick; and when I thought of him, that lofty, magnificent being, now bowed down and desolate, and suing to me for comfort, all my resentment for past neglect was subdued, and a glow of filial affection was awakened within me.

The predominant feeling, however, that overpowered all others was transport at the sudden change in my whole fortunes. A home, a name, a rank, wealth awaited me; and love painted a still more rapturous prospect in the distance. I hastened to Bianca, and threw myself at her feet. "Oh, Bianca," exclaimed I, "at length I can claim you for my own. I am no longer a nameless adventurer, a neglected, rejected outcast. Look—read—behold the tidings that restore me to my name and to myself!"

I will not dwell on the scene that ensued. Bianca rejoiced in the reverse of my situation, because she saw it lightened my heart of a load of care; for her own part she had loved me for myself, and had never doubted that my own merits would command both fame and fortune.

I now felt all my native pride buoyant within me; I no longer walked with my eyes bent to the dust; hope elevated them to the skies; my soul was lit up with fresh fires, and beamed from my countenance.

I wished to impart the change in my circumstances to the count; to let him know who and what I was, and to make formal proposals for the hand of Bianca; but the count was absent on a distant estate. I opened my whole soul to Filippo. Now first I told him of my passion; of the doubts and fears that had distracted me, and of the tidings that had suddenly dispelled them. He overwhelmed me with congratulations and with the warmest expressions of sympathy. I embraced him in the fullness of my heart. I felt compunctions for having suspected him of coldness, and asked him forgiveness for having ever doubted his friendship.

Nothing is so warm and enthusiastic as a sudden expansion of the heart between young men. Filippo entered into our concerns with the most eager interest. He was our confidant and counsellor. It was determined that I should hasten at once to Naples to re-establish myself in my father's affections and my paternal home, and the moment the reconciliation was effected and my father's consent insured, I should return and demand Bianca of the count. Filippo engaged to secure his father's acquiescence; indeed, he undertook to watch over our interests, and was the channel through which we were to correspond.

My parting with Bianca was tender—delicious—agonizing.

It was in a little pavilion of the garden which had been one of our favorite resorts. How often and often did I return to have one more adieu—to have her look once more on me in speechless emotion—to enjoy once more the rapturous sight of those tears streaming down her lovely cheeks—to seize once more on that delicate hand, the frankly accorded pledge of love, and cover it with tears and kisses! Heavens! There is a delight even in the parting agony of two lovers worth a thousand tame pleasures of the world. I have her at this moment before my eyes—at the window of the pavilion, putting aside the vines that clustered about the casement—her light form beaming forth in virgin white—her countenance all tears and smiles—sending a thousand and a thousand adieus after me, as, hesitating, in a delirium of fondness and agitation, I faltered my way down the avenue.

As the bark bore me out of the harbor of Genoa, how eagerly my eyes stretched along the coast of Sestri, till it discerned the villa gleaming from among trees at the foot of the mountain. As long as day lasted, I gazed and gazed upon it, till it lessened and lessened to a mere white speck in the distance; and still my intense and fixed gaze discerned it, when all other objects of the coast had blended into indistinct confusion, or were lost in the evening gloom.

On arriving at Naples, I hastened to my paternal home. My heart yearned for the long-withheld blessing of a father's love. As I entered the proud portal of the ancestral palace, my emotions were so great that I could not speak. No one knew me. The servants gazed at me with curiosity and surprise. A few years of intellectual elevation and development had made a prodigious change in the poor fugitive stripling from the convent. Still that no one should know me in my rightful home was overpowering. I felt like the prodigal son returned. I was a stranger in the house of my father. I burst into tears, and wept aloud. When I made myself known, however, all was changed. I who had once been almost repulsed from its walls, and forced to fly as an exile, was welcomed back with acclamation, with servility. One of the servants hastened to prepare my father for my reception; my eagerness to receive the paternal embrace was so great that I could not await his return; but hurried after him.

What a spectacle met my eyes as I entered the chamber! My father, whom I had left in the pride of vigorous age, whose noble and majestic bearing had so awed my young imagination, was bowed down and withered into decrepitude. A paralysis had ravaged his stately form, and left it a shaking ruin. He sat propped up in his chair, with pale, relaxed visage and glassy, wandering eye. His intellects had evidently shared in the ravage of his frame. The servant was endeavoring to make him comprehend the visitor that was at hand. I tottered up to him and sunk at his feet. All his past coldness and neglect were forgotten in his present sufferings. I remembered only that he was my parent, and that I had deserted him. I clasped his knees; my voice was almost stifled with convulsive sobs. "Pardon—pardon—oh my father!" was all that I could utter. His apprehension seemed slowly to return to him. He gazed at me for some moments with a vague, inquiring look; a convulsive tremor quivered about his lips; he feebly extended a shaking hand, laid it upon my head, and burst into an infantine flow of tears.

From that moment he would scarcely spare me from his sight. I appeared the only object that his heart responded to in the world; all else was as a blank to him. He had almost lost the powers of speech, and the reasoning faculty seemed at an end. He was mute and passive; excepting that fits of child-like weeping would sometimes come over him without any immediate cause. If I left the room at any time, his eye was incessantly fixed on the door till my return, and on my entrance there was another gush of tears.

To talk with him of my concerns, in this ruined state of mind, would have been worse than useless; to have left him, for ever so short a time, would have been cruel, unnatural. Here then was a new trial for my affections. I wrote to Bianca an account of my return and of my actual situation; painting in colors vivid, for they were true, the torments I suffered at our being thus separated; for to the youthful lover every day of absence is an age of love lost. I enclosed the letter in one to Filippo, who was the channel of our correspondence. I received a reply from him full of friendship and sympathy; from Bianca full of assurances of affection and constancy.

Week after week, month after month elapsed, without making any change in my circumstances. The vital flame, which had seemed nearly extinct when first I met my father, kept fluttering on without any apparent diminution. I watched him constantly, faithfully—I had almost said patiently. I knew that his death alone would set me free; yet I never at any moment wished it. I felt too glad to be able to make any atonement for past disobedience; and, denied as I had been all endearments of relationship in my early days, my heart yearned towards a father, who, in his age and helplessness, had thrown himself entirely on me for comfort. My passion for Bianca gained daily more force from absence; by constant meditation it wore itself a deeper and deeper channel. I made no new friends nor acquaintances; sought none of the pleasures of Naples which my rank and fortune threw open to me. Mine was a heart that confined itself to few objects, but dwelt upon those with the intenser passion. To sit by my father, and administer to his wants, and to meditate on Bianca in the silence of his chamber, was my constant habit. Sometimes I amused myself with my pencil in portraying the image that was ever present to my imagination. I transferred to canvas every look and smile of hers that dwelt in my heart. I showed them to my father in hopes of awakening an interest in his bosom for the mere shadow of my love; but he was too far sunk in intellect to take any more than a child-like notice of them.

When I received a letter from Bianca it was a new source of solitary luxury. Her letters, it is true, were less and less frequent, but they were always full of assurances of unabated affection. They breathed not the frank and innocent warmth with which she expressed herself in conversation, but I accounted for it from the embarrassment which inexperienced minds have often to express themselves upon paper. Filippo assured me of her unaltered constancy. They both lamented in the strongest terms our continued separation, though they did justice to the filial feeling that kept me by my father's side.

Nearly eighteen months elapsed in this protracted exile. To me they were so many ages. Ardent and impetuous by nature, I scarcely know how I should have supported so long an absence, had I not felt assured that the faith of Bianca was equal to my own. At length my father died. Life went from him almost imperceptibly. I hung over him in mute affliction, and watched the expiring spasms of nature. His last faltering accents whispered repeatedly a blessing on me. Alas! how has it been fulfilled!

When I had paid due honors to his remains, and laid them in the tomb of our ancestors, I arranged briefly my affairs; put them in a posture to be easily at my command from a distance, and embarked once more, with a bounding heart, for Genoa.

Our voyage was propitious, and oh! what was my rapture when first, in the dawn of morning, I saw the shadowy summits of the Apennines rising almost like clouds above the horizon. The sweet breath of summer just moved us over the long wavering billows that were rolling us on towards Genoa. By degrees the coast of Sestri rose like a sweet creation of enchantment from the silver bosom of the deep. I beheld the line of villages and palaces studding its borders. My eye reverted to a well-known point, and at length, from the confusion of distant objects, it singled out the villa which contained Bianca. It was a mere speck in the landscape, but glimmering from afar, the polar star of my heart.

Again I gazed at it for a livelong summer's day, but oh! how different the emotions between departure and return. It now kept growing and growing, instead of lessening on my sight. My heart seemed to dilate with it. I looked at it through a telescope. I gradually defined one feature after another. The balconies of the central saloon where first I met Bianca beneath its roof; the terrace where we so often had passed the delightful summer evenings; the awning that shaded her chamber window—I almost fancied I saw her form beneath it. Could she but know her lover was in the bark whose white sail now gleamed on the sunny bosom of the sea! My fond impatience increased as we neared the coast. The ship seemed to lag lazily over the billows; I could almost have sprung into the sea and swam to the desired shore.

The shadows of evening gradually shrouded the scene, but the moon arose in all her fulness and beauty and shed the tender light so dear to lovers, over the romantic coast of Sestri. My whole soul was bathed in unutterable tenderness. I anticipated the heavenly evenings I should pass in wandering with Bianca by the light of that blessed moon.

It was late at night before we entered the harbor. As early next morning as I could get released from the formalities of landing I threw myself on horseback and hastened to the villa. As I galloped round the rocky promontory on which stands the Faro, and saw the coast of Sestri opening upon me, a thousand anxieties and doubts suddenly sprang up in my bosom. There is something fearful in returning to those we love, while yet uncertain what ills or changes absence may have effected. The turbulence of my agitation shook my very frame. I spurred my horse to redoubled speed; he was covered with foam when we both arrived panting at the gateway that opened to the grounds around the villa. I left my horse at a cottage and walked through the grounds, that I might regain tranquillity for the approaching interview. I chid myself for having suffered mere doubts and surmises thus suddenly to overcome me; but I was always prone to be carried away by these gusts of the feelings.

On entering the garden everything bore the same look as when I had left it; and this unchanged aspect of things reassured me. There were the alleys in which I had so often walked with Bianca; the same shades under which we had so often sat during the noontide. There were the same flowers of which she was fond; and which appeared still to be under the ministry of her hand. Everything around looked and breathed of Bianca; hope and joy flushed in my bosom at every step. I passed a little bower in which we had often sat and read together. A book and a glove lay on the bench. It was Bianca's glove; it was a volume of the *Metastasio* I had given her. The glove lay in my favorite passage. I clasped them to my heart. "All is safe!" exclaimed I, with rapture, "she loves me! she is still my own!"

I bounded lightly along the avenue down which I had faltered so slowly at my departure. I beheld her favorite pavilion which had witnessed our parting scene. The window was open, with the same vine clambering about it, precisely as when she waved and wept me an adieu. Oh how transporting was the contrast in my situation! As I passed near the pavilion, I heard the tones of a female voice. They thrilled through me with an appeal to my heart not to be mistaken. Before I could think, I *felt* they were Bianca's. For an instant I paused, overpowered with agitation. I feared to break in suddenly upon her. I softly ascended the steps of the pavilion. The door was open. I saw Bianca seated at a table; her back was towards me; she was warbling a soft melancholy air, and was occupied in drawing. A glance sufficed to show me that she was copying one of my own paintings. I gazed on her for a moment in a delicious tumult of emotions. She paused in her singing; a heavy sigh, almost a sob followed. I could no longer contain myself. "Bianca!" exclaimed I, in a half-smothered voice. She started at the sound; brushed back the ringlets that hung clustering about her face; darted a glance at me; uttered a piercing shriek and would have fallen to the earth, had I not caught her in my arms.

"Bianca! My own Bianca!" exclaimed I, folding her to my bosom; my voice stifled in sobs of convulsive joy. She lay in my arms without sense or motion. Alarmed at the effects of my own precipitation, I scarce knew what to do. I tried by a thousand endearing words to call her back to consciousness. She slowly recovered, and half opening her eyes—"Where am I?" murmured she faintly. "Here," exclaimed I, pressing her to my bosom. "Here! Close to the heart that adores you; in the arms of your faithful Ottavio!"

"Oh no! no! no!" shrieked she, starting into sudden life and terror—"away! away! leave me! leave me!"

She tore herself from my arms; rushed to a corner of the saloon, and covered her face with her hands, as if the very sight of me were baleful. I was thunderstruck—I could not believe my senses. I followed her, trembling, confounded. I endeavored to take her hand, but she shrunk from my very touch with horror.

"Good heavens, Bianca," exclaimed I, "what is the meaning of this? Is this my reception after so long an absence? Is this the love you professed for me?"

At the mention of love, a shuddering ran through her. She turned to me a face wild with anguish. "No more of that! No more of that!" gasped she—"talk not to me of love—I—I—am married!"

I reeled as if I had received a mortal blow. A sickness struck to my very heart. I caught at a window frame for support. For a moment or two, everything was chaos around me. When I recovered, I beheld Bianca lying on a sofa; her face buried in a pillow, and sobbing convulsively. Indignation at her fickleness for a moment overpowered every other feeling.

"Faithless! perjured!" cried I, striding across the room. But another glance at that beautiful being in distress, checked all my wrath. Anger could not dwell together with her idea in my soul.

"Oh, Bianca," exclaimed I, in anguish, "could I have dreamt of this; could I have suspected you would have been false to me?"

She raised her face all streaming with tears, all disordered with emotion, and gave me one appealing look. "False to you? they told me you were dead!"

"What," said I, "in spite of our constant correspondence?"

She gazed wildly at me "Correspondence? What correspondence?"

"Have you not repeatedly received and replied to my letters?"

She clasped her hands with solemnity and fervor. "As I hope for mercy, never!"

A horrible surmise shot through my brain, "Who told you I was dead?"

"It was reported that the ship in which you embarked for Naples perished at sea."

"But who told you the report?"

She paused for an instant, and trembled—

"Filippo!"

"May the God of heaven curse him!" cried I, extending my clinched fists aloft.

"Oh do not curse him—do not curse him!" exclaimed she—"He is—he is—my husband!"

This was all that was wanting to unfold the perfidy that had been practised upon me. My blood boiled like liquid fire in my veins. I gasped with rage too great for utterance. I remained for a time bewildered by the whirl of horrible thoughts that rushed through my mind. The poor victim of deception before me thought it was with her I was incensed. She faintly murmured forth her exculpation. I will not dwell upon it. I saw in it more than she meant to reveal. I saw with a glance how both of us had been betrayed. "'Tis well!" muttered I to myself in smothered accents of concentrated fury. "He shall account to me for this!"

Bianca overheard me. New terror flashed in her countenance. "For mercy's sake do not meet him—say nothing of what has passed—for my sake say nothing to him—I only shall be the sufferer!"

A new suspicion darted across my mind—"What!" exclaimed I—"do you then *fear* him—is he *unkind* to you—tell me," reiterated I, grasping her hand and looking her eagerly in the face—"tell me— *dares* he to use you harshly!"

"No! no! no!" cried she faltering and embarrassed; but the glance at her face had told me volumes. I saw in her pallid and wasted features; in the prompt terror and subdued agony of her eye a whole history of a mind broken down by tyranny. Great God! And was this beauteous flower snatched from me to be thus trampled upon? The idea roused me to madness. I clinched my teeth and my hands; I foamed at the mouth; every passion seemed to have resolved itself into the fury that like a lava boiled within my heart. Bianca shrunk from me in speechless affright. As I strode by the window my eye darted down the alley. Fatal moment! I beheld Filippo at a distance! My brain was in a delirium—I sprang from the pavilion, and was before him with the quickness of lightning. He saw me as I came rushing upon him—he turned pale, looked wildly to right and left, as if he would have fled, and trembling drew his sword.

"Wretch!" cried I, "well may you draw your weapon!"

I spake not another word—I snatched forth a stiletto, put by the sword which trembled in his hand, and buried my poniard in his bosom. He fell with the blow, but my rage was unsated. I sprang upon him with the blood-thirsting feeling of a tiger; redoubled my blows; mangled him in my frenzy, grasped him by the throat, until with reiterated wounds and strangling convulsions he expired in my grasp. I remained glaring on the countenance, horrible in death, that seemed to stare back with its protruded eyes upon me. Piercing shrieks roused me from my delirium. I looked round and beheld Bianca flying distractedly towards us. My brain whirled. I waited not to meet her, but fled from the scene of horror. I fled forth from the garden like another Cain, a hell within my bosom, and a curse upon my head. I fled without knowing whither—almost without knowing why—my only idea was to get farther and farther from the horrors I had left behind; as if I could throw space between myself and my conscience. I fled to the Apennines, and wandered for days and days among their savage heights. How I existed I cannot tell—what rocks and precipices I braved, and how I braved them, I know not. I kept on and on—trying to out-travel the curse that clung to me. Alas, the shrieks of Bianca rung forever in my ear. The horrible countenance of my victim was forever before my eyes. The blood of Filippo cried to me from the ground. Rocks, trees, and torrents all resounded with my crime.

Then it was I felt how much more insupportable is the anguish of remorse than every other mental pang. Oh! could I but have cast off this crime that festered in my heart; could I but have regained the innocence that reigned in my breast as I entered the garden at Sestri; could I but have restored my victim to life, I felt as if I could look on with transport even though Bianca were in his arms.

By degrees this frenzied fever of remorse settled into a permanent malady of the mind. Into one of the most horrible that ever poor wretch was cursed with. Wherever I went, the countenance of him I had slain appeared to follow me. Wherever I turned my head I beheld it behind me, hideous with the contortions of the dying moment. I have tried in every way to escape from this horrible phantom; but in vain. I know not whether it is an illusion of the mind, the consequence of my dismal education at the convent, or whether a phantom really sent by heaven to punish me; but there it ever is—at all times—in all places—nor has time nor habit had any effect in familiarizing me with its terrors. I have travelled from place to place, plunged into amusements—tried dissipation and distraction of every kind—all—all in vain.

I once had recourse to my pencil as a desperate experiment. I painted an exact resemblance of this phantom face. I placed it before me in hopes that by constantly contemplating the copy I might diminish the effect of the original. But I only doubled instead of diminishing the misery.

Such is the curse that has clung to my footsteps—that has made my life a burden—but the thoughts of death, terrible. God knows what I have suffered. What days and days, and nights and nights, of sleepless torment. What a never-dying worm has preyed upon my heart; what an unquenchable fire has burned within my brain. He knows the wrongs that wrought upon my poor weak nature; that converted the tenderest of affections into the deadliest of fury. He knows best whether a frail erring creature has expiated by long-enduring torture and measureless remorse, the crime of a moment of madness. Often, often have I prostrated myself in the dust, and implored that he would give me a sign of his forgiveness, and let me die.—

Thus far had I written some time since. I had meant to leave this record of misery and crime with you, to be read when I should be no more. My prayer to heaven has at length been heard. You were witness to my emotions last evening at the performance of the *Miserere*; when the vaulted temple resounded with the words of atonement and redemption. I heard a voice speaking to me from the midst of the music; I heard it rising above the pealing of the organ and the voices of the choir; it spoke to me in tones of celestial melody; it promised mercy and forgiveness, but demanded from me full expiation. I go to make it. To-morrow I shall be on my way to Genoa to surrender myself to justice. You who have pitied my sufferings; who have poured the balm of sympathy into my wounds, do not shrink from my memory with abhorrence now that you know my story. Recollect, when you read of my crime I shall have atoned for it with my blood!

When the Baronet had finished, there was a universal desire expressed to see the painting of this frightful visage. After much entreaty the Baronet consented, on condition that they should only visit it one by one. He called his housekeeper and gave her charge to conduct the gentlemen singly to the chamber. They all returned varying in their stories: some affected in one way, some in another; some more, some less; but all agreeing that there was a certain something about the painting that had a very odd effect upon the feelings.

I stood in a deep bow window with the Baronet, and could not help expressing my wonder. "After all," said I, "there are certain mysteries in our nature, certain inscrutable impulses and influences, that warrant one in being superstitious. Who can account for so many persons of different characters being thus strangely affected by a mere painting?"

"And especially when not one of them has seen it!" said the Baronet with a smile.

"How?" exclaimed I, "not seen it?"

"Not one of them?" replied he, laying his finger on his lips in sign of secrecy. "I saw that some of them were in a bantering vein, and I did not choose that the memento of the poor Italian should be made a jest of. So I gave the housekeeper a hint to show them all to a different chamber!"

Thus end the stories of the Nervous Gentleman.

KIDD THE PIRATE

In old times, just after the territory of the New Netherlands had been wrested from the hands of their High Mightinesses, the Lords States-General of Holland, by King Charles the Second, and while it was as yet in an unquiet state, the province was a great resort of random adventurers, loose livers, and all that class of hap-hazard fellows who live by their wits, and dislike the old-fashioned restraint of law and gospel. Among these, the foremost were the buccaneers. These were rovers of the deep, who perhaps in time of war had been educated in those schools of piracy, the privateers; but having once tasted the sweets of plunder, had ever retained a hankering after it. There is but a slight step from the privateersman to the pirate; both fight for the love of plunder; only that the latter is the bravest, as he dares both the enemy and the gallows.

But in whatever school they had been taught, the buccaneers that kept about the English colonies were daring fellows, and made sad work in times of peace among the Spanish settlements and Spanish merchantmen. The easy access to the harbor of the Manhattoes, the number of hiding-places about its waters, and the laxity of its scarcely organized government, made it a great rendezvous of the pirates; where they might dispose of their booty, and concert new depredations. As they brought home with them wealthy lading of all kinds, the luxuries of the tropics, and the sumptuous spoils of the Spanish provinces, and disposed of them with the proverbial carelessness of freebooters, they were welcome visitors to the thrifty traders of the Manhattoes. Crews of these desperadoes, therefore, the runagates of every country and every clime, might be seen swaggering in open day about the streets of the little burgh, elbowing its quiet mynheers; trafficking away their rich outlandish plunder at half or quarter price to the wary merchant; and then squandering their prize-money in taverns, drinking, gambling, singing, swearing, shouting, and astounding the neighborhood with midnight brawl and ruffian revelry.

At length these excesses rose to such a height as to become a scandal to the provinces, and to call loudly for the interposition of government. Measures were accordingly taken to put a stop to the widely extended evil, and to ferret this vermin brood out of the colonies.

Among the agents employed to execute this purpose was the notorious Captain Kidd. He had long been an equivocal character; one of those nondescript animals of the ocean that are neither fish, flesh, nor fowl. He was somewhat of a trader, something more of a smuggler, with a considerable dash of the picaroon. He had traded for many years among the pirates, in a little rakish, mosquito-built vessel, that could run into all kinds of waters. He knew all their haunts and lurking-places; was always hooking about on mysterious voyages, and was as busy as a Mother Gary's chicken in a storm.

This nondescript personage was pitched upon by government as the very man to hunt the pirates by sea, upon the good old maxim of "setting a rogue to catch a rogue"; or as otters are sometimes used to catch their cousins-german, the fish.

Kidd accordingly sailed for New York, in 1695, in a gallant vessel called the Adventure Galley, well armed and duly commissioned. On arriving at his old haunts, however, he shipped his crew on new terms; enlisted a number of his old comrades, lads of the knife and the pistol; and then set sail for the East. Instead of cruising against pirates, he turned pirate himself; steered to the Madeiras, to Bonavista, and Madagascar, and cruised about the entrance of the Eed Sea. Here, among other maritime robberies, he captured a rich Quedah merchantman, manned by Moors, though commanded by an Englishman. Kidd would fain have passed this off for a worthy exploit, as being a kind of crusade against the infidels; but government had long since lost all relish for such Christian triumphs.

After roaming the seas, trafficking his prizes, and changing from ship to ship, Kidd had the hardihood to return to Boston, laden with booty, with a crew of swaggering companions at his heels.

Times, however, were changed. The buccaneers could no longer show a whisker in the colonies with impunity. The new governor, Lord Bellamont, had signalized himself by his zeal in extirpating these offenders; and was doubly exasperated against Kidd, having been instrumental in appointing him to the trust which he had betrayed. No sooner, therefore, did he show himself in Boston, than the alarm was given of his reappearance, and measures were taken to arrest this cutpurse of the ocean. The daring character which Kidd had acquired, however, and the desperate fellows who followed like bull-dogs at his heels, caused a little delay in his arrest. He took advantage of this, it is said, to bury the greater part of his treasures, and then carried a high head about the streets of Boston. He even attempted to defend himself when arrested, but was secured and thrown into prison, with his followers. Such was the formidable character of this pirate and his crew, that it was thought advisable to dispatch a frigate to bring them to England. Great exertions were made to screen him from justice, but in vain; he and his comrades were tried, condemned, and hanged at Execution Dock in London. Kidd died hard, for the rope with which he was first tied up broke with his weight, and he tumbled to the ground. He was tied up a second time, and more effectually; hence came, doubtless, the story of Kidd's having a charmed life, and that he had to be twice hanged.

Such is the main outline of Kidd's history; but it has given birth to an innumerable progeny of traditions. The report of his having buried great treasures of gold and jewels before his arrest, set the brains of all the good people along the coast in a ferment. There were rumors on rumors of great sums of money found here and there, sometimes in one part of the country, sometimes in another; of coins with Moorish inscriptions, doubtless the spoils of his eastern prizes, but which the common people looked upon with superstitious awe, regarding the Moorish letters as diabolical or magical characters.

Some reported the treasure to have been buried in solitary, unsettled places, about Plymouth and Cape Cod; but by degrees various other parts, not only on the eastern coast, but along the shores of the Sound, and even of Manhattan and Long Island, were gilded by these rumors. In fact, the rigorous measures of Lord Bellamont spread sudden consternation among the buccaneers in every part of the provinces: they secreted their money and jewels in lonely out-of-the-way places, about the wild shores of the rivers and sea-coast, and dispersed themselves over the face of the country. The hand of justice prevented many of them from ever returning to regain their buried treasures, which remained, and remain probably to this day, objects of enterprise for the money-digger.

This is the cause of those frequent reports of trees and rocks bearing mysterious marks, supposed to indicate the spots where treasures lay hidden; and many have been the ransackings after the pirate's booty. In all the stories which once abounded of these enterprises, the devil played a conspicuous part. Either he was conciliated by ceremonies and invocations, or some solemn compact was made with him. Still he was ever prone to play the money-diggers some slippery trick. Some would dig so far as to come to an iron chest, when some baffling circumstance was sure to take place. Either the earth would fall in and fill up the pit, or some direful noise or apparition would frighten the party from the place: sometimes the devil himself would appear, and bear off the prize when within their very grasp; and if they revisited the place the next day, not a trace would be found of their labors of the preceding night.

All these rumors, however, were extremely vague, and for a long time tantalized, without gratifying, my curiosity. There is nothing in this world so hard to get at as truth, and there is nothing in this world but truth that I care for. I sought among all my favorite sources of authentic information, the oldest inhabitants, and particularly the old Dutch wives of the province; but though I flatter myself that I am better versed than most men in the curious history of my native province, yet for a long time my inquiries were unattended with any substantial result.

At length it happened that, one calm day in the latter part of summer, I was relaxing myself from the toils of severe study, by a day's amusement in fishing in those waters which had been the favorite resort of my boyhood. I was in company with several worthy burghers of my native city, among whom were more than one illustrious member of the corporation, whose names, did I dare to mention them, would do honor to my humble page. Our sport was indifferent. The fish did not bite freely, and we frequently changed our fishing-ground without bettering our luck. We were at length anchored close under a ledge of rocky coast, on the eastern side of the island of Manhatta. It was a still, warm day. The stream whirled and dimpled by us, without a wave or even a ripple; and everything was so calm and quiet, that it was almost startling when the kingfisher would pitch himself from the branch of some high tree, and after suspending himself for a moment in the air, to take his aim, would souse into the smooth water after his prey. While we were lolling in our boat, half drowsy with the warm stillness of the day, and the dulness of our sport, one of our party, a worthy alderman, was overtaken by a slumber, and, as he dozed, suffered the sinker of his drop-line to lie upon the bottom of the river. On waking, he found he had caught something of importance from the weight. On drawing it to the surface, we were much surprised to find it a long pistol of very curious and outlandish fashion, which, from its rusted condition, and its stock being worm-eaten and covered with barnacles, appeared to have lain a long time under water. The unexpected appearance of this document of warfare occasioned much speculation among my pacific companions. One supposed it to have fallen there during the

revolutionary war; another, from the peculiarity of its fashion, attributed it to the voyagers in the earliest days of the settlement; perchance
to the renowned Adrian Block, who explored the Sound, and discovered Block Island, since so noted for its cheese. But a third, after
regarding it for some time, pronounced it to be of veritable Spanish
workmanship.

"I'll warrant," said he, "if this pistol could talk, it would tell
strange stories of hard fights among the Spanish Dons. I've no doubt
but it is a relic of the buccaneers of old times,—who knows but it
belonged to Kidd himself?"

"Ah! that Kidd was a resolute fellow," cried an old iron-faced
Cape-Cod whaler.—"There's a fine old song about him, all to the
tune of—

My name is Captain Kidd,
    As I sailed, as I sailed;—

and then it tells about how he gained the devil's good graces by
burying the Bible:—

I had the Bible in my hand,
    As I sailed, as I sailed,
And I buried it in the sand,
    As I sailed. —

"Odsfish, if I thought this pistol had belonged to Kidd, I should
set great store by it, for curiosity's sake. By the way, I recollect a
story about a fellow who once dug up Kidd's buried money, which
was written by a neighbor of mine, and which I learnt by heart. As
the fish don't bite just now, I'll tell it to you, by way of passing
away the time."—And so saying, he gave us the following narration.

THE DEVIL AND TOM WALKER

A few miles from Boston, in Massachusetts, there is a deep inlet winding several miles into the interior of the country from Charles Bay, and terminating in a thickly-wooded swamp, or morass. On one side of this inlet is a beautiful dark grove; on the opposite side the land rises abruptly from the water's edge, into a high ridge on which grow a few scattered oaks of great age and immense size. It was under one of these gigantic trees, according to old stories, that Kidd the pirate buried his treasure. The inlet allowed a facility to bring the money in a boat secretly and at night to the very foot of the hill. The elevation of the place permitted a good lookout to be kept that no one was at hand, while the remarkable trees formed good landmarks by which the place might easily be found again. The old stories add, moreover, that the devil presided at the hiding of the money, and took it under his guardianship; but this, it is well known, he always does with buried treasure, particularly when it has been ill-gotten. Be that as it may, Kidd never returned to recover his wealth; being shortly after seized at Boston, sent out to England, and there hanged for a pirate.

About the year 1727, just at the time when earthquakes were prevalent in New England, and shook many tall sinners down upon their knees, there lived near this place a meagre, miserly fellow of the name of Tom Walker. He had a wife as miserly as himself; they were so miserly that they even conspired to cheat each other. Whatever the woman could lay hands on she hid away; a hen could not cackle but she was on the alert to secure the new-laid egg. Her husband was continually prying about to detect her secret hoards, and many and fierce were the conflicts that took place about what ought to have been common property. They lived in a forlorn-looking house, that stood alone and had an air of starvation. A few straggling savin-trees, emblems of sterility, grew near it; no smoke ever curled from its chimney; no traveller stopped at its door. A miserable horse, whose ribs were as articulate as the bars of a gridiron, stalked about a field where a thin carpet of moss, scarcely covering the ragged beds of pudding-stone, tantalized and balked his hunger; and sometimes he would lean his head over the fence, looked piteously at the passer-by, and seem to petition deliverance from this land of famine.

The house and its inmates had altogether a bad name. Tom's wife was a tall termagant, fierce of temper, loud of tongue, and strong of arm. Her voice was often heard in wordy warfare with her husband; and his face sometimes showed signs that their conflicts were not confined to words. No one ventured, however, to interfere between them; the lonely wayfarer shrunk within himself at the horrid clamor and clapper-clawing; eyed the den of discord askance, and hurried on his way, rejoicing, if a bachelor, in his celibacy.

One day that Tom Walker had been to a distant part of the neighborhood, he took what he considered a short cut homeward through the swamp. Like most short cuts, it was an ill-chosen route. The swamp was thickly grown with great gloomy pines and hemlocks, some of them ninety feet high; which made it dark at noonday, and a retreat for all the owls of the neighborhood. It was full of pits and quagmires, partly covered with weeds and mosses; where the green surface often betrayed the traveller into a gulf of black smothering mud; there were also dark and stagnant pools, the abodes of the tadpole, the bull-frog, and the water-snake, and where trunks of pines and hemlocks lay half drowned, half rotting, looking like alligators, sleeping in the mire.

Tom had long been picking his way cautiously through this treacherous forest; stepping from tuft to tuft of rushes and roots which afforded precarious footholds among deep sloughs; or pacing carefully, like a cat, among the prostrate trunks of trees; startled now and then by the sudden screaming of the bittern, or the quacking of a wild duck, rising on the wing from some solitary pool. At length he arrived at a piece of firm ground, which ran out like a peninsula into the deep bosom of the swamp. It had been one of the strongholds of the Indians during their wars with the first colonists. Here they had thrown up a kind of fort which they had looked upon as almost impregnable, and had used as a place of refuge for their squaws and children. Nothing remained of the Indian fort but a few embankments gradually sinking to the level of the surrounding earth, and already overgrown in part by oaks and other forest trees, the foliage of which formed a contrast to the dark pines and hemlocks of the swamp.

It was late in the dusk of evening that Tom Walker reached the old fort, and he paused there for a while to rest himself. Any one but he would have felt unwilling to linger in this lonely, melancholy place, for the common people had a bad opinion of it from the stories handed down from the time of the Indian wars; when it was asserted that the savages held incantations here and made sacrifices to the evil spirit. Tom Walker, however, was not a man to be troubled with any fears of the kind.

He reposed himself for some time on the trunk of a fallen hemlock, listening to the boding cry of the tree-toad, and delving with his walking-staff into a mound of black mould at his feet. As he turned up the soil unconsciously, his staff struck against something hard. He raked it out of the vegetable mould, and lo! a cloven skull with an Indian tomahawk buried deep in it, lay before him. The rust on the weapon showed the time that had elapsed since this death blow had been given. It was a dreary memento of the fierce struggle that had taken place in this last foothold of the Indian warriors.

"Humph!" said Tom Walker, as he gave the skull a kick to shake the dirt from it.

"Let that skull alone!" said a gruff voice. Tom lifted up his eyes and beheld a great black man, seated directly Opposite him on the stump of a tree. He was exceedingly surprised, having neither seen nor heard any one approach, and he was still more perplexed on observing, as well as the gathering gloom would permit, that the stranger was neither negro nor Indian. It is true, he was dressed in a rude, half Indian garb, and had a red belt or sash swathed round his body, but his face was neither black nor copper color, but swarthy and dingy and begrimed with soot, as if he had been accustomed to toil among fires and forges. He had a shock of coarse black hair, that stood out from his head in all directions; and bore an axe on his shoulder.

He scowled for a moment at Tom with a pair of great red eyes.

"What are you doing in my grounds?" said the black man, with a hoarse growling voice.

"Your grounds?" said Tom, with a sneer; "no more your grounds than mine: they belong to Deacon Peabody."

"Deacon Peabody be damned," said the stranger, "as I flatter myself he will be, if he does not look more to his own sins and less to those of his neighbor's. Look yonder, and see how Deacon Peabody is faring."

Tom looked in the direction that the stranger pointed, and beheld one of the great trees, fair and flourishing without, but rotten at the core, and saw that it had been nearly hewn through, so that the first high wind was likely to blow it down. On the bark of the tree was scored the name of Deacon Peabody. He now looked round and found most of the tall trees marked with the names of some great men of the colony, and all more or less scored by the axe. The one on which he had been seated, and which had evidently just been hewn down, bore the name of Crowninshield; and he recollected a mighty rich man of that name, who made a vulgar display of wealth, which it was whispered he had acquired by buccaneering.

"He's just ready for burning!" said the black man, with a growl of triumph. "You see I am likely to have a good stock of firewood for winter."

"But what right have you," said Tom, "to cut down Deacon Peabody's timber?"

"The right of prior claim," said the other. "This woodland belonged to me long before one of your white-faced race put foot upon the soil."

"And pray, who are you, if I may be so bold?" said Tom.

"Oh, I go by various names. I am the Wild Huntsman in some countries; the Black Miner in others. In this neighborhood I am known by the name of the Black Woodsman. I am he to whom the red men devoted this spot, and now and then roasted a white man by way of sweet-smelling sacrifice. Since the red men have been exterminated by you white savages, I amuse myself by presiding at the persecutions of quakers and anabaptists; I am the great patron and prompter of slave dealers, and the grand master of the Salem witches."

"The upshot of all which is, that, if I mistake not," said Tom, sturdily, "you are he commonly called Old Scratch."

"The same at your service!" replied the black man, with a half civil nod.

Such was the opening of this interview, according to the old story, though it has almost too familiar an air to be credited. One would think that to meet with such a singular personage in this wild, lonely place, would have shaken any man's nerves; but Tom was a hard-minded fellow, not easily daunted, and he had lived so long with a termagant wife, that he did not even fear the devil.

It is said that after this commencement they had a long and earnest conversation together, as Tom returned homeward. The black man told him of great sums of money which had been buried by Kidd the pirate, under the oak trees on the high ridge not far from the morass. All these were under his command and protected by his power, so that none could find them but such as propitiated his favor. These he offered to place within Tom Walker's reach, having conceived an especial kindness for him: but they were to be had only on certain conditions. What these conditions were may easily be surmised, though Tom never disclosed them publicly. They must have been very hard, for he required time to think of them, and he was not a man to stick at trifles where money was in view. When they had reached the edge of the swamp the stranger paused. "What proof have I that all you have been telling me is true?" said Tom. "There is my signature," said the black man, pressing his finger on Tom's forehead. So saying, he turned off among the thickets of the swamp, and seemed, as Tom said, to go down, down, down, into the earth, until nothing but his head and shoulders could be seen, and so on until he totally disappeared.

When Tom reached home he found the black print of a finger burnt, as it were, into his forehead, which nothing could obliterate.

The first news his wife had to tell him was the sudden death of Absalom Crowninshield, the rich buccaneer. It was announced in the papers with the usual flourish, that "A great man had fallen in Israel."

Tom recollected the tree which his black friend had just hewn down, and which was ready for burning. "Let the freebooter roast," said Tom, "who cares!" He now felt convinced that all he had heard and seen was no illusion.

He was not prone to let his wife into his confidence; but as this was an uneasy secret, he willingly shared it with her. All her avarice was awakened at the mention of hidden gold, and she urged her husband to comply with the black man's terms and secure what would make them wealthy for life. However Tom might have felt disposed to sell himself to the devil, he was determined not to do so to oblige his wife; so he flatly refused out of the mere spirit of contradiction. Many and bitter were the quarrels they had on the subject, but the more she talked the more resolute was Tom not to be damned to please her.

At length she determined to drive the bargain on her own account, and if she succeeded, to keep all the gain to herself. Being of the same fearless temper as her husband, she sat off for the old Indian fort towards the close of a summer's day. She was many hour's absent. When she came back she was reserved and sullen in her replies. She spoke something of a black man whom she had met about twilight, hewing at the root of a tall tree. He was sulky, however, and would not come to terms; she was to go again with a propitiatory offering, but what it was she forebore to say.

The next evening she sat off again for the swamp, with her apron heavily laden. Tom waited and waited for her, but in vain: midnight came, but she did not make her appearance; morning, noon, night returned, but still she did not come. Tom now grew uneasy for her safety; especially as he found she had carried off in her apron the silver tea pot and spoons and every portable article of value. Another night elapsed, another morning came; but no wife. In a word, she was never heard of more.

What was her real fate nobody knows, in consequence of so many pretending to know. It is one of those facts that have become confounded by a variety of historians. Some asserted that she lost her way among the tangled mazes of the swamp and sunk into some pit or slough; others, more uncharitable, hinted that she had eloped with the household booty, and made off to some other province; while others assert that the tempter had decoyed her into a dismal quagmire, on top of which her hat was found lying. In confirmation of this, it was said a great black man with an axe on his shoulder was seen late that very evening coming out of the swamp, carrying a bundle tied in a check apron, with an air of surly triumph.

The most current and probable story, however, observes that Tom Walker grew so anxious about the fate of his wife and his property that he sat out at length to seek them both at the Indian fort. During a long summer's afternoon he searched about the gloomy place, but no wife was to be seen. He called her name repeatedly, but she was no where to be heard. The bittern alone responded to his voice, as he flew screaming by; or the bull-frog croaked dolefully from a neighboring pool. At length, it is said, just in the brown hour of twilight, when the owls began to hoot and the bats to flit about, his attention was attracted by the clamor of carrion crows that were hovering about a cypress tree. He looked and beheld a bundle tied in a check apron and hanging in the branches of a tree; with a great vulture perched hard by, as if keeping watch upon it. He leaped with joy, for he recognized his wife's apron, and supposed it to contain the household valuables.

"Let us get hold of the property," said he consolingly to himself, "and we will endeavor to do without the woman."

As he scrambled up the tree the vulture spread its wide wings, and sailed off screaming into the deep shadows of the forest. Tom seized the check apron, but, woful sight! found nothing but a heart and liver tied up in it.

Such, according to the most authentic old story, was all that was to be found of Tom's wife. She had probably attempted to deal with the black man as she had been accustomed to deal with her husband; but though a female scold is generally considered a match for the devil, yet in this instance she appears to have had the worst of it. She must have died game, however; from the part that remained unconquered. Indeed, it is said Tom noticed many prints of cloven feet deeply stamped about the tree, and several handfuls of hair that looked as if they had been plucked from the coarse black shock of the woodsman. Tom knew his wife's prowess by experience. He shrugged his shoulders as he looked at the signs of a fierce clapper-clawing. "Egad," said he to himself, "Old Scratch must have had a tough time of it!"

Tom consoled himself for the loss of his property by the loss of his wife; for he was a little of a philosopher. He even felt something like gratitude towards the black woodsman, who he considered had done him a kindness. He sought, therefore, to cultivate a further acquaintance with him, but for some time without success; the old black-legs played shy, for whatever people may think, he is not always to be had for calling for; he knows how to play his cards when pretty sure of his game.

At length, it is said, when delay had whetted Tom's eagerness to the quick, and prepared him to agree to anything rather than not gain the promised treasure, he met the black man one evening in his usual woodman dress, with his axe on his shoulder, sauntering along the edge of the swamp, and humming a tune. He affected to receive Tom's advance with great indifference, made brief replies, and went on humming his tune.

By degrees, however, Tom brought him to business, and they began to haggle about the terms on which the former was to have the pirate's treasure. There was one condition which need not be mentioned, being generally understood in all cases where the devil grants favors; but there were others about which, though of less importance, he was inflexibly obstinate. He insisted that the money found through his means should be employed in his service. He proposed, therefore, that Tom should employ it in the black traffic; that is to say, that he should fit out a slave ship. This, however, Tom resolutely refused; he was bad enough, in all conscience; but the devil himself could not tempt him to turn slave dealer.

Finding Tom so squeamish on this point, he did not insist upon it, but proposed instead that he should turn usurer; the devil being extremely anxious for the increase of usurers, looking upon them as his peculiar people.

To this no objections were made, for it was just to Tom's taste.

"You shall open a broker's shop in Boston next month," said the black man.

"I'll do it to-morrow, if you wish," said Tom Walker.

"You shall lend money at two per cent a month."

"Egad, I'll charge four!" replied Tom Walker.

"You shall extort bonds, foreclose mortgages, drive the merchant to bankruptcy—"

"I'll drive them to the d——l," cried Tom Walker, eagerly.

"You are the usurer for my money!" said black-legs, with delight. "When will you want the rhino?"

"This very night."

"Done!" said the devil.

"Done!" said Tom Walker.—So they shook hands and struck a bargain.

A few days' time saw Tom Walker seated behind his desk in a counting house in Boston. His reputation for a ready-moneyed man, who would lend money out for a good consideration, soon spread abroad. Everybody remembers the days of Governor Belcher, when money was particularly scarce. It was a time of paper credit. The country had been deluged with government bills; the famous Land Bank had been established; there had been a rage for speculating; the people had run mad with schemes for new settlements; for building cities in the wilderness; land jobbers went about with maps of grants, and townships, and Eldorados, lying nobody knew where, but which everybody was ready to purchase. In a word, the great speculating fever which breaks out every now and then in the country, had raged to an alarming degree, and everybody was dreaming of making sudden fortunes from nothing. As usual, the fever had subsided; the dream had gone off, and the imaginary fortunes with it; the patients were left in doleful plight, and the whole country resounded with the consequent cry of "hard times."

At this propitious time of public distress did Tom Walker set up as a usurer in Boston. His door was soon thronged by customers. The needy and the adventurous; the gambling speculator; the dreaming land-jobber; the thriftless tradesman; the merchant with cracked credit; in short, every one driven to raise money by desperate means and desperate sacrifices, hurried to Tom Walker.

Thus Tom was the universal friend of the needy, and he acted like a "friend in need;" that is to say, he always exacted good pay and good security. In proportion to the distress of the applicant was the hardness of his terms. He accumulated bonds and mortgages; gradually squeezed his customers closer and closer; and sent them, at length, dry as a sponge from his door.

In this way he made money hand over hand; became a rich and mighty man, and exalted his cocked hat upon 'Change. He built himself, as usual, a vast house, out of ostentation; but left the greater part of it unfinished and unfurnished out of parsimony. He even set up a carriage in the fulness of his vainglory, though he nearly starved the horses which drew it; and as the ungreased wheels groaned and screeched on the axle trees, you would have thought you heard the souls of the poor debtors he was squeezing.

As Tom waxed old, however, he grew thoughtful. Having secured the good things of this world, he began to feel anxious about those of the next. He thought with regret on the bargain he had made with his black friend, and set his wits to work to cheat him out of the conditions. He became, therefore, all of a sudden, a violent church-goer. He prayed loudly and strenuously as if heaven were to be taken by force of lungs. Indeed, one might always tell when he had sinned most during the week, by the clamor of his Sunday devotion. The quiet Christians who had been modestly and steadfastly travelling Zionward, were struck with self-reproach at seeing themselves so suddenly outstripped in their career by this new-made convert. Tom was as rigid in religious, as in money matters; he was a stern supervisor and censurer of his neighbors, and seemed to think every sin entered up to their account became a credit on his own side of the page. He even talked of the expediency of reviving the persecution of quakers and anabaptists. In a word, Tom's zeal became as notorious as his riches.

Still, in spite of all this strenuous attention to forms, Tom had a lurking dread that the devil, after all, would have his due. That he might not be taken unawares, therefore, it is said he always carried a small Bible in his coat pocket. He had also a great folio Bible on his counting-house desk, and would frequently be found reading it when people called on business; on such occasions he would lay his green spectacles on the book, to mark the place, while he turned round to drive some usurious bargain.

Some say that Tom grew a little crack-brained in his old days, and that fancying his end approaching, he had his horse new shod, saddled and bridled, and buried with his feet uppermost; because he supposed that at the last day the world would be turned upside down; in which case he should find his horse standing ready for mounting, and he was determined at the worst to give his old friend a run for it. This, however, is probably a mere old wives' fable. If he really did take such a precaution it was totally superfluous; at least so says the authentic old legend, which closes his story in the following manner:

One hot afternoon in the dog days, just as a terrible black thunder-gust was coming up, Tom sat in his counting-house in his white linen cap and India silk morning-gown. He was on the point of foreclosing a mortgage, by which he would complete the ruin of an unlucky land speculator for whom he had professed the greatest friendship. The poor land jobber begged him to grant a few months' indulgence. Tom had grown testy and irritated and refused another day.

"My family will be ruined and brought upon the parish," said the land-jobber.

"Charity begins at home," replied Tom, "I must take care of myself in these hard times."

"You have made so much money out of me," said the speculator.

Tom lost his patience and his piety—"The devil take me," said he, "if I have made a farthing!"

Just then there were three loud knocks at the street door. He stepped out to see who was there. A black man was holding a black horse which neighed and stamped with impatience.

"Tom, you're come for!" said the black fellow, gruffly. Tom shrunk back, but too late. He had left his little Bible at the bottom of his coat pocket, and his big Bible on the desk buried under the mortgage he was about to foreclose: never was sinner taken more unawares. The black man whisked him like a child astride the horse and away he galloped in the midst of a thunder-storm. The clerks stuck their pens behind their ears and stared after him from the windows. Away went Tom Walker, dashing down the street; his white cap bobbing up and down; his morning-gown fluttering in the wind, and his steed striking fire out of the pavement at every bound. When the clerks turned to look for the black man he had disappeared.

Tom Walker never returned to foreclose the mortgage. A countryman who lived on the borders of the swamp, reported that in the height of the thunder-gust he had heard a great clattering of hoofs and a howling along the road, and that when he ran to the window he just caught sight of a figure, such as I have described, on a horse that galloped like mad across the fields, over the hills and down into the black hemlock swamp towards the old Indian fort; and that shortly after a thunder-bolt fell in that direction which seemed to set the whole forest in a blaze.

The good people of Boston shook their heads and shrugged their shoulders, but had been so much accustomed to witches and goblins and tricks of the devil in all kinds of shapes from the first settlement of the colony, that they were not so much horror-struck as might have been expected. Trustees were appointed to take charge of Tom's effects. There was nothing, however, to administer upon. On searching his coffers all his bonds and mortgages were found reduced to cinders. In place of gold and silver, his iron chest was filled with chips and shavings; two skeletons lay in his stable instead of his half-starved horses, and the very next day his great house took fire and was burnt to the ground.

Such was the end of Tom Walker and his ill-gotten wealth. Let all griping money-brokers lay this story to heart. The truth of it is not to be doubted. The very hole under the oak trees, from whence he dug Kidd's money, is to be seen to this day; and the neighboring swamp and old Indian fort is often haunted in stormy nights by a figure on horseback, in a morning-gown and white cap, which is doubtless the troubled spirit of the usurer. In fact, the story has resolved itself into a proverb, and is the origin of that popular saying prevalent throughout New England, of "The Devil and Tom Walker."

Such, as nearly as I can recollect, was the tenor of the tale told by the Cape Cod whaler. There were divers trivial particulars which I have omitted, and which wiled away the morning very pleasantly, until the time of tide favorable for fishing being passed, it was proposed that we should go to land, and refresh ourselves under the trees, till the noontide heat should have abated.

We accordingly landed on a delectable part of the island of Manhatta, in that shady and embowered tract formerly under dominion of the ancient family of the Hardenbrooks. It was a spot well known to me in the course of the aquatic expeditions of my boyhood. Not far from where we landed, was an old Dutch family vault, in the side of a bank, which had been an object of great awe and fable among my schoolboy associates. There were several mouldering coffins within; but what gave it a fearful interest with us, was its being connected in our minds with the pirate wreck which lay among the rocks of Hell Gate. There were also stories of smuggling connected with it, particularly during a time that this retired spot was owned by a noted burgher called Ready Money Provost; a man of whom it was whispered that he had many and mysterious dealings with parts beyond seas. All these things, however, had been jumbled together in our minds in that vague way in which such things are mingled up in the tales of boyhood.

While I was musing upon these matters my companions had spread a repast, from the contents of our well-stored pannier, and we solaced ourselves during the warm sunny hours of mid-day under the shade of a broad chestnut, on the cool grassy carpet that swept down to the water's edge. While lolling on the grass I summoned up the dusky recollections of my boyhood respecting this place, and repeated them like the imperfectly remembered traces of a dream, for the entertainment of my companions. When I had finished, a worthy old burgher, John Josse Vandermoere, the same who once related to me the adventures of Dolph Heyliger, broke silence and observed, that he recollected a story about money-digging which occurred in this very neighborhood. As we knew him to be one of the most authentic narrators of the province we begged him to let us have the particulars, and accordingly, while we refreshed ourselves with a clean long pipe of Blase Moore's best tobacco, the authentic John Josse Vandermoere related the following tale.

WOLFERT WEBBER,
OR GOLDEN DREAMS

In the year of grace one thousand seven hundred and—blank—for I do not remember the precise date; however, it was somewhere in the early part of the last century, there lived in the ancient city of the Manhattoes a worthy burgher, Wolfert Webber by name. He was descended from old Cobus Webber of the Brille in Holland, one of the original settlers, famous for introducing the cultivation of cabbages, and who came over to the province during the protectorship of Oloffe Van Kortlandt, otherwise called the Dreamer.

The field in which Cobus Webber first planted himself and his cabbages had remained ever since in the family, who continued in the same line of husbandry, with that praiseworthy perseverance for which our Dutch burghers are noted. The whole family genius, during several generations was devoted to the study and development of this one noble vegetable; and to this concentration of intellect may doubtless be ascribed the prodigious size and renown to which the Webber cabbages attained.

The Webber dynasty continued in uninterrupted succession; and never did a line give more unquestionable proofs of legitimacy. The eldest son succeeded to the looks, as well as the territory of his sire; and had the portraits of this line of tranquil potentates been taken, they would have presented a row of heads marvellously resembling in shape and magnitude the vegetables over which they reigned.

The seat of government continued unchanged in the family mansion:—a Dutch-built house, with a front, or rather gable-end of yellow brick, tapering to a point, with the customary iron weathercock at the top. Everything about the building bore the air of long-settled ease and security. Flights of martins peopled the little coops nailed against the walls, and swallows built their nests under the eaves; and every one knows that these house-loving birds bring good luck to the dwelling where they take up their abode. In a bright sunny morning in early summer, it was delectable to hear their cheerful notes, as they sported about in the pure, sweet air, chirping forth, as it were, the greatness and prosperity of the Webbers.

Thus quietly and comfortably did this excellent family vegetate under the shade of a mighty button-wood tree, which, by little and little, grew so great as entirely to overshadow their palace. The city gradually spread its suburbs round their domain. Houses sprung up to interrupt their prospects. The rural lanes in the vicinity began to grow into the bustle and populousness of streets; in short, with all the habits of rustic life they began to find themselves the inhabitants of a city.

Still, however, they maintained their hereditary character, and their hereditary possessions, with all the tenacity of petty German princes in the midst of the Empire. Wolfert was the last of the line, and succeeded to the patriarchal bench at the door, under the family tree, and swayed the sceptre of his fathers, a kind of rural potentate in the midst of a metropolis.

To share the cares and sweets of sovereignty, he had taken unto himself a helpmate, one of that excellent kind called stirring women; that is to say, she was one of those notable little housewives who are always busy when there is nothing to do. Her activity however, took one particular direction; her whole life seemed devoted to intense knitting; whether at home or abroad; walking or sitting, her needles were continually in motion, and it is even affirmed that by her unwearied industry she very nearly supplied her household with stockings throughout the year. This worthy couple were blessed with one daughter, who was brought up with great tenderness and care; uncommon pains had been taken with her education, so that she could stitch in every variety of way; make all kinds of pickles and preserves, and mark her own name on a sampler. The influence of her taste was seen also in the family garden, where the ornamental began to mingle with the useful; whole rows of fiery marigolds and splendid hollyhocks bordered the cabbage-beds; and gigantic sunflowers lolled their broad, jolly faces over the fences, seeming to ogle most affectionately the passers-by.

Thus reigned and vegetated Wolfert Webber over his paternal acres, peaceably and contentedly. Not but that, like all other sovereigns, he had his occasional cares and vexations. The growth of his native city sometimes caused him annoyance. His little territory gradually became hemmed in by streets and houses, which intercepted air and sunshine. He was now and then subject to the irruptions of the border population, that infest the streets of a metropolis, who would sometimes make midnight forays into his dominions, and carry off captive whole platoons of his noblest subjects. Vagrant swine would make a descent, too, now and then, when the gate was left open, and lay all waste before them; and mischievous urchins would often decapitate the illustrious sunflowers, the glory of the garden, as they lolled their heads so fondly over the walls. Still all these were petty grievances, which might now and then ruffle the surface of his mind, as a summer breeze will ruffle the surface of a mill-pond; but they could not disturb the deep-seated quiet of his soul. He would seize a trusty staff, that stood behind the door, issue suddenly out, and anoint the back of the aggressor, whether pig or urchin, and then return within doors, marvellously refreshed and tranquillized.

The chief cause of anxiety to honest Wolfert, however, was the growing prosperity of the city. The expenses of living doubled and trebled; but he could not double and treble the magnitude of his cabbages; and the number of competitors prevented the increase of price; thus, therefore, while every one around him grew richer, Wolfert grew poorer, and he could not, for the life of him, perceive how the evil was to be remedied.

This growing care which increased from day to day, had its gradual effect upon our worthy burgher; insomuch, that it at length implanted two or three wrinkles on his brow; things unknown before in the family of the Webbers; and it seemed to pinch up the corners of his cocked hat into an expression of anxiety, totally opposite to the tranquil, broad-brimmed, low-crowned beavers of his illustrious progenitors.

Perhaps even this would not have materially disturbed the serenity of his mind had he had only himself and his wife to care for; but there was his daughter gradually growing to maturity; and all the world knows when daughters begin to ripen no fruit or flower requires so much looking after. I have no talent at describing female charms, else fain would I depict the progress of this little Dutch beauty. How her blue eyes grew deeper and deeper, and her cherry lips redder and redder; and how she ripened and ripened, and rounded and rounded in the opening breath of sixteen summers, until, in her seventeenth spring, she seemed ready to burst out of her bodice like a half-blown rose-bud.

Ah, well-a-day! could I but show her as she was then, tricked out on a Sunday morning in the hereditary finery of the old Dutch clothes-press, of which her mother had confided to her the key. The wedding dress of her grandmother, modernized for use, with sundry ornaments, handed down as heirlooms in the family. Her pale brown hair smoothed with buttermilk in flat waving lines on each side of her fair forehead. The chain of yellow virgin gold, that encircled her neck; the little cross, that just rested at the entrance of a soft valley of happiness, as if it would sanctify the place. The—but pooh!—it is not for an old man like me to be prosing about female beauty: suffice it to say, Amy had attained her seventeenth year. Long since had her sampler exhibited hearts in couples desperately transfixed with arrows, and true lovers' knots worked in deep blue silk; and it was evident she began to languish for some more interesting occupation than the rearing of sunflowers or pickling of cucumbers.

At this critical period of female existence, when the heart within a damsel's bosom, like its emblem, the miniature which hangs without, is apt to be engrossed by a single image, a new visitor began to make his appearance under the roof of Wolfert Webber. This was Dirk Waldron, the only son of a poor widow, but who could boast of more fathers than any lad in the province; for his mother had had four husbands, and this only child, so that though born in her last wedlock, he might fairly claim to be the tardy fruit of a long course of cultivation. This son of four fathers united the merits and the vigor of his sires. If he had not a great family before him, he seemed likely to have a great one after him; for you had only to look at the fresh gamesome youth, to see that he was formed to be the founder of a mighty race.

This youngster gradually became an intimate visitor of the family. He talked little, but he sat long. He filled the father's pipe when it was empty, gathered up the mother's knitting-needle, or ball of worsted when it fell to the ground; stroked the sleek coat of the tortoise-shell cat, and replenished the teapot for the daughter from the bright copper kettle that sung before the fire. All these quiet little offices may seem of trifling import, but when true love is translated into Low Dutch, it is in this way that it eloquently expresses itself. They were not lost upon the Webber family. The winning youngster found marvellous favor in the eyes of the mother; the tortoise-shell cat, albeit the most staid and demure of her kind, gave indubitable signs of approbation of his visits, the tea-kettle seemed to sing out a cheering note of welcome at his approach, and if the sly glances of the daughter might be rightly read, as she sat bridling and dimpling, and sewing by her mother's side, she was not a wit behind Dame Webber, or grimalkin, or the tea-kettle in good-will.

Wolfert alone saw nothing of what was going on. Profoundly wrapt up in meditation on the growth of the city and his cabbages, he sat looking in the fire, and puffing his pipe in silence. One night, however, as the gentle Amy, according to custom, lighted her lover to the outer door, and he, according to custom, took his parting salute, the smack resounded so vigorously through the long, silent entry as to startle even the dull ear of Wolfert. He was slowly roused to a new source of anxiety. It had never entered into his head, that this mere child, who, as it seemed but the other day, had been climbing about his knees, and playing with dolls and baby-houses, could all at once be thinking of lovers and matrimony. He rubbed his eyes, examined into the fact, and really found that while he had been dreaming of other matters, she had actually grown into a woman, and what was more, had fallen in love. Here were new cares for poor Wolfert. He was a kind father, but he was a prudent man. The young man was a very stirring lad; but then he had neither money or land. Wolfert's ideas all ran in one channel, and he saw no alternative in case of a marriage, but to portion off the young couple with a corner of his cabbage garden, the whole of which was barely sufficient for the support of his family.

Like a prudent father, therefore, he determined to nip this passion in the bud, and forbade the youngster the house, though sorely did it go against his fatherly heart, and many a silent tear did it cause in the bright eye of his daughter. She showed herself, however, a pattern of filial piety and obedience. She never pouted and sulked; she never flew in the face of parental authority; she never fell into a passion, or fell into hysterics, as many romantic novel-read young ladies would do. Not she, indeed! She was none such heroical rebellious trumpery, I warrant ye. On the contrary, she acquiesced like an obedient daughter; shut the street-door in her lover's face, and if ever she did grant him an interview, it was either out of the kitchen window, or over the garden fence.

Wolfert was deeply cogitating these things in his mind, and his brow wrinkled with unusual care, as he wended his way one Saturday afternoon to a rural inn, about two miles from the city. It was a favorite resort of the Dutch part of the community from being always held by a Dutch line of landlords, and retaining an air and relish of the good old times. It was a Dutch-built house, that had probably been a country seat of some opulent burgher in the early time of the settlement. It stood near a point of land, called Corlears Hook, which stretches out into the Sound, and against which the tide, at its flux and reflux, sets with extraordinary rapidity. The venerable and somewhat crazy mansion was distinguished from afar, by a grove of elms and sycamores that seemed to wave a hospitable invitation, while a few weeping willows with their dank, drooping foliage, resembling falling waters, gave an idea of coolness, that rendered it an attractive spot during the heats of summer.

Here, therefore, as I said, resorted many of the old inhabitants of the Manahattoes, where, while some played at shuffle-board and quoits and nine-pins, others smoked a deliberate pipe, and talked over public affairs.

It was on a blustering autumnal afternoon that Wolfert made his visit to the inn. The grove of elms and willows was stripped of its leaves, which whirled in rustling eddies about the fields.

The nine-pin alley was deserted, for the premature chilliness of the day had driven the company within doors. As it was Saturday afternoon, the habitual club was in session, composed principally of regular Dutch burghers, though mingled occasionally with persons of various character and country, as is natural in a place of such motley population.

Beside the fireplace, and in a huge leather-bottomed armchair, sat the dictator of this little world, the venerable Rem, or, as it was pronounced, Ramm Rapelye. He was a man of Walloon race, and illustrious for the antiquity of his line, his great grandmother having been the first white child born in the province. But he was still more illustrious for his wealth and dignity: he had long filled the noble office of alderman, and was a man to whom the governor himself took off his hat. He had maintained possession of the leathern-bottomed chair from time immemorial; and had gradually waxed in bulk as he sat in his seat of government, until in the course of years he filled its whole magnitude. His word was decisive with his subjects; for he was so rich a man, that he was never expected to support any opinion by argument. The landlord waited on him with peculiar officiousness; not that he paid better than his neighbors, but then the coin of a rich man seems always to be so much more acceptable. The landlord had always a pleasant word and a joke, to insinuate in the ear of the august Ramm. It is true, Ramm never laughed, and, indeed, maintained a mastiff-like gravity, and even surliness of aspect, yet he now and then rewarded mine host with a token of approbation; which, though nothing more nor less than a kind of grunt, yet delighted the landlord more than a broad laugh from a poorer man.

"This will be a rough night for the money-diggers," said mine host, as a gust of wind howled round the house, and rattled at the windows.

"What, are they at their works again?" said an English half-pay captain, with one eye, who was a frequent attendant at the inn.

"Aye, are they," said the landlord, "and well may they be. They've had luck of late. They say a great pot of money has been dug up in the field, just behind Stuyvesant's orchard. Folks think it must have been buried there in old times by Peter Stuyvesant, the Dutch governor."

"Fudge!" said the one-eyed man of war, as he added a small portion of water to a bottom of brandy.

"Well, you may believe, or not, as you please," said mine host, somewhat nettled; "but everybody knows that the old governor buried a great deal of his money at the time of the Dutch troubles, when the English red-coats seized on the province. They say, too, the old gentleman walks; aye, and in the very same dress that he wears in the picture which hangs up in the family house."

"Fudge!" said the half-pay officer.

"Fudge, if you please!—But didn't Corney Van Zandt see him at midnight, stalking about in the meadow with his wooden leg, and a drawn sword in his hand, that flashed like fire? And what can he be walking for, but because people have been troubling the place where he buried his money in old times?"

Here the landlord was interrupted by several guttural sounds from Ramm Rapelye, betokening that he was laboring with the unusual production of an idea. As he was too great a man to be slighted by a prudent publican, mine host respectfully paused until he should deliver himself. The corpulent frame of this mighty burgher now gave all the symptoms of a volcanic mountain on the point of an eruption. First, there was a certain heaving of the abdomen, not unlike an earthquake; then was emitted a cloud of tobacco smoke from that crater, his mouth; then there was a kind of rattle in the throat, as if the idea were working its way up through a region of phlegm; then there were several disjointed members of a sentence thrown out, ending in a cough; at length his voice forced its way in the slow, but absolute tone of a man who feels the weight of his purse, if not of his ideas; every portion of his speech being marked by a testy puff of tobacco smoke.

"Who talks of old Peter Stuyvesant's walking?—puff—Have people no respect for persons?—puff—puff—Peter Stuyvesant knew better what to do with his money than to bury it—puff—I know the Stuyvesant family—puff—every one of them—puff—not a more respectable family in the province—puff—old standers—puff—warm householders—puff—none of your upstarts—puff—puff—puff.— Don't talk to me of Peter Stuyvesant's walking—puff—puff—puff— puff."

Here the redoubtable Ramm contracted his brow, clasped up his mouth, till it wrinkled at each corner, and redoubled his smoking with such vehemence, that the cloudly volumes soon wreathed round his head, as the smoke envelopes the awful summit of Mount Etna.

A general silence followed the sudden rebuke of this very rich man. The subject, however, was too interesting to be readily abandoned. The conversation soon broke forth again from the lips of Peechy Prauw Van Hook, the chronicler of the club, one of those narrative old men who seem to grow incontinent of words, as they grow old, until their talk flows from them almost involuntarily.

Peechy, who could at any time tell as many stories in an evening as his hearers could digest in a month, now resumed the conversation, by affirming that, to his knowledge, money had at different times been dug up in various parts of the island. The lucky persons who had discovered them had always dreamt of them three times beforehand, and what was worthy of remark, these treasures had never been found but by some descendant of the good old Dutch families, which clearly proved that they had been buried by Dutchmen in the olden time.

"Fiddlestick with your Dutchmen!" cried the half-pay officer. "The Dutch had nothing to do with them. They were all buried by Kidd, the pirate, and his crew."

Here a key-note was touched that roused the whole company. The name of Captain Kidd was like a talisman in those times, and was associated with a thousand marvellous stories.

The half-pay officer was a man of great weight among the peaceable members of the club, by reason of his military character, and of the gunpowder scenes which, by his own account, he had witnessed.

The golden stories of Kidd, however, were resolutely rivalled by the tales of Peechy Prauw, who, rather than suffer his Dutch progenitors to be eclipsed by a foreign freebooter, enriched every spot in the neighborhood with the hidden wealth of Peter Stuyvesant and his contemporaries.

Not a word of this conversation was lost upon Wolfert Webber. He returned pensively home, full of magnificent ideas of buried riches. The soil of his native island seemed to be turned into gold dust; and every field teemed with treasure. His head almost reeled at the thought how often he must have heedlessly rambled over places where countless sums lay, scarcely covered by the turf beneath his feet. His mind was in a vertigo with this whirl of new ideas. As he came in sight of the venerable mansion of his forefathers, and the little realm where the Webbers had so long and so contentedly flourished, his gorge rose at the narrowness of his destiny.

"Unlucky Wolfert!" exclaimed he, "others can go to bed and dream themselves into whole mines of wealth; they have but to seize a spade in the morning, and turn up doubloons like potatoes; but thou must dream of hardship, and rise to poverty—must dig thy field from year's end to year's end, and—and yet raise nothing but cabbages!"

Wolfert Webber went to bed with a heavy heart; and it was long before the golden visions that disturbed his brain, permitted him to sink into repose. The same visions, however, extended into his sleeping thoughts, and assumed a more definite form. He dreamt that he had discovered an immense treasure in the centre of his garden. At every stroke of the spade he laid bare a golden ingot; diamond crosses sparkled out of the dust; bags of money turned up their bellies, corpulent with pieces of eight, or venerable doubloons; and chests, wedged close with moidores, ducats, and pistareens, yawned before his ravished eyes, and vomited forth their glittering contents.

Wolfert awoke a poorer man than ever. He had no heart to go about his daily concerns, which appeared so paltry and profitless; but sat all day long in the chimney-corner, picturing to himself ingots and heaps of gold in the fire. The next night his dream was repeated. He was again in his garden, digging, and laying open stores of hidden wealth. There was something very singular in this repetition. He passed another day of reverie, and though it was cleaning-day, and the house, as usual in Dutch households, completely topsy-turvy, yet he sat unmoved amidst the general uproar.

The third night he went to bed with a palpitating heart. He put on his red nightcap, wrong side outwards for good luck. It was deep midnight before his anxious mind could settle itself into sleep. Again the golden dream was repeated, and again he saw his garden teeming with ingots and money-bags.

Wolfert rose the next morning in complete bewilderment. A dream three times repeated was never known to lie; and if so, his fortune was made.

In his agitation he put on his waistcoat with the hind part before, and this was a corroboration of good luck. He no longer doubted that a huge store of money lay buried somewhere in his cabbage-field, coyly waiting to be sought for, and he half repined at having so long been scratching about the surface of the soil, instead of digging to the centre.

He took his seat at the breakfast-table full of these speculations; asked his daughter to put a lump of gold into his tea, and on handing his wife a plate of slap-jacks, begging her to help herself to a doubloon.

His grand care now was how to secure this immense treasure without it being known. Instead of working regularly in his grounds in the day-time, he now stole from his bed at night, and with spade and pickaxe, went to work to rip up and dig about his paternal acres, from one end to the other. In a little time the whole garden, which had presented such a goodly and regular appearance, with its phalanx of cabbages, like a vegetable army in battle array, was reduced to a scene of devastation, while the relentless Wolfert, with night-cap on head, and lantern and spade in hand, stalked through the slaughtered ranks, the destroying angel of his own vegetable world.

Every morning bore testimony to the ravages of the preceding night in cabbages of all ages and conditions, from the tender sprout to the full-grown head, piteously rooted from their quiet beds like worthless weeds, and left to wither in the sunshine. It was in vain

Wolfert's wife remonstrated; it was in vain his darling daughter wept over the destruction of some favorite marygold. "Thou shalt have gold of another guess sort," he would cry, chucking her under the chin; "thou shalt have a string of crooked ducats for thy wedding necklace, my child." His family began really to fear that the poor man's wits were diseased. He muttered in his sleep at night of mines of wealth, of pearls and diamonds and bars of gold. In the daytime he was moody and abstracted, and walked about as if in a trance. Dame Webber held frequent councils with all the old women of the neighborhood, not omitting the parish dominie; scarce an hour in the day but a knot of them might be seen wagging their white caps together round her door, while the poor woman made some piteous recital. The daughter, too, was fain to seek for more frequent consolation from the stolen interviews of her favored swain, Dirk Waldron. The delectable little Dutch songs with which she used to dulcify the house grew less and less frequent, and she would forget her sewing and look wistfully in her father's face as he sat pondering by the fireside.

Wolfert caught her eye one day fixed on him thus anxiously, and for a moment was roused from his golden reveries—"Cheer up, my girl," said he, exultingly, "why dost thou droop?—thou shalt hold up thy head one day with the Brinckerhoffs, and the Schermerhorns, the Van Hornes, and the Van Dams. By Saint Nicholas, but the patroon himself shall be glad to get thee for his son!"

Amy shook her head at his vainglorious boast, and was more than ever in doubt of the soundness of the good man's intellect.

In the meantime Wolfert went on digging, but the field was extensive, and as his dream had indicated no precise spot, he had to dig at random. The winter set in before one-tenth of the scene of promise had been explored. The ground became too frozen and the nights too cold for the labors of the spade. No sooner, however, did the returning warmth of spring loosen the soil, and the small frogs begin to pipe in the meadows, but Wolfert resumed his labors with renovated zeal. Still, however, the hours of industry were reversed. Instead of working cheerily all day, planting and setting out his vegetables, he remained thoughtfully idle, until the shades of night summoned him to his secret labors. In this way he continued to dig from night to night, and week to week, and month to month, but not a stiver did he find. On the contrary, the more he digged the poorer he grew. The rich soil of his garden was digged away, and the sand and gravel from beneath were thrown to the surface, until the whole field presented an aspect of sandy barrenness.

In the meantime the seasons gradually rolled on. The little frogs that had piped in the meadows in early spring, croaked as bull-frogs in the brooks during the summer heats, and then sunk into silence. The peach-tree budded, blossomed, and bore its fruit. The swallows and martins came, twittered about the roof, built their nests, reared their young, held their congress along the eaves, and then winged their flight in search of another spring. The caterpillar spun its winding-sheet, dangled in it from the great button-wood tree that shaded the house, turned into a moth, fluttered with the last sunshine of summer, and disappeared; and finally the leaves of the button-wood tree turned yellow, then brown, then rustled one by one to the ground, and whirling about in little eddies of wind and dust, whispered that winter was at hand.

Wolfert gradually awoke from his dream of wealth as the year declined. He had reared no crop to supply the wants of his household during the sterility of winter. The season was long and severe, and for the first time the family was really straightened in its comforts. By degrees a revulsion of thought took place in Wolfert's mind, common to those whose golden dreams have been disturbed by pinching realities. The idea gradually stole upon him that he should come to want. He already considered himself one of the most unfortunate men in the province, having lost such an incalculable amount of undiscovered treasure, and now, when thousands of pounds had eluded his search, to be perplexed for shillings and pence was cruel in the extreme.

Haggard care gathered about his brow; he went about with a money-seeking air, his eyes bent downwards into the dust, and carrying his hands in his pockets, as men are apt to do when they have nothing else to put into them. He could not even pass the city almshouse without giving it a rueful glance, as if destined to be his future abode.

The strangeness of his conduct and of his looks occasioned much speculation and remark. For a long time he was suspected of being crazy, and then everybody pitied him; at length it began to be suspected that he was poor, and then everybody avoided him.

The rich old burghers of his acquaintance met him, outside of the door when he called, entertained him hospitably on the threshold, pressed him warmly by the hand on parting, shook their heads as he walked away, with the kind-hearted expression of "poor Wolfert," and turned a corner nimbly, if by chance they saw him approaching as they walked the streets. Even the barber and cobbler of the neighborhood, and a tattered tailor in an alley hard by, three of the poorest and merriest rogues in the world, eyed him with that abundant sympathy which usually attends a lack of means, and there is not a doubt but their pockets would have been at his command, only that they happened to be empty.

Thus everybody deserted the Webber mansion, as if poverty were contagious, like the plague; everybody but honest Dirk Waldron, who still kept up his stolen visits to the daughter, and indeed seemed to wax more affectionate as the fortunes of his mistress were on the wane.

Many months had elapsed since Wolfert had frequented his old resort, the rural inn. He was taking a long lonely walk one Saturday afternoon, musing over his wants and disappointments, when his feet took instinctively their wonted direction, and on awaking out of a reverie, he found himself before the door of the inn. For some moments he hesitated whether to enter, but his heart yearned for companionship; and where can a ruined man find better companionship than at a tavern, where there is neither sober example nor sober advice to put him out of countenance?

Wolfert found several of the old frequenters of the tavern at their usual posts, and seated in their usual places; but one was missing, the great Ramm Rapelye, who for many years had filled the chair of state. His place was supplied by a stranger, who seemed, however, completely at home in the chair and the tavern. He was rather under-size, but deep-chested, square, and muscular. His broad shoulders, double joints, and bow-knees, gave tokens of prodigious strength. His face was dark and weather-beaten; a deep scar, as if from the slash of a cutlass, had almost divided his nose, and made a gash in his upper lip, through which his teeth shone like a bull-dog's. A mop of iron-gray hair gave a grizzly finish to his hard-favored visage. His dress was of an amphibious character. He wore an old hat edged with tarnished lace, and cocked in martial style, on one side of his head; a rusty blue military coat with brass buttons, and a wide pair of short petticoat trousers, or rather breeches, for they were gathered up at the knees. He ordered everybody about him with an authoritative air; talked in a brattling voice, that sounded like the crackling of thorns under a pot; damned the landlord and servants with perfect impunity, and was waited upon with greater obsequiousness than had ever been shown to the mighty Ramm himself.

Wolfert's curiosity was awakened to know who and what was this stranger who had thus usurped absolute sway in this ancient domain. He could get nothing, however, but vague information. Peechy Prauw took him aside, into a remote corner of the hall, and there in an under voice, and with great caution, imparted to him all that he knew on the subject. The inn had been aroused several months before, on a dark stormy night, by repeated long shouts, that seemed like the howlings of a wolf. They came from the water-side; and at length were distinguished to be hailing the house in the seafaring manner. "House-a-hoy!" The landlord turned out with his head waiter, tapster, hostler, and errand boy—that is to say with his old negro Cuff. On approaching the place from whence the voice proceeded, they found this amphibious-looking personage at the water's edge, quite alone, and seated on a great oaken sea-chest. How he came there, whether he had been set on shore from some boat, or had floated to land on his chest, nobody could tell, for he did not seem disposed to answer questions, and there was something in his looks and manners that put a stop to all questioning. Suffice it to say, he took possession of a corner room of the inn, to which his chest was removed with great difficulty. Here he had remained ever since, keeping about the inn and its vicinity. Sometimes, it is true, he disappeared for one, two, or three days at a time, going and returning without giving any notice or account of his movements. He always appeared to have plenty of money, though often of very strange, outlandish coinage; and he regularly paid his bill every evening before turning in.

He had fitted up his room to his own fancy, having slung a hammock from the ceiling instead of a bed, and decorated the walls with rusty pistols and cutlasses of foreign workmanship. A great part of his time was passed in this room, seated by the window, which commanded a wide view of the Sound, a short old-fashioned pipe in his mouth, a glass of rum toddy at his elbow, and a pocket telescope in his hand, with which he reconnoitred every boat that moved upon the water. Large square-rigged vessels seemed to excite but little attention; but the moment he descried any thing with a shoulder-of-mutton sail, or that a barge, or yawl, or jolly boat hove in sight, up went the telescope, and he examined it with the most scrupulous attention.

All this might have passed without much notice, for in those times the province was so much the resort of adventurers of all characters and climes that any oddity in dress or behavior attracted but little attention. But in a little while this strange sea monster, thus strangely cast up on dry land, began to encroach upon the long-established customs and customers of the place; to interfere in a dictatorial manner in the affairs of the nine-pin alley and the bar-room, until in the end he usurped an absolute command over the little inn. It was in vain to attempt to withstand his authority. He was not exactly quarrelsome, but boisterous and peremptory, like one accustomed to tyrannize on a quarter deck; and there was a dare-devil air about every thing he said and did, that inspired a wariness in all bystanders. Even the half-pay officer, so long the hero of the club, was soon silenced by him; and the quiet burghers stared with wonder at seeing their inflammable man of war so readily and quietly extinguished.

And then the tales that he would tell were enough to make a peaceable man's hair stand on end. There was not a sea-fight, or marauding or freebooting adventure that had happened within the last twenty years but he seemed perfectly versed in it. He delighted to talk of the exploits of the buccaneers in the West Indies and on the Spanish Main. How his eyes would glisten as he described the waylaying of treasure ships, the desperate fights, yard arm and yard arm—broadside and broadside—the boarding and capturing of large Spanish galleons! With what chuckling relish would he describe the descent upon some rich Spanish colony; the rifling of a church; the sacking of a convent! You would have thought you heard some gormandizer dilating upon the roasting of a savory goose at Michaelmas as he described the roasting of some Spanish Don to make him discover his treasure—a detail given with a minuteness that made every rich old burgher present turn uncomfortably in his chair. All this would be told with infinite glee, as if he considered it an excellent joke; and then he would give such a tyrannical leer in the face of his next neighbor, that the poor man would be fain to laugh out of sheer faint-heartedness. If any one, however, pretended to contradict him in any of his stories he was on fire in an instant. His very cocked hat assumed a momentary fierceness, and seemed to resent the contradiction.—"How the devil should you know as well as I! I tell you it was as I say!" and he would at the same time let slip a broadside of thundering oaths and tremendous sea phrases, such as had never been heard before within those peaceful walls.

Indeed, the worthy burghers began to surmise that he knew more of these stories than mere hearsay. Day after day their conjectures concerning him grew more and more wild and fearful. The strangeness of his manners, the mystery that surrounded him, all made him something incomprehensible in their eyes. He was a kind of monster of the deep to them—he was a merman—he was a behemoth—he was a leviathan—in short, they knew not what he was.

The domineering spirit of this boisterous sea urchin at length grew quite intolerable. He was no respecter of persons; he contradicted the richest burghers without hesitation; he took possession of the sacred elbow chair, which time out of mind had been the seat of sovereignty of the illustrious Ramm Rapelye. Nay, he even went so far in one of his rough jocular moods, as to slap that mighty burgher on the back, drink his toddy and wink in his face, a thing scarcely to be believed. From this time Ramm Rapelye appeared no more at the inn; his example was followed by several of the most eminent customers, who were too rich to tolerate being bullied out of their opinions, or being obliged to laugh at another man's jokes. The landlord was almost in despair, but he knew not how to get rid of this sea-monster and his sea-chest, which seemed to have grown like fixtures, or excrescences, on his establishment.

Such was the account whispered cautiously in Wolfert's ear, by the narrator, Peechy Prauw, as he held him by the button in a corner of the hall, casting a wary glance now and then towards the door of the bar-room, lest he should be overheard by the terrible hero of his tale.

Wolfert took his seat in a remote part of the room in silence; impressed with profound awe of this unknown, so versed in free-booting history. It was to him a wonderful instance of the revolutions of mighty empires, to find the venerable Ramm Rapelye thus ousted from the throne; a rugged tarpaulin dictating from his elbow chair, hectoring the patriarchs, and filling this tranquil little realm with brawl and bravado.

The stranger was on this evening in a more than usually communicative mood, and was narrating a number of astounding stories of plunderings and burnings upon the high seas. He dwelt upon them with peculiar relish, heightening the frightful particulars in proportion to their effect on his peaceful auditors. He gave a long swaggering detail of the capture of a Spanish merchantman. She was laying becalmed during a long summer's day, just off from an island which was one of the lurking places of the pirates. They had reconnoitred her with their spy-glasses from the shore, and ascertained her character and force. At night a picked crew of daring fellows set off for her in a whale boat. They approached with muffled oars, as she lay rocking idly with the undulations of the sea and her sails flapping against the masts. They were close under her stern before the guard on deck was aware of their approach. The alarm was given; the pirates threw hand-grenades on deck and sprang up the main chains sword in hand.

The crew flew to arms, but in great confusion; some were shot down, others took refuge in the tops; others were driven overboard and drowned, while others fought hand to hand from the main-deck to the quarter-deck, disputing gallantly every inch of ground. There were three Spanish gentlemen on board with their ladies, who made the most desperate resistance; they defended the companion-way, cut down several of their assailants, and fought like very devils, for they were maddened by the shrieks of the ladies from the cabin. One of the Dons was old and soon despatched. The other two kept their ground vigorously, even though the captain of the pirates was among their assailants. Just then there was a shout of victory from the main deck. "The ship is ours!" cried the pirates.

One of the Dons immediately dropped his sword and surrendered; the other, who was a hot-headed youngster, and just married, gave the captain a slash in the face that laid all open. The captain just made out to articulate the words "no quarter."

"And what did they do with their prisoners?" said Peechy Prauw, eagerly.

"Threw them all overboard!" said the merman.

A dead pause followed this reply. Peechy Prauw shrunk quietly back like a man who had unwarily stolen upon the lair of a sleeping lion. The honest burghers cast fearful glances at the deep scar slashed across the visage of the stranger, and moved their chairs a little farther off. The seaman, however, smoked on without moving a muscle, as though he either did not perceive or did not regard the unfavorable effect he had produced upon his hearers.

The half-pay officer was the first to break the silence; for he was continually tempted to make ineffectual head against this tyrant of the seas, and to regain his lost consequence in the eyes of his ancient companions. He now tried to match the gunpowder tales of the stranger by others equally tremendous. Kidd, as usual, was his hero, concerning whom he had picked up many of the floating traditions of the province. The seaman had always evinced a settled pique against the red-faced warrior. On this occasion he listened with peculiar impatience. He sat with one arm a-kimbo, the other elbow on a table, the hand holding on to the small pipe he was pettishly puffing; his legs crossed, drumming with one foot on the ground and casting every now and then the side glance of a basilisk at the prosing captain. At length the latter spoke of Kidd's having ascended the Hudson with some of his crew, to land his plunder in secrecy.

"Kidd up the Hudson!" burst forth the seaman, with a tremendous oath; "Kidd never was up the Hudson!"

"I tell you he was," said the other. "Aye, and they say he buried a quantity of treasure on the little flat that runs out into the river, called the Devil's Dans Kammer."

"The Devil's Dans Kammer in your teeth!" cried the seaman. "I tell you Kidd never was up the Hudson. What the plague do you know of Kidd and his haunts?"

"What do I know?" echoed the half-pay officer; "why, I was in London at the time of his trial, aye, and I had the pleasure of seeing him hanged at Execution Dock."

"Then, sir, let me tell you that you saw as pretty a fellow hanged as ever trod shoe-leather. Aye!" putting his face nearer to that of the officer, "and there was many a coward looked on, that might much better have swung in his stead."

The half-pay officer was silenced; but the indignation thus pent up in his bosom glowed with intense vehemence in his single eye, which kindled like a coal.

Peechy Prauw, who never could remain silent, now took up the word, and in a pacifying tone observed that the gentleman certainly was in the right. Kidd never did bury money up the Hudson, nor indeed in any of those parts, though many affirm the fact. It was Bradish and others of the buccaneers who had buried money, some said in Turtle Bay, others in Long Island, others in the neighborhood of Hell Gate. Indeed, added he, I recollect an adventure of Sam, the negro fisherman, many years ago, which some think had something to do with the buccaneers. As we are all friends here, and as it will go no further, I'll tell it to you.

"Upon a dark night many years ago, as Sam was returning from fishing in Hell Gate—"

Here the story was nipped in the bud by a sudden movement from the unknown, who, laying his iron fist on the table, knuckles downward, with a quiet force that indented the very boards, and looking grimly over his shoulder, with the grin of an angry bear. "Heark'ee, neighbor," said he, with a significant nodding of the head, "you'd better let the buccaneers and their money alone— they're not for old men and old women to meddle with. They fought hard for their money, they gave body and soul for it, and wherever it lies buried, depend upon it he must have a tug with the devil who gets it."

This sudden explosion was succeeded by a blank silence throughout the room. Peechy Prauw shrunk within himself, and even the red-faced officer turned pale. Wolfert, who, from a dark corner of the room, had listened with intense eagerness to all this talk about buried treasure, looked with mingled awe and reverence on this bold buccaneer, for such he really suspected him to be. There was a chinking of gold and a sparkling of jewels in all his stories about the Spanish Main that gave a value to every period, and Wolfert would have given any thing for the rummaging of the ponderous sea-chest, which his imagination crammed full of golden chalices and crucifixes and jolly round bags of doubloons.

The dead stillness that had fallen upon the company was at length interrupted by the stranger, who pulled out a prodigious watch of curious and ancient workmanship, and which in Wolfert's eyes had a decidedly Spanish look. On touching a spring it struck ten o'clock; upon which the sailor called for his reckoning, and having paid it out of a handful of outlandish coin, he drank off the remainder of his beverage, and without taking leave of anyone, rolled out of the room, muttering to himself as he stamped upstairs to his chamber.

It was some time before the company could recover from the silence into which they had been thrown. The very footsteps of the stranger, which were heard now and then as he traversed his chamber, inspired awe.

Still the conversation in which they had been engaged was too interesting not to be resumed. A heavy thunder-gust had gathered up unnoticed while they were lost in talk, and the torrents of rain that fell forbade all thoughts of setting off for home until the storm should subside. They drew nearer together, therefore, and entreated the worthy Peechy Prauw to continue the tale which had been so discourteously interrupted. He readily complied, whispering, however, in a tone scarcely above his breath, and drowned occasionally by the rolling of the thunder, and he would pause every now and then, and listen with evident awe, as he heard the heavy footsteps of the stranger pacing overhead.

THE LEGEND OF DON MUNIO
SANCHO DE HINOJOSA

In the cloisters of the ancient Benedictine convent of San Domingo, at Silos, in Castile, are the mouldering yet magnificent monuments of the once powerful and chivalrous family of Hinojosa. Among these reclines the marble figure of a knight, in complete armor, with the hands pressed together, as if in prayer. On one side of his tomb is sculptured in relief a band of Christian cavaliers, capturing a cavalcade of male and female Moors; on the other side, the same cavaliers are represented kneeling before an altar. The tomb, like most of the neighboring monuments, is almost in ruins, and the sculpture is nearly unintelligible, excepting to the keen eye of the antiquary. The story connected with the sepulchre, however, is still preserved in the old Spanish chronicles, and is to the following purport.

In old times, several hundred years ago, there was a noble Castilian cavalier, named Don Munio Sancho de Hinojosa, lord of a border castle, which had stood the brunt of many a Moorish foray. He had seventy horsemen as his household troops, all of the ancient Castilian proof; stark warriors, hard riders, and men of iron; with these he scoured the Moorish lands, and made his name terrible throughout the borders. His castle hall was covered with banners, and scimitars, and Moslem helms, the trophies of his prowess. Don Munio was, moreover, a keen huntsman; and rejoiced in hounds of all kinds, steeds for the chase, and hawks for the towering sport of falconry. When not engaged in warfare, his delight was to beat up the neighboring forests; and scarcely ever did he ride forth, without hound and horn, a boar-spear in his hand, or a hawk upon his fist, and an attendant train of huntsmen.

His wife, Donna Maria Palacin, was of a gentle and timid nature, little fitted to be the spouse of so hardy and adventurous a knight; and many a tear did the poor lady shed, when he sallied forth upon his daring enterprises, and many a prayer did she offer up for his safety.

As this doughty cavalier was one day hunting, he stationed himself in a thicket, on the borders of a green glade of the forest, and dispersed his followers to rouse the game, and drive it toward his stand. He had not been here long, when a cavalcade of Moors, of both sexes, came prankling over the forest lawn. They were unarmed, and magnificently dressed in robes of tissue and embroidery, rich shawls of India, bracelets and anklets of gold, and jewels that sparkled in the sun.

At the head of this gay cavalcade, rode a youthful cavalier, superior to the rest in dignity and loftiness of demeanor, and in splendor of attire; beside him was a damsel, whose veil, blown aside by the breeze, displayed a face of surpassing beauty, and eyes cast down in maiden modesty, yet beaming with tenderness and joy.

Don Munio thanked his stars for sending him such a prize, and exulted at the thought of bearing home to his wife the glittering spoils of these infidels. Putting his hunting horn to his lips, he gave a blast that rung through the forest. His huntsmen came running from all quarters, and the astonished Moors were surrounded and made captives.

The beautiful Moor wrung her hands in despair, and her female attendants uttered the most piercing cries. The young Moorish cavalier alone retained self-possession. He inquired the name of the Christian knight, who commanded this troop of horsemen. When told that it was Don Munio Sancho de Hinojosa, his countenance lighted up. Approaching that cavalier, and kissing his hand, "Don Munio Sancho," said he, "I have heard of your fame as a true and valiant knight, terrible in arms, but schooled in the noble virtues of chivalry. Such do I trust to find you. In me you behold Abadil, son of a Moorish alcayde. I am on the way to celebrate my nuptials with this lady; chance has thrown us in your power, but I confide in your magnanimity. Take all our treasure and jewels; demand what ransom you think proper for our person, but suffer us not to be insulted or dishonored."

When the good knight heard this appeal, and beheld the beauty of the youthful pair, his heart was touched with tenderness and courtesy. "God forbid," said he, "that I should disturb such happy nuptials. My prisoners in troth shall ye be, for fifteen days, and immured within my castle, where I claim, as conqueror, the right of celebrating your espousals."

So saying, he despatched one of his fleetest horsemen in advance, to notify Dona Maria Palacin of the coming of this bridal party; while he and his huntsmen escorted the cavalcade, not as captors, but as a guard of honor. As they drew near to the castle, the banners were hung out, and the trumpets sounded from the battlements; and on their nearer approach, the draw-bridge was lowered, and Dona Maria came forth to meet them, attended by her ladies and knights, her pages and her minstrels. She took the young bride, Allifra, in her arms, kissed her with the tenderness of a sister, and conducted her into the castle. In the mean time, Don Munio sent forth missives in every direction, and had viands and dainties of all kinds collected from the country round; and the wedding of the Moorish lovers was celebrated with all possible state and festivity. For fifteen days, the castle was given up to joy and revelry. There were tiltings and jousts at the ring, and bull-fights, and banquets, and dances to the sound of minstrelsy. When the fifteen days were at an end, he made the bride and bridegroom magnificent presents, and conducted them and their attendants safely beyond the borders. Such, in old times, were the courtesy and generosity of a Spanish cavalier.

Several years after this event, the King of Castile summoned his nobles to assist him in a campaign against the Moors. Don Munio Sancho was among the first to answer to the call, with seventy horsemen, all staunch and well-tried warriors. His wife, Dona Maria, hung about his neck. "Alas, my lord!" exclaimed she, "how often wilt thou tempt thy fate, and when will thy thirst for glory be appeased?"

"One battle more," replied Don Munio, "one battle more, for the honor of Castile, and I here make a vow, that when this is over, I will lay by my sword, and repair with my cavaliers in pilgrimage to the sepulchre of our Lord at Jerusalem." The cavaliers all joined with him in the vow, and Dona Maria felt in some degree soothed in spirit: still, she saw with a heavy heart the departure of her husband, and watched his banner with wistful eyes, until it disappeared among the trees of the forest,

The king of Castile led his army to the plains of Salmanara, where they encountered the Moorish host, near to Ucles. The battle was long and bloody; the Christians repeatedly wavered, and were as often rallied by the energy of their commanders. Don Munio was covered with wounds, but refused to leave the field. The Christians at length gave way, and the king was hardly pressed, and in danger of being captured.

Don Munio called upon his cavaliers to follow him to the rescue. "Now is the time," cried he, "to prove your loyalty. Fall to, like brave men! We fight for the true faith, and if we lose our lives here, we gain a better life hereafter."

Rushing with his men between the king and his pursuers, they checked the latter in their career, and gave time for their monarch to escape; but they fell victims to their loyalty. They all fought to the last gasp. Don Munio was singled out by a powerful Moorish knight, but having been wounded in the right arm, he fought to disadvantage, and was slain. The battle being over, the Moor paused to possess himself of the spoils of this redoubtable Christian warrior. When he unlaced the helmet, however, and beheld the countenance of Don Munio, he gave a great cry, and smote his breast. "Woe is me!" cried he: "I have slain my benefactor! The flower of knightly virtue! the most magnanimous of cavaliers!"

While the battle had been raging on the plain of Salmanara, Donna Maria Palacin remained in her castle, a prey to the keenest anxiety. Her eyes were ever fixed on the road that led from the country of the Moors, and often she asked the watchman of the tower, "What seest thou?"

One evening, at the shadowy hour of twilight, the warden sounded his horn. "I see," cried he, "a numerous train winding up the valley. There are mingled Moors and Christians. The banner of my lord is in the advance. Joyful tidings!" exclaimed the old seneschal: "my lord returns in triumph, and brings captives!" Then the castle courts rang with shouts of joy; and the standard was displayed, and the trumpets were sounded, and the draw-bridge was lowered, and Dona Maria went forth with her ladies, and her knights, and her pages, and her minstrels, to welcome her lord from the wars. But as the train drew nigh, she beheld a sumptuous bier, covered with black velvet, and on it lay a warrior, as if taking his repose: he lay in his armor, with his helmet on his head, and his sword in his hand, as one who had never been conquered, and around the bier were the escutcheons of the house of Hinojosa.

A number of Moorish cavaliers attended the bier, with emblems of mourning, and with dejected countenances: and their leader cast himself at the feet of Dona Maria, and hid his face in his hands. She beheld in him the gallant Abadil, whom she had once welcomed with his bride to her castle, but who now came with the body of her lord, whom he had unknowingly slain in battle!

The sepulchre erected in the cloisters of the Convent of San Domingo was achieved at the expense of the Moor Abadil, as a feeble testimony of his grief for the death of the good knight Don Munio, and his reverence for his memory. The tender and faithful Dona Maria soon followed her lord to the tomb. On one of the stones of a small arch, beside his sepulchre, is the following simple inscription: "*Hic jacet Maria Palacin, uxor Munonis Sancij De Finojosa*:" Here lies Maria Palacin, wife of Munio Sancho de Hinojosa.

The legend of Don Munio Sancho does not conclude with his death. On the same day on which the battle took place on the plain of Salmanara, a chaplain of the Holy Temple at Jerusalem, while standing at the outer gate, beheld a train of Christian cavaliers advancing, as if in pilgrimage. The chaplain was a native of Spain, and as the pilgrims approached, he knew the foremost to be Don Munio Sancho de Hinojosa, with whom he had been well acquainted in former times. Hastening to the patriarch, he told him of the honorable rank of the pilgrims at the gate. The patriarch, therefore, went forth with a grand procession of priests and monks, and received the pilgrims with all due honor. There were seventy cavaliers, beside their leader, all stark and lofty warriors. They carried their helmets in their hands, and their faces were deadly pale. They greeted no one, nor looked either to the right or to the left, but entered the chapel, and kneeling before the sepulchre of our Saviour, performed their orisons in silence. When they had concluded, they rose as if to depart, and the patriarch and his attendants advanced to speak to them, but they were no more to be seen. Every one marvelled what could be the meaning of this prodigy. The patriarch carefully noted down the day, and sent to Castile to learn tidings of Don Munio Sancho de Hinojosa. He received for reply, that on the very day specified, that worthy knight, with seventy of his followers, had been slain in battle. These, therefore, must have been the blessed spirits of those Christian warriors, come to fulfil their vow of a pilgrimage to the Holy Sepulchre at Jerusalem. Such was Castilian faith, in the olden time, which kept its word, even beyond the grave.

If any one should doubt of the miraculous apparition of these phantom knights, let him consult the History of the Kings of Castile and Leon, by the learned and pious Fray Prudencio de Sandoval, bishop of Pamplona, where he will find it recorded in the History of the King Don Alonzo VI, on the hundred and second page. It is too precious a legend to be lightly abandoned to the doubter.